CURSE OF THE BEETLE

ANTHONY GIANGREGORIO
AND
RICHARD MARSH

OTHER BOOKS BY STFU PUBLISHING

RANDY AND WALTER: KILLERS
THE CONSERVATORY
MEN OF PERDITION
RAT WAR: AN ANTHOLOGY
DROPPING FEAR
DREAM WEAVERS

PART 1

The Surprising Narration of Robert Holt

Chapter 1

"There's no more room! We're full up for the night!"

The man banged the door in my face, which was the final blow. To think, to have tramped about all day looking for work, to have begged even for a job which would give me money enough to buy a little food, and to have tramped and to have begged in vain, that was bad. But sick at heart, depressed in mind and in body, exhausted by hunger and fatigue, to have been compelled to pocket any little pride I might have left, and solicit, as the penniless, homeless tramp which indeed I was, a night's lodging in the casual ward—and to solicit it in vain—that was worse. Much worse. About as bad as it could get.

I stared stupidly at the door which had just been banged in my face. I could scarcely believe it was possible. I'd hardly expected to figure as a tramp, but supposing it conceivable that I could become one, that I should be refused admission to that abode of all ignominy, the tramp's ward, was to have attained a depth of misery of which never even in nightmares I could have dreamed.

As I stood wondering what I should do, a man in rags slouched towards me from out of the shadows. "Won't let you in, huh?"

"He says it's full," I replied.

"Says it's full, does he? That's the lay at Fulham, they always says it's full. They want to keep the number down. You got a name?" he asked.

"Robert Holt," I said. I looked at the man askance: his head hung forward, his hands were in his pant pockets, his clothes were filthy, he smelled terribly, and his tone was husky.

"Do you mean that they say it's full when it isn't, that they won't let me in although there's room?" I asked.

"That's it exactly. The bloke's messin' with ya," he said.

"But if there's room, aren't they supposed to let me in?"

"Course they are, and blimey, if I was you I'd make 'em do it. Blimey, I would!" He broke into a volley of curses.

"But what am I to do?"

"Why, give 'em another knock— let 'em know you won't be put off!" he said.

I hesitated, then acting on his suggestion, for the second time I rang the bell. The door was flung wide open this time, and the grizzled man who had previously responded to my summons stood in the open doorway, a deep frown on his face. Had he been the Chairman of the Board of a fortune five hundred company he couldn't have addressed me with greater scorn.

"What, here again! What's your game, pal? Ya think I've got nothin' better to do than to wait upon the likes of you?"

"I want to be admitted," I said flatly.

"Then you won't be admitted!"

"I want to see someone in authority."

"Ain't you seein' someone in authority now?" he asked.

"I want to see someone besides you. I want to see the master."

"Then you won't see the master!" He moved to close the door, but prepared for such a move, I thrust my foot sufficiently inside to prevent it from closing.

I continued to address him. "Are you sure that the ward is full?"

"Filled up two hours ago!"

"But what am I to do?"

"I don't know what you're to do. It's not my bloody problem!"

"Which is the next nearest shelter?" I asked.

"Kensington."

Suddenly opening the door as he answered me, he thrust his arm at me, pushing me backwards. Before I could recover the door was closed.

The man in rags had continued a grim spectator of the scene. Now he said, "Nice bloke, ain't he?"

"He's only one of the tramps, is he not; has he any right to act as one of the officials?"

"I tell ya some of them tramps is worse than the officers, a long sight worse!" he said. "They think they own the house, blimey they do. Oh it's a fine world, this is!"

I hesitated. For some time there had been a suspicion of rain in the air. Now it was commencing to fall in a fine but soaking drizzle. It only needed that to fill my cup to overflowing.

My companion regarded me with a sort of sullen curiosity. "Ain't you got any money?" he asked.

"No, nothing."

"Done much of this sort of thing?"

"It's the first time I've been to a place like this, and it doesn't seem as if I'm going to get in now," I said.

"I thought you looked as if you was a bit fresh. What're ya goin' to do?" he asked.

"How far is it to Kensington?"

"About three miles, but if I were you, I'd try St. George's."

"Where's that?"

"In the Fulham Road," he said. "Kensington's only a small place, but they do you well there, and it's always full as soon as the door's opened. You'd have more chance at St George's." He went silent.

I turned his words over in my mind, feeling as little disposed to try the one place as the other.

Presently he said, "I've traveled from Reading this day; tramped every foot. This is a fine country, this is. But I ain't goin' no further than here. I'll have a bed in Hammersmith or I'll know the reason why."

"How are you going to manage it? Have you got any money?" I asked.

"Got any money? My God! Do I look like I have money?"

"How are you going to get a bed then?"

He grinned knowingly at me. "Just watch and learn, my friend." He picked up two stones, one in each hand. The one in his left he flung at the glass which was over the door of the shelter. It crashed through it, and through the lamp beyond. "That's how I'm goin" to get a bed here."

The door was hastily opened. The grizzled pauper reappeared. He shouted as he glared at us in the darkness. "Who did that?"

"I did it, and, if you like, you can see me do another one. It might do your eyesight good." Before the grizzled pauper could interfere, he'd hurled the stone in his right hand through another pane. I felt that it was time for me to go. The man was earning a night's rest at a price which, even in my time of need, I wasn't prepared to pay.

When I left, two or three other tramps had appeared upon the scene, and the man in rags was addressing them with a degree of frankness, which left little to be desired. I crept away unnoticed. I hadn't gone far before I almost decided that I might as well have thrown in my fortune with the bolder wretch, and smashed a window, too. Indeed, more than once my feet faltered, as I all but returned to do the deed which I'd left undone.

A more miserable night for an out-of-door excursion I could hardly have chosen. The rain was like a mist, and was not only drenching me to the skin, but it was rendering it difficult to see more than a little distance in any direction. The neighborhood was badly lighted. It was one in which I was a stranger, I had come to Hammersmith as a last resource. It had seemed to me that I'd tried to find some occupation which would enable me to keep body and soul together in every other part of London, and that now only Hammersmith was left. And, at Hammersmith, even the workhouse would have none of me!

Retreating from the inhospitable shelter, I'd taken the first turn to the left, and at the moment, had been glad to take it. In the darkness and the rain, the locality which I was entering appeared unfinished. I seemed to be leaving civilization behind me. The path was unpaved, the road rough and uneven, as if it had never been properly made. Houses were few and far between. Those which I did encounter seemed in the imperfect light, amid the general desolation, to be cottages which were crumbling to decay.

Exactly where I was I couldn't tell. I had a faint notion that, if I only kept on long enough, I should strike some part of Walham Green. How long I should have to keep on I could only guess. Not a soul seemed to be about of whom I could make inquiries. It was as if I was in a land denuded of life.

I suppose it was between eleven o'clock and midnight. I hadn't given up my quest for work till all the shops were closed, and in Hammersmith—that night at any rate—they were not early closers. Then I had lounged about dispiritedly, wondering what would be the next thing I could do.

It was only because I feared that if I attempted to spend the night in the open air, without food, when the morning came I should be broken up, and fit for nothing, that I sought a night's free board and lodging. It was really hunger which drove me to the workhouse door. That was Wednesday. Since the Sunday night preceding nothing had passed my lips save water from the public fountains—with the exception of a crust of bread which a man had given me whom I'd found crouching at the root of a tree in Holland Park. For three days I'd been fasting, and practically all the time on my feet. It seemed to me that if I had to go hungry till the morning, I would collapse. Yet, in this strange and inhospitable place, where was I to get food at that time of night, and how?

I don't know how far I went. Every yard I covered, my feet dragged even more. I was exhausted, inside and out. I had neither strength nor courage left, and within me there was that frightful craving, which was as though it shrieked aloud. I leaned against a wall, dazed and giddy. If only death had come upon me quickly, painlessly, how true a friend I should have thought it! It was the agony of dying inch by inch which was so hard to take.

It was some minutes before I could collect myself sufficiently to withdraw from the wall and to start afresh. I stumbled blindly over the uneven road. Once, like a drunken man, I lurched forward, and fell to my knees. Such was my backboneless state that for some seconds I remained where I was, half-disposed to let things slide, accept the good the gods had sent me, and make a night of it right there. A long night, I fancy, it would have been, stretching from time unto eternity.

Once I regained my feet, I'd gone perhaps another couple hundred yards along the road. Heaven knows that it seemed to me just then a couple of miles, when there came over me again that overpowering giddiness which, I take it, was born of my agony of hunger. I staggered, helplessly, against a low wall which was at the side of the path. Without it I should have fallen in a heap. The attack inside me appeared to last for hours, though I suppose it was only seconds, and when I came to, it was as though I'd been aroused from sleep—aroused by extreme pain. I yelled out, "For a loaf of bread what wouldn't I do!"

I looked around in a kind of frenzy. As I did so, I for the first time became conscious that behind me was a house. It wasn't a large one. It was one of those so-called villas which were springing up in multitudes all round London, and which were let at rentals for a decent price. It was detached. So far as I could see in the imperfect light, there wasn't another building within twenty or thirty yards on either side of it. It was two stories.

There were three windows in the upper storey. Behind each the blinds were closely drawn. The front door was on my right,; it was approached by walking though a little wooden gate.

The house itself was so close to the public road that by leaning over the low wall, I could have touched either of the windows on the lower floor. There were two of them. One of them was a bow window, which was open about six inches.

Chapter 2

I mentally photographed all the little details of the house in front of which I was standing with what almost amounted to a gleam of preternatural perception. An instant before the world swam before my eyes I saw nothing. But now I saw everything with a clearness which, as it were, was shocking.

Above all, I saw the open window. I stared at it, conscious as I did so, of a curious catching of my breath. It was so near to me, so very near. I had but to stretch out my hand to thrust it through the opening. Once inside, my hand would at least be dry. How it was raining out here! My scanty clothing was soaked; I was wet to the skin! I was shivering, and as each second passed, it seemed to rain harder. My teeth were chattering. The damp was liquefying the very marrow in my bones.

But inside that open window, it had to be so warm, so dry!

There wasn't a soul in sight; not a human being anywhere near. I listened; there wasn't a sound. I alone was at the mercy of the sodden night. Of all God's creatures, the only one unsheltered from the fountains of Heaven which He had opened was me. There was no one to see what I might do; no one to care. Perhaps the house was empty; nay, probably. It was my plain duty to knock at the door, rouse the owners, and call attention to their oversight—namely the open window. The least they could do would be to reward me for my effort.

But suppose the place was empty. Then what would be the use of knocking? All it would do is make a useless clatter, and possibly disturb the neighborhood for nothing. And even if the people were at home, I might go unrewarded. I'd learned in a hard school the world's ingratitude. To have caused the window to be closed— the inviting window, the tempting window, the convenient window— and then to be no better for it after all, but still to be penniless, hopeless, hungry, out in the cold and the rain, better anything than that.

Leaning over the low wall I found that I could very easily put my hand inside the home. How warm it was in there! I could feel the difference in temperature in my fingertips. Very quietly I stepped over the wall. There was just room to stand in comfort between the window and the wall. The ground hard, as if it was cement. Stooping down, I peered through the opening. I could see nothing. It was black as pitch inside. The blind was drawn right up; it seemed incredible that anyone could be at home, and have gone to bed, leaving the blind up and the window open. I placed my ear to the crevice. How still it was! Beyond doubt, the place was empty.

I decided to push the window up another inch or two, so as to enable me to reconnoiter. If anyone caught me in the act, then there would be an opportunity to describe the circumstances, and to explain how I was just on the point of giving the alarm. Only, I needed to go carefully. In such damp weather it was probable that the window would creak.

It didn't, however. It moved as readily and as noiselessly as if it had been oiled. This silence of the window so emboldened me that I raised it more than I intended. In fact, as far as it would go. Not by a sound did it betray me. Bending over the sill, I put my head and half my body into the room. I could see nothing. For all I could tell the room might have been unfurnished. Indeed, the likelihood of such an explanation began to occur to me.

I might have chanced upon an empty house and in the darkness there was nothing to suggest the contrary. What was I to do?

Well, if the house was empty, and in such a plight as mine, I might be said to have a moral—if not a legal—right to its bare shelter. Who, with a heart in his bosom, would deny me? Hardly the most punctilious landlord. So raising myself by means of the sill, I slipped all the way into the house.

The moment I did so I became conscious that, at any rate, the room was not entirely unfurnished. The floor was carpeted. I have had my feet on some good carpets in my time—I know what carpets are—but never did I stand upon a softer one than that. It reminded me of the turf in Richmond Park; it caressed my instep, and sprang beneath my feet. To my poor, travel-worn feet, it was luxury after the sodden, puddle-filled, uneven road I'd traveled. So should I, now that I had ascertained that the room was at least partially furnished, beat a retreat? Or should I push my ¬search further? It would have been rapture to have thrown off my clothes, and to have sunk down on the carpet then and there, to sleep.

But I was so hungry, starving actually; what I wouldn't have given to have found something good to eat!

I moved a step or two forward, gingerly, reaching out with my hands, lest I hit, unawares, against some unseen thing. When I had taken three or four steps, without encountering an obstacle, or indeed anything at all, I began all at once, to wish I hadn't seen the house, that I'd passed it by, that I'd not come through the window, and that I were safely out of it again.

I became aware that something was in the room with me. There was nothing, ostensible, to lead me to such a conviction; it may be that my faculties were unnaturally keen; but all at once, I knew that there was something there. What was more, I had a horrible feeling that, though I was unseeing, I was being seen, that my every movement was being watched.

What was with me I couldn't tell; I couldn't even guess. It was as though something in my mental organization had been stricken by a sudden paralysis. It may seem childish to use such language, but I was overwrought, played out, physically speaking. Then without the slightest warning, I was conscious of a very curious sensation, the like of which I had never felt before, and the like of which I pray that I never would feel again; a sensation of panic fear. I remained rooted to the spot on which I stood, not daring to move, fearing to draw breath. I felt that the presence in the room was something strange, something evil.

I don't know how long I stood there, spell-bound, but it was certainly for considerable time. By degrees, as nothing moved, nothing was seen or heard, and nothing happened, I made an effort to better play a man of courage. I knew that at the moment, I was playing the cur, and endeavored to ask myself what it was I was so afraid of. I was shivering at my own imagination. What could be in the room, to have suffered me to open the window and to enter unopposed? Whatever it was, it was surely as great a coward as I was, or why permit, unchecked, my burglarious entry. Since I had been allowed to enter, the probability was that I should be at liberty to leave, and I had a much keener desire to retreat than I ever had to enter.

I had to put the greatest amount of pressure upon myself before I could summon up sufficient courage to enable me to even turn my head, and the moment I did so I turned it back again. What constrained me I couldn't have said, but I was constrained nonetheless.

My heart was palpitating in my chest; I could hear it beat. I was trembling so that I could scarcely stand. I was overwhelmed by a fresh flood of terror. I stared in front of me with eyes in which, had it been light, would have seen the frenzy of unreasoning fear. My ears strained so that I listened with an acuteness of tension which was painful.

Something moved in the darkness. Silently, with a sound so soft it would have scarcely been audible to other ears save mine. But I heard it. I was looking in the direction from which the movement came, and as I looked, I saw in front of me two specks of light.

They weren't there a moment ago, that I would swear. But they were there now. They were eyes, or I told myself they were eyes. I had heard how a cat's eyes gleam in the dark, though I had never seen them, and I said to myself that these were a cat's eyes, that the thing in front of me was nothing but a cat. But I knew I lied.

I knew that these were eyes, but I knew they weren't cat's eyes, but what eyes they were I didn't know, nor dared to think otherwise.

They moved towards me. The creature to which the eyes belonged was coming closer. So intense was my desire to flee that I would much rather have died than stood there, yet I couldn't control a limb; as if my body wasn't mine. The eyes came closer, noiselessly. At first they were between two and three feet from the floor, but suddenly there was a rustling sound, as if some yielding body had been pushed off the floor. The eyes vanished, to reappear a moment later at what I judged to be a distance of some six inches from the floor.

They again came ever closer.

So it seemed that the creature, whatever it was to which the eyes belonged, was after all small. Why I didn't obey the frantic longing I had to flee I don't know. I only know I could not. I take it that the stress and privations which I had lately undergone, and which I was, even then, still undergoing, had much to do with my conduct at that moment, and with the part I played in all that followed. Ordinarily I believe that I have as high a spirit as the average man, and as solid a resolution, but when one has been dragged through the Valley of Humiliation, and plunged again and again into the Waters of Bitterness and Privation, a man can be forced to a course of action of which, in better times, he would have deemed himself incapable. I know this to be true of myself anyway.

Slowly the eyes came closer with a strange slowness, and as they did, they moved from side to side as if their owner walked unevenly. Nothing could have exceeded the horror with which I awaited their approach, except my incapacity to escape them. Not for an instant did my gaze shift from them. I couldn't have closed my eyes for all the gold in the world, so that as they came closer, I had to look right down to what seemed to be almost the level of my feet.

When at last they reached my feet, they never paused. Suddenly I felt something on my boot, and with a sense of shrinking horror and nausea, I was rendered momentarily helpless.

That was when I realized that the creature was beginning to ascend my legs, to climb my body. Even then what it was I couldn't tell. It mounted me apparently, with as much ease as if I had been horizontal instead of perpendicular. It was as though it were some gigantic spider, though a spider of the nightmares, a monstrous conception of some dreadful vision.

It pressed lightly against my clothing with what might, for all the world, have been spider's legs. There was an amazing host of them; I felt the pressure of each separate one. They embraced me softly, stickily, as if the creature glued and unglued them each time it moved.

Higher and higher! It had gained my loins. It was moving towards the pit of my stomach. The helplessness with which I suffered its invasion was not the least part of my agony, it was the helplessness we all know in dreadful dreams. I understood, quite well, that if I gave myself a hearty shake, the creature would fall off, but I hadn't a muscle at my command.

As the creature moved higher, its eyes began to play the part of two small lamps; they positively emitted rays of light. By their rays I began to perceive faint outlines of its body.

It seemed larger than I had supposed. Either the body itself was slightly phosphorescent, or it was of a peculiar yellow hue. It gleamed in the darkness. What was there was still nothing to positively show, but the impression grew upon me that it was some member of the spider family—some monstrous member—of the like of which I had never heard or read. It was heavy. So heavy that I wondered how, with so slight a pressure, it managed to retain its hold on me. That it did so by the aid of some adhesive substance at the end of its legs I was sure, as I could feel it stick. Its weight increased as it ascended, and it smelled! For some time I'd been aware that it emitted an unpleasant, fetid odor, and as it neared my face it became so intense as to be unbearable.

When it was on my chest I became more and more conscious of an uncomfortable wobbling motion, as if each time it breathed its body heaved. Its forelegs touched the bare skin about the base of my neck; they stuck to it and I shall never forget the feeling; I have it often in my dreams. While it hung on with those in front, it seemed to draw its other legs up after it. It crawled up my neck with hideous slowness, a quarter of an inch at a time, its weight compelling me to brace the muscles of my back.

When it reached my chin it touched my lips, and I stood still and bore it all, while it enveloped my face with its huge, slimy, evil-smelling body, and embraced me with its myriad of legs.

The horror of it made me mad, and I finally broke from my stupor and shook myself like one stricken by illness. I shook the creature off and it fell to the floor. Shrieking like some lost spirit, I turned and dashed towards the window. As I ran, my foot got caught in some obstacle, and I fell headlong to the floor.

Picking myself up as quickly as I could, I resumed my flight, rain or no rain, my only goal to get out of that room! I already had my hand on the sill, knowing in another instant I would be over it, when someone struck a light behind me, chasing the shadows away.

Chapter 3

The illumination which instantly followed was unexpected. It startled me.

"Keep still!" a voice said.

There was a quality in the voice which I can't describe. There was not only an accent of command, but there was something malicious as well. It was a little guttural, though whether it was a man speaking I couldn't have positively said, but I had no doubt it was a foreigner. It was the most disagreeable voice I'd ever heard, and it had the most disagreeable effect on me, for when it said, "Keep still!" I kept still. It was as though there was nothing else for me to do.

"Turn around!"

I did so mechanically, like an automaton. Such passivity was worse than undignified, it was galling; I knew that well. I resented it with secret rage. But in that room, in that presence, I was immobile.

When I turned I found myself confronting someone who was lying in bed in the far corner of the room. At the head of the bed was a shelf, and on it was a small lamp which gave the most brilliant light I'd ever seen. It caught me full in the eyes, and it had on me such a blinding effect that for a few seconds I could see nothing.

Throughout the entire, strange interview I can't affirm that I saw clearly, as the dazzling glare from the lamp caused dancing specks to obscure my vision. But after an interval of time, I did see something, and what I did see I'd rather have left unseen.

I couldn't decide if it was a man or a woman lying in the bed. Indeed, at first I doubted if it was anything human. But afterwards I knew it to be a man of Asian descent, for the reason that it was impossible such a human being could be feminine. The bedclothes were drawn up to his shoulders and only his head was visible. He lay on his left side, his head resting on his left hand, motionless, eyeing me as if he sought to read my inmost soul. And to be truthful, I believe he did read it. I couldn't guess his age, but he was so ancient that such a look of age I had never imagined. Had he asserted that he had been living through the ages, I should have been forced to admit that, at least, he looked it. Yet I felt that it was quite within the range of possibility that he was no older than me; there was a vitality in his eyes which was startling. It might have been that he'd been afflicted by some terrible disease, and it was that which had made him so supernaturally ugly.

There wasn't a hair on his face or head, but to make up for it, the skin, which was saffron yellow, was an amazing mass of wrinkles. The cranium, and indeed, the entire skull, was so small as to be disagreeably suggestive of something animal. The nose on the other hand, was abnormally large; so extravagant were its dimensions, and so peculiar its shape that it resembled the beak of some bird of prey. A characteristic of the face—and an uncomfortable one—was that it stopped short at the mouth. His blubbery lips came immediately underneath the nose, and the chin for all intents and purposes, was nonexistent. This deformity—the absence of a chin—was to give the face the appearance of something not human; that and the eyes. The most prominent feature on the man were his eyes, and it seemed to me that he was nothing but eyes.

His eyes ran, literally, across the entire upper portion of his unwontedly small face, and the top of the nose was razor-edged. The pupils were long, and they looked out of narrow windows, and they seemed to be lighted by some internal radiance, for they shone out like lamps in a lighthouse tower. Escape them I couldn't, while as I endeavored to meet them, it was as if I shriveled into nothingness. Never before had I realized what was meant by the power of the eye. They held me enchained, helpless, spell-bound. I felt that they could do with me as they would; and they did. Their gaze was unfaltering, having the bird-like trick of never blinking; this man could have glared at me for hours and never moved an eyelid.

It was he who broke the silence. I was speechless.

"Close the window," he said with a heavy Asian accent, his voice high like a woman's. I did as he bade me and closed the window.

"Pull down the blind."

I obeyed.

"Turn around again and face me."

I was still obedient.

"What is your name?"

Then I answered him. There was this odd thing about the words I uttered, that they came from me, not in response to my willpower, but in response to his. It was not I who willed that I should speak; it was he. What he willed that I should say, I said. Just that and nothing more. For the time I was no longer a man; my manhood was merged in his. I was, in the extremist sense, an example of passive obedience.

"Robert Holt."

"What are you?"

"A clerk."

"You look as if you were a clerk." There was a flame of scorn in his voice which scorched me even then. "What sort of a clerk are you?"

"I'm not employed at the moment."

"You look as if you're out of work." Again the scorn. "Are you the sort of clerk who is always out of work? You're a thief."

"I'm not a thief."

"Oh? Do clerks come through the window?" I was still, he putting no constraint on me to speak. "Why did you come through the window?"

"Because it was open," I replied.

"So! Do you always come through a window which is open?"

"No."

"Then why through this one?"

"Because I was wet and cold and hungry and tired," The words came from me as if he had dragged them one by one, which in fact, he did.

"Have you a home?"

"No."

"Money?"

"No."

"Friends?"

"No."

"Then what sort of a clerk are you?"

I didn't answer him, I didn't know what it was he wished me to say. I was the victim of bad luck, nothing else, I swear it. Misfortune had followed hard upon misfortune. The firm that I'd been employed with for years had suspended payment. I then obtained a position with one of their creditors, though at a lower salary but then they reduced their staff, which entailed my going. After an interval I obtained a temporary engagement, the occasion which required my services passed, and I with it. After another, and a longer interval, I again found temporary employment, the pay for which was but a pittance.

When that was over I could find nothing. That was nine months ago, and since then I hadn't earned a penny. It's so easy to grow shabby when you're on the everlasting tramp, and are living on your stock of clothes. I'd trudged all over London in search of work of any kind, anything would have been welcome, so long as it would have enabled me to keep body and soul together. But I had trudged in vain. Now I'd been refused admittance in a shelter as a casual; how easy is the descent! But I didn't tell the man lying on the bed all this. I knew he didn't wish to hear, and had he wished he would have made me tell him.

It may be that he read my story, unspoken though it was, by studying me; it's conceivable. His eyes had powers of penetration which were peculiarly their own, that I know.

"Undress!" When he spoke again that was what he said, in that guttural tone of his in which there was a reminiscence of some foreign land. I obeyed, letting my sodden, shabby clothes fall to the floor. A look came on his face as I stood naked in front of him, which if it was meant for a smile, it was a satyr's smile, and it filled me with a sensation of shuddering repulsion.

"What white skin you have, how white! What I wouldn't give for skin as white as that, ah yes!" He paused, devouring me with his eyes, then continued, "Go to the cupboard; you'll find a cloak—put it on."

I went to a cupboard which was in a corner of the room, his eyes following me as I moved. It was full of clothing; garments which might have formed the stock-in-trade of a tailor whose specialty was providing costumes for masquerades. A long dark cloak hung on a peg. My hand moved towards it, apparently of its own volition. I put it on, its ample folds falling to my feet.

"In the other cupboard you will find meat, bread, and wine. Eat and drink."

On the opposite side of the room, near the head of his bed, there was a second cupboard. In this one, upon a shelf, I found what looked like pressed beef, several round cakes of what tasted like rye bread, and some thin, sour wine in a straw-covered flask. But I was in no mood to criticize; I crammed myself like some famished wolf, he watching me in silence the entire the time. When I was done, which was when I'd eaten and drunk as much as I could hold, there returned to his face that satyr's grin.

"I wish that I could eat and drink like that, ah yes! Put back what's left." I put it back, which seemed an unnecessary exertion, as there was so little remaining. "Look me in the face."

I did as he said, and immediately became conscious as I did so, that something was going from me, the capacity as it were, to be myself.

His eyes grew larger and larger, until they seemed to fill all space till I became lost in their immensity. He moved his hand, doing something to me, though I know not what, and as the hand passed through the air, it cut the solid ground from underneath my feet, so that I fell headlong to the floor.

Where I fell, there I lay, like a log. Then the light went out.

Chapter 4

I knew that the light went out. What was not the least odd, nor indeed, the least distressing part of my condition, was the fact that to the best of my knowledge and belief, I never once lost consciousness during the long hours which followed. I was aware of the extinction of the lamp, and of the black darkness which ensued.

I heard a rustling sound, as if the man in the bed was settling himself between the sheets. Then all was still. But throughout that interminable night I remained, my brain awake, my body dead, waiting and watching for the day.

What had happened to me I couldn't guess. That I probably wore some of the external evidences of death my instinct told me; I knew I did. Paradoxical though it may sound, I felt as a man might feel who had actually died. It's very far from certain that feeling necessarily expires with what we call life. I continually asked myself if I could be dead; the inquiry pressed itself on me with awful iteration. Does the body die, and the brain—the I, the ego—still live on? God only knows. But then what of the agony of the thought.

The hours passed. By slow degrees, the silence was eclipsed. Sounds of traffic, of hurrying footsteps—life--were ushers of the morning. Outside the window, sparrows twittered, a cat mewed, a dog barked and there was the clatter of a milk can. Shafts of light stole past the blind, increasing in intensity. It still rained, and now and again it pattered against the glass of the window. The wind must have shifted, because for the first time there came a sudden clang of a distant clock striking the hour—seven. Then, with the interval of a lifetime between each chiming, eight, nine and ten.

So far, in the room itself there hadn't been a sound. When the clock had struck ten, as it seemed to me, years ago, there came a rustling noise from the direction of the bed. Feet stepped upon the floor, moving towards where I was. It was of course, now day, and I presently perceived that a figure, clad in some odd-colored garment, was standing at my side and looking down at me. It stooped, then knelt.

My only covering was unceremoniously thrown off me, so that I lay there in my nakedness. Fingers prodded me then and there, as if I'd been a cow ready for the butcher's stall. A face looked into mine, and in front of me were those dreadful eyes. Then, whether I was dead or living, I said to myself that this could be nothing human, as nothing fashioned in God's image could wear such a shape as that. Fingers were pressed into my cheeks and thrust into my mouth. They touched my staring eyes, closed my eyelids, then opened them again, and—horror of horrors—the blubbery lips were pressed to mine, and the soul of something evil entered into me in the guise of a kiss.

Then this travesty of manhood got to his feet, and said, whether speaking to me or to himself, I couldn't tell, "Dead! Dead! As good as dead! And better! We'll have him buried."

He moved away from me. I heard a door open and close and knew that he was gone. He was gone throughout the day. I had no actual knowledge of his going out into the street, but he must have done so, because the house appeared deserted. What had become of the dreadful creature of the night before I couldn't guess. My first fear was that he had left it behind in the room with me, as a sort of watchdog. But as the minutes and the hours passed, and there was still no sign or sound of anything living, I concluded that if the thing was there, it was possibly as helpless as I was, and that during its owner's absence at any rate, I had nothing to fear from it.

With the exception of myself, the house held nothing human, and I had strong presumptive proof of this more than once in the course of the day. Several times, both in the morning and the afternoon, people outside attempted to attract the attention of whoever was within. Vehicles—probably tradesmen's carts—drew up in front, their stopping being followed by more or less assiduous assaults upon the knocker and the bell.

But in every case their appeals remained unheeded. Whatever it was they wanted, they had to go away unsatisfied.

Lying there, torpid, with nothing to do but listen, it did occur to me that one among the callers was more persistent than the rest.

The distant clock had just struck noon when I heard the gate open outside, and someone approached the front door. Since nothing but silence followed, I supposed that the occupant of the place had returned, and had chosen to do so as silently as when he'd left. Presently however, there came from the doorstep a slight but peculiar call, as if a rat was squeaking. It was repeated three times, and then there was the sound of footsteps quietly retreating, and the gate closing. Between one and two in the afternoon the caller came again; there was a repetition of the same signal, that it was a signal I did not doubt, followed by the same retreat.

At about three the mysterious visitor returned. The signal was repeated, and when there was no response, fingers tapped softly against the panels of the front door. When there was still no answer, the footsteps stole softly round the side of the house, and there came the signal from the rear, and then again the tapping of fingers against what was apparently, the back door. After no notice was taken of these various proceedings, the footsteps returned the way they'd come, and as before the gate was closed.

Shortly after darkness had fallen this persistent caller returned, to make a fourth and more resolute attempt to call attention to his presence. From the peculiar character of his maneuvers it seemed that he suspected that whoever was within had particular reasons for ignoring him. He went through the familiar pantomime of the three squeaky calls both at the front door and the back, followed by the tapping of the fingers on the panels. This time though, he also tried the window panes. I could hear quite distinctly, the clear yet distinct noise of what seemed like knuckles rapping against the windows behind me. Disappointed there, he renewed his efforts at the front. The curiously quiet footsteps came around the house, to pause before the window of the room in which I lay.

Then something odd occurred.

While I waited for the tapping, there came instead, the sound of someone or something scrambling onto the windowsill, as if some creature, unable to reach the window from the floor, was trying to gain the vantage of the sill; some ungainly creature, unskilled in surmounting such an obstacle as a perpendicular brick wall. There was the noise of what seemed to be the scratching of claws, as if it had experienced considerable difficulty in obtaining a hold on the unyielding surface. What kind of creature it was I couldn't imagine and I was astonished to find that it was a creature at all. I had taken it for granted that the persevering visitor was either a woman or a man. If however, as now seemed likely, it was some sort of animal, this explained the squeaking sounds, though what, except a rat, did squeak like that was more than I could say—and the absence of any knocking or ringing.

Whatever it was, it had gained the summit of its desires—the windowsill. It panted as if its efforts at climbing had made it short of breath. Then began the tapping. In the light of my new discovery, I perceived clearly enough, that the tapping was hardly that which was likely to be the product of human fingers, for it was sharp and definite, rather resembling the striking of the point of a nail against the glass. It wasn't loud, but in time—it continued with much persistency—it became plainly vicious. It was accompanied by what I can only describe as the most extraordinary noises. There were squeaks, growing angrier and shriller as the minutes passed, what seemed like someone gasping for breath, and a peculiar buzzing sound like, yet unlike, the purring of a cat.

The creature's resentment at its want of success in attracting attention was unmistakable. The tapping became like the clattering of hailstones; it kept up a continuous noise with its cries and panting. Then there was the sound as of some large body being rubbed against the glass, as if it were extending itself against the window, and trying by force of pressure, to gain an entrance through the glass. So violent did its contortions become that I momentarily anticipated the yielding of the glass and the excited assailant then coming crashing through.

Considerably to my relief the window proved more impregnable than seemed at one time likely. The stolid resistance proved in the end to be too much either for its endurance or its patience. Just as I was looking for some fresh manifestation of fury, it seemed rather to tumble than to spring off the sill; then came once more, the same sound of quietly retreating footsteps, and what under the circumstances seemed odder still, the same closing of the gate.

During the next two or three hours nothing happened at all. But then took place the most surprising incident of all. The clock had struck ten some time before. Since before the striking of the hour nothing and no one had passed along what was evidently the little frequented road in front of the uncanny house I was in. But then two sounds broke the stillness outside: one of someone running and another of cries.

Judging from his hurrying steps, someone seemed to be running for his life to the accompaniment of curious cries. It was only when the runner reached the front of the house that in the cries I recognized the squeaks of the persistent caller. I imagined that he had returned as before, alone, to renew his attacks upon the window, until it was made plain, as it quickly was, that with him was some sort of a companion.

Immediately there arose from without the noise of battle. Two creatures, whose cries were to me of so unusual a character that I found it impossible to even guess their identity, seemed to be waging war upon the doorstep.

After a minute or two of furious battle, victory seemed to rest with one of the combatants, for the other fled, squeaking as with pain. While I listened with strained attention for the next episode in this odd drama, I expected that now would come another assault upon the window, but to my unbounded surprise I heard a key thrust in the keyhole, the lock turned, and the front door was thrown open with a furious bang.

It was closed as loudly as it was opened. Then the door of the room in which I lay was shoved open with the same display of excitement and clamor, and footsteps came hurrying in. The door was slammed with such force that the house shook to its foundations. There was a rustling as of bedclothes, the brilliant illumination of the lamp from night before, and a voice which I had only too good a reason to remember said, "Stand up."

I stood up automatically at the word of command, and faced the bed. There between the sheets, with his head resting on his hand, in the position in which I'd last seen him, was the man I'd made acquaintance with under circumstances which I was never likely to forget.

But there was something different about him.

He was the same, yet not the same.

Chapter 5

That the man in the bed was the one whom, to my cost, I'd suffered myself to stumble on the night before, there could be of course not the faintest doubt. Yet I recognized that some astonishing alteration had taken place in his appearance. To begin with, he seemed younger, the decrepitude of age had given place to something very like the fire of youth. His features had undergone some subtle change. His nose, for instance, was not by any means so grotesque; its beak-like quality was now less conspicuous. Most of his wrinkles had disappeared, as if by magic, and though his skin was still as yellow as saffron, his contours had rounded, and he'd even come into possession of a modest allowance of chin. But the most astounding novelty was around the face; there was something which was essentially feminine. So feminine that I wondered if I could by any possibility have blundered earlier and mistaken a woman for a man.

The effect of the changes which had come about in his appearance— for after all, I told myself that it was impossible that I could have been such a simpleton as to have been mistaken on such a question as gender— was heightened by the self-evident fact that very recently he'd been engaged in some pitched battle. Hand to hand probably, from which he had come away with wounds from opponent's prowess. His antagonist could hardly have been a chivalrous fighter, for his countenance was marked by a dozen different scratches which seemed to suggest that the weapons used had been fingernails.

It was perhaps because the heat of the battle was still in his veins that he was in such a state of excitement. He seemed to be almost overwhelmed by the strength of his own feelings. His eyes seemed literally to flame with fire. The muscles of his face were working as if they were beyond his control. When he spoke, his accent was markedly foreign, the words rushing from his lips in an inarticulate torrent. He kept repeating the same thing over and over again in a fashion which wasn't a little suggestive of insanity.

"So you're not dead! You're not dead, you're alive! You're alive! Well, how does it feel to be dead? I ask you! Is it not good to be dead? To be dead is better, it's the best of all! To have made an end of all things, to cease to strive and to cease to weep, to cease to want and to cease to have, to cease to annoy and to cease to long, to no more care, no, not for anything, to pull from you the curse of life forever! Is that not the best? Oh yes! I tell you! Do I not know? But for you such knowledge is not yet. For you there is the return to life, the coming out of death. You shall live on! For me! Live on!"

He made a movement with his hand to me, and just like before on the previous evening, a metamorphosis took place in the very abysses of my being. I woke from my torpor, as he put it. I came out of death and was alive again. I was still far from being my own man. I realized that he'd exercised on me a degree of mesmeric force which I'd never dreamed that one creature could exercise on another, but at least I was no longer in doubt as to whether I was or wasn't dead. I knew I was alive.

He lay there watching me, as if he was reading the thoughts which occupied my brain, and for all I knew, he was.

"Robert Holt, you're a thief."

"I am not." My own voice as I heard it startled me; it was so long since it had sounded in my ears.

"You're a thief! Only thieves come through windows, did you not come through the window?" I was still, what would my contradiction have availed me? "But it's well that you came through the window, well you are a thief, well for me! For me! It's you that I'm wanting at the happy moment you've dropped yourself into my hands, in the nick of time. For you are my slave, at my beck and call, my familiar spirit, to do with as I will; you know this, eh?"

I did know it, and the knowledge of my impotence was terrible. I felt that if I could only get away from him, only release myself from the bonds with which he had bound me, only remove myself from him, only get one or two square meals and have an opportunity of recovering from the stress of mental and bodily fatigue. I felt that then I might be something like his match, and that a second time, he would endeavor in vain to bring me within the compass of his magic. But as it was, I was conscious that I was helpless, and the consciousness was agony.

"I say you're a thief!" he persisted. "A thief, Robert Holt, a thief! You came through a window for your own pleasure, but now you'll go through a window for me—not this window, but another." Where the jest lay I didn't know, but it tickled him, for a grating sound came from his throat which was meant to be laughter. "This time though, you will go in as a thief, oh yes, be sure of that." He paused to transfix me with his gaze. His unblinking eyes never for an instant left my face. With frightful fascination they constrained me, and how I loathed them!

When he spoke again there was a new intonation in his speech, something bitter, cruel, unrelenting. "Do you know Paul Lessingham?"

He pronounced the name as if he hated it, and yet as if he loved to have it on his tongue.

"What Paul Lessingham?" I asked.

"There is only one Paul Lessingham! *The* Paul Lessingham, the 'great' Paul Lessingham!" He shrieked, rather than said this, with an outburst of rage so frenzied that I thought, for the moment, that he was going to spring on me and tear me apart. I shook all over.

I don't doubt that as I replied, my voice trembled. "All the world knows Paul Lessingham, the politician and statesman."

As he glared at me his eyes dilated. I still stood in expectation of a physical assault, but for the present, he contented himself with words. "Tonight you're going through his window like a thief!"

I had no inkling of his meaning, and apparently, judging from his next words, I looked something of the bewilderment I felt. "You don't understand? No! It's simple! What could be simpler? I say that tonight you're going through his window like a thief. You came through my window, why not through the window of Paul Lessingham, the politician and statesman?"

He repeated my words as if in mockery. I was one of that great multitude that regarded Paul Lessingham as the greatest living force in practical politics, and which I believe, with confidence, the man would carry through that great work of constitutional and social reform which he has set himself to do. I daresay that my tone, in speaking of him, savored of laudation, which plainly, the man in the bed resented. What he meant by his wild words about my going through Paul Lessingham's window like a thief, I still hadn't the faintest notion. They sounded like the ravings of a madman.

As I remained silent, he stared at me. Then there came into his tone another note, a note of tenderness, of which I hadn't deemed him capable. "He's good to look at, Paul Lessingham, is he not good to look at?"

I was aware that physically, Mr. Lessingham was a fine specimen of manhood, but I wasn't prepared for the assertion of the fact in such a quarter, nor for the manner in which the temporary master of my fate continued to harp and enlarge upon the theme.

"He's straight, straight as the mast of a ship, he's tall, his skin is white; he's strong— do you not know that he is strong, how strong! Oh yes! Is there a better thing than to be his wife? His well-beloved? The light in his eyes? Is there for a woman a happier chance? Oh no, not one!" As with soft cadences, he gave vent to these unlooked-for sentiments. Then his countenance changed. A look of longing came into his face, a savage, frantic longing, which un-alluring though it was, for the moment transfigured him. But the mood was transient. "To be his wife, oh yes! The wife of his scorn! The despised and rejected!"

The return to the venom of his former bitterness was rapid. I couldn't help but feel that this was the man in his natural state. Though why a man such as he should go out of his way to apostrophize, in such a manner, a publicist of Mr. Lessingham's stature, surpassed my comprehension. Yet he stuck to his subject like a leech, as if it had been one in which he had an engrossing personal interest.

"He's a devil, hard as the granite rock, cold as the snows of Ararat. In him there is none of life's warm blood—he's accursed! He's false, aye, false as the fables of those who lie for love of lies, he's all treachery. She whom he has taken to his bosom he would put away from him as if she had never been; he would steal from her like a thief in the night, and he would forget she ever was! But the avenger follows after, lurking in the shadows, hiding among the rocks, waiting, watching, until his time shall come. And it shall come! The day of the avenger! Aye, the day has come!"

Raising himself to a sitting position, he threw his arms above his head, and shrieked with a demonic fury. Presently he calmed down and reverted to his recumbent position, resting his head on his hand. He eyed me steadily, then asked me a question which struck me as being under the circumstances, more than a little strange.

"You know his house, the house of the great Paul Lessingham, the politician and statesman?"

"Not I don't."

"You lie! You do!" The words came from him with a sort of snarl, as if he would have lashed me across the face with them.

"I don't. Men in my position aren't acquainted with the residences of men in his position. I may at some time, have seen his address in print, but if so I've forgotten it."

He looked at me intently, for some moments, as if to learn if I spoke the truth, and apparently at last was satisfied that I did.

"You don't know it? Well! I'll show it to you. I'll show the house of the great Paul Lessingham."

What he meant by this I didn't know, but I was soon to learn, and an astounding revelation it proved to be. There was about his manner something hardly human, something which, for want of a better phrase, I'd call vulpine. In his tone there was a mixture of mockery and bitterness, as if he wished his words to have the effect of corrosive acid, and so sear me as he uttered them.

"Listen carefully and give me your undivided attention so that you may do as I bid you. Not that I fear your disobedience." He paused, as if to enable me to fully realize the picture of my helplessness conjured up by his jibes. "You came through my window like a thief but you'll leave through my window like a fool. You'll go to the house of the great Paul Lessingham. You say you do not know it? Well, I will show it you. I will be your guide. Unseen in the darkness and the night, I will stalk beside you, and will lead you to where I would have you go. You will go just as you are, with bare feet, head uncovered, and with but a single garment to hide your nakedness. You will be cold, your feet will be cut and bleeding, but what better does a thief deserve? If any see you, at the least they will take you for a madman. But have no fear; bear a bold heart. None shall see you while I stalk at your side. I will cover you with a cloak of invisibility, so that you may come in safety to the house of the great Paul Lessingham."

He paused again. What he said, wild and wanton though it was, was beginning to fill me with a sense of the most extreme discomfort. His sentences, in some strange, indescribable way, seemed as if they came from his lips, to then warp my limbs, to enwrap themselves about me, to confine me, tighter and tighter, as it were, in swaddling clothes—to make me more and more helpless. I was already conscious that whatever mad mission he chose to set me on, I should have no option but to carry it out.

"When you reach the house, you will stand and look, then seek a window convenient for entry. It may be that you will find one open, as you did mine, but if not, you'll open one. How you do this is your affair, not mine. You will practice the arts of a thief to break into the house."

The monstrosity of his suggestion fought against the spell which he again was casting upon me, and forced me into speech, endowed me with the power to show that there still was in me something of a man, though every second the strands of my manhood, as it seemed, were slipping faster through the fingers which were strained to clutch them.

"I won't do it."

He was silent as he looked at me. The pupils of his eyes dilated, until they seemed all pupil. "You will. Do you hear me? I say you will."

"I'm not a thief, I'm an honest man. Why should I do this thing?"

"Because I bid you."

"Have mercy!"

"On whom—on you, or on Paul Lessingham? Who at any time has shown mercy unto me, that I should show mercy unto them?" He stopped, and then went on, reiterating his former incredible suggestion with an emphasis which seemed to eat its way into my brain.

"You will practice the arts of a thief to steal into his house, and once inside, you will listen. If all is still, you'll make your way to the room he calls his study."

"How shall I find it? I know nothing of his house." The question was wrung from me. I felt that the sweat was standing in great drops on my brow.

"I'll show it you."

"Will you go with me?"

"Aye, I shall go with you. All the time I shall be with you. You won't see me, but I shall be there. Don't be afraid."

His claim to supernatural powers—for what he said amounted to nothing less—was on the face of it preposterous, but then I was in no condition to even hint at its absurdity.

He continued, "When you have gained the study, you will go to a certain drawer, which is in a certain bureau, in a corner of the room. I see it now, when you're there you shall see it too—and you will open it."

"Will it be locked?"

"You'll still open it."

"But how shall I open it if it's locked?"

"By those arts in which a thief is skilled. I say to you again, that is your affair, not mine."

I made no attempt to answer him. Even supposing that he forced me, by what I presumed were hypnotic powers, to carry the adventure to a certain stage—since he could hardly at an instant's notice endow me with the knack of picking locks, should the drawer he alluded to be locked— nothing serious might issue from it after all.

He read my thoughts.

"You will open it, though it will be locked. In it you will find..." He hesitated, as if to reflect. "Some letters; it may be two or three, I know not just how many. They are bound by a silken ribbon. You will take them out of the drawer, then make your way out of the house, and bring them back to me."

"What do I do if anyone comes upon me while I'm engaged in these nefarious proceedings? For instance, what if I should encounter Mr. Lessingham himself?"

"You need have no fear if you encounter him."

"I need have no fear! Even if he finds me in his house at the dead of night committing burglary!"

"You need have no fear of him," he repeated.

"On your account or on my own? At least he will have me arrested."

"I say you need have no fear of him. I say what I mean."

"Then how will I escape his righteous vengeance? He's not the man to suffer a midnight robber to escape him scot-free. Will I have to kill him?"

"You won't hurt him, nor will he hurt you."

"By what spell shall prevent him from this?"

"By the spell of two words."

"What words are they?" I asked.

"Should Lessingham by chance to come upon you and find you in his house, and should he seek to prevent you from whatever it is you may be at, you will not flinch nor flee from him, but will stand still, and say..."

Something in the crescendo accents of his voice, something weird and ominous, caused my heart to press against my ribs, so that when he stopped, in my eagerness I cried out,

"What?"

"The beetle!"

As the words came from him in a kind of screech, the lamp went out, and the place fell into darkness. I knew right then with a sense of loathing that with me in the room was the evil presence of the night before. Two bright specks gleamed in front of me, and something flopped from off the bed and on to the floor. The thing was coming towards me across the floor!

It approached me slowly. I stood still, speechless in the sickness of my horror. Until on my bare feet, it touched me with slimy feelers, and my terror, lest it should creep up my naked body, lent me voice, and I fell shrieking like a soul in agony.

It may be that my shrieking drove it from me. At least, it went away. All became still. Then suddenly, the lamp came on again, and there, lying as before in bed, glaring at me with his baleful eyes, was the being whom in my folly or in my wisdom, I was beginning to credit with the possession of unhallowed, unlawful powers.

"You'll say that to him, those two words. Only them. And you will see what you will see. But Lessingham is a man of resolution. Should he still persist in interfering, or seek to hinder you, you will say those two words again. You need do no more. Twice will suffice, I promise you. Now go. Draw up the blind, open the window, and climb through it. Hasten to do what I have bidden you. I will wait here for your return, and all the while I shall be with you."

Chapter 6

I went to the window, drew up the blind, unlatched the lock, and opened it. Clad, or rather unclad as I was, I clambered through it into the open air. I wasn't only incapable of resistance, I was incapable of distinctly formulating the desire to offer resistance. Some compelling influence moved me onward, with complete disregard of whether I wanted to.

And yet, when I found myself outside, I was conscious of a sense of exultation at having escaped from the miasmic atmosphere of that room of unholy memories. A faint hope began to dawn within me that as I increased the distance between myself and the house, I might shake off something of the nightmare helplessness which numbed and tortured me.

I lingered for a moment by the window, then stepped over the short dividing wall and to the street. Then I lingered again.

My condition was one of dual personality. While I was bound physically, to a considerable extent I was free mentally. But this measure of freedom on my mental side made my plight no better. For among other things, I realized what a ridiculous figure I must be cutting, barefooted and bareheaded, abroad at such an hour of the night in such a boisterous breeze, for I quickly discovered that the wind amounted to something like a gale.

Apart from all other considerations, the notion of parading the streets in such a condition filled me with profound disgust. I do believe that if my tyrannical oppressor had only permitted me to attire myself in my own garments, I should have started with a comparatively light heart on the felonious mission on which he apparently was sending me.

I believe, too, that being aware of my attire, or lack thereof, increased my sense of helplessness, and that had I been dressed as Englishmen are wont to be, who take their walks abroad, he would not have found in me the facile instrument which he had—at least on that occasion,

There was a moment in which the graveled pathway first made itself known to my naked feet, and the cutting wind to my naked flesh. I think it possible that had I gritted my teeth and strained my every nerve, I might have shaken myself free from the bonds which shackled me, and bade defiance to the ancient sinner who, for all I knew, was peering at me through the window. But so depressed was I by the knowledge of the ridiculous appearance I presented, that before I could take advantage of it the moment passed, not to return again that night.

The opportunity passed and it was too late. My tormentor—though unseen—must had seen and tightened his grip. I was whirled around, and sent hastily onwards in a direction in which I certainly had no desire of traveling.

All the way I never met a soul. I've since wondered whether in that respect my experience was not a normal one, whether it might not have happened at all. If so, there are streets in London, long lines of streets, which at a certain period of the night, in a certain sort of weather—probably the weather had something to do with it—are clean and deserted. Streets in which there were neither pedestrians nor vehicles, let alone a policeman.

The greater part of the route along which I was sent was one with which I had some sort of acquaintance. At first it led through what I take it was some part of Walham Green, then along Lillie Road, through Brompton, across Fulham Road, through the network of streets leading to Sloane Street, across Sloane Street and into Lowndes Square. Whoever goes that way goes some distance, and goes through some important thoroughfares, yet not a soul did I see, nor I imagine, was there anyone that saw me.

As I crossed Sloane Street, I fancied that I heard the distant rumbling of a horse-drawn carriage along Knightsbridge Road, but that was the only sound I heard.

It's painful even to recollect the plight in which I was when I was stopped, for stopped I was, as shortly and as sharply as a beast of burden with a bridle in its mouth, when the driver slams on the brakes.

Intermittent gusts of rain were borne on the scurrying wind, and in spite of the pace at which I was moving, I was chilled to the bone, but worst of all, my mud-stained feet, all cut and bleeding, were in great pain.

Unfortunately, I was still susceptible enough to pain that it was agony to have them come into contact with the cold and the slime of the hard, unyielding pavement.

I'd been stopped on the opposite side of the square, that nearest to the hospital, in front of a house which struck me as being somewhat smaller than the rest. It was a house with a portico. About the pillars of this portico was trelliswork, and on the trelliswork some sort of climbing plant. As I stood, shivering, wondering what would happen next, some strange impulse came over me, and to my own unbounded amazement, I immediately found myself scrambling up the trellis towards the verandah above.

I'm no gymnast, either by nature or by education, and I doubt whether previously I'd ever attempted to climb anything more difficult than a step ladder. The result was that though the impulse might have made me attempt such a feat, I still had no skill, and I'd only ascended a yard or so before losing my footing.

I came slithering down upon my back. Bruised and shaken though I was, I wasn't allowed to inspect my injuries. In a moment I was on my feet again, and again I was impelled to climb, only to once, again fall down.

This time the demon, or whatever it was that had entered and was controlling me, seemed to appreciate the impossibility of getting me to the top of that verandah, so it directed me to try another way. I mounted the steps leading to the front door, got onto the low parapet which was at one side, thence on to the sill of the adjacent window. Had I slipped then I would have fallen at least twenty feet to the ground. But the sill was broad, and fortune favored me. I didn't fall.

In my clenched fist I had a stone. With this I struck the pane of glass, as with a hammer. Through the hole which resulted, I could just insert my hand and reach the latch within. In another minute the window was raised and I was in the house.

I had committed burglary.

As I look back and reflect upon the audacity of the entire proceeding, even now I tremble. A hapless slave of another's will though I was, I can't repeat too often that I did realize to the fullest just what it was that I was being compelled to do—a fact which was very far from rendering my situation less distressful!

Every detail of my involuntary actions were projected upon my brain in a series of pictures, whose clear-cut outlines—so long as memory endures—will never fade. Certainly no professional burglar, nor indeed anyone in his senses, would have ventured to emulate my surprising rashness.

The process of smashing the pane of glass—it was plate-glass—was anything but a noiseless one. There was first the blow itself, then the shivering of the glass, then the clattering of fragments onto the floor. One would have thought that the entire thing would have made enough noise to rouse anyone within the home. But here again the weather was on my side.

At the same time that I struck the window, the wind was howling wildly, and it came shrieking across the square surrounding the house. It's possible that the tumult it made drowned out all other sounds.

As I stood inside the room, listening for signs of someone being on the alert, I heard nothing. Within the house there seemed to be the silence of the grave. I closed the window and made for the door.

It proved by no means easy to find. The windows were obscured by heavy curtains, so that the room inside was pitch dark. It appeared to be unusually full of furniture; an appearance due perhaps to my being a stranger in the midst of such Stygian blackness. I had to feel my way, very gingerly, among the various impediments. I seemed like I came into contact with most of the obstacles there were to come into contact with, stumbling more than once over footstools, and over what seemed to be dwarf chairs.

It was a miracle that my movements still continued to be unheard, but I believe that the explanation was that the house was well built, that the servants were the only persons in it at the time, that their bedrooms were on the top floor, that they were fast asleep, and that they were little likely to be disturbed by anything that might occur in the room which I'd entered.

Reaching the door at last, I opened it and listened for any promise of being interrupted, then went across the hall and up the stairs. I passed the first landing, and on the second moved to a door upon the right. I turned the handle, it yielded, the door opened, I entered, then closed it behind me. I went to the wall just inside the door, found a handle, jerked it, and switched on the light—make no doubt that all these things were seen by me from a spectator's point of view as I was being controlled, though naturally a judge and jury would have been difficult to persuade that my actions were not the product of my own volition.

In the brilliant glow of the electric light I took a leisurely survey of the contents of the room. It was, as the man in the bed had said it would be, a study, a fine, spacious apartment, evidently intended rather for work than for show. There were three separate writing desks—one very large and two smaller ones—all covered with an orderly array of manuscripts and papers. A typewriter was at the side of one. On the floor, under and about the desks, were piles of books, portfolios and official-looking documents. Every available foot of wall space on three sides of the room was lined with shelves, all full of books. On the fourth side, facing the door, was a large lock-up oak bookcase, and in the farther corner a quaint old bureau. As soon as I saw this bureau I went straight for it, and it would be no abuse of metaphor to say that I was propelled towards it like an arrow from a bow.

It had drawers below, glass doors above, and between the drawers and the doors was a flap to let down. It was to this flap that my attention was directed. I put out my hand to open it but it was locked at the top. I pulled at it with both hands but it refused to budge.

So this was the lock I was to practice the arts of a thief to open. I was no lock-pick, I'd flattered myself that nothing, and no one, could make me such a thing. Yet now that I found myself confronted by that unyielding flap, I found that pressure, irresistible pressure, was being put upon me to gain by any means, access to its interior.

I had no option but to yield. I looked around in search of some convenient tool with which to ply the felon's trade. I found it close beside me. Leaning against the wall, within a yard of where I stood, were examples of various kinds of weapons, among them spearheads. Taking one of the spearheads, with much difficulty I forced the point between the flap and the bureau. Using the leverage thus obtained, I attempted to open it. The flap held fast and the spearhead snapped in two. I tried another, with the same result then a third time. I failed again. There were no more spearheads. The most convenient thing remaining was an odd, heavy-headed, sharp-edged hatchet. This I took, and brought the sharp edge down with all my force. The hatchet went through easily and it was open.

But I was destined on the occasion of my first—and I trust last— experience of the burglar's calling to carry the part completely through. I'd gained access to the flap itself only to find that at the back were several small drawers, on one of which my observation was brought to bear in a fashion which it was quite impossible to disregard. As a matter of course it was locked, and once more I had to search for something which would serve as a rough-and-ready substitute for the missing key.

There was nothing at all suitable among the weapons. I could hardly for such a purpose use the hatchet for the drawer in question was such a little one that to have done so would have been to shatter it into splinters. On the mantle—in an open leather case—was a pair of revolvers.

Statesmen nowadays sometimes stand in actual peril of their lives. It's possible that Mr. Lessingham, conscious of continually threatened danger, carried them with him as a necessary protection. They were serviceable weapons, large, and somewhat weighty, of the type with which I believe upon occasion the police used. Not only were all the barrels loaded, but in the case itself there was a supply of cartridges more than sufficient to load them again.

I was handling the weapons, wondering— if in my condition, the word was applicable—what use I could make of them to enable me to gain admission to the drawer, when there came from the street the sound of an approaching carriage. There was a whirring within my brain, as if someone was endeavoring to explain to me to what service to apply the revolvers, and I strained every nerve to grasp the meaning of my invisible mentor.

While I did so, the carriage drew rapidly nearer, and just as I was expecting it to go racing by, it stopped in front of the house. My heart leapt in my chest. In a convulsion of frantic terror, I all but burst the bonds that held me, and fled, haphazardly, from the imminent peril. But the bonds were stronger than I; it was as if I had been rooted to the floor.

A key was inserted into the lock on the front door, the lock was turned, the door was thrown open, and firm footsteps entered the house.

If I could have I would left right then, but my actions were still not under my control. Panic and fear raged within me, though outwardly I looked calm. I stood still, turning the revolvers over and over in my hands, asking myself what it could be that I was intended to do with them. Then all at once it came to me in an illuminating flash; I was to fire at the lock of the drawer and blow it open.

It would have been impossible to come up with a more insane scheme. The servants had slept through a good deal of my actions, but they would hardly sleep through the discharge of a revolver in a room below them, not to mention the person who had just entered the house, and whose footsteps were already audible as he came up the stairs.

I struggled to make a futile protest against the insensate folly which was hurrying me to infallible destruction, without success. For me there was only obedience. With a revolver in either hand, I marched towards the bureau. I placed the muzzle of one of the revolvers against the keyhole of the drawer to which my unseen guide had previously directed me, and pulled the trigger. The lock shattered and the contents of the drawer were at my mercy. I snatched up a bundle of letters in which a pink ribbon was wrapped.

There came a noise behind, and startled, I glanced over my shoulder. The door to the room was open, and he was standing with his hand on the knob.

Chapter 7

Paul Lessingham wore a suit. In his left hand he held a small portfolio. If the discovery of my presence startled him, as it could scarcely have failed to do, he allowed no sign of surprise to show on his face. His impenetrability was proverbial. Whether on platforms addressing excited crowds, or in the midst of heated discussion in the House of Commons, all the world knew that he remained unruffled. It's generally understood that he owed his success in the political arena in no slight measure to the adroitness which was born of his invulnerable presence of mind. He gave me a taste of its quality then. Standing in the attitude which had been familiarized to myself and others by caricaturists, his feet apart, his broad shoulders well set back, his handsome head a little advanced, his keen blue eyes having in them something suggestive of a bird of prey considering just when, where, and how to pounce, he regarded me for some seconds in perfect silence. Whether outwardly I flinched I can't say, but I know I did inwardly.

When he spoke, it was without moving from where he stood, and his voice was in the calm, airy tone in which he might have addressed an acquaintance that had just dropped in. "May I ask, sir, as to why I am enjoying the pleasure of your company?" He paused, as if waiting for my answer. When none came, he put his question in another form. Pray, sir, who are you, and on whose invitation do I find you here?"

As I still stood speechless, motionless, and meeting his glance without a twitching of an eyebrow, nor a tremor of the hand, I imagined that he began to consider me with an even closer intentness than before. And that the—to say the least of it—peculiarity of my appearance caused him to suspect that he was face to face with an adventure of a peculiar kind. Whether he took me for a lunatic I can't say, but from his manner, I think it possible he did. He moved towards me from across the room, while addressing me with the utmost courtesy. "Be so good as to give me the revolver, and the papers you're holding in your hand."

As he came on, something entered into me, and forced itself from between my lips, so that I said, in a low, hissing voice, which I vow was never mine, "*The Beetle!*"

Whether it was—or wasn't—owing in some degree to a trick of my imagination, I can't determine, but as the words were spoken, it seemed to me that the lights went low, so that the place was all darkness, and I again was filled with the nauseous consciousness of the presence of something evil in the room.

But if in that matter my abnormally strained imagination played a trick on me, there could be no doubt to the effect which the words had on Mr. Lessingham. When the mist of the blackness—real or supposititious—had passed from before my eyes, I found that he had retreated to the far corner of the room, and was crouching with his back against the bookshelves, clutching at them, in the attitude of a man that had received a staggering blow, from which as yet, he'd had no opportunity of recovering. A most extraordinary change had taken place in the expression of his face; in his countenance amazement, fear, and horror seemed to be struggling for mastery. I was filled with a most discomforting qualm, as I gazed at the frightened figure before me, realizing that it was still the great Paul Lessingham, the god of my political idolatry, who now cowered on the floor.

"Who are you? In God's name, who are you?" he choked. His very voice seemed changed; his frenzied, choking accents would hardly have been recognized by either friend or foe. "Who are you? Do you hear? Who are you? In the name of God, I bid you tell me!"

As I remained still, he began to get excited, which seemed odd, especially as he continued to crouch against the bookshelf, as if he was afraid to stand up straight. Far from exhibiting the calm for which he was renowned, all the muscles in his face and all the limbs of his body seemed to be in motion at once, like he was a man afflicted with the shivering ague. His very fingers were twitching aimlessly, as they were stretched out on either side of him, as if seeking support from the shelves against which he leaned.

"Where have you come from? What do you want? Who sent you here? What concern have you with me? Is it necessary that you should come and play these childish tricks with me? Why?" The questions came from him with astonishing rapidity. When I remained silent, they came even faster, mingled with what sounded to me like a stream of incoherent abuse.

"Why do you stand there in that extraordinary garment, it's worse than nakedness, yes, worse than nakedness! For that alone I could have you punished, and I will if you try to play the fool. Do you think I'm a boy to be bamboozled by every bogey a blunderer may try to conjure up? If so, you're wrong, and whoever sent you might have had the sense enough to let you know this. If you tell me who you are, and who sent you here, and what it is you want, I'll be merciful; if not, the police shall be sent for, and the law shall take its course—to the bitter end! I warn you. Do you hear me? You fool! Tell me who you are?"

The last words came from him in what was very like a burst of childish fury. He seemed conscious the moment after he spoke to realize that his passion was sadly lacking in dignity, and to be ashamed of it. He drew himself straight up. With a pocket-handkerchief which he took from within his coat, he wiped his lips. Then, clutching it tightly in his hand, he eyed me a stare that under any other circumstances, I would have found unbearable.

"Well, sir, is your continued silence part of the business of the role you've set yourself up to play?" His tone was firmer, and his bearing more in keeping with his character. "If it be so, then I presume that I at least have liberty to speak. When I find a gentleman, even one gifted with your eloquence of silence, playing the part of burglar, I think you'll grant that a few words on my part can't justly be considered out of place." Again he paused and then said, "To commence with, may I ask if you've come through London, or through any portion of it, in that costume, or rather, in that want of costume? It would seem out of place in a Cairene street, would it not? Even in the Rue de Rabagas, was it not the Rue de Rabagas?"

He asked the question with an emphasis the meaning of which was lost on me. What he referred to I had no idea, though I would have probably found great difficulty in convincing him of my ignorance.

"I take it that you're a reminiscence of the Rue de Rabagas, am I correct?" A new idea seemed to strike him, born perhaps of my continued silence.

"You look English, is it possible that you're not English? What are you then—French? We shall see!"

He addressed me in a tongue which I recognized as French, but with which I wasn't sufficiently acquainted to understand. Although, I flatter myself that as the present narrative should show, I've not made ill-use of the opportunities which I've had to improve my modest education. I regret that I've never had so much as a ghost of a chance to acquire even a rudimentary knowledge of any language except my own. Recognizing, I suppose, from my looks, that he was addressing me in a tongue to which I didn't know, after a time he stopped, smiled slightly, and then began to talk to me in a lingo in which I was even more a stranger, for this time I hadn't the faintest notion what it was. It might have been gibberish for all I could tell.

Quickly perceiving that he'd succeeded no better than before, he returned to English. "You don't know French, nor the Rue de Rabagas? Very good, then what is it that you do know? Are you under a vow of silence, or are you dumb. Your face is English, what can be seen of it, and I will take it, therefore, that English spoken words convey some meaning to your brain. So listen, sir, to what I have to say, and do me the favor of listening carefully."

He was becoming more and more his former self. In his clear, modulated tone there was a ring of something like a threat, a something which went very far beyond his words.

"You know something of a period which I choose to have forgotten, that's obvious, and you come from a person who probably knows still more. So go back to that person and say that what I've forgotten I've forgotten; nothing will be gained by anyone trying to make me remember. Be very sure on that point; say that nothing will be gained by anyone. That time was one of mirage, of delusion, of disease. I was in a condition, mentally and bodily, in which pranks could've been played on me by any trickster, and such pranks were played. I know that now quite well. I don't pretend to be proficient in the modus operandi of the hanky-panky man, but I know that he has a method, all the same, one susceptible too, of facile explanation. Go back to your friend, and tell him that I'm not again likely to be made the butt of his joke, nor of his new one either. You hear me, sir?"

I remained motionless and silent, an attitude which plainly he resented.

"Are you deaf and dumb? You certainly aren't dumb, for you spoke to me just now. Be advised, sir, don't compel me to resort to measures which will cause you serious discomfort. You hear me, sir?"

Still from me, not a sign of comprehension, to his increased annoyance.

"So be it. Keep your own counsel, if you choose. Yours will be the bitterness, not mine. You may play the lunatic, and play it excellently well, but that you do understand what's said to you is clear. Come to business, sir. Give me that revolver, and the packet of letters which you've stolen from my desk."

He'd been speaking with the air of one who desired to convince himself as much as me, and about his last words there was almost a flavor of braggadocio. I remained unheeding.

"Are you going to do as I require, or are you insane enough to refuse? In which case I shall summon assistance, and there will quickly be an end of this. Pray don't imagine that you can trick me into supposing that you don't grasp the situation. I know better. Once more, are you going to give me that revolver and those letters?"

Still no reply from me. His anger was growing greater and his agitation, too. On my first introduction to Paul Lessingham I wasn't destined to discover in him any one of those qualities of which the world held him to be the undisputed possessor. He showed himself to be as unlike the statesman I'd conceived—and esteemed—as he easily could have been.

"Do you think I stand in awe of you? Do as I tell you, or I'll teach you a much-needed lesson." He raised his voice. In his bearing there was a would-be defiance. He might not have been aware of it, but the repetitions of his threats were in themselves confessions of his weakness. He stood and stepped forward, then stopped short and began to tremble. The perspiration broke out on his brow, and he made spasmodic little dabs at it with his crumpled-up handkerchief. His eyes wandered back and forth, as if searching for something which he feared to see yet was constrained to seek. He began to talk to himself out loud, in odd disconnected sentences, ignoring me entirely.

"What was that? It was nothing. It was my imagination. My nerves are shot. I've been working too hard. I'm not well. What was that?" This last inquiry came from him in a half-stifled shriek, as the door opened to admit an elderly man in a state of considerable undress. He had the tousled appearance of one who had been unexpectedly roused out of slumber, and unwillingly dragged from bed.

Mr. Lessingham stared at him as if he had been a ghost, while he stared back at Mr. Lessingham as if he found a difficulty in crediting the evidence of his own eyes.

It was he who broke the silence, and said in a halting voice, "I am sure I beg your pardon, sir, but one of the maids thought that she heard the sound of a gunshot, so we came down to see if there was anything the matter. I had no idea that you were here, sir." His eyes traveled from Mr. Lessingham to me, suddenly going wider to about twice their previous size when he saw me, "God save us! Who is that?"

The man's self-evident cowardice possibly impressed Mr. Lessingham with the conviction that he himself wasn't cutting the most dignified of figures. At any rate, he made a notable effort to once more assume a bearing of greater determination.

"You're quite right, Matthews, quite right. I'm obliged by your watchfulness. At present you may leave the room, I propose to deal with this fellow myself, only remain with the other men upon the landing, so that if I call, you may come to my assistance."

Matthews did as he was told, leaving the room more rapidly than he'd entered it. Mr. Lessingham turned back to me, his manner distinctly more determined, as if he found his resolution reinforced by the closeness of his retainers.

"Now, my man, you see how the case stands, and at a word from me you'll be overpowered and doomed to undergo a long period of imprisonment. Yet I'm still willing to listen to what you have to say. Put down that revolver, give me those letters, you'll not find me disposed to treat you hardly."

For all the attention I paid him, I might have been a graven image. He misunderstood, or pretended to misunderstand, the cause of my silence.

"Come, I see that you suppose my intentions to be harsher than they really are, don't let us have a scandal and a scene here—be sensible! Give me those letters!" Again he moved in my direction, and again, after he'd taken a step or two, he stumbled and stopped, and looked about him with frightened eyes. He began to mumble to himself aloud once more.

"It's a conjurer's trick! Of course! Nothing more. What else could it be? I'm not to be fooled. I'm older than I was. I've been overdoing it, that's all." Suddenly he broke into cries. "Matthews! Matthews! Help! Help!"

Matthews entered the room, followed by three other men, all younger than him. Evidently all had slipped into the first articles of clothing they could lay their hands on, and each carried a stick, or some similar rudimentary weapon.

Their master spurred them on. Strike the revolver out of his hand, Matthews! Knock him down! Take the letters from him! Don't be afraid, for I am not!" In proof of it, Mr. Lessingham rushed at me, as it seemed half blindly. As he did so, I was constrained to shout out, in tones which I didn't recognize as mine, "*The Beetle!*"

The room was suddenly thrown into darkness, and there were screams as of someone in agony. I felt that something had entered the room, something evil. I don't know how I knew this, but only that it was something of horror.

The next action of which I was conscious of was that under the cover of darkness, I was dashing out the door, propelled by I knew not what.

Chapter 8

Whether anyone pursued me I can't say. I have some dim recollection, as I exited the room, of women huddled against the wall, and of their screaming as I went past them. But whether any effort was made to arrest my progress I couldn't tell. My own impression was that not the slightest attempt to impede my headlong flight was made by anyone.

In what direction I was going I didn't know. I was like a man dashing through the images of a dream, knowing neither how nor whither. I tore along what I suppose was a broad passage, through a door at the end, and into what I believe was a drawing-room.

Across this room I ran, bringing down in the gloom unseen articles of furniture, with myself sometimes on top, and sometimes under them. Each time I fell, I was on my feet again, until I went crashing against a window which was concealed by curtains. It wouldn't have been strange had I crashed through it, but I was spared that.

Thrusting aside the curtains, I fumbled for the fastening of the window. It was a tall French casement, extending so far as I could judge, from floor to ceiling. When I had it open, I stepped through it onto the verandah, to find that I was on the top of the portico which I had vainly tried to climb from below earlier.

I proceeded to climb down it with a breakneck recklessness of which now I shudder to think. It was probably some thirty feet above the pavement, yet I rushed down it with as much disregard for the safety of life and limb as if it had been only three feet. Over the edge of the parapet I went, obtaining with my naked feet, a precarious foothold on the latticework, then down I commenced to scramble.

I never did get a proper hold, and when I'd descended more than half the distance—scraping as it seemed to me every scrap of skin off my body in the process—I lost what little hold I had. Down to the ground I went tumbling, rolling right across the pavement and into the muddy road. It was a miracle I wasn't seriously injured, but in that sense, certainly, that night the miracles were on my side. Hardly was I down, than I was up again, mud and all.

Just as I was getting onto my feet, I felt a firm hand grip me by the shoulder. Turning, I found myself confronted by a tall, slender man with a long, drooping moustache and an overcoat buttoned up to the chin. He held me with a grasp of steel. He looked at me, and I looked back at him.

"After the ball, eh?" he said.

Even then I was struck by something pleasant in his voice, and some quality as of sunshine in his handsome face. Seeing that I said nothing, he continued with a curious, half-mocking smile. "Is that the way to come slithering down the Apostle's pillar? Is it simple burglary, or simpler murder? Tell me the glad tidings that you've killed Paul, and I'll let you go."

Whether he was mad or not I can't say, though there was reason for me thinking so. He didn't look mad, though his words and actions alike were strange.

"Although you've confined yourself to gentle felony, shall I not shower blessings on the head of him who has been robbing Paul? Away with you then!" He removed his grip, giving me a gentle push as he did so, and I was away

I neither stayed nor paused. I knew little of records for running, but if anyone has made a better record than I did that night between Lowndes Square and Walham Green I should like to know just what it was, and I would like to see it done.

In an incredibly short space of time I was once more in front of the house with the open window, the packet of letters—which almost cost me dearly—gripped tightly in my hand.

Chapter 9

I pulled up sharply, as if a brake had been suddenly and even mercilessly applied to bring me to a standstill. I remembered nothing of my travels back; it was like a dream in which I woke to find the memory of it already fading to nothing. I stood shivering in front of the window. A rain shower had recently commenced, the falling rain being blown before the breeze. I was in a terrible sweat, yet trembled like I was cold. Covered with mud, bruised, cut, and bleeding, a piteous an object as you would care to see. Every limb on my body ached, every muscle exhausted; I was done both mentally and physically. If I hadn't been held up, as it were, by the spell which was upon me, I would have sunk down then and there, in a hopeless, helpless, hapless heap.

But my tormentor wasn't yet done with me.

As I stood there, like some broken and beaten hack, waiting for the word of command, it came. It was as if some strong magnetic current had been switched on to me through the window to draw me into the room.

Over the low wall I went, over the windowsill, until once more I stood in that chamber of my humiliation and shame.

Once again I was conscious of that awful sense of the presence of an evil thing. How much of it was fact, and how much of it was the product of imagination I can't say, but looking back, it seemed to me that it was as if I was taken out of my corporeal body to be plunged into the inner chambers of all nameless sin.

There was the sound of something flopping from off the bed and onto the floor, and I knew that the thing was coming at me. My stomach quaked, my heart melted within me; the very anguish of my terror gave me strength to scream and scream! Sometimes late at night, even now I hear those screams of mine ringing through the night, and I bury my face in my pillow, and it's as though I was passing through the very Valley of the Shadow.

The thing stopped and retreated, and I could hear it slipping and sliding across the floor. There was only silence. Then presently, the lamp was lit, and the room was bathed in brightness. There, on the bed, in the familiar position between the sheets, his head resting on his hand, his eyes blazing like living coals, was the dreadful cause of all my agonies. He looked at me with his unpitying, unblinking gaze.

"So! Through the window again! Like a thief! Is it always that way that you come into a house?" He paused, as if to give me time to digest his gibe. "You saw Paul Lessingham then? The great Paul Lessingham! Was he, then, so great?" His rasping voice, with its odd foreign twang, reminded me in some uncomfortable way of a rusty saw. The things he said, and the manner in which he said them, were alike intended to add to my discomfort. It was solely because the feat was barely possible that he only partially succeeded.

"Like a thief you went into his house, did I not tell you that you would? Like a thief he found you; were you not ashamed? Since like a thief he found you, how did you escape? By what robber's artifice have you saved yourself from prison?"

His manner then changed, so that all at once he seemed to snarl at me. "Is he great? Well, is he great, Paul Lessingham? You're small, but he's smaller, your great Paul Lessingham! Was there ever a man so less than nothing?"

With the recollection fresh upon me of Mr. Lessingham as I had so lately seen him I couldn't but feel that there might be a modicum of truth in what, with such an intensity of bitterness, the man suggested. The picture which, in my mental gallery, I'd hung in the place of honor for Lessingham, seemed to say the least, to have become a trifle smudged.

As usual, the man in the bed seemed to experience not the slightest difficulty in deciphering what was passing through my mind.

"That's so, you and he, you're a pair; the great Paul Lessingham is as great a thief as you, and greater, for at least he has more courage."

For some moments he was still, then he exclaimed with sudden fierceness, "Give me what you've stolen!"

I moved towards the bed—most unwillingly—and held out to him the packet of letters which I'd abstracted from the little drawer. Perceiving my disinclination to be near him, he set himself to play with it. Ignoring my outstretched hand, he stared at me straight in the face.

"What ails you? Are you not well? Is it not sweet to stand close at my side? You, with your white skin. If I were a woman, would you not take me for a wife?"

There was something about the manner in which he said this which was so essentially feminine that once more I wondered if I could possibly be mistaken in his sex. I'd have given much to have been able to strike him across the face, or better yet, to have taken him by the neck and thrown him through the window to roll about in the mud.

He pretended to notice for the first time what I was holding out to him.

"So, that's what you've stolen! That's what you took from the drawer in the bureau—the drawer which was locked—and which you used the arts of a thief to enter. Give it to me, thief!"

He snatched the packet from me, scratching the back of my hand as he did so, as if his nails were talons. He turned the packet over and over, glaring at it as he did so; it was strange what a relief it was to have his glance removed from off my face. "You kept it in your inner drawer, Paul Lessingham, where none but you could see it, didn't you? You hid it as one hides a treasure. There should be something here worth having, worth seeing, worth knowing, yes, worth knowing! Since you found it worth your while to hide it up so closely."

As I've said, the packet was bound about by pink ribbon, a fact on which he presently began to comment.

"With what a pretty string you've encircled it, and how neatly it's tied! Surely only a woman's hand could tie a knot like this; who would have guessed yours were such agile fingers? So! An endorsement on the cover! What's this? Let's see what's written! 'The letters of my dear love, Marjorie Lindon.'"

As he read these words, which as he said, were endorsed on the outer sheet of paper that served as a cover for the letters which were enclosed within, his face became transfigured. Never did I suppose that rage could have so possessed a human countenance. His jaw dropped open so that his yellow fangs gleamed though his parted lips; he held his breath so long that each moment I looked he seemed to fall down in a fit. The veins stood out all over his face and head like seams of blood. I don't how long he was speechless, but when his breath returned, it was with chokings and gaspings in the midst of which he hissed out his words, as if their mere passage through his throat brought him near to strangulation.

"The letters of his dear love! Of his dear love! His, Paul Lessingham's! So, it's as I guessed, as I knew, as I saw! Marjorie Lindon! Sweet Marjorie! His dear love! Paul Lessingham's dear love! She with the lily face, the corn-hued hair! What is it his dear love has found in her fond heart to write to him?"

Sitting up in bed, he tore the packet open. It contained perhaps eight or nine letters, some mere notes, some much longer. But short or long, he devoured them with equal appetite, each one over and over again, until I thought he never would be done reading them. They were on thick white paper of a peculiar shade of whiteness with untrimmed edges. On each sheet a crest and an address were stamped in gold, and all the sheets were of the same shape and size. I told myself that if anywhere, at any time, I saw writing paper like that again, I wouldn't fail to know it. The calligraphy was, like the paper, unusual, bold, decided, and I should have guessed, produced by a J pen.

All the time that he was reading he kept emitting sounds, most resembling yelps and snarls than anything more human, like some savage beast nursing its pent-up rage. When he'd finished reading he let his passion have full vent.

"So, that's what his dear love has found in her heart to write Paul Lessingham!"

I can't truly describe the concentrated frenzy of hatred with which the man dwelt upon Lessingham's name—it was demonic.

"It's enough! It's the end! It's his doom! He shall be ground between the upper and the nether stones in the towers of anguish, and all that's left of him will be cast on the accursed sand of the bitter waters, to stink under the blood-grimed sun! And for her—for Marjorie Lindon—for his dear love, it shall come to pass that she shall wish that she was never born, nor he, and the gods of the shadows shall smell the sweet incense of her suffering! It shall be!"

In the madness of his rhapsodically frenzy I believe that he'd actually forgotten I was there. But then glancing aside, he saw me and remembered, and was prompt to take advantage of an opportunity to wreak his rage upon a tangible object, namely me.

"It's you, you thief! You still live! To make a mockery of one of the children of the gods!"

He leaped off the bed, shrieking, and sprang at me, clasping my throat with his horrid hands, bearing me backwards onto the floor. I felt his breath mingle with mine and then God in His mercy, I slipped into oblivion.

PART 2

The Story According To Sydney Atherton

Chapter 10

It was after our second waltz that I did it. In the usual quiet corner, which that time was in the shadow of a palm in the hall. Before I'd gotten into my stride she checked me, touching my sleeve with her fan, turning towards me with startled eyes.

"Please stop, Mr. Atherton!" Marjorie Lindon pleaded.

But I wasn't to be stopped. Cliff Challoner passed by us with Gerty Cazell on his arm. I fancy that, as he passed, he nodded. I didn't care. I was wound up to go, and I went with it. No man knows how he can talk till he does talk to the girl he wants to marry. It's my impression that I gave her recollections of the Restoration poets. She seemed surprised, not having previously detected in me the poetic strain, and insisted on cutting in.

"Mr. Atherton, I'm so sorry," she said.

"Why? Sorry that I love you! Why should you be sorry that you've become the one thing needful in any man's eyes, even in mine? The one thing precious, the one thing to be altogether esteemed! Is it so common for a woman to come across a man who would be willing to lay down his life for her that she should be sorry when she finds him?"

"I didn't know that you felt like this, though I confess that I've had my doubts."

"Doubts! I thank you."

"You're quite aware, Mr. Atherton, that I like you very much."

"Like me! Bah!" I said.

"I can't help liking you, though it may be 'bah.' "

"I don't want you to like me. I want you to love me."

"Precisely, that's your mistake," she said.

"My mistake in wanting you to love me! When I love you…"

"Then you shouldn't, though I can't help thinking that you're mistaken even there," she said.

"Mistaken in supposing that I love you! When I assert and reassert it with the whole force of my being! What do you want me to do to prove I love you, take you in my arms and crush you to my bosom, and make a spectacle of you before everyone in the place?"

"I'd rather you wouldn't, and perhaps you wouldn't mind not talking quite so loud. Mr. Challoner seems to be wondering what you're shouting about."

I glanced over my shoulder and saw that indeed, the man was watching us.

"You shouldn't torture me," I said.

She opened and closed her fan, and as she looked down at it I'm disposed to suspect that she smiled.

"I'm glad we've had this little explanation, because of course, you're my friend."

"I'm not your friend," I said.

"Pardon me, you are."

"I say I'm not. If I can't be something else, I'll be no friend."

She frowned, calmly ignoring me, playing with her fan. "As it happens, I'm just now in rather a delicate position in which a friend is welcome," she said.

"What's the matter? Who's been worrying you; your father?"

"Well, he hasn't, as yet, but he may be soon."

"What's in the wind?"

"Mr. Lessingham." She dropped her voice, and her eyes. For the moment I didn't catch her meaning.

"What?"

"Your friend, Mr. Lessingham," she said.

"Excuse me, Miss Lindon, but I am by no means sure that anyone is entitled to call Mr. Lessingham a friend of mine."

"What! Not when I'm going to be his wife?"

That took me aback. I'd had my suspicions that Paul Lessingham was more with Marjorie than he had any right to be, but I'd never supposed that she could see anything desirable in a stick of a man like that. Not to mention a hundred and one other considerations, Lessingham on one side of the House, and her father on the other, and old Lindon girding at him anywhere and everywhere— with his high-dried Tory notions of his family importance, to say nothing of his fortune.

I don't know if I looked what I felt; if I did, I looked uncommonly blank.

"You've chosen an appropriate moment, Miss Lindon, to tell me this."

She chose to disregard my irony.

"I'm glad you think so, because now you'll understand what a difficult position I'm in," she said.

"I offer you my hearty congratulations."

"And I thank you for them, Mr. Atherton, in the spirit in which they're offered, because from you I know they mean so much."

I bit my lip, for the life of me I couldn't tell how she wished me to read her words.

"Do I understand that this announcement has been made to me as one of the public?" I asked.

"You do not. It's made to you in confidence, as my friend—as my greatest friend—because a husband is something more than friend." My pulses tingled. "Will you be on my side?" She paused and I stayed silent.

"On your side, or Mr. Lessingham's?"

"His side is my side, and my side is his side; you'll be on our side?" she asked.

"I'm not sure that I altogether follow you."

"You're the first I've told. When Papa hears it's possible that there will be trouble, as you know. He thinks so much of you and of your opinion, so when that trouble comes I want you to be on our side...on my side."

"Why should I? What does it matter?" I asked. "You're stronger than your father. And though it's just possible that Lessingham is stronger than you, together, from your father's point of view, you'll be invincible."

"You're my friend, are you not my friend?" she asked.

"In effect, you offer me an Apple of Sodom."

"Thank you. I didn't think you so unkind."

"And you, are you kind? I make you an avowal of my love, and straightway, you ask me to act as chorus to the love of another."

"How could I tell you loved me, as you say!" she said. "I had no notion. You've known me all your life, yet you've never breathed a word of it until now."

"And If I'd spoken before?" I imagine that there was a slight movement of her shoulders, almost amounting to a shrug.

"I don't know that it would've made any difference," she said. "I don't pretend that it would. But I do know this; I believe that you yourself have only discovered the state of your own mind within the last half-hour."

If she'd come right out and slapped my face she couldn't have startled me more. I'd no notion if her words were uttered at random, but they came so near the truth that they held me breathless. It was a fact that only during the last few minutes had I really realized how things were with me; only since the end of that first waltz that the flame had burst out in my soul which was now consuming me. She'd read me by what seemed so like a flash of inspiration that I hardly knew what to say to her.

I tried to be stinging. "You flatter me, Miss Lindon, you flatter me at every point. Had you only discovered to me the state of your mind a little sooner, I wouldn't have shared the state of my mind at all."

"We'll consider it terra incognita then," she said.

"Very well."

Her provoking calmness stung me, and I had the suspicion that she was laughing at me in her sleeve.

"But at the same time, since you assert that you've so long been innocent, I beg that you'll continue so no more. At least, your innocence shall be without excuse. For I wish you to understand that I love you, Miss Lindon, that I have loved you, that I shall continue to love you. Any understanding you may have with Mr. Lessingham won't make the slightest difference to me. I warn you, Miss Lindon, that until death you'll have to write me down as your lover."

She looked at me with wide-open eyes, as if I almost frightened her. To be frank, that was what I wished to do.

"Mr. Atherton!"

"Miss Lindon?"

"That's not like you at all."

"Well, we seem to be making each other's acquaintance for the first time."

She continued to gaze at me with her big eyes, which to be candid, I found difficult to meet. Then suddenly her face was lighted by a smile, which I resented.

"Not after all these years, not after all these years!" she said. "I know you, and though I daresay you're not flawless, I fancy you'll be married soon enough."

Her manner was almost sisterly—an older-sister. I could have shaken her. Then Hartridge, coming to claim his dance, gave me an opportunity to escape with as much remnants of my dignity as I could gather about me.

Hartridge dawdled up, his thumbs as usual in his waistcoat pockets. "I believe, Miss Lindon, this is our dance," he said.

She acknowledged it with a bow and rose to take his arm. I left her without a word. As I crossed the hall I chanced on Percy Woodville. He was in his familiar state of fluster, and was gaping about him as if he'd mislaid the Koh-i-noor, and wondered where in thunder it had gotten to. When he saw me he caught me by the arm.

"I say, Atherton, have you seen Miss Lindon?"

"I have."

"No! Have you? By Jove! Where? I've been looking for her all over the place, except in the cellars and the attics, and I was just going to check them too. This is our dance."

"In that case, she's shunted you."

"No! Impossible!" His mouth went like an O and his eyes too, his eyeglass clattering down onto the front of his shirt. "I expect the mistake's mine. Fact is, I've made a mess of my program. It's either the last dance or this dance, or the next that I've booked with her, but I'm hanged if I know which. Just take a look at it, there's a good chap, and tell me which one you think it is."

I took a look since he held the thing within an inch of my nose. I could hardly help it; one look and that was enough and more. Some men's ball programs are studies in impressionism, but Percy's seemed to me to be a study in madness. It was covered with hieroglyphics, but what they meant or why they were there was anyone's guess. Proverbially, the man's a champion hasher.

"I regret, my dear Percy, that I'm not an expert in cuneiform writing. If you have any doubt as to which dance is yours, you'd better ask the lady; she'll feel flattered."

Leaving him to do his own addling I went to find my coat. I wanted to get out into the open air. As for dancing, I loathed it. Just as I neared the cloak-room someone stopped me. It was Dora Grayling.

"Have you forgotten that this is our dance?" she inquired with a smile.

I'd totally forgotten, and I hadn't been obliged by her reminding me. As I looked at her sweet, gray eyes and at the soft contours of her gentle face, I felt that I deserved a good kicking for forgetting. She was an angel, one of the best, but I was in no mood for angels. Not for a million pounds would I have gone through that dance just then, nor with Dora Grayling by my side. So I looked her in the eyes and flat-out lied. "You must forgive me, Miss Grayling, but I'm not feeling very well, and I don't think I'm up to any more dancing. Goodnight."

Chapter 11

The weather outdoors was in tune with my frame of mind, I was in a hell of a mood, and it was a hell of a night. A harsh, northeast wind warranted to take the skin right off you, was playing catch with intermittent gusts of blinding rain. Though it wasn't fit for a dog outside—and I didn't want to take a cab—there was no choice but to walk.

I went down Park Lane, and the wind and rain went with me, and also thoughts of Dora Grayling. What an idiot I'd been, and was! If there was anything in worse taste than to book a lady for a dance, only to then leave her in the lurch, I should like to know what that thing is—when found it ought to be made a note of. If any man of my acquaintance allowed himself to be guilty of such a felony in the first degree, I would cut him immediately and demand he apologize to said woman. I almost wished someone would try to cut me, though I should like to see him try.

It was all Marjorie's fault, all of it! Past, present, and what was to come. I'd known that girl when she was in pigtails. And all that time I've loved her. If I had not mentioned it, it was because I'd suffered my affection, 'like the worm, to lie hidden in the bud,' or whatever it is the fellows says.

At any rate, I was perfectly positive that if I'd had the faintest notion that she would ever seriously consider such a man as Lessingham, I would have told her that I loved her long ago.

Lessingham! Why, he was old enough to be her father, at least he was a good many years older than I was. And an ass! Though it's true that on certain points I'm what some people would call an ass as well, but I'm not an ass of his caliber. Thank Heaven, no! No doubt in the past I have admired traits in his character, but now that I've learned of him and her together, I'm even prepared to admit that he's a man of ability, in his own way of course.

Which is emphatically not my way. But to think of him in connection with such a girl as Marjorie Lindon—preposterous! Why, the man's as dry as a stick, drier even! And cold as an iceberg. Nothing but a politician, absolutely. He a lover! Ridiculous! Laughable even. Both by education and by nature, he was incapable of even playing such a part; it's utterly absurd!

If you were to sink a shaft from the top of his head to the soles of his feet, you'd find inside him nothing but the dry bones of parties and politics.

What my Marjorie—if everyone had his own, she is mine, and in that sense, she will always be mine—could see in such a dry-as-dust bloke out of which even to construct the rudiments of a husband was beyond my fathoming.

Suchlike agreeable reflections were fit company for the wind and rain, so they bore me company all down the lane. I crossed at the corner, going around the hospital towards the square. Not realizing where I was until I was there, this path brought me to the home of Paul Lessingham.

Like the idiot I was, I went out into the middle of the street, and stood a while in the mud to curse him and his house. On the whole when one considers that that is the kind of man I could be, it's perhaps not surprising that Marjorie disdained me.

"May your following both in the House and out of it, no longer regard you as a leader," I shouted. "May your party follow after other gods! May your political aspirations wither, and your speeches be listened to by empty benches! May the Speaker persistently and strenuously refuse to allow you to catch his eye, and at the next election, may your constituency reject you!

Until that moment I'd appeared to be the only lunatic at large, either outside the house or in it, but suddenly a second lunatic came on the scene, and that one with a vengeance. Suddenly, a window in Lessingham's house shattered from within—the one over the front door—and someone came flying through it and onto the top of the portico. At first I assumed it was a case of intended suicide, and I began to hope that I was about to witness the death of Paul Lessingham.

But I wasn't so sure when the individual in question began to scramble down the pillar of the porch in the most extraordinary fashion I've ever witnessed, when he came tumbling down to lay sprawling in the mud at my feet.

I fancy, if I'd performed that portion of the act I should have stood quiet for a second or two, to take in the scene more clearly. There was no question the stranger wasn't Lessingham, and by the way he moved and how he landed it was like he was made out of India-rubber—or ought to have been—as before he was down he was up again, and it was all I could do to grab at him before he was off like a rocket.

Such a figure he presented was seldom seen, well, at least in the streets of London. What he'd done with the rest of his apparel I'm not in a position to say, but all that was left of his clothes were a long, dark cloak which he attempted to wrap around him. Save for that, and mud, he was as bare as the palm of my hand. Yet it was his face that held me. In my time I've seen strange expressions on men's faces, but never before one such as I saw on his. He looked like a man might look who, after living a life of undiluted crime, at last finds himself face to face with the devil. It wasn't the look of a madman—far from it—it was something worse.

It was the expression on his face, as much as anything else, which made me behave as I did. I said something to him, some nonsense, I know not what. He regarded me with a silence which was supernatural. I spoke to him again, but not a word issued from his rigid lips. There wasn't even a tremor in his awful eyes, eyes which I was tolerably convinced saw something that I'd never seen, or would want to. Then I took my hand off his shoulder and let him go. I don't know why but I did.

He'd remained as motionless as a statue while I held him, and for any evidence of life he gave he might as well have been a statue, but when my grasp was loosened, how he ran! He turned the corner and was out of sight before I could say, "Wait!"

It was only then, when he was gone, and I realized the lightning rate at which he'd taken his departure, that it occurred to me of what an extremely sensible act I'd been guilty of in letting him go at all. Here was an individual who had been committing burglary, or something very like it, in the house of a budding cabinet minister, and who had tumbled plump into my arms, so that all I had to do was call a policeman and get him arrested, but I'd done nothing of the sort.

"Some hero I am!" I said to myself, "I catch someone in the act robbing Paul and all I do is let him go. Well, the least I can do is see how Paul's doing."

So I went to Lessingham's front door and knocked. I knocked once, twice, three times, and on the third time I made the echoes ring, but still not a soul answered.

"If this is a case of a murder, and the gentleman in the cloak has made a fair clearance of every living person the house contains, perhaps it's just as well I've chanced upon the scene, still I do think that one of the corpses might get up to answer the door. If it's possible to make noise enough to waken the dead, you bet I'm up to it."

And I was up to it. I punished that knocker until I warrant the pounding I gave it was audible on the other side of Green Park. At last I woke the dead, or rather, I roused the house servant Matthews.

He opened the door about six inches, and through the crack he protruded his ancient nose. "Who's there?" he asked.

"Nothing, my dear sir; nothing and no one. It must have been your vigorous imagination which made you to believe that there was; you let it run away with you."

Then he knew me, and opened the door about two feet.

"Oh, it's you, Mr. Atherton. I beg your pardon, sir. I thought it might have been the police."

"What then? Do you stand in terror of the minions of the law at last?"

Matthews was a most discreet servant, and just the fellow for a budding cabinet minister. He glanced over his shoulder; I had suspected the presence of a colleague at his back, now I was assured. He put his hand up to his mouth, and I thought how exceedingly discreet he looked, in his trousers and stockinged feet, with his hair all rumpled, and his nightshirt creased.

"Well, sir, I have received instructions not to admit the police," he said.

"The hell you have! From whom?"

Coughing behind his hand, then leaning forward, he addressed me with an air which was flatteringly confidential. "From Mr. Lessingham, sir."

"Possibly Mr. Lessingham isn't aware that a robbery has been committed on his premises, and that the burglar has just come out of his drawing-room window with a hop, skip, and a jump. Why, the bloke bounded out of the window like a tennis-ball, before rounding the corner like a rocket."

Again Matthews glanced over his shoulder, as if not clear which way discretion lay, whether fore or aft. "Thank you, sir. I believe that Mr. Lessingham is aware of something of the kind." He seemed to come to a sudden resolution, dropping his voice to a whisper, he said, "The fact is, sir, that I fancy Mr. Lessingham's a good deal upset."

"Upset?" I stared at him. There was something in his manner I didn't understand. "What do you mean by upset? Has the scoundrel attempted violence?"

"Who's there?" The voice was Lessingham's, calling to Matthews from the staircase, though for an instant, I hardly recognized it—it was so curiously petulant. Pushing past Matthews, I stepped into the hall. A young man, I suppose a footman, in the same undress as Matthews, was holding a candle; it seemed the only light about the place. By its glimmer I perceived Lessingham standing halfway up the stairs. He was in full attire, and as he isn't the sort of man who dresses for the House, I took it that he'd been mixing pleasure with business.

"It's I, Lessingham, Atherton. Do you know that a fellow has jumped out of your drawing-room window?"

It was a second or two before he answered. When he did, his voice had lost its petulance. "Has he escaped?"

"Clean. He's a mile away by now."

It seemed to me that in his tone, when he spoke again, there was a note of relief. "I wondered if he had. Poor fellow! More sinned against than sinning! Take my advice, Atherton, and keep out of politics. They bring you into contact with all the lunatics at large. Now goodnight! I'm much obliged to you for checking on us. Matthews, close the door."

I didn't expect to receive such treatment. I expected to be listened to with deference, and to hear all that there was to hear, and not to be sent away before I had a chance of really opening my lips. Before I knew it— almost—the door was closed, and I was on the doorstep. Confound the politician's impudence! Next time he might have his house burned down— and him in it—before I took the trouble to touch his dirty knocker.

What did he mean by his allusion to lunatics in politics, did he think to fool me? I realized then that there was more happening here than met the eye, and a good deal more than he wished to share with me, hence his insolence. The bastard.

What Marjorie Lindon could see in such an fool surpassed my comprehension, especially when there was a man of my sort walking about, who adored the very ground she trod upon.

Chapter 12

All through the night, waking and sleeping, and in my dreams, I wondered what Marjorie could see in him! In those same dreams I satisfied myself that she could, and did, see nothing in him, but everything in me— oh the comfort! The misfortune was that when I awoke I knew it was the other way around, so that it was a sad awakening—an awakening to thoughts of murder.

So, I went into my laboratory to plan murder—legalized murder—on the biggest scale it has ever been planned. I was on the track of a weapon which would make war not only an affair of a single campaign, but of a single half hour. It wouldn't want an army to work it either. Once an individual, or two or three at most, were in possession of my weapon-that-was-to-be, and they got within a mile or so of even the largest body of disciplined troops that a nation could put into the field and—poof!— in about the time it takes you to say the word they would all be dead men.

If weapons of precision, which may be relied upon to slay, are preservers of the peace—and any man is a fool who says that they are not—then I was within reach of the finest preserver of the peace imagination has ever conceived.

What a sublime thought to think that in the hollow of my own hand lay the life and death of nations.

I had in front of me some of the finest destructive agents any man could wish to light upon: carbon-monoxide, chlorine-trioxide, mercuric-oxide, conine, potassamide, potassium-carboxide, cyanogens. When Edwards entered I was wearing a mask of my own invention, a thing that covered ears and head and everything, something like a diver's helmet. I was dealing with gases a sniff of which meant death and only a few days before, unmasked, I'd been doing some fool's trick with a couple of acids—sulphuric and cyanide of potassium—when somehow, my hand slipped, and before I knew it minute portions of them combined. By the mercy of Providence I fell backwards instead of forwards. About an hour afterwards, Edwards found me on the floor, and it took the remainder of that day, and most of the doctors in town, to bring me back to life again.

Edwards announced his presence by touching me on the shoulder; when I'm wearing that mask it isn't always easy to make me hear.

"Someone wishes to see you, sir."

"Then tell that someone that I don't wish to see them."

The well-trained servant he was, Edwards walked off with the message as decorously as you please. I thought that was the end to it, but it wasn't.

I was regulating the valve of a cylinder in which I was fusing some oxides when once more, someone touched me on the shoulder. Without turning I took it for granted it was Edwards back again.

"I have only to give a tiny twist to this tap, my good fellow, and you will be in the land where the bogies bloom. Why would you come where you're not wanted?"

Then I looked around. "Who the devil are you?"

For it wasn't Edwards at all, but quite a different class of character. I found myself confronting an individual who might almost have sat for one of the bogies I'd just alluded to. His attire was reminiscent of the 'Algerians' whom one finds all over France, and who are the most persistent, insolent and amusing of peddlers. I remember one who used to haunt the repetitions at the Alcazar at Tours. This individual was like the originals, yet not exactly; he was less gaudy, and a good deal dingier than his Gallic prototypes were apt to be. He wore a burnoose, the yellow, grimy-looking article of the Arab of the Sudan, not the spick and span Arab of the boulevard. But the largest difference of all was that his face was clean shaven. I ask you: whoever saw an Algerian of Paris whose finest glory was not his well-trimmed moustache and beard?

I expected that he would address me in the lingo which these gentlemen call French, but he didn't.

"You're Mr. Atherton?" he inquired.

"Who are you? How did you come here? Where's my servant?"

The fellow held up his hand. As he did so, as if in accordance with a pre-arranged signal, Edwards came into the room looking excessively startled.

I turned to Edwards. "Is this the person who wished to see me?"

"Yes, sir."

"Didn't I tell you to say that I didn't wish to see him?"

"Yes, sir."

"Then why didn't you do as I told you?"

"I did, sir."

"Then how come he's here?"

"Really, sir." Edwards put his hand up to his head as if he was half asleep. "I don't quite know."

"What do you mean by you don't know? Why didn't you stop him?"

"I think, sir, that I must have had a touch of sudden faintness, because I tried to put out my hand to stop him and I couldn't."

"You're an idiot. Go!" He left. I turned to the stranger. "Pray, sir, are you a magician?"

He replied to my question with another. "You, Mr. Atherton, are you also a magician?" He was staring at my mask with an evident lack of comprehension.

"I wear this because, in this place, death lurks in so many subtle forms, so that without it, I dare not breathe."

He inclined his head, though I doubt if he understood.

"Be so good as to tell me briefly, what it is you wish of me," I said.

He slipped his hand into the folds of his burnoose, and taking out a slip of paper, laid it on the table by which we were standing. I glanced at it, expecting to find a petition on it, or a testimonial, or a true statement of his sad case, but instead it contained two words only: 'Marjorie Lindon.' The sight of that well-loved name brought the blood into my cheeks.

"You come from Miss Lindon?" I asked.

He narrowed his shoulders, brought his fingertips together, and inclined his head in a fashion that was peculiarly Oriental, but not particularly explanatory.

I repeated my question. "Do you wish me to understand that you come from Miss Lindon?"

Again he slipped his hand into his burnoose, and produced another slip of paper. He placed it on the table beside the first one. I glanced at it. Nothing was written on it but a name: 'Paul Lessingham.'

"Well? I see Paul Lessingham. What then?"

"She's good, he's bad; is it not so?" He touched first one scrap of paper, then the other.

I stared. "Pray how do you happen to know this?"

"He shall never have her, eh?"

"What on earth do you mean?"

"Ah! What do I mean!" he said.

"Precisely, what do you mean? And also, and at the same time, who the devil are you?"

"It's as a friend I come to you."

"Then in that case you may go; I happen to be overstocked in that line just now," I said with a frown,

"Not with the kind of friend I am!"

"The saints forefend!"

"You love her, you love Miss Lindon! Can you bear to think of him in her arms?" he asked.

I took off my mask, feeling that the occasion required it. As I did so he brushed aside the hanging folds of the hood of his burnoose, so that I saw more of his face. I was immediately conscious that in his eyes there was, in an especial degree, what for want of a better term one may call the mesmeric quality. That his was one of those morbid organizations which are oftener found—thank goodness—in the east than in the west, and which are apt to exercise an uncanny influence over the weak and the foolish folk with whom they come in contact, the kind of man for whom it is always just as well to keep a seasoned rope close by and handy.

I was, also, conscious that he was taking advantage of the removal of my mask to try his will on me, which he couldn't have found a more difficult job. The sensitive something which is found in the hypnotic subject is entirely absent in me.

"I see you're a mesmerist," I said.

He started. "I'm nothing, merely a shadow!"

"And I'm a scientist. I should like, with your permission—or without it—to try an experiment or two on you."

He moved further back. There came a gleam into his eyes which suggested that he possessed his hideous power to an unusual degree, that in the estimation of his own people he was qualified to take his standing as a regular devil-doctor.

"We'll try experiments together, you and I, on Paul Lessingham," he said.

"Why on him?"

"You don't know?"

"I do not."

"Why do you lie to me?" he asked.

"I don't lie to you. I haven't the faintest notion what is the nature of your interest in Mr. Lessingham."

"My interest? That's another thing; it's your interest of which we're speaking," he said.

"Pardon me, but it's yours."

"Listen! You love her! A word from you he shall not have her, ever! It is I who say it. I!"

"And, once more, sir, who are you?" I asked.

"I am of the children of Isis!"

"Is that so? It occurs to me that you have made a slight mistake; this is London, not a dog-hole in the desert."

"I know that. What does it matter? You shall see! There will come a time when you will want me; you'll find that you can't bear to think of him in her arms, her whom you love! When you call to me I will come, and of Paul Lessingham there shall be an end."

While I was wondering whether he was really as mad as he sounded, or whether he was some impudent charlatan who had an axe of his own to grind with Lessingham—and thought that he had found in me a grindstone—he turned and exited the room.

I went after him. "Hey there! Stop!" I cried out.

He moved faster than I could ever have imagined. Before I had a foot in the hall, I heard the front door slam, and when I reached the door and stepped out onto the street, intent on calling him back, there was no sign of him.

Chapter 13

"I wonder what that man really means, and who he happens to be?" I said to myself when I returned to the laboratory. "If it's true and Providence does write a man's character on his face, then there can't be the slightest shred of a doubt that a curious one's been written on his. I wonder what his connection is with Paul Lessingham, or if it's only part of his game."

I strode up and down; for the moment my interest in the experiments I was conducting had waned.

"If it was all bluff I never saw a better piece of acting, and yet what sort of finger can such a man as Paul have in such a pie? The fellow seemed to squirm at the mere mention of his name. Can the objection be political? Let me consider; what has Lessingham done which could offend the religious or patriotic susceptibilities of the most fanatical of Orientals? Politically, I can recall nothing. Foreign affairs, as a rule, he has carefully eschewed. If he has offended—and if he hasn't the seeming was uncommonly good—the cause will have to be sought upon some other track. But then what track?"

The more I strove to puzzle it out, the greater the puzzlement grew.

"Absurd! The rascal has had no more connection with Paul than St. Peter. The probability is that he's a crackpot, and if he isn't, he has some scam going, which he tried on me, but couldn't. As for Marjorie. My Marjorie! Only she isn't mine, confound it! If I'd had my senses about me, I should have broken his head in several places for daring to allow her name to pass his lips, the unbaptized bastard! Now to return to the chase of splendid murder!"

I snatched up my mask. By the way, it's one of the most ingenious inventions of recent years. If the armies of the future wear my mask they will defy my weapon! I was about to re-adjust it in its place, when someone knocked at the door.

"Who's there? Come in!"

It was Edwards. He looked around him as if surprised. "I beg your pardon, sir, I thought you were engaged. I didn't know that…that thee gentleman had gone."

"He went up the chimney, as all that kind of gentlemen do. Why the hell did you let him in when I told you not to?"

"Really, sir, I don't know. I gave him your message, and he looked at me, and…that's all I remember until I found myself standing in this room."

Had it not been Edwards I might have suspected him of having had his palm well-greased, but in his case, I knew better. It was as I thought, my visitor was a mesmerist of the first class; he'd actually played some of his tricks, in broad daylight, on my servant at my own front door. No doubt a man worth studying.

"There's someone else who wishes to see you, sir," Edwards continued. "Mr. Lessingham is here."

"Mr. Lessingham!" At that moment the coincidence of him arriving here now seemed odd.

"Yes sir," Mathews said and left.

A minute later entered Paul.

I have to confess that in a sense I do admire the man, so long as he doesn't presume to thrust himself into a certain position. He possesses physical qualities I also admire. The fellow's lithe and active, agile, clean built, the sort of man who might be relied upon to make a good recovery. You might beat him in a sprint, mental or physical, but in a cross country race he would eventually prevail. I don't know if he's exactly the kind of man whom I would trust. He's too calm, too self-contained, with the knack of looking all around him even in moments of extreme peril, and for whatever he does he has a good excuse.

He has the reputation, both in the House and out of it, of being a man of iron nerve, and with some reason; yet I'm not so sure. Unless I read him wrongly he's one of those men who, confronted by certain events, would rise to the occasion, only to collapse the moment the trial had passed. However, he would show no trace of this.

And this was the man whom Marjorie loved. Well, she could show some cause. He was a man of position, and destined probably, to rise much higher. He always did the right thing, at the right time, and in the right way.

He was dressed as a gentleman should be dressed: black frock coat, black vest, dark gray trousers, stand-up collar, smartly-tied bow, gloves of the proper shade, neatly brushed hair, and a smile, which if it wasn't child-like, at any rate was bland.

"I hope I'm not disturbing you," he said.

"Not at all."

"Are you sure? I never enter a place like this, where a man is matching himself with nature, to wrest from her secrets, without feeling that I'm crossing the threshold of the unknown. The last time I was in this room was just after you'd taken out the final patents for your System of Telegraphy at Sea, which the Admiralty purchased wisely. What is it you're doing now?"

"Death."

"Really? What do you mean?"

"If you're a member of the next government, you'll possibly learn, as I may offer them the refusal of a new wrinkle in the art of murder."

"I see; a new projectile. How long is this race to continue between attack and defense?" he asked.

"Until the sun grows cold."

"And then?"

"There'll be no defense, nothing to defend."

He looked at me with his calm, grave eyes. "The theory of the Age of Ice towards which we're advancing isn't a cheerful one." He began to finger a glass tube which lay on the table. "By the way, it was very good of you to check on me last night. I'm afraid you thought me impolite, so I've come to apologize."

"I don't know that I thought you impolite; I thought you odd, given the circumstances."

"Yes I can see how I would appear like that." He glanced at me with that expressionless look on his face which he could summon at will, and which is at the bottom of the superstition of his iron nerve. "I was simply concerned, that's all. Besides, one doesn't care to be burgled, even by a maniac."

"Was he a maniac?"

"Did you see him?" he asked.

"Very clearly."

"Where?"

"In the street."

"How close were you to him?" he inquired with a raise of his left eyebrow.

"Closer than I am to you."

"Indeed. I didn't know you were so close to him as that. Did you try to stop him?"

"Easier said than done; he took off before I knew what was happening."

"Did you see how he was dressed, or rather, undressed?"

"I did."

"In nothing but a cloak on such a night. Who but a fanatic would have attempted burglary in such a costume?"

"Did he take anything?"

"Absolutely nothing," he replied.

"It seems to have been a curious episode."

He moved his eyebrows—according to members of the House the only gesture in which he has been known to indulge.

"We become accustomed to curious episodes I suppose. Oblige me by not mentioning it to anyone will you? Not to anyone." He repeated the last three words, as if to give them emphasis. I wondered if he was thinking of Marjorie. "I'm communicating with the police, you know. Until they find the intruder I don't want it to get into the papers, or be talked about. It's a worry, you understand," he said with a slight nod.

I nodded in reply.

He changed topics. "This that you're engaged upon, is it a projectile or a weapon?"

"If you're a member of the next government you will possibly know; if you aren't you possibly won't."

"Yes, well, I suppose you have to keep this sort of thing a secret."

"I do. As it seems that matters of much less importance you wish to keep secret."

"You mean that business of last night? If even a hint of that sort of thing gets into the papers, or gets talked about it will explode…you have no notion how we're pestered. It becomes an almost unbearable nuisance. Jones the Unknown can commit murder with less inconvenience to himself than Jones the Notorious can have his pocket picked—there's not much exaggeration in there either. Well, then I should be going. Goodbye, and thanks for your promise."

I'd given him no promise, but that was irrelevant.

He turned to go, then stopped. "There's one more thing. I believe you're a specialist on questions of ancient superstitions and extinct religions."

"I'm interested in such subjects, yes, but I'm not a specialist."

"Can you tell me what were the exact tenets of the worshippers of Isis?"

"No, neither I nor any man, with scientific certainty anyway. As you know, she had a brother, and the cult of Osiris and Isis was one and the same. What precisely were its dogmas, its practices, or anything about it, none now can tell. The Papyri, hieroglyphics and so on, which remain, are very far from being exhaustive, and our knowledge of those which do remain is still less so."

"I suppose that the marvels which are told of it are purely legendary?"

"To what marvels do you particularly refer?"

"Weren't supernatural powers attributed to the priests of Isis?" he asked.

"Broadly speaking, at that time, supernatural powers were attributed to all the priests of all the creeds."

"I see. I presume that her cult is long since extinct, that none of the worshippers of Isis exist today," he said.

I hesitated. I was wondering why he'd hit on such a subject; if he really had a reason, or if he was merely asking questions as a cover for something else, for you see, I knew Paul and how he acted. "That is not so sure."

He looked at me with that passionless, yet searching glance of his. "You think that she's still worshipped?" he asked.

"I think it possible, even probable, that here and there she has followers. Africa is a large order! Homage is paid to Isis, quite in the good old way."

"Do you know that as a fact?" he asked.

"Excuse me, but do you know it's a fact? Are you aware that you're treating me as if I was on the witness stand? Have you any special purpose in making these inquiries?"

He smiled. "In a kind of a way I have. I've recently come across a rather curious story. I'm trying to get to the bottom of it."

"What's the story?"

"I'm afraid that at present I'm not at liberty to tell you, but when I am, I will. I can assure you that you'll find it interesting as an instance of a peculiar survival. Didn't the followers of Isis believe in transmigration?"

"Some of them, no doubt."

"What did they understand by transmigration?" he inquired.

"Transmigration?"

"Yes, but of the soul or of the body," he explained.

"How do you mean? Transmigration is transmigration. Are you driving at something in particular? If you'll tell me fairly and squarely what it is, I'll do my best to give you the information you require; as it is, your questions are a bit perplexing."

"Oh, it doesn't matter, as you say, transmigration is transmigration."

I was eyeing him keenly. I seemed to detect in his manner an odd reluctance to continue on the subject he himself had started. "Hadn't the followers of Isis a—what is it? A sacred emblem?"

"How?"

"Hadn't they a special regard for some sort of a— wasn't it some sort of a beetle?" he inquired.

"You mean Scarabaeus sacer—according to Latreille, Scarabaeus Egyptiorum? Undoubtedly, the scarab was venerated throughout Egypt, indeed, speaking generally, most things that had life, such as cats. As you know, Orisis continued among men in the figure of Apis, the bull."

"Weren't the priests of Isis—or some of them—supposed to assume after death the form of a scarabaeus?" he asked.

"I never heard of it."

"Are you sure? Think!"

"I shouldn't like to answer such a question positively, offhand, but I don't on the spur of the moment recall any supposition of the kind."

"Don't laugh at me, he said. "I'm not a lunatic! But I understand that recent researches have shown that even in some of the most astounding of the ancient legends there was a substratum of fact. Is it absolutely certain that there could be no shred of truth in such a belief?"

"In what belief?"

"In the belief that a priest of Isis—or anyone—assumed after death the form of a scarabaeus?" he said.

"It seems to me, Lessingham, that you've lately come across some uncommonly interesting data, and of a kind which it's your binding duty to give to the world, or at any rate, to that portion of the world which is represented by me. Come, tell me all about it! What are you afraid of?"

"I'm afraid of nothing, and some day you shall be told, but not now. At present, answer my question."

"Then repeat your question, clearly."

"Is it absolutely certain that there could be no foundation of truth in the belief that a priest of Isis—or anyone—assumed after death the form of a beetle?" he repeated.

"I know no more than the man in the moon; how the dickens should I? Such a belief may have been symbolical. Christians believe that after death the body takes the shape of worms, and so in a sense, it does, and sometimes as eels."

"That's not what I mean."

"Then what do you mean?"

"Listen. If a person, of whose veracity there could not be a vestige of a doubt, assured you that he had seen such a transformation actually take place, could it conceivably be explained on natural grounds?" he inquired.

"Seen a priest of Isis assume the form of a beetle?"

"Yes, or a follower of Isis?"

"Before or after death?"

He hesitated. I'd seldom seen him look so interested—and to be frank, I was keenly interested too—but suddenly there came into his eyes a glint of something that was almost terror. When he spoke, it was with the most unwonted awkwardness. "In…in the very act of dying."

"In the very act of dying?"

"Yes, if someone had seen a follower of Isis in—the very act of dying, assume—the form of a beetle, on any conceivable grounds would such a transformation be easily explained?"

I stared, as who would not? Such an extraordinary question was rendered more extraordinary by coming from such a man, yet I was almost beginning to suspect that there was something behind it more extraordinary still.

"Look here, Lessingham, I can see you've a capital tale to tell, so tell it, man! Unless I'm mistaken, it's not the kind of tale in which ordinary scruples can have any part or parcel, anyhow, it's hardly fair of you to get my curiosity going full speed, only to then leave it unappeased."

He eyed me steadily, the appearance of interest fading more and more, until presently, his face assumed its wonted expressionless mask; somehow I was conscious that what he saw in my face wasn't altogether to his liking.

His voice was once more bland and self-contained. "I perceive you're of an opinion that I've been told a fairytale. I suppose I have."

"But what is the fairytale? Don't you see I'm dying to know?"

"Unfortunately, Atherton, I'm on my honor. Until I have permission I'm afraid my tongue is tied." He picked up his hat and umbrella from where he'd placed them on the table. Holding them in his left hand, he advanced to me with his right outstretched. "It's very good of you to suffer my continued interruption; I know to my sorrow what such interruptions mean, believe me, I'm not ungrateful." His eyes glanced at something to the right of me and said, "What's this?"

On the shelf within a foot or so from where I stood was a sheet of paper, the size and shape of half a sheet of post note. At this he stooped to get a better look. As he did so, something surprising occurred. At that exact instant a look came onto his face which literally terrified him. His hat and umbrella fell from his grasp onto the floor. He retreated, gibbering, his hands held out as if to ward something off from him, until he reached the wall on the other side of the room. A more amazing spectacle than he presented I'd never seen.

"Lessingham!" I exclaimed. "What's wrong with you?"

My first impression was that he'd been struck by a fit of epilepsy, though anyone less like an epileptic subject it would be hard to find. In my bewilderment I looked around to see what could be the immediate cause.

My gaze fell on the sheet of paper and I stared at it with considerable surprise. I hadn't noticed it there previously, as I'd not put it there. Then where had it come from? The curious thing was that on it was an illustration of a species of beetle with which I felt I ought to be acquainted with, and yet was not. It was of a dull golden green, and the color was well brought out, even to the extent of seeming to scintillate, and the whole thing was so dexterously done that the creature seemed alive. In fact, the semblance of reality was so vivid that it needed a second glance to be sure that it was a mere trick of the picture. Its presence there was odd, especially after what we'd been talking about; it needed an explanation, but it was absurd to suppose that the picture alone could have had such an effect on a man like Lessingham.

With the picture in my hand, I crossed to where he was, pressing his back against the wall; he'd shrunk lower inch by inch until he was actually crouching on his haunches.

"Lessingham! Come, man, what's wrong with you?" Taking him by the shoulder, I shook him with some vigor. My touch had the effect of seeming to wake him out of a dream, of restoring him to consciousness, and against the nightmare horrors with which he was struggling. He gazed up at me with a look of cunning on his face which one associates with abject terror.

"Atherton? Is it you? It's all right, quite right. I'm well, very well." As he spoke, he slowly drew himself up, until he was standing tall.

"Then, in that case, all I can say is that you have an odd way of being very well."

He put his hand up to his mouth, as if to hide the trembling of his lips. "It's the pressure of overwork. I've had one or two attacks like this, but it's nothing, temporary."

I observed him keenly; to my thinking there was something about him which was very odd indeed.

"Only temporary! If you take my strongly-urged advice, you'll get a medical opinion without delay, if you haven't been wise enough to have done so already."

"Yes, I'll go today; at once, but I know it's only stress."

"You're sure it's nothing to do with this?" I held up the picture of the beetle. As I did so, he backed away from me, shrieking, trembling as with palsy.

"Take it away! Take it away!" he screamed.

I stared at him for some seconds, astonished into speechlessness. Then I found my tongue. "Lessingham! It's only a picture! Are you stark mad?"

He persisted in his screams. "Take it away! Take it away! Tear it up! Burn it!"

His agitation was so unnatural, and fearing the recurrence of the attack from which he'd just recovered, I did as he bade me. I tore the sheet of paper into quarters, and striking a match, set fire to each separate piece.

He watched the process of incineration as if fascinated. When it was concluded, and nothing but ashes remained, he gave a gasp of relief.

"Lessingham," I said, "you're either mad already, or you're going mad; which is it?"

"I think it's neither. I believe I'm as sane as you, Atherton. It's that story of which I was speaking; it seems curious, but I'll tell you all about it some day. As I observed, I think you'll find it an interesting instance of a peculiar survival." He made an obvious effort to gather himself. "It's extremely unfortunate, Atherton, that I should have troubled you with such a display of weakness, especially as I'm able to offer you so scant an explanation. One thing I would ask of you is to observe strict confidence. What's taken place here has to remain between us. I'm in your hands. I'm your friend. I know I can rely on you not to speak of it to anyone, and in particular not to breathe a word of it to Miss Lindon."

"Why in particular, not to Miss Lindon?"

"Can't you guess?"

I hunched my shoulder. "If what I guess is what you mean, then isn't that a good reason why silence would be unfair to her?"

"It's for me alone to tell her, and I shall not fail to do what should be done. Give me your promise that you won't mention a word to her of what you have so unfortunately seen?"

I gave him the promise he required.

* * *

There was no more work for me that day. Paul's stories and his beetles and his Arabian friend, these things were as microbes which, acting on a system already predisposed for their reception, produced a high fever in me. Though I was in a fever it was one of unrest. My brain was in a whirl! Marjorie, Paul, Isis, beetles, mesmerism, all in delirious jumble. Love's upsetting, and in itself is a sufficiently severe disease, but when complications intervene, suggestive of mystery and novelties, so that you don't know if you're going up or down it can be quite maddening.

I tried to think things out, and if I'd kept on trying, something would have happened, so I went out on the river instead.

Chapter 14

That night was the Duchess of Datchet's ball, and the first person I saw as I entered the dancing-room was Dora Grayling.

I went straight up to her. "Miss Grayling, I behaved very badly to you last night, I've come to say I'm sorry and beg your forgiveness!"

"My forgiveness?" Her head went back; she has a pretty bird-like trick of cocking it a little to one side. "Why Atherton, that's most gentlemanly of you?"

"So you forgive me? Then would you honor me with a dance for the one I lost last night?"

She rose. A man came up, a stranger to me; Miss Grayling is one of the most desired women in England.

"This is my dance, Miss Grayling," the new arrival said.

She looked at him. "You must excuse me but I'm afraid I have made a mistake. I'd forgotten that I was already engaged."

I was shocked. She took my arm, and away we went, leaving her suitor staring after us.

"It's he who's the sufferer now," I whispered as we danced— oh how she can waltz!

"You think so?" she said. "To me, a dance with you means something." She went all red, adding as an afterthought, "Nowadays so few men really dance. I expect it's because you dance so well."

"Thank you."

We danced the waltz right through, then we went to an impromptu shelter which had been rigged up on a balcony where we talked. There's something sympathetic about Miss Grayling which leads one to talk about one's self, and before I was half aware of it, I was telling her all about my plans and projects, actually telling her of my latest notion which, ultimately, was to result in the destruction of entire armies as by a flash of lightning. She took an amount of interest in it which was surprising.

"What really stands in the way of things of this sort is not theory but practice, one can prove one's facts on paper, or on a small scale in a room, but what is really wanted is proof on a large scale, by actual experiment. If for instance, I could take my plant to one of the forests of South America, where there is plenty of animal life but no humans, I could demonstrate the soundness of my position then and there."

"Why don't you?"

"Think of the money it would cost."

"I thought I was a friend of yours," she said.

"I'd hoped you were."

"Then why don't you let me help you out?"

"Help me? How?"

"By letting you have the money for your South American experiment; it would be an investment on which I'd expect to receive good interest of course."

I fidgeted. "That's very nice of you, Miss Grayling, to offer but…."

She became quite frigid. "Stop right there! I perceive quite clearly that you're going to turn me down, and that you're trying to do it as delicately as you know how."

"Miss Grayling!"

"I understand that it was an impertinence on my part to volunteer assistance which was unasked; you've made that sufficiently plain."

"I assure you…."

"Pray don't. Of course, if it had been Miss Lindon it would have been different; she would at least have received a civil answer. But we're not all Miss Lindon."

I was aghast. The outburst was so uncalled for, I hadn't the faintest notion what I'd said or done to cause it; she was in such a surprising passion— and it suited her! I thought I'd never seen her look more beautiful. I could do nothing else but stare.

So she went on, "Have I offended you so irremediably that it'll be impossible for you to dance with me again?"

"Miss Grayling! I shall be only too delighted." She handed me her dance card. "Which may I have?"

"For your own sake you'd better place it as far off as you possibly can."

"They all seem taken."

"That doesn't matter; strike off any name you please, anywhere, and put your own instead." She was giving me an almost embarrassingly free hand. With a wave she left me then, returning to the dance. I booked myself for the next waltz—who it was that would have to give way to me I didn't trouble to inquire.

"Mr. Atherton! Is that you?" came a voice from behind me.

It was Marjorie! As soon as I saw her I knew that there was only one woman in the world for me; the mere sight of her sent the blood tingling through my veins. Turning to her attendant cavalier, she dismissed him with a bow. She seated herself in the chair Miss Grayling had just vacated. I sat down beside her. She glanced at me with laughter in her eyes. I felt my stomach flutter as she looked at me.

"You remember that last night I told you that I might require your friendly services in diplomatic intervention?" she asked.

I nodded. I felt that the allusion was unfair.

"Well, the occasion's come, or at least it's very near." She was still, and I said nothing to help her. "You know how unreasonable Papa can be."

I did. Never was there a more pig-headed man in England than Geoffrey Lindon. But just then, I wasn't prepared to admit it to his daughter.

"You know what an absurd objection he has to— Paul." There was an appreciative hesitation before she uttered his name, so that when it came it was with an accent of tenderness which stung me like a gadfly. To speak to me, of all men, of the fellow in such a tone was like I was merely her friend.

"Has Mr. Lindon no notion of how things stand between you?" I inquired.

"Only what he suspects. That's where you are to come in, Sydney. Papa thinks so much of you— I want you to sound Paul's praises in his ear, to prepare him for what must come."

Was ever a rejected lover burdened with such a task? Its enormity kept me still. "Sydney, you've always been my friend, my truest, dearest friend. When I was a little girl, you used to come between Papa and me, to shield me from his wrath. Now that I'm a big girl I want you to be on my side once more, to shield me still." Her voice softened. She laid her hand on my arm. How, under her touch, I burned.

"But I don't understand what cause there's been for secrecy; why should there have been any secrecy at all?"

"It was Paul's wish that Papa shouldn't be told," she said.

"Is Mr. Lessingham ashamed of you?"

"Sydney!"

"Or does he fear your father?"

"You're being unkind. You know perfectly well that Papa has been prejudiced against him all along. You know that his political position is just now one of the greatest difficulty, that every nerve and muscle is kept on the continual strain, that it's in the highest degree essential that further complications of every and any sort should be avoided. He's quite aware that his suit will not be approved of by Papa, and he simply wishes that nothing shall be said about it till the end of the session, that's all."

"I see! Mr. Lessingham is cautious even in love-making; politician first, and lover afterwards."

"Well! Why not? Would you have him injure the cause he has at heart for want of a little patience?" she said.

"It depends what cause it is he has at heart."

"What's the matter with you? Why do you speak to me like that? It's not like you at all." She looked at me shrewdly, with flashing eyes. "Is it possible that you're jealous? That you were in earnest in what you said last night? I thought that was the sort of thing you said to every girl."

I would have given a great deal to take her in my arms, and press her to my bosom then and there; to think that she should taunt me with what I said to her, as if I professed my love to every woman I knew. "What do you know of Mr. Lessingham?" I asked.

"What all the world knows, that history will be made by him."

"There are kinds of history in the making of which one wouldn't want to be associated to. What do you know of his private life? That was what I was referring to."

"Really, Sydney, you go too far. I know that he's one of the best, just as he's one of the greatest of men; for me that's sufficient."

"If you do know that, it's sufficient," I replied.

"I do know it, all the world knows it," she said. "Everyone with whom he comes in contact is aware—must be aware—that he's incapable of a dishonorable thought or action."

"Take my advice; don't appreciate any man too highly. In the book of every man's life there is a page which he would wish to keep turned down."

"There's no such page in Paul's, there may be in yours; I think that probable," she said.

"Thank you. I fear it's more than probable. I fear that, in my case, the page may extend to several. There's nothing political about me, not even the name."

"Sydney, you're unendurable! It's the more strange to hear you talk like this since Paul regards you as his friend."

"He flatters me."

"Are you not his friend?"

"Isn't sufficient to be yours?"

"No, who is against Paul is against me," she said, her jaw taut.

"That's hard."

"How is it hard? Who's against the husband can hardly be for the wife, when the husband and the wife are one."

"But you're not 'one' yet. Is my cause so hopeless?"

"What do you call your cause? Are you thinking of that nonsense you were talking about last night?" she laughed.

"You call it nonsense. You ask for sympathy, and give so much!"

"I'll give you all the sympathy you need, I promise! My poor, dear Sydney, don't be so absurd! Do you think that I don't know you? You're the best of friends, and the worst of lovers, as the one, so true; so fickle as the other. To my certain knowledge, with how many girls have you been in love, and out again? It's true that, to the best of my knowledge and belief, you've never been in love with me before, but that's the merest accident. Believe me, my dear, dear Sydney, you'll be in love with someone else tomorrow, if you're not halfway there tonight already. I confess, quite frankly, that in that direction, all the experience I've had of you has in no way strengthened my prophetic instinct. Cheer up! One never knows!" Her gaze shifted past me. "Who's that's coming?"

It was Dora Grayling who was coming back for me. I went off with her without a word; we were halfway through the dance before she spoke to me.

"I'm sorry that I was cross with you a while ago, and disagreeable," I said. "Somehow I always seem destined to show to you my most unpleasant side."

"The blame was mine, what sort of side do I show you? You're far kinder to me than I deserve, now and always," she said.

"Pardon me, it's true, otherwise how come I'm alone without a friend?" I asked.

"You! Without a friend! I've never known any man who had so many! I never knew a person of whom so many men and women join in speaking well of too!"

"Miss Grayling!" I gasped.

"As for never having done anything worth doing, think of what you've done. Think of your discoveries, of your inventions, think of— but never mind! The world knows you've done great things, and it confidently looks to you to do still greater. You talk of being friendless, and yet when I ask as a favor—as a great favor—to be allowed to do something to show my friendship, you well, you snub me."

"I snub you!"

"You know you snubbed me," she said.

"Do you really mean that you take an interest in my work?"

"You know I mean it." She turned to me, her face all glowing, and I did know it.

"Will you come to my laboratory tomorrow morning?"

"Will I! Won't I!"

"With your aunt?"

"Yes, with my aunt," She smiled.

"I'll show you around, and tell you all there is to be told, and then if you still think there's anything in it, I'll accept your offer about that South American experiment, that is, if it still holds good."

"Of course it still holds good," she grinned.

"And we'll be partners."

"Partners? Yes, we'll be partners.

"It will cost a terrific sum.

"There are some things which never can cost too much," she said.

"That's not my experience."

"I hope it'll be mine."

"It's a bargain?" I asked.

"On my side, I promise you that it's a bargain," she said.

When I left the dance I found that Percy Woodville was at my side. His round face was, in a manner of speaking as long as my arm. He took out his eyeglasses, and rubbed them with his handkerchief, then put them back, only to take them out yet again and begin rubbing. I don't think that I've never seen him in such a state of fluster, and when one speaks of Woodville, that means something.

"Atherton, I'm in a devil of a stew." He looked it, too. "I've had a blow which I shall never get over!"

"Then get under."

Woodville is one of those fellows who'll insist on telling me their most private matters, even to what they owe their washerwomen for the ruination of their shirts. Why he does this I have no idea; heaven knows I'm not sympathetic.

"Don't be an idiot! You don't know what I'm suffering! I'm as nearly as possible stark mad," he said in a fluster.

"That's all right, old chap. I've seen you that way more than once before."

"Don't talk like that, you're not a perfect brute!"

"I bet you a shilling that I am."

"Don't torture me, Atherton, you're not!" He seized me by the lapels of my coat, seeming half beside himself; fortunately he'd drawn me into a recess, so that we were noticed by few observers. "What do you think has happened?"

"My dear chap, how on earth am I to know?" I said.

"She's refused me!"

"Has she! Well I never! Buck up, try some other address, there are more fish in the sea as ever came out of it."

"Atherton, you're a blackguard."

He'd crumpled his handkerchief into a ball, and was actually bobbing at his eyes with it; the idea of Percy Woodville being dissolved in tears was excruciatingly funny, only right then I could hardly tell him so.

"There's not a doubt of it, it's my way of being sympathetic. Don't be so down, man, try her again!" I said.

"It's not the slightest use—I know it isn't—from the way she treated me."

"Don't be so sure; women often say what they mean least. Who's the lady?"

"Who?" he asked. "Are there more women in the world than one for me, or has there ever been? You ask me who! What does the word mean to me but Marjorie Lindon!"

"Marjorie Lindon?" I fancy that my jaw dropped open. I turned and strode away—leaving him staring at my back—and all but ran into Marjorie's arms.

"I'm just leaving. Will you see me to the carriage, Mr. Atherton?" I did so. "Are you off? Can I give you a lift?"

"Thank you, I'm not thinking of being off," I said.

"I'm going to the House of Commons, won't you come?"

"What are you going there for?"

The second she spoke of it I knew why she was going, and she knew that I knew, as her words showed.

"You're quite well aware of why. You're not so ignorant not to know that the Agricultural Amendment Act is on tonight, and that Paul is to speak there. I always try to be there when he is to speak, and I mean to always keep on trying."

"He's a fortunate man," I said.

"Indeed he is. A man with such gifts as his are inadequately described as 'fortunate.' But I must be off. He expected to be up before, but I heard from him a few minutes ago that there has been a delay, and that he'll be up within half an hour. Until our next meeting." I watched her leave, then I returned to the house. In the hall I met Percy Woodville. He had his hat on.

"Where are you off to?"

"I'm off to the House," he replied.

"To hear Paul Lessingham?"

"Damn Paul Lessingham!" he said.

"With all my heart!"

"There's a division expected, I've got to go," he said

"Someone else has gone to hear Paul Lessingham, too," I said. "Marjorie Lindon."

"No! You don't say so! By Jove! I say, Atherton, I wish I could make a speech. I never can. When I'm running for election I have to have my speeches written for me, and then I have to read 'em. But, by Jove, if I knew Miss Lindon was in the gallery, and if I knew anything about the thing, or could get someone to tell me something, well, hang me if I wouldn't speak. I'd show her I'm not the fool she thinks I am!"

"Speak, Percy, speak! You'd knock 'em silly, sir! I tell you what I'll do, I'll come with you! I'll go to the House as well! Paul Lessingham shall have an audience of three at the least."

Chapter 15

The House was full. Percy and I went upstairs to the gallery which is theoretically supposed to be reserved for what are called 'distinguished strangers.' Trumperton was talking, hammering out those sentences which smell, not so much of the lamp as of the dunderhead. Nobody was listening, except the men in the Press Gallery.

It wasn't until Trumperton had finished that I discovered Lessingham. The tedious ancient Trumperton resumed his seat amidst a murmur of sounds which, I have no doubt, some of the pressmen interpreted next day as 'loud and continued applause.' There was movement in the House, possibly expressive of relief, and with a hum of voices, men came flocking in. Then from the Opposition benches, there rose a sound which was applause, and I perceived that—on a cross bench close to the gangway— Paul Lessingham was standing up.

I eyed him critically, as a collector might eye a valuable specimen, or a pathologist a curious subject. During the last twenty-four hours my interest in him had grown. Right then, to me, he was the most interesting man in the world.

When I remembered how I'd seen him that same morning, a nerveless, terror-stricken wretch, groveling like some craven cur on the floor, frightened, to the verge of imbecility, by a shadow, no, less than a shadow, I was confronted by two hypotheses. Either I'd exaggerated his condition then, or I exaggerated his condition now. So far as appearance went, it was incredible that this man could look as composed as he did.

I confess that my feeling rapidly became one of admiration. I love the fighter. I quickly recognized that here we had him in perfection. To his fingertips he was a fighting man. I'd never realized it so clearly before. He was coolness itself. He had all his faculties under complete command.

While never for a moment really exposing himself, he would be swift in perceiving the slightest weakness in his opponent's defense, and as soon as he saw it, like lightning, he would slip in a telling blow. And even if he was defeated, he would hardly be disgraced, and one might easily believe that their very victories would be so expensive to his assailants, that in the end they would actually contribute to his triumph.

"Damn it!" I said to myself. "I can see what Marjorie sees in him." For I perceived how a clever and imaginative young woman, seeing him at his best, holding his own like a gallant knight against overwhelming odds, in the lists in which he was so much at home, might come to think of him as if he were always and only there, ignoring altogether the kind of man he was when the joust was finished.

It did me good to hear him, I do know that, and I could easily imagine the effect he had on one particular auditor who was in the Ladies' Cage. It was very far from being an 'oration' in the American sense, as it had little or nothing of the fire and fury of the French Tribune; it was marked neither by the ponderosity nor the sentiment of the eloquent German, yet it was as satisfying as are the efforts of either of the three, producing without doubt, precisely the effect which the speaker intended.

His voice was clear and calm, not exactly musical, yet distinctly pleasant, and it was so managed that each word he uttered was as audible to every person present as if it had been addressed particularly to him. His sentences were short and crisp; the words which he used were not big ones, but they came from him with an agreeable ease, and he spoke just fast enough to keep one's interest alert without invoking a strain on the attention.

He commenced by making, in the quietest and most courteous manner, sarcastic comments on the speeches and methods of Trumperton and his friends, which tickled the House amazingly. But he didn't make the mistake of pushing his personalities too far. To a speaker of a certain sort, nothing is easier than to sting to madness. If he likes, his every word is barbed. Wounds so given fester, and they are not so easily forgiven—it's essential to a politician that he should have his firmest friends among the fools, or his climbing days will soon be over.

Soon his sarcasms were at an end, and he began to exchange them for sweet-sounding phrases. He actually began to say pleasant things to his opponents, and apparently meant them. To put them in a good conceit with themselves, no doubt. He pointed out how much truth there was in what they said, and then as if by accident, with what ease and at how little cost, amendments might be made. He found their arguments, and took them for his own, and flattered them, whether they would or would not, by showing how firmly they were founded upon fact, and grafted other arguments upon them. He transformed them, and drove them hither and thither, and brought them—their own arguments—to a round, irrefutable conclusion, which was diametrically the reverse of that to which they themselves had brought them. And he did it all with an aptness, a readiness, a grace, which was incontestable. So that, when he finally sat down, he'd performed that most difficult of all feats: he'd delivered what in a House of Commons' sense, was a practical, statesman-like speech, and yet one which left his hearers in an excellent humor.

It was a great success, an immense success. A parliamentary triumph of almost the highest order. Paul Lessingham had been coming on by leaps and bounds. When he resumed his seat, amidst applause which this time really was applause, there were probably few who doubted that he was destined to go even farther still. How much farther only time alone could tell, but so far as appearances went, all the prizes, which are as the crown and climax of a statesman's career, were well within his reach.

For my part, I was delighted. I'd enjoyed an intellectual exercise, a species of enjoyment not as common as it might be. Paul had almost persuaded me that the political game was one worth playing, and that its triumphs were things to be desired. It's something, after all, to be able to appeal successfully to the passions and aspirations of your peers, to gain their plaudits, to prove your skill at the game you yourself have chosen, and to be looked up to and admired. And when a woman's eyes look down on you, and her ears drink in your every word, and her heart beats time with yours—each man to his own temperament—and when that woman is the woman whom you love, to know that your triumph means her glory, and her happiness. To me that would be the best part of it all.

In that hour, I almost wished that I were a politician too!

Soon, the division was over. The business of the night was practically done and I found myself back in the lobby. The theme of conversation was Paul's speech and on every side they talked of it.

Suddenly Marjorie was at my side. Her face was glowing. I'd never seen her look more beautiful, or happier. She seemed to be alone.

"So you've come after all!" she said to me. "Wasn't it splendid? Wasn't it magnificent? Isn't it grand to have such great gifts, and to use them to such good purpose? Speak, Sydney! Don't feign a coolness which is foreign to your nature!"

I saw that she was hungry for me to praise the man whom she delighted to honor. But somehow, her enthusiasm cooled mine.

"It wasn't a bad speech, of a kind."

"Of a kind!" How her eyes flashed fire! With what disdain she treated me! "What do you mean by 'of a kind'? My dear Sydney, are you not aware that it's only a small mind that would attempt to belittle those which are greater? Even if you're conscious of inferiority, it's unwise to show it. Mr. Lessingham's was a great speech, of any kind, and your incapacity to recognize the fact simply reveals your lack of intelligence."

"Well, it's fortunate for Mr. Lessingham that there's at least one person in whom intelligence is so bountifully developed. Apparently, in your judgment, he who discriminates is lost."

I thought she was going to let her temper lose, but instead, laughing, she placed her hand on my shoulder. "Poor Sydney! I understand! It's so sad! Do you know you're like a little boy who, when he's beaten, declares that the victor has cheated him. Never mind! As you grow older, you'll learn better."

She'd stung me almost beyond bearing, I cared not what I said. "You, unless I'm mistaken, will learn better before you're older, too."

"What do you mean?" she asked.

Before I could say anything more, Paul Lessingham joined us.

"I hope I've not kept you waiting; I've been delayed longer than I expected," he said with a wide smile.

"Not at all, though I'm quite ready to get away; it's a little tiresome waiting here." With a mischievous glance towards him, a glance which compelled Lessingham to notice me, I said, "You don't often favor us."

"I don't. Normally I have better things to do," he said.

"You're wrong. It's the slant of the day to underrate the House of Commons, and the work which it performs; don't you suffer yourself to join in the chorus of the simpletons. Your time can't be better employed than in endeavoring to improve the body politic," I said.

"I'm obliged to you."

"I hope you're feeling better than when I saw you last," I said.

A gleam came into his eyes, fading as quickly as it came. He showed no other sign of comprehension, surprise, or resentment. "Thank you. I'm very well."

Marjorie perceived that I meant more than met the eye, and that what I meant was unpleasant.

"Come, let us be off. It's Mr. Atherton tonight who's not well." She slipped her arm through Lessingham's just as her father approached. Old Lindon stared at her on Paul's arm, as if he could hardly believe that it was she.

"I thought that you were at the Duchess' ?" he asked.

"I was Papa, and now I'm here."

"Here!" Old Lindon began to stutter and stammer, and to grow red in the face, as is his wont when he gets excited. "W…what do you mean by here? Wh…where's the carriage?"

"Where should it be, except waiting for me outside, unless the horses have run away," she replied.

"I…I…I'll take you down to it. I…I don't approve of y…your w…w…waiting in a place like this."

"Thank you, Papa, but Mr. Lessingham is going to take me down. I'll see you afterwards. Goodbye." Anything cooler than the way in which she walked off I don't think I ever saw. There was no doubt that this was the age of feminine advancement. Young women think nothing of twisting their mothers around their fingers, let alone their fathers, but the fashion in which that young woman walked off, on Paul's arm, and left her father standing there, was in its way, a study for all women.

Old Lindon seemed scarcely able to realize that the pair of them had gone. Even after they'd disappeared in the crowd he stood staring after them, growing redder and redder, until the veins stood out on his forehead, and I thought that an apoplectic seizure threatened to overtake him.

Then, with a gasp, he turned to me and said, "Damned scoundrel!"

I assumed he was referring to Paul, even though his following words hardly suggested it. "Only this morning I forbade her to have anything to do with him, and n…now He's w…walked off with her! C…confounded adventurer! That's what he is, an adventurer, and before many hours have passed I'll take the liberty to tell him so!"

Jamming his fists into his pockets and puffing like a grampus in distress, he left, and it was time he did, for his words were as audible as they were pointed, and already people were wondering what the matter was.

Woodville came up as Old Lindon was leaving, looking just as sorely distressed as ever. "She went away with Lessingham, did you see her?" he asked.

"Of course I saw her," I said. "When a man makes a speech like Lessingham's any girl would go away with him, and be proud to. When you're endowed with such great powers as his, and use them for such lofty purposes, she'll walk away with you, but till then, never."

He was at his old trick of polishing his eyeglasses.

"It's bitter hard," he said. "When I knew that she was there, I'd half a mind to make a speech myself, upon my word I had, only I didn't know what to talk about, and I can't speak anyhow, how can a fellow speak when he's shoved into the gallery?"

"As you say, how can he? He can't stand on the railing and shout, even with a friend holding him behind," I said.

"I know I shall speak one day, bound to, and then she won't be there."

"It'll be better for you if she isn't."

"Think so?" he asked. "Perhaps you're right. I'd be safe to make a mess of it, and then, if she were to see me at it, it'd be the devil! "On my word, I've been wishing lately I was clever." He rubbed his nose with the rim of his eyeglasses, looking the most comically disconsolate figure.

"Put it all behind you, Percy! Buck up, my boy! The division's over, you're free. Now we'll go 'on the fly.'"

And we did 'go on the fly.'

Chapter 16

I took Percy to dinner at the Helicon. All the way in the cab he was trying to tell me the story of how he proposed to Marjorie, and he was very far from being through with it when we reached the club. There was the usual crowd of diners, but we got a little table to ourselves in a corner of the room, and before anything was brought for us to eat he was at it again. A good many of the people were pretty near to shouting, and as they seemed to be all speaking at once, and the band was playing, and as the Helicon band is not piano, Percy didn't have it quite all to himself. Still, considering the delicacy of his subject, he talked as loudly as was decent, getting more so as he went on. But Percy is peculiar.

"I don't know how many times I've tried to tell her, over and over again," he said.

"Have you now?"

"Yes, pretty near every time I've met her, but I never seem to quite get to it, don't you know."

"How's that?"

"Why, just when I'm about to start with, 'Miss Lindon, may I offer you the gift of my affection?' my nerve breaks and I stop."

"Was that how you invariably intended to begin?"

"Well, not always; one time like that, and another time another way. Fact is, I memorized a little speech, and I know it by heart, but I never got a chance to reel it off, so I made up my mind to just say anything."

"And what did you say?" I asked.

"Well, nothing, you see, I never got there. Just as I was feeling my way, she'd ask me if I preferred big sleeves to little ones, or top hats to billycocks, or some nonsense of the kind."

"Would she now?"

"Yes, and of course I had to answer, and by the time I'd answered the chance was lost." Percy was polishing his eyeglasses. "I tried to get there so many times, and she choked me off so often, that I can't help thinking that she suspected what it was I was after."

"You think she did?"

"She must have done," he nodded. "Once I followed her down Piccadilly, and into a glove shop in the Burlington Arcade. I meant to propose to her in there. I hadn't had a wink of sleep all night through dreaming of her, and I was just about desperate."

"Did you propose?"

He shook his head. "The girl behind the counter made me buy a dozen pairs of gloves instead. They turned out to be three sizes too large for me too. I believe she thought I'd gone to spoon the glove girl; she went out and left me there. The girl at the counter loaded me with all sorts of things when Miss Lindon was gone. I couldn't get away! She held me with her blessed eye, a gaze I couldn't break. I believe it was a glass one."

"Miss Lindon's? Or the glove girl's?"

"The glove girl's obviously. She sent me home with a whole cartload of green ties and declared I'd ordered them. I shall never forget that day. I've never been up the Arcade since, and never mean to."

"You gave Miss Lindon a wrong impression."

"I don't know, perhaps," he sighed. "It seems that I was always giving her wrong impressions. Once she said that she knew I wasn't a marrying man, that I was the sort of chap who never would marry, because she saw it in my face."

"Under the circumstances, that was trying."

"Bitter hard." Percy sighed again. "I shouldn't mind if I wasn't so flustered. I'm not a fellow who does get flustered easily, but when I do…" He trailed off and shrugged.

"I tell you what, Percy, have a drink, you'll feel better!"

"I don't drink, you know that."

"You talk of your heart being broken, and of your not drinking in the same breath, if your heart were really broken you'd throw abstinence to the winds."

"Do you think so? Why?"

"Because men whose hearts are broken always do; you'd swallow a magnum at the least."

Percy groaned. "When I drink I'm always ill, but I'll have a try."

He did, making a good beginning by emptying the glass which the waiter had just now filled. Then he relapsed into melancholy.

"Tell me, Percy—honest Indian—do you really love her?"

"Love her?" His eyes grew round as saucers. "Didn't I tell you that I love her?"

"Yes you did, but that sort of thing is easy telling. What does it make you feel like, this love you talk so much about?"

"Feel like? You should have a look inside me, then you'd know."

"I see. It's like that, is it? Suppose she loved another man, what sort of feeling would you feel towards him?"

"Does she love another man?" he asked.

"I say, suppose."

"I dare say she does. I expect that's it. What an idiot I am not to have thought of that before." He sighed and refilled his glass. "He's a lucky chap, whoever he is. I'd like to tell him so."

"You'd like to tell him so?"

"He's such a jolly lucky chap, you know," he said.

"Possibly, but his jolly good luck is your jolly bad luck. Would you be willing to give her to him without a word?"

"If she loves him."

"But you say you love her."

"Of course I do," he said.

"Well then?"

"You don't suppose that, because I love her, I shouldn't like to see her happy? I'm not such a beast! I'd sooner see her happy than anything else in all the world."

"I see. Even happy with another man? Well, Percy, I'm afraid my philosophy isn't like yours. If I loved Miss Lindon, and she loved another man, I'm afraid I shouldn't feel like that towards him at all."

"What would you feel like?" he asked.

"Murderous. Percy, you come home with me tonight, we've begun the night together, so let's end it together. I'll show you one of the finest notions for committing murder on a scale of real magnificence that you've ever dreamed of. I would like to make use of it to show my feelings towards this fictionist man Miss Lindon loves. He'd know what I felt for him once he was introduced to it."

Percy went with me without a word. He hadn't had much to drink, but it was still too much for him, and he was in a condition of maundering sentimentality. I got him into a cab and we dashed along Piccadilly.

He was silent, and sat looking in front of him with an air of vacuous sullenness which ill-became his normal countenance. I bade the cabman pass though Lowndes Square. As we passed Paul Lessingham's, I had the driver pull over. I pointed out the place to Percy Woodville.

"You see, Percy, That's Lessingham's house! That's the house of the man who went away with Marjorie!"

"Yes." Words came from him slowly, with a quite unnecessary stress on each. "Because he made a speech. I'd like to make a speech. One day I'll make a speech."

"Because he made a speech, only that and nothing more! When a man speaks with such a quick-witted tongue, he can catch any woman in the land." Then I saw, or thought I saw, someone or something glide up the steps and withdraw into the shadow of the doorway, as if unwilling to be seen. When I hailed no one answered. I called again. "Hello, who's that there? Lessingham, is that you? Don't be shy, my friend!"

I sprang out of the cab, ran across the road and up the steps. To my surprise, there was no one in the doorway. It seemed incredible, but the place was empty. I felt about me with my hands, as if I'd been playing at blind man's buff, and grasped at only air. I came down a step or two.

"Ostensibly, there's a vacuum, which nature abhors. I say, driver, did you see someone come up these steps?"

"I thought I did, sir. I could have sworn I did."

"So could I. It's very odd."

"Perhaps whoever it was has gone into the house, sir."

"I don't see how. We would have heard the door open, even if we hadn't seen it. It's not so dark as that. I've half a mind to ring the bell and inquire."

"I shouldn't do that if I was you, sir," the driver said. "You jump in, and I'll get along. This is Mr. Lessingham's home, the 'great' Mr. Lessingham's."

I believe the cabman thought I was drunk, and not respectable enough to claim acquaintance with the 'great' Mr. Lessingham.

"Wake up, Percy! Do you know I believe there's some mystery about this place. I feel assured of it. I feel as if I were in the presence of something uncanny, something which I can neither see, nor touch, nor hear."

The cabman bent down from his seat, wheedling me. "Jump in, sir, and we'll be getting along."

I jumped in, and we got along, but not far. Before we had gone a dozen yards I was out again, without troubling the driver to stop.

He pulled up, aggrieved. "Well, sir, what's the matter now? You'll be damaging yourself before you're done, and then you'll be blaming me."

I'd caught sight of a cat crouching in the shadow of the railings—a black one. That cat was my quarry. Either the creature was unusually sleepy, slow, stupid, or it had lost its wits—which a cat seldom does lose. Without making an attempt to escape, it allowed me to grab it by the nape of the neck.

As soon as we were inside my laboratory, I put the cat into my glass box.

Percy stared. "What have you put it there for?" he asked.

"That, my dear Percy, is what you're shortly about to see. You're about to be the witness of an experiment which, to a legislator such as you are, ought to be of the greatest possible interest. I'm going to demonstrate, on a small scale, the action of the force which, on a large scale, I propose to employ on behalf of my native land."

He showed no signs of being interested. Sinking into a chair, he said, "I hate cats! Do let it go! I'm always miserable when there's a cat in the room."

"Nonsense, that's ridiculous! What you want is a taste of whisky, then you'll be as chirpy as a cricket."

"I don't want anything more to drink! I've had too much already!"

I paid no heed to what he said. I poured two stiff doses into a couple of tumblers. Without seeming to be aware of what it was he was doing, he disposed of the better half of the one I gave him. Putting his glass upon the table, he dropped his head on his hands and groaned.

"What would Marjorie think of me if she saw me now?"

"Think? Nothing. Why should she think of a man like you, when she has so much better fish to fry?" I said.

"I'm feeling frightfully ill! I'll be drunk before I've done!"

"Then be drunk! Only for gracious sake, be a lively drunk, not a deadly doleful. Cheer up, Percy!" I clapped him on the shoulder, almost knocking him off his seat and onto the floor. "I'm now going to show you that little experiment of which I was speaking! You see that cat?"

"Of course I see it—the foul thing! I wish you'd let it go!"

"Why should I let it go? Do you know whose cat that is? That cat's Paul Lessingham's."

"Paul Lessingham's?" he said.

"Yes, Paul Lessingham's, the man who made the speech, the man whom Marjorie went away with."

"How do you know it's his?"

"I don't know it's his, but I believe it is. I choose to believe it is! I intend to believe it is! I figure it was outside his house, therefore it's his cat. I can't get Lessingham inside that box, so I'll get his cat instead."

"Whatever for?"

"You'll see. You observe how happy it is?"

"It doesn't seem happy."

"We've all our ways of seeming happy. That's its way." The cat was behaving like a cat gone mad, dashing itself against the sides of its glass prison, leaping to and fro, and from side to side, squealing with rage, or with terror, or with both. Perhaps it foresaw what was coming, there is no fathoming the intelligence of what we call the lower animals.

I held up an object. "Observe this little toy, you've seen something of its kind before. It's a spring gun; you pull the spring, drop the charge into the barrel, release the spring, and the charge is fired. I'll unlock this safe, which is built into the wall. It's a letter lock, the combination just now is 'whisky,' you see. That's a hint to you. You'll notice the safe is strongly made; it's airtight, fire-proof, the outer casing is of triple-plated drill-proof steel, the contents are valuable and devilish dangerous, and I'd pity the thief who in his innocent ignorance broke into it. Look inside. You see it's full of balls, glass balls, each in its own little separate nest. Light as feathers and transparent; you can see right through them. Here are a couple, see, they're like tiny pills. They contain neither dynamite nor cordite, nor anything of the kind, yet given a fair field and no favor, they'll work more mischief than all the explosives man has fashioned. Say you heart is broken. Take hold of one and squeeze it under your nose. Just use a gentle pressure, and in less time than no time you'll be in the land where they say there are no broken hearts."

Percy shrunk back. "I don't know what you're talking about. I don't want the thing. Take it away."

"Think twice, you may not get a second chance."

"I tell you I don't want it," he said.

"Are you sure?"

"Of course I'm sure!"

"Then the cat shall have it."

"Let the poor thing go!"

"The poor thing's going to the land which is so near, and yet so far. Once more, if you please, pay attention. Notice what I do with this toy gun. I pull back the spring, I insert this small glass pellet, and I thrust the muzzle of the gun through the opening in the glass box which contains Lessingham's cat. You'll observe it fits quite close, which on the whole is perhaps fortunate for us. I'm about to release the spring. Close attention, please. Notice the effect."

"Atherton, let the thing go!"

"The thing's gone! I've released the spring—the pellet has been discharged—and it's struck against the roof of the glass box. It's been broken by the contact, and presto! The cat lays dead, and that in the face of its nine lives. You perceive how still it is, how still! Let's hope that now it's really happy. The cat which I choose to believe is Paul Lessingham's has received its due, and in the morning I'll send it back to him. He'll miss it no doubt! Now, Percy, think of a huge bomb, filled with what will be called Atherton's Magic Vapor, fired say, from a hundred and twenty ton gun, bursting at a given elevation over the heads of an opposing force. Properly managed, in less than an instant of time, a hundred thousand men—quite possibly more—would drop down dead as if smitten by the lightning of the skies. Isn't that something like a weapon, sir?"

"I'm not well! I want to get away! I wish I'd never come!" Percy said as he stared at the dead cat.

That was all Percy had to say.

"Rubbish! You're adding to your stock of information every second, and in these days when a member of Parliament is supposed to know all about everything, information's the one thing everyone wants. Empty your glass, man. It's that time of day for you!"

I handed him his tumbler. He drained what was left of its contents, then in a fit of tipsy, childish temper, flung the tumbler from him. I'd placed— carelessly enough—the second pellet within a foot of the edge of the table.

The shock of the glass striking the board close to it set it rolling. I was at the other side. I started forward to stop its motion, but I was too late. Before I could reach the crystal globule, it had fallen off the edge of the table and onto the floor at Woodville's feet, shattering. As it smashed, he was looking down, wondering no doubt in his stupidity, what was going on, for I was shouting and making something of a clatter in my efforts to prevent the catastrophe which I knew was coming. As the vapor from the broken pellet gained access to the air, Percy inhaled and fell forward onto his face. Rushing to him, I snatched his limp body from the floor, and dragged it staggeringly, towards the door which opened onto the yard.

Flinging the door open, I got him into the open air. As I did so, I found I had a new visitor who stood outside watching me.

It was Lessingham's mysterious Egypto-Arabian friend.

Chapter 17

The passage into the yard from the electrically lit laboratory was a passage from brilliancy to gloom. The shrouded figure, standing in the shadow, was like some object in a dream. My own senses reeled.

It was only because I'd resolutely held my breath, and kept my face averted that I hadn't succumbed to the same fate which had overtaken Percy. Had I been a moment longer in gaining the open air, it would have been too late. As it was, in placing Percy on the ground, I stumbled over him and my senses left me. Even as they went I was conscious of remembering the saying about the hangman being hanged by his own noose.

My sensations on returning to consciousness were curious. I found myself being supported in someone's arms, a stranger's face was bending over me, and the most extraordinary pair of eyes I'd ever seen were looking into mine.

"Who are you?" I asked. Then, I recalled that it was my uninvited visitor, and with scant ceremony I drew myself away from him. By the light which was streaming through the laboratory door, I saw that Percy was lying close beside me, stark and still.

"Is he dead?" I cried. "Percy, speak, man! It's not as bad with you as that!"

But it was pretty bad, so bad that as I bent down and looked at him, my heart beat uncomfortably fast. His heart seemed still, for the vapor took effect directly on the cardiac centers. To revive their action, and that instantly, was indispensable. Yet my brain was in such a whirl that I couldn't even think of how to set about beginning. Had I been alone, it's more than probable Percy would have died. As I stared at him, senselessly, aimlessly, the stranger, passing his arms beneath his body, extended himself at full length upon Percy's motionless form. Putting his lips to Percy's, he seemed to be pumping life from his own body into the unconscious man's. As I gazed bewildered, surprised, presently there came a movement of Percy's body. His limbs twitched, as if he was in pain. By degrees, the motions became convulsive, until suddenly he stirred to such an effect that the stranger was rolled right off him. I bent down to find that the Percy's condition still seemed very far from satisfactory. There was a rigidity about the muscles of his face, a clamminess about his skin, a disagreeable suggestiveness about the way in which his teeth and the whites of his eyes were exposed, which was uncomfortable to contemplate.

The stranger must have seen what was passing through my mind, as it wasn't a very difficult thing to see. Pointing to the prone Percy, he said, with that odd foreign twang of his, which whatever it had seemed like in the morning, sounded musical enough just then, "All will be well with him."

"I'm not so sure," I replied.

The stranger didn't answer. He was kneeling on one side of the victim of modern science, myself on the other. Passing his hand back and forth in front of Percy face, as if by magic all semblance of discomfort vanished from his features, and to all appearances he looked placidly asleep.

"Have you hypnotized him?"

"What does it matter?" he asked.

If it was a case of hypnotism, it was very neatly done. The conditions were both unusual and trying, and the effect produced seemed all that could be desired. The change brought about in half a dozen seconds was quite remarkable. I began to be aware of a feeling of quasi-respect for Paul Lessingham's friend. His morals might be peculiar, and his manners were nonexistent, but in this case at any rate, the end seemed to have justified the means.

"He sleeps," he said. "When he awakes he will remember nothing that has been. Leave him, the night is warm, all will be well."

As he said, the night was warm, and it was dry. Percy would come to little harm by being allowed to enjoy the pleasant breeze for a while. So I acted on the stranger's advice, and left him lying in the yard, while I had a little interview with the impromptu physician.

Chapter 18

The laboratory door was closed, the stranger standing a foot or two away from it. I was further within the room, and was subjecting him to as keen a scrutiny as circumstances permitted. Beyond doubt he was conscious of my observation, yet he bore himself with an air of indifference, which was suggestive of absolute unconcern. The fellow was oriental to the fingertips, that much was certain, yet in spite of a pretty wide personal knowledge of oriental people, I couldn't make up my mind as to the exact part of the east from which he came. He was hardly an Arab, he was not a fellah, he wasn't, unless I'd erred, a Mohammedan at all, and there was something about him which was distinctly not Mussulmanic. So far as looks were concerned, he wasn't a flattering example of his race, whatever his race might be. The portentous size of his beak-like nose would have been, in itself, sufficient to damn him in any court of beauty. His lips were thick and shapeless, and this, joined to another peculiarity in his appearance, seemed to suggest that in his veins there ran more than a streak of African blood.

The peculiarity alluded to was his semblance of great age. As one looked at him one was reminded of the legends told of people who are supposed to have retained something of their pristine vigor after having lived for centuries. But as one continued to gaze, one began to wonder if he really was so old as he seemed, and if indeed he was exceptionally old at all. Negroes, and especially negresses, are apt to age with extreme rapidity. Among colored folk, one sometimes encounters women whose faces seem to have been lined by the passage of centuries, yet whose actual tale of years would entitle them to regard themselves, here in England anyway, as in the prime of their life. Besides, the senility of the fellow's countenance was contradicted by the youthfulness of his eyes. No really old man could have had eyes like that. They were curiously shaped, reminding me of the elongated, faceted eyes of some odd creature, with whose appearance I was familiar, although I couldn't, at the instant, recall its name. They glowed not only with the force and fire, but also with the frenzy of youth, owing probably to some peculiar formation of the optic-nerve. I felt as I met his gaze that he was looking right through me. More obvious danger signals never yet were placed in a man's head.

It happens that I am endowed with an unusual tenacity of vision. I could, for instance, easily outstare any man I ever met. Yet, as I continued to stare at this man, I was conscious that it was only by an effort of will that I was able to resist a baleful something which seemed to be passing from his eyes to mine. It might have been my imagination, but in that sense I'm not an imaginative man, and if it was my imagination, then it was of an unpleasantly vivid kind. I could understand how, in the case of a nervous or a sensitive temperament, the fellow might exercise by means of the peculiar quality of his glance alone an influence of a most disastrous sort, which given an appropriate subject in the manifestation of its power might approach almost to the supernatural. If ever man was endowed with the traditional evil eye, in which Italians among modern nations are such profound believers, it was he.

When we had stared at each other for five minutes or so, I began to think I'd had about enough of it, so by way of breaking the ice, I asked, "May I ask how you found your way into my backyard?"

He didn't reply in words, but by raising his hands and then lowering them, palms downward, with a gesture which was peculiarly oriental.

"Indeed? Is that so? Your meaning may be understood to you, but for my benefit perhaps you wouldn't mind translating it into words. Once more I ask: how did you find your way into my backyard?"

Again nothing but the gesture.

"Possibly you're not sufficiently acquainted with English manners and customs to be aware that you've placed yourself within reach of the pains and penalties of the law. Were I to call in the police, you'd find yourself in an awkward situation, and unless you're presently more explanatory, call them I will."

By way of answer he indulged in a distortion of his countenance which might have been meant as a smile, and which seemed to suggest that he regarded the police with a contempt which was too great for words.

"Why do you laugh? Do you think that being threatened with the police is a joke? You're not likely to find it so. Have you suddenly been bereft of the use of your tongue?"

He proved that he hadn't by using it. "I have still the use of my tongue," he said.

"That, at least, is something. Perhaps, since the subject of how you got into my backyard seems to be a delicate one, will you tell me why you were there."

"You know why I have come."

"Pardon me if I appear to flatly contradict you, but that's precisely what I don't know."

"You do know," he said.

"Do I? Then in that case, I presume that you're here for the reason which appears upon the surface to be to commit a felony."

"You call me thief?"

"What else are you?"

"I am no thief. You know why I have come." He raised his head a little. A look came into his eyes which I felt that I ought to understand, yet to the meaning of which I knew not. I shrugged my shoulders.

"I have come because you wanted me," he said.

"Because I wanted you! On my word! That's rich!"

"All night you have wanted me, do I not know? When she talked to you of him, and the blood boiled in your veins, when he spoke, and all the people listened, and you hated him because he put love in her eyes."

I was startled. Either it was incredible what he meant or there was confusion somewhere.

"Take my advice, my friend, and don't try to become the '*bunco-steerer*' over me, I'm a bit in that line myself, you know."

This time the score was mine, he was puzzled.

"I don't understand," he said

"In that case we're equal, I don't understand you either."

His manner, for him at least, was childlike and bland. "What is it you do not know? This morning did I not say: if you want me, then I come?"

"I fancy I've some faint recollection of your being so good as to say something of the kind, but—where's the application?"

"Do you not feel for him the same as I?" he asked.

"Who?"

"Paul Lessingham." It was spoken quietly, but with a degree of—to put it gently—spitefulness which showed that at least the will to do Paul harm wouldn't be lacking.

"And, pray, what is the common feeling which we have for him?"

"Hate."

Plainly, with this gentleman, hate meant hate in the solid oriental sense. I should hardly have been surprised if the mere utterance of the words had seared his lips.

"By no means am I prepared to admit that I have this feeling which you attribute to me, but even granting that I have, what then?"

"Those who hate are kin," he said.

"That also I should be slow to admit, but to go a step further; what has all this to do with your presence on my premises?"

"You love her." This time I didn't ask him to supply the name, being unwilling that it should be soiled by the traffic of his lips. "She loves him, that is not well. If you choose, she shall love you; that will be well," he said.

"Indeed. And pray how is this consummation which is so devoutly to be desired to be brought about?"

"Put your hand into mine. Say that you wish it and it shall be done."

Moving a step forward, he stretched out his hand towards me. I hesitated. There was something in the fellow's manner which for the moment, had an unwholesome fascination for me. Memories flashed through my mind of stupid stories which have been told of deals made with the devil. I almost felt as if I was standing in the actual presence of one of the powers of evil. I thought of my love for Marjorie, which had revealed itself after all these years; of the delight of holding her in my arms, of feeling the pressure of her lips to mine. As my gaze met his, the lower side of what the conquest of this fair lady would mean burned in my brain, and fierce imaginings blazed before my eyes. To win her over as mine….forever!

But what nonsense was he talking about? What empty promises was he making? Suppose, just for the sake of the joke, I did put my hand in his, and did wish, right out, what it was he offered. If I wished, what harm would it do? It would be the purest jest. Out of his own mouth he would be shown the fool, for it was certain that nothing would come of it. Why shouldn't I do it then?

I would act on his suggestion. I would carry the thing right through. I was already advancing towards him when I stopped. I don't know why. At that moment, my thoughts went off at a tangent.

What sort of a blackguard did I call myself that I should take a woman for the sake of playing a fool's tricks with such scum of the earth as the hideous vagabond in front of me? Rage took hold of me. "You bastard!" I cried.

In my sudden passage from one mood to another, I was filled with the desire to shake the life out of him. But as soon as I moved a step in his direction, intending war instead of peace, he altered the position of his hand, holding it palm up, as if forbidding my approach. As he did so, quite involuntarily, I pulled up dead, as if my progress had been stayed by bars of iron and walls of steel.

For the moment I was astonished to the verge of stupefaction. The sensation was peculiar. I was as incapable of advancing another inch in his direction as if I'd lost the use of my limbs. I was even incapable of attempting to advance. At first I could only stare and gape but then I began to have an inkling of what had happened.

The scoundrel had almost succeeded in hypnotizing me.

That was a nice thing to happen to a man of my sort at my time of life. A shiver went down my back; what might have occurred if I hadn't pulled up in time? What pranks might a man of his character not have been disposed to play? It was the old story of the peril of playing with edged tools; I'd made the dangerous mistake of underrating the enemy's strength. Evidently, in his own line, the fellow was altogether something out of the usual way.

I believe that even as it was, he thought he had me. As I turned away, and leaned against the table at my back, I fancy that he shivered, as if this proof of my being my own master still was unexpected. I was silent; it took some seconds to enable me to recover from the shock of the discovery of the peril in which I'd been standing. Then I resolved that I'd endeavor to do something which should make me equal to this gentleman of many talents.

"Take my advice, my friend, and don't attempt to play any of that hanky-panky on me again."

"I don't know what you talk of," he said.

"Don't lie to me, or I'll burn you into ashes." Behind me was an electrical machine that gave an eighteen inch spark. It was set in motion by a lever fitted into the table, which I could easily reach from where I was. As I spoke the visitor was treated to a little exhibition of electricity. The change in his bearing was amusing. He shook with terror then he salaamed down to the floor.

"My Lord! My Lord! Have mercy, oh my Lord!" he pleaded.

"Then you be careful, that's all. You may suppose yourself to be something of a magician, but as it happens, unfortunately for you, that I can do a bit in that line myself, and perhaps I'm a trifle better at the game than you. Especially as you've ventured into my stronghold, which contains magic enough to make a show of a hundred thousand such as you."

Taking down a bottle from a shelf, I sprinkled a drop or two of its contents on the floor. Immediately flames arose, accompanied by a blinding vapor. It was a sufficiently simple illustration of one of the qualities of phosphorous-bromide, but its effect on my visitor was as startling as it was unexpected. If I could believe the evidence of my own eyes, in the very act of giving utterance to a scream of terror he disappeared; how it happened there was nothing to show, and in his place, where he'd been standing on the floor, there seemed to be a dim object of some sort in a state of frenzied agitation. The phosphorescent vapor was confusing; the lights appeared to be suddenly burning low. Before I had sense enough to go and see if there was anything there, and if so, what the flames had vanished, the man himself reappeared, and prostrated on his knees, was salaaming in a condition of abject terror.

"My Lord! My Lord!" he whined. "I entreat you, my Lord, to use me as your slave!"

"I'll use you as my slave!" Whether he or I was the one more agitated it would've been difficult to say.

"Stand up!"

He stood up. I eyed him with an interest which, so far as I was concerned, was of a distinctly new and original sort. Whether or not I'd been the victim of an ocular delusion I couldn't be sure. It was incredible to suppose that he could have disappeared as he'd seemed to disappear, and it was also incredible that I could have imagined his disappearance. If the thing had been a trick, I hadn't the faintest notion how it had been worked, and if it wasn't a trick, then what was it? Was it something new in scientific marvels? Could he give me as much instruction in the qualities of unknown forces as I could him?

In the meantime, he stood in an attitude of complete submission, with downcast eyes, hands crossed upon his chest. I started to cross-examine him.

"I'm going to ask you some questions. So long as you answer them promptly, truthfully, you'll be safe. Otherwise you'd best beware."

"Ask, oh my Lord."

"What's the nature of your objection to Mr. Lessingham?"

"Revenge."

"What has he done to you that you should wish revenge on him?"

"It is the feud of the innocent blood."

"What do you mean by that?"

"On his hands is the blood of my kin. It cries out for vengeance."

"Who has he killed?"

"That, my Lord, is for me, and for him to know," he said.

"I see. Am I to understand that you don't choose to answer me, and that I'm again to use my magic?"

He quivered. "My Lord, he has spilled the blood of her who has lain upon his breast."

I hesitated. What he meant appeared clear enough. Perhaps it would be as well not to press for further details. The words pointed to what it might be courteous to call an Eastern Romance, though it was hard to conceive of Lessingham figuring as the hero of such a story. It was the old tale retold, that to the life of every man there's a background, and that it's precisely in the unlikeliest cases that the background is darkest. What would Lessingham make of such a story if it were blazoned through the land?

" 'Spilling blood' is a figure of speech; pretty, perhaps, but vague. If you mean that Mr. Lessingham has killed someone, then your best and most effective revenge would be to appeal to the law."

"What has the Englishman's law to do with me?" he asked.

"Well, if you can prove that he's guilty of murder it would have a great deal to do with you. I assure you that at any rate, in that sense, the Englishman's law is honorable. Show him to be guilty, and it would hang Paul Lessingham as indifferently and as cheerfully as it would hang any other guilty man."

"Is that so?"

"It is, and you'll be easily able to prove it to your own entire satisfaction."

He had raised his head, and was looking at something which he seemed to see in front of him with a maleficent glare in his sensitive eyes. I found it unsettling.

"He would be shamed?" he asked.

"Indeed, he would be shamed."

"Before all men?"

"Before all men, and I take it, before all women, too."

"And he would hang?"

"If shown to have been guilty of willful murder, yes."

His hideous face was lighted up by a sort of diabolical exultation which made it, if that were possible, more hideous still. I'd apparently given him information which pleased him.

"Perhaps I will do that in the end, in the end!" He opened his eyes to their widest limits, then closed them tight, as if to gloat on the picture which his mind painted. Then reopened them. "In the meantime, I will have vengeance in my own fashion. He already knows that the avenger is upon him, and he has good reason to know it. And through the days and the nights the knowledge shall be with him still, and it shall be to him as the bitterness of death, aye, of many deaths. For he will know that there is no escape, none, and that for him there shall be no more sun in the sky, and that the terror shall be with him by night and by day, at his rising up and at his lying down, wherever his eyes shall turn it shall be there, yet behold, the sap and the juice of my vengeance is in this: in that he shall be very sure that the days of his death is coming and shall be on him—when I will it!"

The fellow spoke like an inspired maniac. If he meant even half of what he said, and if he didn't then his looks and his tones belied him, then a doom-filled future was in store for Lessingham, and also, with circumstances being as they were, for Marjorie. It was this latter reflection which gave me pause. Either this fanatic would have to be disposed of—either by Lessingham himself or by someone acting on his behalf—or Marjorie would have to be warned. To allow Marjorie to irrevocably link her fate with Paul's, without being first made aware of what he was—which was to all intents and purposes a haunted man—was unheard of.

"You employ large phrases, sir. I wonder if these phrases are full of hot air." My words cooled his heated blood. Once more his eyes were cast down, and his hands crossed over his chest.

"I crave my Lord's pardon. My wound is still fresh."

"By the way, what was the secret history of that little incident of the cockroach this morning?"

He glanced up quickly. "Cockroach? I know not what you say."

"Well, was it a beetle, then?"

"Beetle!" He seemed, all at once, to have lost his voice, the word was gasped.

"After you left, I found on a sheet of paper a capitally executed drawing of a beetle, which I fancy you must have left behind. Scarabaeus sacer, wasn't it?"

"I know not what you talk of."

"Its discovery seemed to have quite an strange effect on Mr. Lessingham. Now, why was that?"

"I know nothing," he said.

"Oh yes you do, and, before you go, I mean to know something too."

The man was trembling, looking this way and that, showing signs of marked discomfiture. There was something about that ancient scarab, which figured so largely in the still unraveled tangles of the Egyptian mythologies, and the effect which the mere sight of it had had on such a seasoned man as Paul Lessingham. It might be well worth my finding out more about it, and I felt convinced that the man's demeanor, on my referring to the matter, told its own plain tale. I made up my mind to get to the bottom of it, then and there.

"Listen to me, my friend. I'm a plain man, and I use plain speech. You'll give me the information I require, and that at once, or I'll pit my magic against yours, in which case I think it extremely probable that you'll come off worst from the encounter."

I reached out for the lever, and the exhibition of electricity began anew.

Immediately his tremors were redoubled. "My Lord, I know not of what you talk."

"No more of your lies. Tell me why at the sight of the thing on that sheet of paper, Paul Lessingham went green and yellow."

"Ask him, my Lord."

"Later on that's probably what I'll do, but right now I'm asking you. Answer, or else."

The electrical exhibition was going on. He was glaring at it as if he wished it would stop. As if ashamed of his cowardice, he drew himself up with what amounted to an air of dignity.

"I am a child of Isis!"

It struck me that he made this remark, not so much to impress me, but to elevate his own low spirits,

"Are you really? Then in that case, I regret that I'm unable to congratulate the lady on her offspring."

When I said that, a ring came into his voice which I hadn't heard before.

"Silence!" he barked. "You know not of what you speak! I warn you, as I warned Paul Lessingham, be careful not to go too far. Be not like him; heed my warning."

"What is it I'm being warned against? *'The Beetle'*?"

"Yes, the beetle!" he shouted.

I wondered whether this *child of Isis* wasn't playing the fool with me. His performance was realistic enough, but still; was he mad or simply befuddled?

He was standing about ten feet of where I leaned against the edge of the table. The light was full on, so that it was difficult to suppose that I could make a mistake as to what took place in front of me next. As he replied to my mocking allusion to the beetle by echoing my own words, he suddenly vanished, or rather, I saw him taking a different shape before my eyes.

His loose clothes fell off him, and as they were in the very act of falling, there issued a monstrous creature of the beetle type, and the man himself was gone. On the point of size I wish to make myself clear. My impression, when I saw it first was that it was as large as the man had been, and that it was, in some way, standing up on end with the legs towards me. But the moment it came into view, it began to dwindle, and so rapidly that in a couple of seconds at the most, a little heap of clothing was lying on the floor, and on it was a truly astonishing example of the coleoptera. It appeared to be a beetle. It was perhaps six or seven inches high, and about a foot in length. Its scales were of a vivid golden green. I could distinctly see where the wings were sheathed along the back. As I watched in amazement I saw the wings open and the thing take wing.

I was so astonished, and who wouldn't have been, that for an appreciable space of time I was practically in a state of stupefaction. I could do nothing but stare.

I was acquainted with the legendary transmigrations of Isis, and with the story of the beetle which issued from a woman's womb through all eternity, and with the other colorful tales, but to be an actual spectator was something new. If the man with whom I'd just been speaking was gone, where had he gone to? And if this glittering creature was there in his stead, whence had it come?

After the first shock of surprise had passed, I retained my presence of mind. I felt as an investigator might feel who has stumbled, haphazard, on some astounding discovery. I was conscious that I should make the best use of my mental faculties if I was to take full advantage of something so astonishing. I kept my gaze riveted on the creature, with the idea of photographing it in my brain. I believe that if it were possible to take a retinal print—which it someday will be no doubt—I would have a perfect picture of what it was I saw. Beyond doubt it was a lamellicorn, one of the copridae, and with the exception of its monstrous size, the characteristics in plain view: the convex body, the large head, the projecting clypeus. More, its smooth head and throat seemed to suggest that it was a female. Equally beyond a doubt, apart from its size, there were unusual features present, too. The eyes were not only unwontedly conspicuous, they gleamed as if they were lighted by internal flames, and in some indescribable fashion they reminded me of my vanished visitor. The coloring was superb, and the beetle appeared to have the chameleon-like faculty of lightening and darkening the shades at will. Its least curious feature was its restlessness. It was in a state of continual agitation, and as if it resented my inspection, the more I looked at it the more its agitation grew. I expected every moment to see it take wing and circle through the air.

I tried to think what I could use to capture it. I did consider killing it, and wish I'd tried to, as there were dozens of things lying ready to my hand, any one of which would have severely hurt it, but on the spur of the moment the only method of taking it alive which occurred to me was to pop over it a big tin canister which had contained soda-lime. The canister was on the floor to my left. I moved towards it as nonchalantly as I could, keeping an eye on that shining wonder all the time. When I moved, its agitation perceptibly increased; it was, so to speak, all one whirr of tremblement. It scintillated, as if its colored scales had been so many prisms, and it began to unsheathe its wings, as if it had finally decided that it would make use of them. Picking up the tin, I sprang towards my intended victim. Its wings opened wide; obviously it was about to rise, but it was too late. Before it had cleared the floor, the tin was over it.

It remained over it, however, for only an instant. I'd stumbled in my haste, and in my effort to save myself from falling face first on the floor, I was compelled to remove my hands from the tin. Before I was able to replace them, the tin was sent flying. While I was still partially recumbent, within eighteen inches of me the beetle swelled, until it had assumed its former portentous dimensions. Then it was enveloped by a human shape, and in less time than no time there stood in front of me, naked from head to toe, my truly versatile oriental friend. His nudity revealed one startling fact. I had been mistaken on the question of sex. My visitor was not a man, but a woman, and judging from the brief glimpse which I had of her body, by no means was she old or ill-shaped.

That transformation was a bewildering one to see. The most level-headed scientist would have temporarily lost his mental facilities upon witnessing such a quick change within a span or two of his own nose. I wasn't only witless, I was breathless, too. I could only gape. And, while I gaped, the woman, stooping down, picked up her clothes and began to pull them on her as she ran towards the door which led into the backyard. When I observed this last maneuver, to some extent I did rise to the requirements of the situation.

Leaping up, I rushed to halt her. "Stop!" I shouted.

But she was too quick for me. Before I could reach her, she'd opened the door and was through it, and what was more, she slammed it in my face.

In my excitement, I did some fumbling with the handle. When I finally got the door open and was standing in the yard, she was out of sight. I did fancy I saw a dim form disappearing over the wall at the far side, and I made for it as fast as could. I clambered onto the wall, looking this way and that, but there was no one to be seen.

I listened for the sound of retreating footsteps, but all was still. Apparently I had the entire neighborhood to myself. My visitor had vanished and time devoted to the pursuit of her I felt would be time ill-spent.

As I returned across the yard, Percy, who still was taking his rest under the open canopy of heaven, sat up. It appeared my approach had roused him from his slumber.

At sight of me he rubbed his eyes, yawned, and blinked. "I say," he remarked, not at all unreasonably. "Where am I?"

"You're on holy—or on haunted—ground. Damn if I know which, but that's where you are, my boy."

"My, I'm feeling quite odd! I've got a headache, too, don't you know."

"I shouldn't be in the least surprised at anything you have, or haven't, in fact I'm beyond surprised. It's a drop of whisky you're wanting now I bet, and what I'm wanting too, only for goodness sake, no drops! I want a bottle of the stuff at the least."

I put my arm through his, and we went into the laboratory. When we were inside, I closed and locked the door.

Chapter 19

Dora Grayling stood in the doorway.

"I told your servant he needn't trouble to show me in, and I've come without my aunt. I hope I'm not intruding." She came into the room with twinkling eyes, looking radiantly happy; the sort of look that made even a plain young woman attractive. "Am I intruding? I believe I am." She held out her hand while she was still a dozen feet away, and when I didn't at once dash forward to make a clutch at it, she shook her head and made a little mouth at me. "What's the matter with you? Aren't you well?" she asked, cocking her head to the side.

I wasn't well. I was very far from well in fact. I was as unwell as I could be without being positively ill, and any person of common discernment would have perceived it at a glance. But at the same time, I wasn't going to admit anything of the kind to her.

"Thank you, I'm perfectly well."

"Then, if I were you," she said, "I'd try to become imperfectly well. A little imperfection in that direction might make you appear to more advantage."

"I'm afraid that I'm not one of those people who ever do appear to much advantage; didn't I tell you so last night?"

"I believe you did say something of the kind, it's very good of you to remember," she said. "Have you forgotten something else which you said to me last night?"

"You can hardly expect me to keep fresh in my memory all the follies of which my tongue is guilty."

"Thank you. That's quite enough. Good day." She turned as if to go.

"Miss Grayling!"

"Mr. Atherton?"

"What's the matter?"

"Last night you invited me to come and see you this morning. Is that one of the follies of which your tongue was guilty?"

The engagement had escaped my recollection, and my face betrayed me.

"You'd forgotten?" Her cheeks flamed; her eyes sparkled. "You must pardon my stupidity for not having understood that the invitation was of the general kind which is never meant to be acted on." She was halfway to the door before I stopped her, I had to take her by the shoulder to do it.

"Miss Grayling! You're hard on me."

"I suppose I am. Is anything harder than to be intruded on by an undesired, and unexpected, guest?" she asked.

"Now you're harder still. If you knew what I've gone through since our conversation last night, I think you'd be more merciful."

"Indeed? What have you gone through?"

I hesitated. What I'd actually gone through I certainly didn't propose to tell her and wasn't able to come with a plausible tale on the spur of the moment.

So I fenced, or tried to. "For one thing, I've had no sleep." I hadn't either, not one single wink. When I did get between the sheets, I suffered from that worst form of nightmare, the nightmare of the man who is wide awake. Before my fevered eyes there was continually the strange figure of that 'nameless thing.' I'd often smiled at tales of haunted folk, and now here I was one of them. My feelings weren't rendered more agreeable by a strengthening conviction that if I'd only retained the normal attitude of a scientific observer I would in all probability have solved the mystery of my oriental friend, and that his example of the genus of copridae might have been pinned by a very large pin on a piece—a monstrous piece—of cork!

It was galling to reflect that he and I had played together a game of bluff, a game at which had proved to be a failure. She couldn't have seen all this in my face, but she did see something, because her own visage softened.

"You do look tired." She seemed to be casting about in her own mind for a cause. "You've been worrying." She glanced around my large labora- tory. "Have you been spending the night in this—wizard's cave?"

"Pretty much."

"Oh!" The monosyllable, as she uttered it, was big with meaning. Unin- vited, she seated herself in an armchair, a huge old thing, of faded leather, which would have held half a dozen of her. She looked demure in it, like an agreeable reminiscence, alive, and a little up-to-date of the women of long ago. Her dove gray eyes seemed to perceive so much more than they cared to show.

"How is it that you've forgotten that you asked me to come here? Didn't you mean it?"

"Of course I meant it."

"Then how is it you've forgotten?" she asked.

"I didn't forget."

"Don't tell fibs. Something's the matter; tell me what it is. Is it that I'm too early?"

"Nothing of the sort, you couldn't be too early."

"Thank you. When you pay a compliment, even so neat a one as that, sometimes you should look as if you mean it. It's early. I know it's early, but afterwards I want you to come to lunch with me. I told my aunt that I'd bring you back with me."

"You're much better to me than I deserve."

"Perhaps." A tone came into her voice which was almost pathetic. "I think that to some men women are almost better than they deserve. I don't know why. I suppose it pleases them. It's odd." There was a different intonation, a dryness. "Have you forgotten what I came for?"

"No, I remember clearly. You came to see a demonstration of that pleasant little fancy of mine for slaughtering my fellows. But the truth is, I'm hardly in a mood for that right now. I've been demonstrating it too much already."

"What do you mean?"

"Well, for one thing, it's been murdering Lessingham's cat."

"Mr. Lessingham's cat?" she asked, her eyes wide.

"Then it almost murdered Percy Woodville."

"Mr. Atherton! I wish you wouldn't talk like that."

"It's a fact. It was an accident, I assure you, but if it hadn't been for something very much like a miracle, he'd be dead now."

"I wish you wouldn't have anything to do with such things—I hate them."

I stared. "Hate them? I thought you'd come to see a demonstration."

"And pray what was your notion of this demonstration?"

"Well, another cat would have had to be killed, at least."

"And do you suppose that I would have sat still while a cat was being killed for my amusement?"

"It needn't necessarily have been a cat, but something would have had to be killed. How can I demonstrate the death-dealing propensities of a weapon of that sort without it?"

"Is it possible that you truly believed that I came here to see something killed?"

"If not, then why did you come?" I don't know what there was about the question which was startling, but as soon as it was out, she went fiery red.

"Because I was a fool, sir."

I was bewildered. Either she had gotten out of the wrong side of bed, I had, or we both had. Here she was assailing me, hammer and tongs, as far as I could see, for absolutely nothing.

"You're pleased to be satirical at my expense, I see," I said.

"I shouldn't dare. Your detection of me would be so painfully rapid."

I was in no mood for jangling. I turned a little away from her. Immediately she was at my elbow.

"Mr. Atherton?"

"Miss Grayling."

"Are you cross with me?" she asked.

"Why should I be? If it pleases you to laugh at my stupidity, then you're completely justified."

"But you're not stupid."

"No? Nor are you satirical."

"You're not stupid, and you know you're not stupid; it was only stupidity on my part to pretend that you were."

"It's very good of you to say so. But I fear that I'm an indifferent host. Although you wouldn't care for a demonstration, there may be other things which you might find amusing."

"Why do you keep on snubbing me?" she asked.

"I keep on snubbing you! Whatever do you mean?"

"You're always snubbing me, you know you are. Some times I feel as if I hate you for it, too."

"Miss Grayling!"

"I do! I do!"

"After all, it's only natural."

"That's how you talk, as if I were a child, and you were, oh I don't know what. Well, Mr. Atherton, I'm sorry to be obliged to leave you. I've enjoyed my visit very much. I only hope I haven't seemed too intrusive."

She flounced—'flounce' was the only appropriate word—out of the room before I could stop her. I caught her in the passage.

"Miss Grayling, please…"

"Don't 'please' me Mr. Atherton." Standing still she turned to me. "I'd rather show myself to the door as I showed myself in, but if that's impossible, might I ask you not to speak to me between now and the street?"

The hint was broad enough, even for me. I escorted her through the hall without a word; in perfect silence she shook the dust of my home from off her feet.

I'd made a pretty good mess of things. I felt it as I stood on the top of the steps and watched her leave that she was walking off at four miles an hour; I hadn't even ventured to ask to be allowed to call a cab for her.

I decided that it would be a good time to try to get some sleep, and I was just returning into the house with the intention of putting myself into my flannels, when a cab drew up, and old man Lindon got out of it.

Chapter 20

Mr. Lindon was excited, there was no mistaking it when he was, because with him excitement means perspiration, and as soon as he was out of the cab, he took off his hat and began to wipe the lining.

"Atherton, I want to speak to you; most particularly, somewhere in private," he said.

I took him into my laboratory. It's my rule to take no one there; it's a workshop, not a playroom. The place is private, but recently my rules had become dead letters. Once he was inside, Lindon began puffing and stewing, wiping his forehead, throwing out his chest, as if he were impressed by a sense of his own importance. Then he started talking at the top of his voice, and it's not a low one either.

"Atherton, I…I've always looked on you as kind of a son."

"That's very kind of you."

"I've always regarded you as a…a level-headed fellow; a man from whom sound advice can be obtained when sound advice…is…is most to be desired."

"That's also very kind of you."

"And therefore I make no apology for coming to you at…at what may be regarded as a…a strictly domestic crisis; at a moment in the history of the Lindons when delicacy and common sense are… are essentially required."

This time I contented myself with nodding. Already I perceived what was coming; somehow when I'm talking with a man, I feel so much more clear-headed than I do when I'm with a woman. I realize so much better the nature of the ground on which I'm standing.

"What do you know of this man Lessingham?" he asked.

I knew it was coming. "What all the world knows," I replied.

"And what does all the world know of him? I ask you that! A flashy, plausible, shallow-pated carpet-bagger. That's what all the world knows of him. The man's a political adventurer; he snatches a precarious and criminal notoriety by trading on the follies of his fellow countrymen. He's devoid of decency, destitute of principle, and impervious to all the feelings of a gentleman. What do you know of him besides this?"

"I'm not prepared to admit that I do know more."

"Oh yes you do! Don't talk nonsense! You choose to screen the fellow! I say what I mean, I've always said and I always shall say too. What do you know of him outside politics, of his family, of his private life?"

"Well, not very much."

"Of course you don't!" he said. "Nor does anybody else! The man's a mushroom, or a toadstool, rather, and has sprung up in the course of a single night, apparently out of some dirty ditch. Why, sir, not only is he without ordinary intelligence, he's even without a substitute for manners."

He'd worked himself into a state of heat in which his countenance presented a not too agreeable assortment of scarlets and purples. He flung himself into a chair, threw his coat wide open, and his arms too, and started off again.

"The family of the Lindons is at this moment represented by a…a young woman, by my daughter, sir. She represents me, and it's her duty to represent me adequately—adequately, sir! And what's more, between ourselves, sir, it's her duty to marry. My property's my own, and I wouldn't have it pass to either of my confounded brothers on any account. They're next door to fools, and…and they don't represent me in any possible sense of the word. My daughter, sir, can marry whom she pleases, whom she pleases! There's no one in England, peer or commoner, who wouldn't esteem it an honor to have her for his wife. I've told her so, yes, sir, I've told her, though you…you'd think that she, of all people in the world, wouldn't require telling. Yet what do you think she does? She…she actually carries on what I can't help calling a…a compromising acquaintance with this man Lessingham!"

"No!"

"But I say yes, Atherton! And I wish to heaven I didn't. I've warned her against the scoundrel more than once. I've told her to cut him dead. And yet, as you saw yourself last night in…in the face of the assembled House of Commons, after that clap-trap speech of his, in which there was not one sound sentiment, nor an idea which would hold water, she positively went away with him in…in the most ostentatious and…and disgraceful fashion on his arm, and…and actually snubbed her father. It's monstrous that a parent—a father—should be subjected to such a treatment by his child."

The poor old boy polished his brow with his pocket-handkerchief.

"When I got home I told her what I thought of her, I promise you that, and I told her what I thought of him," he said. "I didn't mince my words with her. There are occasions when plain speaking is demanded, and that was one. I positively forbade her to speak to the fellow again, or to recognize him if she met him on the street. I pointed out to her, with perfect candor, that the fellow was an infernal scoundrel; that and nothing else! And that he would bring disgrace on whoever came into contact with him. And what do you think she said?"

"She promised to obey you, I make no doubt," I said.

"Did she, sir! By gad, did she! That shows how much you know her! She said, and by gad, by her manner and…and the way she went on, you'd have thought that she was the parent and I was the child. She said that I…I grieved her, that she was disappointed in me, that times have changed, yes, sir, she said that times have changed! That nowadays, parents weren't Russian autocrats, no, sir, not Russian autocrats! That she was sorry she couldn't oblige me, yes, sir, that was how she put it. She was sorry she couldn't oblige me, but it was altogether out of the question to suppose that she could put a period to a friendship which she valued, simply on account of…of my unreasonable prejudices, and…and in short, she told me to go the devil, sir!"

"And did you?"

I was on the point of asking him if he went, but I checked myself in time.

"Let us look at the matter as men of the world. What do you know against Lessingham, apart from his politics?"

"That's just it, I know nothing," I said. "In a sense, isn't that in his favor?"

"I don't see how you make that out. I…I don't mind telling you that I…I've had inquiries made. He's not been in the House six years; this is his second Parliament. He's jumped up like a Jack-in-the-box. His first constituency was Harwich. They've got him still, and much good may he do 'em! But how he came to stand for the place, or who, or what, or where he was before he stood for the place, no one seems to have the faintest notion."

"Hasn't he been a great traveler?" I inquired.

"I never heard of it."

"Not in the East?"

"Has he told you so?" he asked.

"No, I was only wondering, Well, it seems to me that to find out that nothing is known about him is something in his favor!"

"My dear Sydney Atherton, don't talk nonsense. What it proves is simply that he's a nothing and a nobody. Had he been anything or anyone, something would have been known about him, either for or against. I don't want my daughter to marry a man who…who's shot up through a trap, simply because nothing is known against him. Hang me, if I wouldn't ten times sooner she should marry you."

When he said that, my heart leaped in my chest. I had to turn away. "I'm afraid that is out of the question."

He stopped in his tramping, and looked at me askance. "Why?"

I felt that, if I wasn't careful, I should be done for, and probably in his present mood, Marjorie too.

"My dear Mr. Lindon, I can't tell you how grateful I am to you for your suggestion, but I can only repeat that unfortunately, anything of the kind is out of the question."

"I don't see why."

"Perhaps not."

"You…you're a handsome man, upon my word!" he said.

"Thank you."

"I want you to tell her that Lessingham is a damned scoundrel," he said.

"I see. But I would suggest that if I was to use the influence with which you credit me to the best advantage, or to preserve a shred of it, I'd hardly better state the fact to her quite so bluntly."

"I don't care how you state it, state it as you like. Only I want you to soak her mind with a loathing of the fellow. I…I want you to paint him in his true colors, in…in fact, I…want you to keep him away from her."

While he still struggled with his words, and with the perspiration on his brow, Edwards entered. I turned to him and said, "What is it, Edwards?"

"Miss Lindon, sir, wishes to see you at once."

At that moment I found the announcement a trifle perplexing, though it delighted Lindon. He began to stutter and to stammer, "T…the very thing! C…couldn't have been better! Show her in here! H…hide me somewhere, I don't care where, behind that screen! Y…you use your influence with her, g…give her a good talking to. T…tell her what I've told you, and at…at the critical moment I'll come in, and then…then if we can't manage her between us, it'll be a wonder."

The proposition staggered me.

"But, my dear Mr. Lindon, I fear that I can't…" But he cut me short. "Here she comes!"

Before I could stop him he was behind the screen. I hadn't seen him move with such agility before, and before I could try and reason with him some more, Marjorie was in the room. Something which was in her bearing, her face, her eyes, quickened the beating of my pulse; she looked as if something had come into her life, and taken the joy clean out of it.

Chapter 21

"Sydney!" Marjorie cried, "I'm so glad that I can see you!"

She might be, but at the moment I could scarcely assert that I was a sharer of her joy.

"I told you that if trouble overtook me I would come to you, and I'm in trouble now. Such strange trouble."

So was I, and in perplexity as well. An idea occurred to me; I'd outwit her eavesdropping father. "Come with me into the house, tell me all about it there."

She refused to budge. "No, I'll tell you all about it here." She looked around her, and it struck me oddly. "This is just the sort of place in which to unfold a tale like mine. It looks uncanny."

"But…"

"But me no buts! Sydney, don't torture me, let me stop here where I am; don't you see I'm haunted?"

She'd seated herself. Now she stood up, holding her hands out in front of her in a state of extraordinary agitation, her manner as wild as her words. "Why are you staring at me like that? Do you think I'm mad? I wonder if I'm going mad. Sydney, do people suddenly go mad? You're a bit of everything, you're a bit of a doctor, too. Feel my pulse; there it is! Tell me if I'm ill!"

I felt her pulse, it didn't need its swift beating to inform me that fever of some sort was in her veins. I gave her something in a glass. She held it up to the level of her eyes.

"What's this?"

"It's a decoction of my own. You might not think it, but my brain sometimes gets into a whirl. I use it as a sedative. It'll do you good."

She drained the glass. "It's done me good already, I believe it has. That's being something like a doctor. Well, Sydney, the storm has almost burst. Last night Papa forbade me to speak to Paul Lessingham, by way of a prelude."

"Exactly. Mr. Lindon…"

"Yes, Mr. Lindon. That's Papa. I fancy we almost quarreled. I know Papa said some surprising things, but it's a way he has. He's apt to say surprising things. He's the best father in the world, but it's not in his nature to like a really clever person; your good high dried old Tory never can; I've always thought that that was why he's so fond of you."

"Thank you, I presume that's the reason, though it hadn't occurred to me before," I said.

Since her entry, I'd to the best of my ability, been turning the position over in my mind. I came to the conclusion that, all things considered, her father had probably as much right to be a sharer of his daughter's confidence as I had, even from the vantage of the screen, and that for him to hear a few home truths proceeding from her lips might serve to clear the air. From such a distance the lady wouldn't be likely to come off worst. I hadn't the faintest inkling of what was the actual purpose of her visit.

She started off, as it seemed to me, at a tangent. "Did I tell you last night about what took place yesterday morning, about the adventure of my finding the man?" she asked.

"Not a word."

"I believe I meant to; I'm half disposed to think he's brought me trouble. Isn't there some superstition about evil befalling whoever shelters a homeless stranger?"

"We'll hope not, for humanity's sake."

"I fancy there is, I feel sure there is," she said. "Anyhow, listen to my story. Yesterday morning, before breakfast to be accurate, between eight and nine, I looked out of the window and I saw a crowd in the street. I sent our servant Peter out to see what was the matter. He came back and said there was a man in a fit. I went out to look at the man in the fit. I found, lying on the ground, in the center of the crowd, a man who but for the tattered remnants of what had apparently once been a cloak, would have been stark naked. He was covered with dust, dirt, and blood—a dreadful sight. As you know, I've had my smattering of instruction in First Aid to the injured, and that kind of thing, so as no one else seemed to have any sense, and the man seemed as good as dead, I thought I'd try my hand. Directly I knelt down beside him, and what do you think he said?"

"Thank you."

"Nonsense. He said, in a hollow, croaking voice, 'Paul Lessingham.' I was dreadfully startled. To hear a perfect stranger, and a man in his condition, utter that name in such a fashion—to me, of all people in the world— took me aback. The policeman who was holding his head remarked, 'That's the first time he's opened his mouth. I thought he was dead.' He opened his mouth a second time and a convulsive movement came over him, and he exclaimed with the strangest earnestness, and so loudly that you might have heard him at the other end of the street, Be warned, Paul Lessingham, be warned! It was very silly of me, perhaps, but I can't tell you how his words, and his manner—the two together—affected me. Well, the long and the short of it was, that I had him taken into the house, washed, put to bed. I had the doctor sent for. The doctor could make nothing of it at all. He reported that the man seemed to be suffering from some sort of cataleptic seizure. I could see that he thought it likely to turn out almost as interesting a case as I did."

"Did you acquaint your father with the addition to his household?"

She looked at me, quizzically. "You see, when one has such a father as mine one can't tell him everything at once. There are occasions on which one requires time."

I felt that this would be wholesome hearing for old man Lindon.

"Last night, after Papa and I had exchanged our little courtesies, which it is to be hoped, were to Papa's satisfaction, since they weren't to be mine, I went to see the patient. I was told that he had neither eaten nor drunk a thing, nor moved or spoken. But as soon as I approached his bed, he showed signs of agitation. He half raised himself on his pillow, and he called out, as if he'd been addressing some large assembly. I can't describe to you the dreadful something which was in his voice and on his face, 'Paul Lessingham! Beware! *The Beetle!*'

When she said that, I was startled. "Are you sure those were the exact words he used?"

"Quite sure," she said. "Do you think I could mistake them, especially after what has happened since? I hear them ringing in my ears, they haunt me all the time." She put her hands up to her face, as if to veil something from her eyes.

I was becoming more and more convinced that there was something about Paul's connection with his Oriental friend which needed probing to the bottom. "What sort of a man is this patient of yours? What does he look like?"

I had my doubts as to the gentleman's identity, which her words dissolved, only however, to increase my mystification in another direction.

"He seems to be between thirty and forty," she said. "He has light hair and straggling sandy whiskers. He's so thin as to be nothing but skin and bone; the doctor says it's a case of starvation."

"You say he has light hair and sandy whiskers. Are you sure the whiskers are real?"

She opened her eyes. "Of course they're real. Why wouldn't they be real?"

"Does he strike you as being a foreigner?" I asked.

"Certainly not. He looks like an Englishman, and he speaks like one, and not, I should say, of the lowest class. It's true that there's a very curious, a weird, quality in his voice, what I've heard of it anyway, but it's not un-English. If it's catalepsy he's suffering from, then it's a kind of catalepsy I've never heard of. Have you ever seen a clairvoyant?" I nodded. "He seems to me to be in a state of clairvoyance. Of course the doctor laughed when I told him so, but we know what doctors are, and I still believe that he's in some condition of the kind. When he said that last night he struck me as being under what those sort of people call 'influence' and that whoever had him under the influence was forcing him to speak against his will, for the words came from his lips as if they'd been wrung from him in agony."

Knowing what I did know, that struck me as being rather a remarkable conclusion for her to have reached, by the exercise of her own unaided powers of intuition, but I didn't choose to let her know this.

"My dear Marjorie, you who pride yourself on having an imagination so strictly under control, seem to be imagining quite a bit!"

"It's a fact that I pride myself on not making wild assertions at any rate. Listen to me. When I left that unfortunate man's room, I'd had a nurse sent for. I left him in her charge. When I reached my own bedroom, I was possessed by a profound conviction that some appalling, intangible, but very real danger was at that moment threatening Paul."

"Remember, your patient's words came at the end of a very exciting evening, and a discussion with your father."

"That's what I told myself, or rather, that was what I tried to tell myself, because in some extraordinary fashion, I'd lost the command of my powers of reflection."

"Precisely."

"It wasn't precisely in the sense you mean. You may laugh at me, Sydney, but I'd an altogether indescribable feeling, a feeling which amounted to knowledge that I was in the presence of the supernatural."

"Nonsense!"

"It was not nonsense. I wish it had been nonsense. As I've said, I was conscious, completely conscious, that some frightful peril was assailing Paul. I didn't know what it was, but I did know that it was something altogether awful, of which merely to think was to shudder. I wanted to go to his assistance, I tried to, more than once, but I couldn't, and I knew that I couldn't. I knew that I couldn't move as much as a finger to help him." I opened my mouth to speak but she held her hand before me and said, "Stop, let me finish! I told myself that it was absurd, but it wouldn't do; absurd or not, there was the terror with me in the room. I knelt down and I prayed, but the words wouldn't come. I tried to ask God to remove this burden from my brain, but my longings wouldn't shape themselves into words, and my tongue was palsied. I don't know how long I struggled, but at last I came to understand that, for some cause, God had chosen to leave me to fight alone. So I got up, undressed, went to bed, and that was the worst of all. I'd sent my maid away in the first rush of my terror, afraid and I think, ashamed to let her see my fear. Now I would have given anything to summon her back again, but I couldn't do it, I couldn't even ring the bell. So, as I say, I got into bed."

She paused, as if to collect her thoughts. To listen to her words, and to think of the suffering which they meant to her was almost more than I could endure. I would have thrown away the world to have been able to take her in my arms and soothe her fears. I knew her to be, in general, the least hysterical of young women, little wont to become the prey of mere delusions, and incredible though it sounded, I had an innate conviction that even in its wildest parts, her story had some sort of basis in solid fact. What that basis amounted to it would be my business, at any and every cost, quickly to determine.

"You know how you've always laughed at me because of my objection to cockroaches and how in the Spring, the neighborhood of Maybugs has always made me uneasy," she said. "As soon as I got into bed I felt that something of the kind was in the room."

"Something of what kind?" I asked.

"Some kind of—beetle. I could hear the whirring of its wings and its droning in the air. I knew it was hovering above my head, that it was coming lower and lower, nearer and nearer. I hid myself, covering myself all over with the clothes, then I felt it bumping against the coverlet." She drew closer. Her blanched cheeks and frightened eyes made my heart bleed. Her voice became but an echo of itself. "And, Sydney, it followed me."

"Marjorie!"

"It got into the bed."

"You imagined it."

"I didn't imagine it. I heard it crawl along the sheets, until it found a way between them, and then it crawled towards me. Then I felt it against my face—it's here now."

"Where?"

She raised the forefinger of her left hand. "There! Can't you hear it droning?" She listened, intently.

I listened, too. Oddly enough, at that instant the droning of an insect did become audible.

"It's only a bee, child, which has found its way through the open window."

"I wish it were only a bee, I wish it were. Sydney, don't you feel as if you were in the presence of evil? Don't you want to get away from it, back into the presence of God?"

"Marjorie!"

"Pray, Sydney, pray! I can't! I don't know why, but I can't!"

She flung her arms around my neck, and pressed herself against me in paroxysmal agitation. The violence of her emotion threatened to unman me as well. It was so unlike Marjorie, and I would have given my life to save her from a toothache. She kept repeating her own words, as if she couldn't help it.

"Pray, Sydney, pray!"

At last I did as she wished me. At least, there's no harm in praying, I never heard of it bringing hurt to anyone. I repeated aloud the Lord's Prayer, the first time for I know not how long. As the divine sentences came from my lips, her tremors ceased. She became calmer. Until, as I reached the last great petition, "Deliver us from evil." She released her arms from around my neck and dropped to her knees, close to my feet. She joined me in the closing words, as a sort of chorus.

"For Thine is the Kingdom, the Power, and the Glory, for ever and ever. Amen."

When the prayer was ended, we were both still. She with her head bowed and her hands clasped, and I with something tugging at my heart-strings which I hadn't felt there for many a year, almost as if it had been my mother's hand. I daresay that sometimes she does stretch out her hand from her place among the angels, to touch my heart-strings.

As the silence still continued, I chanced to glance up, and there was old man Lindon peeping at us from his hiding-place behind the screen. The look of amazed perplexity which was on his big red face struck me with such a keen sense of the incongruous that it was all I could do to keep from laughter Apparently, the sight of us did nothing to lighten the fog which was in his brain, for he stammered out, in what was possibly intended for a whisper, "Is…is she m…mad?"

The whisper, if it was meant as a whisper, was more than sufficiently audible to catch his daughter's ear. She started, raised her head, sprang to her feet, turned, and saw her father.

"Papa!"

Immediately her sire was seized with an access of stuttering. "W…w…what the d…devil's the m…m…meaning of this?"

Her utterance was clear enough. I fancy her parent found it almost painfully clear. "Rather it's for me to ask, what's the meaning of this! Is it possible that all this time you've actually been concealed behind that screen?"

Unless I'm mistaken, the old gentleman cowered before the directness of his daughter's gaze, and tried to conceal the fact by an explosion of passion.

D...don't you s...speak to me l...like that, you un...undutiful girl! I...I'm your father!"

"You certainly are my father, though I was unaware until now that my father was capable of playing the part of eavesdropper."

Rage rendered him speechless, or at any rate, he chose to let us believe that it was the determining cause of his continuing silence. So Marjorie turned to me and on the whole, I'd rather she had not. Her manner was very different from what it had been a moment ago, it was more than civil, it was freezing.

"Am I to understand, Mr. Atherton, that this has been done with your knowledge? That while you suffered me to pour out my heart to you unchecked, you were aware the entire time that there was a listener behind the screen?"

I was suddenly keenly aware that I'd borne my share in deceiving her. I'd have liked to have thrown old man Lindon through the window right then, too.

"It wasn't my idea. Had I the opportunity, I would have compelled Mr. Lindon to face you when you came in. But your distress caused me to lose my balance. And you'll do me the justice to remember that I tried to induce you to come with me into another room."

"But I don't seem to remember your hinting at there being any particular reason why I should have gone with you," she said.

"You never gave me a chance."

"Sydney! I'd never have thought that you'd play such a trick me!" When she said that in such a tone, the woman I loved, I could have hammered my head against the wall. What a dog I was for treating her so shabbily!

Perceiving I was crushed, she turned again to face her father, and cool, calm and stately, she was once more the Marjorie with whom I was familiar. The demeanor of parent and child was in striking contrast. If appearances were true, then the odds were heavy that in any encounter which might be coming it would be the senior who would suffer.

"I hope, Papa, that you're going to tell me that there has been some curious mistake, and that nothing was farther from your intention than to listen at a keyhole. What would you have thought—and said—if I'd attempted to spy on you? And I've always understood that men were so particular on points of honor."

Old man Lindon was still hardly fit to do much else than sputter, and certainly not prepared to do battle with phrases with his sharp-tongued daughter. "D...don't talk to me li...like that, girl! I believe you're s...stark mad!" He turned to me. "W...what was that tomfoolery she was talking to you about?"

"To what do you allude?" I asked.

"That rub...rubbish about a b...beetle, and goodness alone knows what d...diseased and morbid imagination, r...reared on the literature of the gutter! I never thought that a child of mine could have s...sunk to such a depth! Now, Atherton, I ask you to t...tell me frankly, what do you think of a child who behaves as she has done? Who t...takes a nameless vagabond into the house and con...conceals his presence from her father? And mark the sequel! Even the vagabond warns her against the r...rascal Lessingham! Now, Atherton, tell me what you think of a girl who behaves like that?"

I shrugged my shoulders.

"I...I know very well what you d...do think of her, don't be afraid to say now because she's p...present."

"No, Sydney, don't be afraid," she said.

I saw that her eyes were dancing, and in a manner of speaking, her looks brightened under the sunshine of her father's displeasure.

"Let's hear what you think of her as a m...man of the world!"

"Pray, Sydney, do!" she said.

"What you feel for her in your...your heart of hearts!"

"Yes, Sydney, what do you feel for me in your heart of hearts?" she beamed with heartless sweetness; she was mocking me.

Her father turned as if he would have killed her. "D...don't you speak until you're spoken to! Now, Atherton, I...I hope I'm not deceived in you; I...I hope you're the man I...I took you for; that you're willing and...and ready to play the part of a...an honest friend to this mis...misguided simpleton. T...this isn't the time for mincing words, it...it's the time for candid speech. Tell this...this weak-minded young woman, right out, whether this man Lessingham is, or is not, a damned scoundrel."

"Papa, do you really think that Sydney's opinion, or your opinion, is likely to alter the facts?"

"Do you hear me, Atherton? Tell this wretched girl the truth!"

"My dear Mr. Lindon, I've already told you that I know nothing either for or against Mr. Lessingham except what is known to all the world."

"Exactly, and all the world knows him to be a miserable adventurer who is scheming to entrap my daughter," he said.

"I'm bound to say, since you press me, that your language appears to me to be unnecessarily strong," I said.

"Atherton, I…I'm ashamed of you!" he snapped.

"You see, Sydney," she said, "even Papa is ashamed of you; now you're outside the pale. My dear Papa, if you'll allow me to speak, I'll tell you what I know to be the truth, the whole truth, and nothing but the truth. That Mr. Lessingham is a man with great gifts goes without saying, Papa! He's a man of genius, of honor. He's a man of the loftiest ambitions, and the highest aims. He's dedicated his entire life to the improvement of the conditions amidst which the less fortunate of his fellow countrymen are at present compelled to exist. That seems to me to be an object well worth having. He's asked me to share his life-work, and I've told him that I will: when, where and how he wants me to. And I will. I don't suppose his life has been free from peccadilloes. I have no delusion on the point. What man's life has? Who among men can claim to be without sin? Even the members of our highest families sometimes hide behind screens. But I know that he is, at least, as good a man as I've ever met, and I believe that I shall never meet a better man, and I thank God that I've found favor in his eyes." She turned to me and said, "Goodbye, Sydney." Then she looked back at her father and added, "I suppose I'll see you again, Papa."

With the merest inclination of her head to both of us she straightway left the room but Mr. Lindon would have stopped her.

"S…stay, y…y…y…you…" he stuttered.

I caught him by the arm, halting him. "If you would be advised by me, you'll let her go. Nothing good will be served by arguing with her any more."

"Atherton, I…I'm disappointed in you. You…you haven't behaved as I expected. I haven't received from you the assistance which I hoped for."

"My dear Mr. Lindon, it seems to me that your method of diverting the young lady from the path which she's set herself to tread is calculated to send her furiously along it."

"C…confound all women! And c…confound her! I don't mind telling you, in c…confidence, that at…at times, her mother was the devil, and I'll be hanged if her daughter isn't worse. What was the tomfoolery she was talking to you about? Is she mad?"

"No, I don't think she's mad."

"I never heard such stuff: it made my blood run cold to hear her. What's the matter with her?"

"Well, you must excuse my saying that I don't fancy you quite understand women," I said.

"I...I don't, and I...I don't want to either."

I hesitated, then resolved to explain in Marjorie's interest. "Marjorie is high-strung and extremely sensitive. Her imagination is quickly aflame. Perhaps last night, you drove her as far as was safe. You heard for yourself how, in consequence, she suffered. Now, you don't want people to say you've driven her into a lunatic asylum."

"I...good heavens, no! I...I'll send for the doctor directly once I get home. I...I'll have the best one in town."

"You'll do nothing of the kind; you'll only make her worse. What you have to do is to be patient with her, and let her have peace. As for this affair of Lessingham's, I have a suspicion that it may not be all such plain sailing as she supposes."

"What do you mean?"

"I mean nothing," I replied. "I only wish you to understand that until you hear from me again you'd better let matters slide. Give the girl her space."

"Give her space! H...haven't I...I given the girl her space all her l...life!" He looked at his watch. "Why, the day's half gone!" He began scurrying towards the front door, I following at his heels. "I've got a committee meeting on at the club, m...most important! For weeks they've been giving us the worst food you ever tasted in your life, p...played havoc with my digestion, and I'm going to tell them if things aren't changed, they...they'll have to pay my doctor's bills. As for that man, Lessingham..." As he spoke, he opened the hall door, and there, standing on the step was 'that man Lessingham' himself. Mr. Lindon was a picture of surprise.

Paul was as cool as a cucumber. He held out his hand and said, "Good morning, Mr. Lindon. What delightful weather we're having."

Old man Lindon put his hand behind his back in rebuttal, and behaved as stupidly as was possible. "You'll u...understand, Mr. Lessingham, that in the future, I d...don't know you, and I shall d...decline to recognize you anywhere, and that what I say applies equally to any m...member of my family."

With his hat very much on the back of his head, he went down the steps like an inflated turkey.

Chapter 22

Lessingham evinced not a trace of discomposure. It was as if to have received such a discourteous response from his future father-in-law might have been the most commonplace of incidents. So far as I could judge, he took no notice of the episode whatever, behaving exactly as if nothing had happened. He merely waited till Mr. Lindon was well off the steps, then he turned to me and placidly observed, "I'm interrupting you again see.

The sight of him had set up such a turmoil in my veins, that for the moment I couldn't trust myself to speak. I felt acutely that an explanation with him was, of all things, the thing most to be desired, and that quickly. Providence couldn't have thrown him more opportunely in the way. If before he went away, we didn't understand each other a good deal more clearly—upon certain points at least—the fault shouldn't be mine. Without a reply I turned on my heels and led the way into the laboratory.

Whether he noticed anything peculiar in my demeanor I couldn't tell. Once we were inside he looked around with that purely facial smile, the sight of which had always engendered in me a certain distrust of him.

"Do you always receive visitors in here?" he asked.

"By no means."

"What is this?" Stooping down, he picked up something from the floor. It was a lady's purse, a gorgeous affair made of crimson leather and gleaming gold. Whether it was Marjorie's or Miss Grayling's I couldn't tell. He watched me as I examined it.

"Is it yours?" he inquired with a mischievous grin.

"No. It's not mine."

Placing his hat and umbrella on a chair, he sat on another very leisurely. Crossing his legs, and laying his folded hands on his knees, he looked at me. I was quite conscious of his observation, but endured it in silence, being a little wishful that he should begin.

Presently he had enough of looking at me, and said, "Atherton, what is the matter with you? Have I done something to offend you, too?"

"Why do you ask?"

"Your manner seems a little stiff."

"You think so?"

"I do."

"What have you come to see me about?"

"Just now, nothing. I like to know where I stand though," he said. His manner was courteous, easy, even graceful. I was outmaneuvered. I understood the man sufficiently well to be aware that when once he was on the defensive, the first blow would have to come from me. So I struck it.

"I also like to know where I stand. Lessingham, I'm aware, and you know that I'm aware, that you've made certain overtures to Miss Lindon. That's a fact in which I'm keenly interested."

"Why?"

"The Lindons and the Athertons aren't the acquaintances of one generation only. Marjorie Lindon and I have been friends since childhood. She looks upon me as a brother."

"As a brother?" he said.

"As a brother."

"Okay."

"Mr. Lindon thinks of me as a son. He's given me his confidence, as I believe you're aware, and Marjorie has given me hers, and now I want you to give me yours."

"What do you want to know?"

"I wish to explain my position before I say what I have to say, because I want you to understand me clearly. I believe, honestly, that the thing I most desire in this world is to see Marjorie Lindon happy. If I thought she would be happy with you, I should say, God speed you both! And I should congratulate you with all my heart, because I think that you would have won the best girl in the whole world to be your wife."

"I think so too," he said.

"Yes but before I did that, I should have to see at least some reasonable probability that she would be happy with you."

"Why wouldn't she?" he asked.

"Will you answer a question?"

"What's the question?"

"What's the story in your life of which you stand in such hideous terror of a picture of a beetle?"

There was a perceptible pause before he answered, "Explain yourself, sir."

"No explanation is needed; you know perfectly well what I mean."

"You credit me with miraculous insight."

"Don't dodge the topic, Lessingham, be frank!"

"The frankness shouldn't be all on one side. There's that in your frankness, although you may be unconscious of it, which some men might not unreasonably resent."

"Do you resent it?" I asked.

"That depends. If you're saying it's your right to place yourself between Miss Lindon and me, I do resent it, strongly."

"Answer my question!"

"I'll answer no question that is addressed to me in such a tone." He was as calm as you please. I recognized that already I was in peril of losing my temper, which wasn't at all what I desired. I watched him intently, he returning the same look. His face betrayed no sign of a guilty conscience; I hadn't seen him more completely at ease. He smiled, though it seemed it was to ridicule me. I'm bound to admit that his bearing showed not the faintest shadow of resentment, and that in his eyes there was a gentleness, a softness, which I hadn't observed in them before. I could almost have suspected him of being sympathetic.

"In this matter you must know that I speak for Mr. Lindon," I said.

"Well?"

"Surely you must understand that before anyone is allowed to think of marriage with Marjorie Lindon he will have to show that his past will have to bear the fullest investigation."

"Is that so? Will your past bear the fullest investigation as well?"

I winced. "At any rate, it's known to all the world."

"Is it? Forgive me if I say, Atherton, that I doubt it. I doubt if that can be said with truth of any wise man. In all our lives there are episodes which we keep to ourselves."

I felt that that was so true that for the instant, I hardly knew what to say. "But there are episodes and episodes, and when it comes to a man being haunted, one draws the line," I finally said.

"Haunted?" he asked.

"As you are."

He got up. "Atherton, I think that I understand you, but I fear that you don't understand me." He went to where a self-acting mercurial air-pump was standing on a shelf. "What's this curious arrangement of glass tubes and bulbs?"

"I don't think that you do understand me, or you would know that I'm in no mood to be trifled with."

"Is it some kind of an exhauster?" he asked, curious.

"My dear Mr. Lessingham, I intend to have an answer to my question before you leave this room, but in the meantime if you're so curious about my gadgets, let me show you. There are some very interesting things here which you might care to see."

"Marvelous, is it not, how the human intellect progresses from conquest unto conquest," he said,

"Among the ancients the progression had proceeded farther than with us."

"In what respect?" he asked.

"For instance, in the affair of the Apotheosis of the Beetle, I saw it take place last night."

"Where?" he asked.

"Here, within a few feet of where you're standing."

"Are you serious?" he gasped.

"Perfectly."

"What did you see?"

"I saw the legendary Apotheosis of the Beetle performed last night before my eyes, with a gaudy magnificence at which the legends never hinted."

"That's odd. I once thought that I saw something of the kind myself," he said.

"So I understand."

"From whom?" he asked.

"From a friend of yours."

"From a friend of mine? Are you sure it was from a friend of mine?"

His attempt at coolness did him credit, but it didn't deceive me. That he thought I was trying to bluff him out of his secret I perceived quite clearly, and that it was a secret which he would only render with his life I was beginning to suspect. Had it not been for Marjorie, I would have cared nothing—his affairs were his affairs—though I realized perfectly well that there was something about him which, from the scientist's point of view, might be well worth finding out. Still, if it hadn't been for Marjorie, I would have let it go, but since she was so intimately concerned in it, I wondered more and more what it could be.

My attitude towards what is called the supernatural is an open one. That all things are possible I unhesitatingly believe. I have, even in my short time, seen so many so-called impossibilities proved possible. That we know everything I doubt that our great-great-great-great-grandsires, our forebears of thousands of years ago, of the extinct civilizations, knew more on some subjects than we do. I think it's at least probable. All the legends can hardly be false.

Because men claimed to be able to do things in those days which we can't do, and which we don't know how they did them, we profess to think that their claims are finally dismissed by exclaiming lies! But it's not so sure.

For my part, what I'd seen I'd seen. I'd seen some devil's trick played before my very eyes. Some trick of the same sort seemed to have been played upon my Marjorie, as well, I repeat that I write 'my Marjorie' because to me, she'll always be 'my' Marjorie! It had driven her half out of her senses. As I looked at Lessingham, I saw her at his side, as I'd seen her not long ago, with her white, drawn face, and staring eyes, dumb with an agony of fear. Her life was bidding fair to be knit with his, what tree of horror was rooted in his very bones? The thought that her sweet purity was likely to be engulfed in a devil's slough in which he was swallowing wasn't to be endured. As I realized that the man was more than my match at the game which I was playing, in which such vital interests were at stake, my hands itched to grab him by the throat and try another way.

Doubtless my face revealed my feelings, because presently he said, "Are you aware of how strangely you're looking at me, Atherton? Were my face a mirror I think you'd be surprised to see in it your own."

I drew back from him sullenly. "Not as surprised as yesterday morning, when you would have been able see yours at the mere sight of a pictured scarab."

"How easily you quarrel," he said.

"I don't quarrel."

"Then perhaps it's I, and if that is so, then at once the quarrel's ended. It's done. Mr. Lindon I fear because politically we differ, and he regards me as cursed. Has he put some of his spirit into you? Surely you're a wiser man than that," he said.

"I'm aware that you're adept with words. But this is a case in which words will not only serve."

"Then what will serve?" he asked.

"I'm beginning to wonder that myself."

"And I."

"As you so courteously suggest, I believe I'm wiser than Lindon. I don't care one fig for your politics, or for what you call your politics. I don't care if you're as other men are, as I am, not unspotted from the world. But I do care if you're leprous. And I believe you are."

"Atherton!" he gasped.

"Ever since I've known you I've been conscious of there being some-thing about you which I found it difficult to diagnose— in an unwholesome sense, something out of the common, non-natural, an atmosphere of your own. Events so far as you're concerned, have during the last few days moved quickly. They've thrown an uncomfortably lurid light on that peculiarity of yours which I've noticed. Unless you can explain them to my satisfaction, you'll withdraw your claim to Miss Lindon's hand, or I shall place certain facts before that lady, and if necessary, publish them to the world."

He grew visibly paler but he smiled. "You have your own way of con-ducting a conversation, Mr. Atherton.

"What are the events to whose rapid transit you're referring? Who was the individual, practically stark naked, who came out of your house in such an odd fashion, at the dead of night?"

"Is that one of the facts with which you propose to tickle the public's ear?" he asked.

"Is that the only explanation which you have to offer?"

"Proceed, for the present, with your indictment."

"I'm not so unobservant as you appear to imagine, Mr. Lessingham. There were features about the episode which struck me forcibly at the time, and which have struck me even more forcibly since. To suggest, as you did yesterday morning, that it was an ordinary case of burglary, or that the man was a lunatic, is an absurdity.

"Pardon me, but I did nothing of the kind," he said.

"Then what do you suggest?"

"I suggested, and do suggest now, nothing. All the suggestions come from you."

"You went very much out of your way to beg me to keep the matter quiet. There's an appearance of suggestion about that."

"You take a jaundiced view of all my actions, Mr. Atherton. Nothing to me could seem more natural. However, proceed." He had his hands behind his back, and he now rested them on the edge of the table against which he was leaning. He was undoubtedly ill at ease, but so far I hadn't made the impression on him—either mentally or morally—which I desired.

"Who's your Oriental friend?" I asked.

"I don't follow you."

"Are you sure?"

"I'm certain. Repeat your question," he said with a wave.

"Who's your Oriental friend?"

"I wasn't aware that I had one."

"Do you swear that?"

He laughed—a strange laugh. "Do you seek to catch me in a lie? You conduct your case with too much hostility. You must allow me to grasp the exact meaning of your inquiry before I can undertake to reply to it."

"Are you not aware that at present there's in London an individual who claims to have had a very close, and a very curious, acquaintance with you in the East?"

"I'm not," he replied flatly.

"That you swear?"

"I do."

"That is odd."

"Why?"

"Because I fancy that this individual haunts you."

"Haunts me?" he said.

"Yes."

"Surely you're joking."

"You think so? Do you remember that picture of the beetle which yesterday morning frightened you into a state of semi-idiocy?"

"I know what you allude to," he said and crossed his arms over his chest.

"Do you mean to say that you don't know that you were indebted for that to your Oriental friend?"

"I don't understand you."

"Are you sure?"

"Certainly I'm sure," he said. "It occurs to me, Mr. Atherton, that an explanation is demanded from you rather than from me. Are you aware that the meaning of my presence here is to ask you how that picture found its way into your room?"

"It was projected by the Lord of the Beetle." The words were chance ones, but they struck a mark.

"The Lord..." He faltered and stopped. He showed signs of discomposure. "I'll be frank with you, since frankness is what you seek." His smile now was obviously forced. "Recently I've been the victim of delusions..." There was a pause before he finished, "Of an odd kind. I've feared that they were the result of mental overstrain. Is it possible that you can enlighten me as to their source?"

I was silent. He was putting a great strain on himself; the twitching of his lips betrayed him. A little more and I would reach the other side of Mr. Lessingham, the side which he kept hidden from the world.

"Who is this individual whom you speak of as my Oriental friend?" he asked.

"Being your friend, you should know him better than I do."

"What sort of man is he to look at?"

"I didn't say it was a man."

"But I presume it is a man," he said.

"I didn't say so."

He seemed for a moment to hold his breath, and he looked at me with eyes which weren't friendly. Then, with a display of self-command which did him credit, he drew himself upright with an air of dignity which well became him.

"Atherton, consciously or unconsciously, you're doing me a serious injustice. I don't know what ideas you've formed about me, or on what they're founded, but I protest that to the best of my knowledge I'm as reputable, honest, and as righteous a man as you are."

"But you're haunted."

"Haunted?" He stood taller, looking me straight in the face. Then a shiver went all over him; the muscles of his mouth twitched, and in an instant he was livid. He staggered against the table. "Yes, God knows it's true, I'm haunted."

"So either you're mad and therefore unfit to marry, or else you've done something that places you outside the tolerably generous boundaries of civilized society, and are therefore still more unfit to marry. You're on the horns of a dilemma."

"I'm the victim of a delusion," he said.

"What's the nature of the delusion? Does it take the shape of a beetle?"

"Atherton!" Without the slightest warning, he collapsed. He sank in a heap on the floor, held up his hands above his head, and gibbered like some frenzied animal. A more uncomfortable spectacle than he presented it would be difficult to find. I've seen it matched in the padded rooms of lunatic asylums, but nowhere else. The sight of him set every nerve of my body on edge.

"In Heaven's name, what's the matter with you, man? Are you stark-raving mad? Here, drink this!" Filling a tumbler with brandy, I forced it between his quivering fingers. Then it was some moments before I could get him to understand what it was I wanted him to do. When he did get the glass to his lips, he swallowed its contents as if they were so much water. Slowly, his senses returned to him. He stood up and looked around with a smile which was positively ghastly.

"It's a delusion," he said.

"It's a very strange kind of a delusion, if it is." I eyed him curiously. He was evidently making the most strenuous efforts to regain his self-control, all the while with that horrible smile on his lips.

"Atherton, you take advantage." I was still. "Who's your Oriental friend you speak of?"

"My Oriental friend, you mean yours? I supposed at first that the individual in question was a man, but it appears that she's a woman."

"A woman? Oh. How do you mean?" he asked.

"Well, the face is a man's, of an uncommonly disagreeable type, of which the powers forbid that there are many, and the voice is a man's, also of a kind, but the body—as last night I chanced to discover—is a woman's."

"That sounds very strange." He closed his eyes. I could see that his cheeks were clammy. "Do you—do you believe in witchcraft?"

"That depends."

"Have you heard of Obi?" he asked.

"I have."

"I've been told that an Obeah man can put a spell on someone which compels them to see whatever he—the Obeah man—may please. Do you think that's possible?"

"It's not a question to which I should be disposed to answer either yes or no," I said.

He looked at me out of his half-closed eyes. It struck me that he was making conversation, saying anything for the sake of gaining time.

"I remember reading a book entitled 'Obscure Diseases of the Brain.' It contained some interesting data on the subject of hallucinations," he said.

"Possibly."

"Be honest, would you recommend me to place myself in the hands of a mental pathologist?"

"I don't think that you're insane, Lessingham, if that's what you mean."

"No? That's good to hear. Of all diseases, insanity is the most to be dreaded. Well, Atherton, I'm keeping you. The truth is that, insane or not, I'm very far from well. I think I must give myself a holiday." He moved towards his hat and umbrella.

"There's something else which you must do," I said.

"What's that?"

"You must resign your pretensions to Miss Lindon's hand."

"My dear Atherton, if my health is really failing me, I will resign everything—everything!" He repeated the word with a little movement of his hands which was pathetic.

"Understand me, Lessingham. What else you do is no affair of mine. I'm only concerned with Miss Lindon. You must give me your definite promise, before you leave this room, to terminate your engagement with her before tonight."

His back was towards me. "There will come a time when your conscience will prick you because of your treatment of me, Atherton. When you'll realize that I'm the most unfortunate of men."

"I realize that now. And it's because I realize it that I'm so desirous that the shadow of your evil fortune shall not fall upon an innocent girl."

He turned to face me. "Atherton, what's your actual position with reference to Marjorie Lindon?"

"She regards me as a brother."

"And do you regard her as a sister? Are your sentiments towards her purely fraternal?"

"You know that I love her."

"And do you suppose that my removal will clear the path for you?" he asked.

"I suppose nothing of the kind. You may believe me or not, but my one desire is for her happiness, and surely if you love her, that's your desire, too."

"That is so." He paused. An expression of sadness stole over his face of which I hadn't thought possible. "That is so to an extent of which you don't dream. No man likes to have his hand forced, especially by one that he regards—may I say it—as a possible rival. But I'll tell you this much. If the blight which has fallen on my life is likely to continue, I'd not wish to join her fate with mine, not for all that the world could offer me." He stopped and I waited. Presently he continued, "When I was younger I was subject to a...similar delusion. But it vanished; I saw no trace of it for years. I thought I was done with it for good. Recently, however, it's returned, as you've witnessed. I'll institute inquiries into the cause of its reappearance, and if it seems likely to be irremovable, or even if it bids fair to be prolonged, I'll not only, as you phrase it, 'withdraw my claim' to Miss Lindon's hand, but to all my other ambitions. In the interim, as regards Miss Lindon, I'll be careful to hold myself on the footing of a mere acquaintance."

"You promise me?"

"I do," he nodded. "And on your side, Atherton, in the meantime, deal with me more gently. Judgment in my case has still to be given. You'll find that I'm not the guilty wretch you make me out to be. There are few things more disagreeable to one's self-esteem than to learn, too late, that one has persisted in judging another man too harshly. Think of all that the world has, at this moment, to offer me, and what it'll mean if I have to turn my back on it, owing to a mischievous twist of fortune's wheel."

He turned, is if to go. Then stopped and looked around in an attitude of listening. "What's that?"

There was a sound of droning. I recalled what Marjorie had said of her experiences of the night before; it was like the droning of a beetle. The instant Paul heard it, his countenance began to change; it was pitiable to witness.

I rushed to him. "Lessingham, don't be a fool! Be strong!"

He gripped my left arm with his right hand until it felt as if it were being compressed in a vice. "Then I shall have to have some more brandy," he said.

Fortunately the bottle was within reach from where I stood, otherwise I doubt if he would have released my arm to let me get at it. I gave him the decanter and the glass. He helped himself to generous helping. By the time he'd swallowed it, the droning sound had gone. He put down the empty tumbler and said, "When a man has to resort to alcohol to keep his nerves up to concert pitch, things are in a bad way with him, you may be sure of that, but then you've never known what it is to stand in momentary expectation of a tête-à-tête with the devil." Again he turned to leave, and this time he actually left. I let him go alone. I heard his footsteps passing along the corridor leading out, then the hall door close.

I sat in an armchair, stretched my legs out in front of me, thrust my hands in my pants pockets, and wondered about it all. I'd been there perhaps four or five minutes when there was a slight noise to my side. Glancing around, I saw a sheet of paper come fluttering through the open window. It fell almost at my feet. I picked it up. It was a picture of a beetle, a facsimile of the one which had such an extraordinary effect on Mr. Lessingham the day before.

"If this was intended for Lessingham, it's a trifle late, unless…" I could hear that someone was approaching along the corridor. I looked up, expecting to see Paul reappear but I was happily disappointed. The newcomer was feminine. It was Miss Grayling. As she stood in the open doorway, I saw that her cheeks were red as roses.

"I hope I'm not interrupting you again, but I left my purse here." As an afterthought she added, "And I want you to have lunch with me."

I locked the picture of the beetle in the drawer, and went to have lunch with Dora Grayling.

PART 3

Marjorie Lindon Tells The Tale

Chapter 23

I'm the happiest woman in the world! I wonder how many women have said that of themselves in their time, but I am. Paul has told me that he loves me. Oh, how long I've made inward confession of my love for him, I'm ashamed to say. It sounds prosaic, but I believe it's a fact that the first stirring of my pulse was caused by reading a speech of his which was in the Times.

It was on the Eight Hours' Bill. Papa was most unflattering over Paul though. He said that Paul was an oily spouter, an ignorant agitator, an irresponsible firebrand, and a good deal more to the same effect. I remember very well how Papa fidgeted with the paper, declaring that it read even worse than it sounded, and goodness knew that it had sounded bad enough. He was so emphatic that when he'd gone, I thought I would see what all the bother was about, and read the speech for myself. So I read it. It affected me quite differently than it did Papa. The speaker's words showed such knowledge, charity, and sympathy that they went straight to my heart.

After that I read everything of Paul Lessingham's which I came across, and the more I read the more I was impressed. But it was some time before we met. Considering what Papa's opinions were, it wasn't likely that he'd go out of his way to facilitate a meeting. To him, the mere mention of the name was like a red rag to a bull. But at last we did meet, and then I knew that he was stronger, greater, better even than his words.

It's so often the other way; one finds that men, and women too, are so apt to put their best, as it were, into their shop windows, that the discovery was as novel as it was delightful.

Once the ice was broken, we often met. We didn't plan our meetings— at first, at any rate—yet we seemed to always meet. Seldom a day passed when we didn't meet, sometimes two to three times. It was odd how we were always running into each other in the most unlikely places. I believe we didn't notice it at the time, but looking back I can see that we must have managed our engagements so that somewhere, somehow, we would be certain to have an opportunity of exchanging half a dozen words. Those constant encounters couldn't have all been chance ones.

But I never supposed he loved me, never. I'm not even sure that, for some time, I was aware that I loved him. We were great on friendship, both of us. I was quite aware that I was his friend, and that he regarded me as his friend; he told me so more than once.

"I tell you this," he would say, referring to this, that or the other thing, "because I know that, in speaking to you, I'm speaking to a friend."

Those weren't just empty words either. All kinds of people talk to one another like that—especially men. It's a kind of formula which they use with every woman who shows herself disposed to listen. But Paul isn't like that. He's sparing with his words, and not by any means a woman's man. I tell him that's his weakest point. If the past doesn't lie, few politicians have achieved prosperity without the aid of women. He tells me he's not a politician; that he never meant to be a politician. He simply wished to work for his country, and if his country doesn't need his services, well, let it be.

Papa's political friends have always so many axes of their own to grind, that at first to hear a member of Parliament talk like that was almost disquieting. I'd dreamed of men like that, but I'd never encountered one until I met Paul Lessingham.

Our friendship was a pleasant one, and it became pleasanter and pleasanter as time passed. Until there came a time when he told me everything: the dreams he dreamed, the plans which he'd planned, and the great purposes which, if health and strength were given him, he intended to carry to a great fulfillment. Then at last, he told me something else.

It was after a meeting at a Working Women's Club in Westminster. He'd spoken, and I'd spoken, too. I didn't know what Papa would have said, if he had known, but I had. A formal resolution had been proposed, and I'd seconded it, in perhaps a couple of hundred words, but that would have been quite enough for Papa to have regarded me as an 'Abandoned Wretch,' Papa always puts those sort of words into capitals. Papa regards a speechifying woman as a thing of horror. I have known him to look askance at a Primrose Dame.

The night was fine. Paul proposed that I should walk with him down the Westminster Bridge Road, until we reached the House, and then he would see me into a cab. I did as he suggested. It was still early, not yet ten, and the streets were alive with people. Our conversation, as we went, was entirely political. The Agricultural Amendment Act was then before the Commons, and Paul felt very strongly that it was one of those measures which gives with one hand, while taking with the other. The committee stage was at hand, and already several amendments were threatened, the effect of which would be to strengthen the landlord at the expense of the tenant. More than one of these was to be proposed by Papa. Paul was pointing out how it would be his duty to oppose these tooth and nail, when all at once, he stopped walking and said, "I sometimes wonder how you really feel upon this matter."

"What matter?" I asked.

"On the difference of opinion in political matters, which exists between your father and myself. I'm conscious that Mr. Lindon regards my action as a personal question, and resents it so keenly, that I'm sometimes moved to wonder if at least a portion of his resentment isn't shared by you."

"I've already explained, I consider Papa the politician as one person, and Papa the father as quite another."

"You're his daughter," he said.

"Certainly I am; but would you, on that account, wish me to share his political opinions, even though I believe them to be wrong?"

"You love him," he stated.

"Of course I do, he's the best of fathers."

"Your defection will be a grievous disappointment."

I looked at him out of the corner of my eye. I wondered what was passing through his mind. The subject of my relations with Papa was one which, without saying anything at all about it, we had agreed not to discuss.

"I'm not so sure. I'm permeated with a suspicion that Papa has no politics," I said.

"Miss Lindon! I fancy that I can submit proof to the contrary."

"I believe that if Papa were to marry again, within three weeks his wife's politics would be his own."

Paul thought before he spoke, then he smiled. "I suppose that men sometimes do change their coats to please their wives, even their political ones."

"Papa's opinions are the opinions of those with whom he mixes," I said. "The reason why he consorts with Tories of the crusted school is because he fears that if he associated with anyone else—with Radicals, say—before he knew it, he would be a Radical, too. With him, association is synonymous with logic."

Paul laughed outright. By this time we'd reached Westminster Bridge. Standing, we looked down upon the river. A long line of lanterns was gliding mysteriously over the water; it was a tug towing a string of barges. For some moments neither of us spoke, then Paul recurred to what I'd just been saying.

"And you, do you think marriage would color your convictions?" he asked.

"Would it yours?"

"That depends." He was silent. Then he said, in that tone which I'd learned to look for when he was most earnest, "It depends on whether you would marry me."

I was still. His words were so unexpected that they took my breath away. I knew not what to make of them. My head was in a whirl. Then he addressed to me a monosyllabic interrogation, "Well?"

"I found my voice, or a part of it. "Well? To what?"

He came a little closer. "Will you be my wife?" he asked.

The part of my voice which I'd found was lost again. Tears came to my eyes and I shivered. I hadn't thought that I could be so absurd. Just then the moon came from behind a cloud, and the rippling waters were tipped with silver.

He spoke again, so gently that his words just reached my ears. "You know that I love you."

Then I knew that I loved him, too. That what I had fancied was a feeling of friendship was something very different. It was as if someone, in tearing a veil from before my eyes, had revealed a spectacle which dazzled me. I was speechless.

He misconstrued my silence. "Have I offended you?" he asked.

"No." I fancy that he noted the tremor which was in my voice, and read it rightly. For he remained still. Presently, his hand stole along the parapet, and fastened upon mine, holding it tight.

And that was how it came about. Other things were said, but they were hardly of the first importance, though I believe we took some time in saying them. Of myself I can say with truth that my heart was too full for copious speech. I was filled with a great happiness. And, I believe, I can say the same of Paul. He told me as much when we were parting.

It seemed that we'd only just arrived when Paul turned and stared up at Big Ben.

"Midnight! The House up! Impossible!" he cried.

But it was more than possible, it was fact. We'd actually been on the bridge for two hours, and it hadn't seemed ten minutes. Never had I supposed that the flight of time could have been so entirely unnoticed. Paul was considerably taken aback. His legislative conscience pricked him. He excused himself—in his own fashion.

"Fortunately, for once in a way, my business in the House wasn't as important as my business out of it," he said with a grin.

He had his arm through mine. We were standing face to face.

"So you call this business!" I said.

He laughed.

He not only saw me into a cab, but he saw me home in it, and once in the cab, he kissed me. I fancy I was a little out of sorts that night. My nervous system was, perhaps, demoralized. Because when he kissed me, I did a thing which I never do. I have my own standard of behavior, and that sort of thing is quite outside of it. But this night I behaved like a sentimental chit. I cried and it took him all the way to my father's door to comfort me.

I can only hope that, perceiving the strangeness of the occasion, he consented to excuse me for how I acted.

Chapter 24

Sydney Atherton has asked me to be his wife. It's not only annoying, it's absurd.

This is the result of Paul's wish that our engagement should not be announced. He's afraid of Papa. The atmosphere of the House is charged with electricity. Party feeling runs high. They're at each other, hammer and tongs, about this Agricultural Amendment Act. The strain on Paul is tremendous. I'm beginning to feel positively concerned. Little things which I've noticed about him lately convince me that he's being overwrought. I suspect him of having sleepless nights. The amount of work which he's been getting through lately has been too much for any single human being, no matter who he is. He himself admits that he will be glad when the session is at an end. So will I.

But for the time being, it's his desire that nothing shall be said about our engagement until the House rises. It's reasonable enough. Papa is sure to be violent, and lately the barest allusion to Paul's name has been enough to make him explode. When he does find out, he'll be unmanageable, I foresee it clearly.

From little incidents which have happened recently I predict the worst. He'll be capable of making a scene within the precincts of the House. And, as Paul says, there's some truth in the saying that the last straw breaks the camel's back. He'll be better able to face Papa's wild wrath when the House has risen.

Of course Paul is right, and what he wishes I wish too. Still, it's not all such plain sailing for me as he might think. My domestic atmosphere with Papa is almost as electrical as that in the House. Papa is like the terrier who has scented a rat; he's always sniffing the air. He's not actually forbidden me to speak to Paul, for his courage isn't quite at the sticking point, but he's constantly making uncomfortable allusions to persons who number among their acquaintance 'political adventurers,' 'grasping carpet-baggers,' 'Radical riff-raff,' and that kind of thing. Sometimes I venture to call my soul my own, but such a tempest invariably follows that I become discreet again as soon as I possibly can. So, as a rule, I suffer in silence.

Still, I would with all my heart that the concealment were at an end. No one should ever think that I'm ashamed of being married to Paul, Papa least of all. On the contrary, I'm as proud of it as a woman can be. Sometimes, when he's said or done something unusually wonderful, I fear that my pride will burst, I feel it so strong within me. I should be delighted to have a trial of strength with Papa, anywhere, at any time, and I shouldn't be as rude to him as he is to me. I believe that at the bottom of his heart Papa knows that I'm the more sensible of the two, and after a pitched battle or so he would understand it better still. I know Papa! I haven't been his daughter for all these years in vain. I feel like hot-blooded soldiers must feel, who burning to attack the enemy in the open field, are ordered to skulk behind boulders and hedges and be shot at.

One result is that Sydney has actually made a proposal of marriage—he of all people! It's too comical. The best of it was that he took himself quite seriously. I don't know how many times he's confided to me the sufferings which he's endured for love of other women—some of them, I'm sorry to say, decent married women too, but this is the first occasion on which the theme has been a personal one. He was so frantic, as he's wont to be, that to calm him I told him about Paul, which under the circumstances I felt myself at liberty to do. In return, he was melodramatic, hinting darkly at I know not what.

I was almost cross with him.

He's a curious person, Sydney Atherton. I suppose it's because I've known him all my life, and have always looked upon him, in cases of necessity at least, as a capital substitute for a brother. In some respects he's a genius, but at other times he can be a…. I'll not say 'fool,' for that he never is, though he's often done some extremely foolish things. The fame of his inventions is in the mouths of all men, though the half of them has never been told. He's the most extraordinary mixture. The things which most people would like to have proclaimed in the street, he keeps tightly locked within himself, while those things he should be only too glad to conceal, he shouts from the rooftops.

A very famous man once told me that if Mr. Atherton chose to become a specialist, to take up one branch of inquiry, and devote his life to it, then his fame before he died would bridge the spheres. But sticking to one thing isn't in Sydney's line at all. He prefers, like a bee, to roam from flower to flower.

As for his being in love with me, that's ridiculous. He's as much in love with the moon. I can't think what has put the idea into his head. Some girl must have been ill-using him, or he imagines that she has.

The girl he ought to marry, and who he ultimately will marry, is Dora Grayling. She's young, charming, immensely rich, and deeply in love with him, and even If she wasn't, then he is most definitely in love with her. I believe he's very near it as it is; sometimes he's so very rude to her.

It's a characteristic of Sydney's that he's apt to be rude to a girl that he really likes. As for Dora, I suspect she dreams of him. He's tall, straight, very handsome, with a big moustache, and the most extraordinary eyes—I fancy that those eyes of his have as much to do with Dora's state as anything.

I've heard it said that he possesses the hypnotic power to an unusual degree, and that if he chose to exercise it, he might become a danger to society. In fact, I believe he's hypnotized Dora.

He makes an excellent brother for me however. I've gone to him many a time for help, and some excellent advice I've received. I daresay I will consult him still. There are matters of which I would hardly dare talk to Paul about. In all things he is the great man. He could hardly condescend to chiffons. Now Sydney can and does.

When he's in the mood on the vital subject of dressmaking, a woman couldn't appeal to a sounder authority. I tell him, if he'd been a dressmaker, he would have been magnificent!

Chapter 25

This morning I had an adventure.

I was in the breakfast room and Papa, as usual, was late for breakfast. I was wondering whether I should begin without him, when chancing to look around, something caught my eye in the street. I went to the window to see what it was.

There was a small crowd of people in the middle of the road, and they were all staring at something which, apparently, was lying on the ground. What it was I couldn't see.

The butler happened to be in the room and I said to him, "Peter, what's the matter in the street? Go and see."

He did as I said and presently he returned. Peter is an excellent servant, but the fashion of his speech, even when conveying the most trivial information, is slightly long winded with far too many words. He would have made a capital cabinet minister at question time, as he wraps up the smallest petitions of meaning in the largest possible words.

"An unfortunate individual appears to have been the victim of a catastrophe. I'm informed that he is dead. The constable asserts that he is drunk," Peter informed me.

"Drunk? Dead? Do you mean that he's dead drunk? At this hour!" I said.

"He is either one or the other. I did not behold the individual myself. I derived my information from a bystander."

That wasn't a sufficient explanation for me. I gave way to a seemingly quite causeless impulse of curiosity, and went out into the street to see for myself. It probably wasn't the most sensible thing I could have done, and Papa would have been shocked, but I'm always shocking Papa. It had been raining in the night, and the shoes which I wore weren't well suited for the mud.

I made my way to the scene. "What's the matter?" I asked.

A workman, with a bag of tools over his shoulder, answered me. "There's something wrong with someone. Policeman says he's drunk, but he looks to me as if he was somethin' worse."

"Will you let me pass, please?"

When they saw I was a woman, they permitted me to reach the center of the crowd. A man was lying on his back, in the dirt of the road. He was so plastered with mud that it was difficult at first to be sure that he really was a man. His head and feet were bare. His body was partially covered by a long ragged cloak. It was obvious that one wretched, dirt-stained, sopping wet rag was all the clothing he had on. A large constable was holding his shoulders in his hands, and was regarding him as if he couldn't make him out at all. He seemed uncertain as to whether it was or wasn't a case of shamming.

He spoke to the man as if he was some stubborn child. "Come, my lad, this won't do! Wake up! What's the matter with you?"

But the man neither woke up, nor explained what was the matter. I took hold of his hand. It was icy cold. Apparently the wrist had no pulse. Clearly this was no ordinary case of drunkenness.

"There's something seriously wrong, Officer," I said. "Medical assistance ought to be had at once."

"Do you think he's in a fit, miss?"

"That a doctor should be able to tell you better than I can. There seems to be no pulse. I shouldn't be surprised to find that he was…"

The word 'dead' was actually on my lips when the stranger saved me from making a glaring exposure of my ignorance by snatching his wrist away from me and sitting up in the mud. He held out his hands in front of him, opened his eyes, and exclaimed in a loud, but painfully raucous tone of voice, as if he was suffering from a very bad cold, "Paul Lessingham!"

I was so surprised that I all but sat down in the mud. To hear Paul—my Paul—spoken of by an individual of his appearance, in that fashion, was something which I hadn't expected. The moment the words were uttered, he closed his eyes again, sank backward, and seemingly relapsed into unconsciousness, the constable gripping him by the shoulder just in time to prevent him banging the back of his head against the road.

The officer shook him, and not gently.

"Now, my lad, it's plain that you're not dead! What's the meaning of this? Move yourself!"

Looking around, I found that Peter was behind me. Apparently he'd been struck by the oddness of his mistress' behavior, and had followed to see that it didn't meet with the reward which it deserved.

"Peter, let someone go at once for Dr. Cotes!" I told him.

Dr. Cotes lives just round the corner, and since it was evident that the man's lapse into consciousness had made the constable skeptical as to his case being as serious as it seemed, I thought it might be advisable that a competent opinion should be obtained without delay.

Peter was starting to leave when again the stranger returned to consciousness, that is, if it really was consciousness—of which I was more than a little in doubt. He repeated his previous words, sat up in the mud, stretched out his arms, opened his eyes unnaturally wide—and yet they appeared unseeing—as a sort of convulsion went all over him, and shrieked, "Be warned, Paul Lessingham. Be warned!"

It really amounted to shrieking, as a man might shriek who was in mortal terror. For my part, that settled it. There was a mystery here which needed to be unraveled. Twice had he called out Paul's name, and in the strangest fashion! It was for me to learn the reason; to ascertain what connection there was between this strange man and Paul Lessingham, for providence must have cast him there before my door and I might be entertaining an angel unawares. My mind was made on that instant.

"Peter, hasten for Dr. Cotes," I said. Peter passed the word, and immediately a footman started running as fast as his legs would carry him.

"Officer, I'll have this man taken into my father's house. Will some of you men help to carry him?" I said.

There were volunteers enough, and to spare. Once we were back in the house, and in the hall, I asked Peter, "Is Papa down yet?"

"Mr. Lindon has sent down to say for you to please not wait for him for breakfast. He has issued instructions to have his breakfast conveyed to him upstairs."

"That's all right." I nodded towards the poor wretch who was being carried through the hall. "You'll say nothing to him about this unless he particularly asks. You understand?"

Peter bowed. He's discretion itself. He knows I'm impulsive. The doctor was in the house almost as soon as the stranger was laid down.

"Needs a good washing," the doctor remarked directly upon seeing his patient.

That certainly was true. I never saw a man that stood more obviously in need of soap and water. Then the doctor went through the usual medical formula, I watching all the while. So far as I could see, the man showed not the slightest sign of life.

"Is he dead?" I asked.

"He will be soon if he doesn't have something to eat. The fellow's starving."

The doctor asked the policeman what he knew of him. That sagacious officer's reply was vague. A boy had run up to him crying that a man was lying dead in the street. He'd straightway followed the boy, and discovered the stranger. That was all he knew.

"What is the matter with the man?" I inquired of the doctor, when the constable had left.

"Don't know. It may be catalepsy, and it might not be. When I do know, you may ask again." Dr. Cotes' manner was a trifle brusque, particularly I believe, to me. I remember that once he threatened to box my ears. When I was a small child I used to think nothing of boxing his, although now the idea was at the forefront of my mind.

Realizing that no satisfaction was to be found from a speechless man, particularly as regards to his mysterious references to Paul, I went upstairs. I found that Papa was under the impression that he was suffering from a severe attack of gout. But as he was eating a capital breakfast, and apparently enjoying it, while I was still fasting, I ventured to hope that the matter wasn't as serious as he feared.

I mentioned nothing to him about the person that I'd found in the street, lest it should aggravate his gout. When he's like this, the slightest thing can set him off.

Chapter 26

Paul has stormed the House of Commons with one of the greatest speeches he's ever delivered, and I've quarreled with Papa. And, also, I've very nearly quarreled with Sydney.

Sydney's little affair is nothing. He actually still persists in thinking himself in love with me, as if since last night, when he did what he calls 'proposed' to me. Then when I told him that he falls in and out of love every so often, he became quite disagreeable. Now, Sydney being disagreeable is about as nice as Sydney any other way, but when it comes to his defaming Paul, I object. If he imagines that anything he can say, or hint at, will lessen my estimation of Paul Lessingham by one hair's breadth, he has less wisdom even than I gave him credit for. By the way, Percy Woodville asked me to be his wife tonight, too, which is also nothing. He's been trying to do it for the last three years, though under the circumstances it's a little trying, but he wouldn't spit venom merely because I preferred another man, and I believe he does care for me.

Papa's affair is serious. It's the first clashing of the foils, and this time I imagine, the buttons are really off. This morning he said a few words, but not so much to me, as at me. He informed me that Paul was expected to speak tonight, as if I didn't know it, and availed himself of the opening to load him with the abuse which, in his case, he thinks isn't unbecoming to a gentleman. I don't know, or rather, I do know what he would think if he heard another man use—in the presence of a woman—the kind of language which he habitually employs. However, I said nothing. I had a motive for allowing the chaff to fly before the wind.

But tonight issue was joined. I of course, went to hear Paul speak, as I've done over and over again before. Afterwards, Paul came and fetched me. He had to leave me for a moment while he gave someone a message, and in the lobby I saw Sydney sneering! I could have pinched him, and just as I was coming to the conclusion that I should have to stick a pin into his arm, Paul returned. Sydney was so rude to him that I was ashamed, even if Mr. Atherton was not.

As if it wasn't enough that Paul should be insulted by a mere popinjay, at the very moment when he'd been adding another stone to the fabric of his country's glory, Papa came up. He actually wanted to take me away from Paul. I should have liked to see him do it. Of course I went down with Paul to the carriage, leaving Papa to follow if he chose. He didn't choose, but nonetheless, he managed to be home within three minutes after I'd myself returned.

Then the battle began.

It's impossible for me to give an idea of Papa in a rage. There may be men who look well when they lose their temper, but if there are, Papa is certainly not one of them. He's always talking about the magnificence and the high breeding of the Lindons, but anything less high-bred than the head of the Lindons, in his moments of wrath, would be hard to conceive. His language I won't attempt to portray, but his observations consisted, mainly, of abuse of Paul, glorification of the Lindons, and orders to me.

"I forbid you. I forbid you…" When Papa wishes to be impressive he repeats himself. I don't know if he imagines that they're improved by repetition; if he does, he's wrong. "I forbid you ever again to speak to that…that…"

Here followed language. I was silent. My cue was to keep cool. I believe that, with the exception perhaps, of being a little white, and exceedingly sorry that Papa should so forget himself, I was about the same as I generally am.

"Do you hear me? Do you hear what I say? Do you hear me, miss?"

"Yes, Papa; I hear you."

"Then…then promise me that you'll do as I tell you! Mark my words, my girl, you shall promise before you leave this….this room!"

"My dear Papa, do you intend me to spend the remainder of my life in the drawing room?"

"Don't you be impertinent! Do…don't you speak to me like that! I won't have it!"

"I tell you what it is, Papa, if you don't take care you'll have another attack of gout."

"Damn gout."

That was the most sensible thing he said, and if such a tormentor as gout can be consigned to the nether regions by the mere utterance of a word, then by all means let the word be uttered.

Off he went again. "The man's a ruffian, a rascal…" And so on. "There's not such a villainous vagabond in all of London." And all the rest of it. "I order you, I'm a Lindon, and I order you! I'm your father, and I order you! I order you never to speak to such a…such a…" Various vain repetitions. "I order you never to look at him!"

"Listen to me, Papa. I'll promise you that I'll never speak to Paul Lessingham again, if you'll promise me never to speak to Lord Cantilever again, or to recognize him if you meet him on the street."

You should have seen how Papa glared. Lord Cantilever is the head of his party. It's august, and I presume, reverenced leader. He's Papa's favorite. I'm not sure that he does regard him as being any lower than the angels, but if he does it's certainly something in decimals. My suggestion seemed as outrageous to Papa as his suggestion seemed to me. But it's Papa's misfortune that he can only see one side of a question, and that's his own.

"You, you dare to compare Lord Cantilever to…to that…that…!"

"I'm not comparing them. I'm not aware of there being anything in particular against Lord Cantilever that is against his character. But of course, I shouldn't dream of comparing a man of his caliber with one of real ability, like Paul Lessingham. It would be to treat his Lordship with too much severity."

I couldn't help it, but that did it. The rest of Papa's conversation was a jumble of explosions. It was all so sad. Papa poured all the vials of his wrath upon Paul, to his own sore disfigurement. He threatened me with all the pains and penalties of the inquisition if I didn't immediately promise to hold no further communication with Mr. Lessingham; of course I did nothing of the kind.

He cursed me by bell, book, and candle, and by ever so many other things as well. He called me the most dreadful names. Me! His only child. He warned me that I should find myself in prison before I was done. I'm not sure but I believe he even hinted darkly at the gallows. Finally, he forced me from the room in a whirlwind of curses.

Chapter 27

When I left Papa, or rather, when he'd driven me from him, I went straight to the man tat I'd found on the street. It was late, and I was feeling both tired and worried, so that I only thought of seeing for myself how he was. In some way, he seemed to be a link between Paul and myself, and at that moment, links of that kind were precious. I couldn't have gone to bed without learning something of his condition.

The nurse received me at the door.

"Well, nurse, how's the patient?" I asked.

The nurse was a plump, motherly woman, who had attended more than one odd protégé of mine, and whom I kept pretty constantly at my beck and call.

She held out her hands. "It's hard to tell. He hasn't moved since I arrived."

"Not moved? Is he still insensible?"

"He seems to me to be in some sort of a trance," she said. "He doesn't appear to breathe, and I can detect no pulse, but the doctor says he's still alive, it's the weirdest case I've ever seen."

I went farther into the room, and as I did so, the man in the bed gave signs of life which were sufficiently unmistakable.

The nurse hastened to him. "Why, he's moving!" she exclaimed. "He must have heard you enter!"

As I approached the bed, he raised himself to a sitting posture, like he'd done in the street, As if he was addressing someone, he cried out, "Paul Lessingham! Beware! *The Beetle!*" I can't describe the almost more-than-human agony which was in his voice.

What he meant I hadn't the slightest idea. That probably was why what seemed more like a pronouncement of delirium than anything else had such an extraordinary effect on my nerves. No sooner had he spoken than a sort of blank horror seemed to settle down on my mind. I actually found myself trembling at the knees. I felt, all at once, as if I was standing in the immediate presence of something awful yet unseen.

As for the speaker, no sooner were the words out of his lips, than he relapsed into a condition of a trance.

The nurse, bending over him, said, "He's gone off again! What an extraordinary thing! I suppose it is real." It was clear from the tone of her voice that she shared the doubt which had troubled the constable. "There's not a trace of a pulse. From the look of things he might be dead. Of one thing I'm sure is there's something unnatural about the man. No natural illness I've ever heard of takes hold of a man like this." Glancing up, she saw that there was something unusual in my face, an appearance which startled her. "Why, Miss Marjorie, what's the matter! You look quite ill!"

I did feel ill, worse than ill, but at the same time I was quite incapable of describing what I felt to the nurse, For some inscrutable reason I'd even lost the control of my tongue, and I stammered, "I…I'm not feeling very well, nurse, I think I'll go to bed."

As I spoke, I staggered towards the door, conscious all the while that the nurse was staring at me with her eyes wide open. When I left the room, it seemed that in some incomprehensible fashion as if something had left it with me, and that it and I were alone together in the hallway. So overcome was I by the consciousness of its immediate proximity that all at once I found myself cowering against the wall—as if I expected something or someone to strike me.

How I reached my bedroom I don't know. I found my maid Fanchette awaiting me. Her presence was a positive comfort, until I realized the amazement with which she was regarding me.

"Mademoiselle is not well?" she asked.

"Thank you, Fanchette, I'm rather tired. I'll undress myself tonight; you can go to bed."

"But if mademoiselle is so tired, will she not permit me to assist her?"

The suggestion was reasonable enough, and kindly too, for to say the least of it, she had as much cause for fatigue as I did. I hesitated. I would have liked to throw my arms around her neck and beg her not to leave me, but the plain truth is that I was ashamed. In my inner consciousness I was persuaded that the sense of terror which had suddenly overcome me was so absolutely causeless, that I couldn't bear the notion of playing the coward in my maid's eyes.

While I hesitated, something seemed to sweep past me through the air, and to brush against my cheek in passing. I caught at Fanchette's arm.

"Fanchette! Is there something with us in the room?"

"Something with us in the room? Mademoiselle? What do you mean?" She looked disturbed, which was excusable. Fanchette isn't exactly a strong-minded person, and not likely to be much of a support when a support was most required. If I was going to play the fool, I would be my own audience. So I sent her off. "Didn't you hear me tell you that I'll undress myself? You're to go to bed."

She went did as I bade, and the instant that she was out of the room, I wished her back again. Such a paroxysm of fear came over me that I was incapable of stirring from the spot on which I stood, and it was all I could do to prevent myself from collapsing in a heap on the floor.

Until then, I'd never had reason to suppose that I was a coward, nor suspected myself of being the possessor of 'nerves.' I was as little likely as anyone to be frightened by shadows. I told myself that the whole thing was sheer absurdity, and that I should be thoroughly ashamed of my own conduct when the morning came. "If you don't want to be self-branded as a contemptible idiot, Marjorie Lindon, you'll call up your courage and these foolish fears will fly away." But it wouldn't do. Instead of flying, they grew worse. I became convinced, and the process of conviction was terrible beyond words that there actually was something with me in the room, that some invisible horror might become visible at any moment.

I seemed to understand with a sense of agony which nothing can describe, that this thing which was with me was with Paul, too. That we were linked together by the bond of a common and a dreadful terror. That, at that moment, the same awful peril which was threatening me was also threatening him, and that I was powerless to move a finger to aid him. As with a sort of second sight, I saw out of the room in which I was, into another, in which Paul was crouching on the floor, covering his face with his hands and shrieking.

The vision came again and again with a degree of vividness of which I can't give the least conception. At last the horror, and the reality of it, goaded me to a frenzy. "Paul! Paul!" I screamed, and as soon as I found my voice, the vision faded. Once more I understood that, as a matter of simple fact, I was standing in my own bedroom, that the lights were burning brightly, and that I hadn't yet commenced to undress. "Am I going mad?" I wondered. I'd heard of insanity taking extraordinary forms, but what could have caused the softening of the brain in me I hadn't the faintest notion.

Surely that sort of thing doesn't come on—in such a wholly unmitigated form—without the slightest notice, and that my mental faculties were sound enough a few minutes back I was certain. The first premonition of anything of the kind had come upon me after the melodramatic utterance of the man I'd found in the street.

"Paul Lessingham! Beware! *The Beetle!*" The words were ringing in my ears. Then there was a buzzing sound behind me. I turned to see what it was. It moved as I moved, so that it was still at my back. I swung around swiftly on my heels. It still eluded me, it was still behind. I stood and listened. What was it that hovered so persistently at my back?

The buzzing was distinctly audible. It was like the humming of a bee. Or could it be a…beetle?

My entire life I've had an antipathy to beetles of any sort or kind, though I've objected neither to any of the thousand and one other creatures, animate or otherwise, to which so many people have a rooted, and apparently, illogical dislike. My one—and only—horror has always been beetles.

The mere suspicion of a harmless, and I'm told, necessary cockroach, being within several feet of me has always made me seriously uneasy. The thought that a great, winged beetle—to me, a flying beetle is the horror of horrors—was with me in my bedroom, and goodness alone knew how it had got there, was unendurable. Anyone who had beheld me during the next few moments would have certainly assumed that I was deranged. I turned and twisted, sprang from side to side, screwed myself into impossible positions, in order to obtain a glimpse of the detested visitant, but it was all in vain. I could hear it all the time, but see it—never! The buzzing sound remained continually behind me.

The terror returned to me, and I began to think that my brain must be softening. I dashed to the bed. Flinging myself on my knees, I tried to pray. But I was speechless—words wouldn't come. My thoughts wouldn't take shape. All at once I became conscious as I struggled to ask God's help, that I was wrestling with something evil, that if I only could ask help of Him, evil would flee. But I couldn't. I was helpless. I hid my face in the bed-clothes, cramming my fingers into my ears. But the buzzing continued behind me the entire time.

I sprang up, striking out blindly, wildly, right and left, hitting nothing; the buzzing always came from a point at which at the moment I wasn't aiming.

I tore off my clothes. I had on a lovely frock which I'd worn for the first time that night. I'd had it specially made for the occasion of the Duchess' ball, and—more especially—in honor of Paul's great speech. I'd said to myself, when I saw my image in the mirror, that it was the most exquisite gown I'd ever had, that it suited me to perfection, and that it should continue in my wardrobe for many a day, if only as a souvenir of a memorable night.

Now, in the madness of my terror, all reflections of that sort were forgotten. My only desire was to be away with it. I tore it off, letting it fall in rags to the floor. All else that I had on I flung in the same way after it; it was a veritable holocaust of dainty garments, I acting as relentless executioner who is, as a rule, normally so tender with my things. I leaped upon the bed, switched off the light, hurried into bed, burying myself over head and all, and burrowed deep down between the sheets.

I'd hoped that by turning off the light, I might regain my senses. That in the darkness I might have opportunity for sane reflection. But I'd made a grievous error. I'd exchanged bad for worse. The darkness lent an added terror. The light hadn't been out for five seconds before I'd have given all that I was worth to be able to switch it on again.

As I cowered beneath the bedclothes, I heard the buzzing sound above my head. The sudden silence of the darkness had rendered it more audible than it had been before.

The thing, whatever it was, was hovering above the bed. It came nearer and grew clearer with each passing second. I felt it alight upon the coverlet, shall I ever forget the sensations with which I did feel it? It weighed upon me like a ton of lead. How much of the seeming weight was real, and how much imaginary, I can't pretend to say, but that it was much heavier than any beetle I've ever seen or heard of, I'm sure.

For a time it was still, and during that time I doubt if I even drew a breath. Then I felt it begin to move in wobbling fashion, with awkward, ungainly gait, stopping every now and then, as if for rest.

I was conscious that it was progressing, slowly, yet surely, towards the head of the bed. The emotion of horror with which I realized what this progression might mean, will be I fear, with me to the end of my life, not only in dreams, but too often also, in my waking hours.

My heart, as the Psalmist has it, melted like wax within me. I was incapable of movement, dominated by something as hideous as, and infinitely more powerful than, the fascination of the serpent.

When it reached the head of the bed, what I feared would happen, did happen. It began to find its way inside, to creep between the sheets—the wonder of it all is that I didn't die right there!

I felt it coming nearer and nearer, inch by inch. I knew it was upon me, that there was no escape. I felt something touch my hair.

And then for the first time in my life I swooned, and all became darkness.

Chapter 28

I've been anticipating for some weeks past that things would become exciting—and they have. But hardly in the way which I foresaw. It's the old story of the unexpected happening. It seems that suddenly, events of the most extraordinary nature have come crowding in on me from the most unlooked-for quarters.

Let me try to take them in something like their proper order.

To begin with, Sydney has behaved very badly. So badly that it seems likely that I will have to re-cast my whole conception of his character. It was nearly nine o'clock this morning when I…well, I can't say woke up, because I don't believe that I'd really been asleep, but when I returned to consciousness I found myself sitting up in bed and trembling like some frightened child.

What had actually happened to me I didn't know, couldn't guess. I was conscious of an overwhelming sense of nausea, and generally, I was feeling very far from well. I attempted to arrange my thoughts and to decide upon some plan of action. Finally, I decided to go for advice and help where I'd so often gone before—to Sydney Atherton.

I went and told him the whole, gruesome story. He couldn't help but see what a deep impression the events of the night had made on me. He heard me to the end with every appearance of sympathy, and then all at once I discovered that the entire time Papa had been concealed behind a large screen which was in the room, listening to every word I'd been saying.

That I was dumfounded goes without saying. It was bad enough in Papa, but in Sydney it seemed like it was such treachery. He and I have told each other secrets all our lives, and it's never entered my imagination, as he very well knows, to play him false, not one bit, and I've always understood that in this sort of matter, men pride themselves on their sense of honor being so much keener than a woman's. I told them some plain truths, and I fancy that I left them both feeling heartily ashamed of themselves.

One result the experience had on me was that it wound me up. It had on me the revivifying effect of a cold cloth. I realized also that mine was a situation in which I would have to help myself.

When I returned home, I learned that the man whom I'd found in the street was himself again, and was conscious. Burning with curiosity to learn the nature of the connection which existed between Paul and him, and what was the meaning of his words, I merely paused to remove my hat before hastening into his room.

When he saw me, and heard who I was, the expressions of his gratitude were painful in their intensity. Tears streamed down his cheeks. He looked to me like a man that had very little life left in him. He looked weak, white, and worn to a shadow. He'd probably never been robust, and it was only too plain that privation had robbed him of what little strength he'd ever had. He was nothing but skin and bone. Physical and mental debility was written all over him.

He wasn't bad looking, however, in a milk and watery sort of way. He had pale blue eyes and very fair hair, and I daresay, at one time had been a spruce enough clerk. It was difficult to guess his age, as one ages so rapidly under the stress of misfortune, but I would have said he was about forty. His voice, though faint enough at first, was that of an educated man, and as he went on and gathered courage, and became more and more in earnest, he spoke with a simple directness which was akin to eloquence. It was a curious story which he had to tell.

So curious, so astounding indeed, that by the time it was finished, I was in such a state of mind that I could perceive no alternative but to forgive Sydney, and in spite of his recent and scandalous misbehavior, again appeal to him for assistance.

It seemed, if the story told by the man I'd found in the street was true, and incredible though it sounded—he spoke like a truthful man—that Paul was threatened by some dreadful, and to me, wholly incomprehensible danger.

But though it was a case in which time was of the essence, I was in a position in which I couldn't move alone. The shadow of the terror of the night was still with me, and with that fresh in my memory how could I hope, single-handedly, to act effectually against the mysterious being of whom this amazing tale was told?

I believed that Sydney did care for me, in his own peculiar way, and I knew that he was quick, cool, and fertile in resource, and that he showed to most advantage in a difficult situation. It was possible that he had a conscience, of a sort, and that this time, I might not appeal to it in vain.

So I sent a servant off to fetch him.

As luck would have it, the servant returned with him within five minutes. It appeared that he'd been lunching with Dora Grayling, who lives just at the end of the street, and the footman had met him coming down the steps. I had him shown to my own room.

"I want you to go to the man I found in the street, and listen to what he has to say."

"With pleasure," he said with a bow.

"Can I trust you, Sydney?"

"To listen to what he has to say? I believe so."

"Can I trust you to respect my confidence?"

He wasn't at all abashed. I never saw Sydney Atherton when he was abashed. Whatever the offence of which he's been guilty, he always seems completely at his ease.

His eyes twinkled. "You can. I won't breathe a syllable even to your father."

"In that case, come! But you understand, I'm going to put to the test the affirmations which you've made during all these years, and to prove if you have any of the feeling for me which you pretend."

Soon we were in the stranger's room. Sydney marched straight up to the bed, stared at the man who was lying in it, crammed his hands into his trouser pockets, and whistled. I was amazed.

"So!" he exclaimed. "It's you!"

"Do you know this man?" I asked.

"I'm hardly prepared to go so far as to say that I know him, but I chance to have a memory for faces, and it happens that I have met this gentleman on at least one previous occasion. Perhaps he remembers me. Do you, sir?"

The stranger seemed uneasy, as if he found Sidney's tone and manner disconcerting. "I do. You're the man in the street."

"Precisely. I am that— individual. And you're the man who came through out window, and are now in a much more comfortable condition you appear to be than when first I saw you." Sydney turned to me. "It's just possible, Miss Lindon, that I may have a few remarks to make to this gentleman which would be better made in private, if you don't mind."

"But I do mind, I mind very much. What do you suppose I sent for you here for in the first place?"

Sydney smiled that absurd, provoking smile of his, as if the occasion weren't sufficiently serious. "To show that you still have a vestige of confidence in me."

"Don't talk nonsense. This man has told me a most extraordinary story, and I've sent for you, as you may believe, not too willingly." Sydney bowed again. "In order that he may repeat it in your presence, and in mine."

"Is that so? Well! Permit me to offer you a chair, in case this tale may turn out to be a trifle long."

To humor him I accepted the chair he offered, though I should have preferred to stand. He seated himself on the side of the bed, fixing his keen, quizzical, and not too merciful eyes of his on the stranger.

"Well, sir, we're at your service, if you'll be so good as to favor us with a second edition of that pleasant yarn you've been spinning. But let's begin at the right end! What's your name?"

"Robert Holt."

"Is that so? Then, Mr. Robert Holt, please begin!"

Thus encouraged, Mr. Holt repeated the tale which he'd told me, only in more connected fashion than before. I fancy that Sydney's glances exercised on him a sort of hypnotic effect, and this kept him to the point. He scarcely needed a word of prompting from the first syllable to the last.

He told how, tired, wet, hungry, desperate and despairing he'd been, and how he was refused admittance to the shelter of those who have abandoned even hope. How he'd come upon an open window in an apparently empty house, and thinking of nothing but shelter from the inclement night, he had clambered through it. How he'd found himself in the presence of an extraordinary being, who in his debilitated and nervous state, had seemed to him to be only half human. How this dreadful man had given utterance to wild sentiments of hatred towards Paul Lessingham, my Paul! How the man had taken advantage of Holt's enfeebled state to gain over him the most complete, horrible, and almost incredible ascendancy. How he actually had sent Holt, practically naked, into the storm-swept streets, to commit burglary at Paul's house, and how he, Holt, had actually gone without being able to offer even a shadow of opposition. How Paul, suddenly returning home, had come upon Holt engaged in the very act of committing burglary, on Paul hearing Holt make a reference to some mysterious beetle, the manhood had gone out of Paul and he'd suffered the intruder to make good his escape without an effort to detain him.

The story had seemed sufficiently astonishing the first time, and it seemed still more astonishing the second, but as I watched Sydney listening, what struck me most was the conviction that he'd heard it all before.

I asked him directly when Holt had finished. "This isn't the first time you've been told this tale."

"Pardon me, but it is. Do you suppose I live in an atmosphere of fairy tales?" he said.

Something in his manner made me feel sure he was deceiving me. Sydney! Don't tell me a story! Paul has told you!"

"I'm not telling you a story, at least on this occasion, and Mr. Lessingham hasn't told me. Suppose we postpone these details to a little later, all right? Perhaps in the interim, you'll permit me to put a question or two to Mr. Holt."

I let him have his way, though I knew he was concealing something from me. That he'd a more intimate acquaintance with Mr. Holt's strange tale than he chose to confess I had no doubt, and for some reason, his reticence annoyed me.

He looked at Mr. Holt in silence for a second or two. Then he said, with the quizzical little air of bland impertinence which is peculiarly his own, "I presume, Mr. Holt, you've been entertaining us with a novelty in fables, and that we're expected to believe this pleasant little yarn of yours."

"I expect nothing. But I have told you the truth, and you know it," Mr. Holt said.

This seemed to take Sydney aback. "I protest that, like Miss Lindon, you credit me with a more extensive knowledge than I possess. However, we'll let it pass. I take it that you paid particular attention to the mysterious man of this mysterious dwelling."

Mr. Holt shuddered. "I'm not likely ever to forget him."

"Then, in that case, you'll be able to describe him to us," Sydney said.

"To do so adequately would be beyond my powers. But I'll do my best," Mr. Holt replied.

If the original was more remarkable than the description which he gave of the man, then the man must have been remarkable indeed. The impression conveyed to my mind was rather of a monster than a human being. I watched Sydney attentively as he followed Mr. Holt's somewhat lurid language, and there was something in his demeanor which made me more and more persuaded that Sydney was more behind the scenes in this strange business than he pretended, or than the speaker suspected.

Sydney put a question which seemed uncalled for by anything which Mr. Holt had said. "You're sure this thing of beauty was a man?"

"No, sir, that's exactly what I'm not sure of."

There was a note in Sydney's voice which suggested that he'd received precisely the answer which he'd expected. "Did you think it was a woman?"

"I did think so, more than once," Mr. Holt said. "Though I can hardly explain what made me think so. There was certainly nothing womanly about the face." He paused, as if to reflect. Then added, "I suppose it was a question of instinct."

"I see. Just so. It occurs to me, Mr. Holt, that you're rather strong on questions of instinct." Sydney got off the bed. He stretched, as if fatigued, which is a way he has about him. "I won't do you the injustice to hint that I don't believe a word of your charming and simple narrative. On the contrary, I'll demonstrate my belief by remarking that I haven't the slightest doubt that you'll be able to point out to me to my particular satisfaction, the residence in which this mysterious man lives."

Mr. Holt's face became red. Sydney's tone could scarcely have been more significant.

"You must remember, sir, that it was a dark night, that I'd never been in that neighborhood before, and that I wasn't in a condition to pay much attention to locality," Mr. Holt said.

"All of which is granted, but how far was it from Hammersmith Workhouse?"

"Possibly under half a mile."

"Then, in that case, surely you can remember which turning you took on leaving Hammersmith Workhouse. I suppose there aren't many turnings you could have taken," Sydney said.

"I think I could remember."

"Then you'll have an opportunity to try. It isn't very far to Hammersmith. Do you think you're well enough to drive there now, just you and I together in a cab?"

"I should say so," Mr. Holt replied. "I do want to get up this morning. It's only by the doctor's orders that I've stayed in bed."

"Then for once the doctor's orders will be ignored, as I prescribe fresh air." Sydney turned to me. "Since Mr. Holt's wardrobe seems rather lacking, don't you think a suit might fit him, if Mr. Holt wouldn't mind waiting for the moment? Then, by the time you've finished dressing, Mr. Holt, I'll be ready."

While they were ascertaining which suit of clothes would be best adapted to his figure, I went with Sydney to my room. As soon as we were inside, I let him know that this wasn't a matter in which I intended to be trifled with.

"Of course you understand, Sydney, that I'm coming with you."

He pretended not to know what I meant. "Coming with me? I'm delighted to hear it, but where?"

"To the house of which Mr. Holt has been speaking."

"Nothing could give me greater pleasure, but might I point out that Mr. Holt has to find it still?"

"I'll come help you to help him find it."

Sydney laughed, but I could see he didn't altogether relish the suggestion.

"Three in a small carriage?"

"There is such a thing as a four-wheeled cab, or I could order a carriage if you'd like one."

Sydney looked at me out of the corner of his eye, then began to walk up and down the room with his hands in his pockets. Presently, he began to talk nonsense. "I needn't say how happy I'll be of taking a drive with you, even in a four-wheeled cab, but were I in your place, I fancy that I wouldn't allow Holt and your humble servant to go hunting out this house alone. It may prove a more tedious business than you imagine. I promise that after the hunt is over, I'll describe the proceedings to you with the most literal accuracy."

"I daresay. Do you think I don't know you've been deceiving me all the time?" I said.

"Deceiving you? Me!"

"Yes, you! Do you think I'm an idiot?"

"My dear Marjorie!"

"Do you think I can't see that you know all about what Mr. Holt's been telling us? Perhaps more about it than he knows himself?"

"On my word! You credit me with far too much knowledge."

"Yes, I do, or discredit you, rather. If I were to trust you, I think that you would tell me just as much as you chose, which would be nothing. I'm coming with you, and that's final."

"Very well. Do you happen to know if there are any revolvers in the house?" he inquired. He knew better than to continue arguing with me. When I've made up my mind there would be no deterring me from my goal.

"Revolvers? Whatever for?"

"Because I should like to borrow one," he said. "I won't conceal from you—since you press me—that this is a case in which a revolver is quite likely to be required."

"You're trying to frighten me, Sydney."

"I'm doing nothing of the kind, only under the circumstances, I'm bound to point out to you what it is you might expect."

"Oh, you think that you're bound to point that out, do you? Fine then your duty's done. As for there being any revolvers in the house, Papa has a perfect arsenal; would you like to take them all?"

"Thanks, but I daresay I shall be able to manage with one, unless you'd like one, too. You may find yourself in need of it."

"I'm obliged to you, but on this occasion, I don't think I'll bother. I'll run the risk. Oh, Sydney, what a hypocrite you are!"

"It's for your sake if I seem to be. I tell you most seriously that I earnestly advise you to allow Mr. Holt and myself to manage this affair alone. I don't mind going so far as to say that this is a matter with which, in days to come, you'll wish you hadn't allowed yourself to be associated."

"What do you mean by that? Do you dare to insinuate anything against Paul?"

"I insinuate nothing," he said. "What I mean, I say right out, and my dear Marjorie, what I actually do mean is this; that if in spite of my urgent solicitations you'll persist in accompanying us on this the expedition, so far as I'm concerned, it will be postponed."

"That is what you do mean, isn't it? Then that's settled." I rang the bell and the servant came. "Order a four-wheeled cab at once," I ordered him. "And let me know the moment Mr. Holt is ready." The servant nodded and left. I turned to Sydney and said, "If you'll excuse me, I'll go and put my hat on. You're of course at liberty to please yourself as to whether you will or won't go, but if you don't, then I will go alone with Mr. Holt."

I moved to the door. He stopped me.

"My dear Marjorie, why will you persist in treating me with such injustice? Believe me, you have no idea what sort of adventure this is which you're setting out upon, or you'd hear reason. I assure you that you're gratuitously proposing to thrust yourself into imminent peril."

"What sort of peril? Why do you beat about the bush, why don't you speak outright?"

"I can't speak out right, there are circumstances which render it practically impossible, and that's the plain truth, but the danger is nonetheless real on that account. I'm not joking, I'm in earnest. Won't you take my word for it?"

"It's not a question of taking your word, it's a question of something else. I haven't forgotten my adventures of last night, and Mr. Holt's story is mysterious enough in itself, but there's something more mysterious still at the back of it, something which you appear to suggest points unpleasantly at Paul. My duty is clear, and nothing you can say will turn me from it. Paul, as you're very well aware, is already overwhelmed with affairs of state, other-wise I would take the tale to him, and he would talk to you after a fashion on his own. But with things being as they are, I propose to show you that, although I'm not yet Paul's wife, I can make his interests my own as com-pletely as though I were. I can therefore, only repeat that it's for you to decide what you intend to do, but if you prefer to stay, I will be going with Mr. Holt without you."

He sighed, then said, "Understand that when the time for regret comes, as it will come, you're not to blame me for having done what I advised you not to do."

"My dear, Sydney, I'll undertake to do my utmost to guard your spotless reputation. I'd also be sorry if anyone held you responsible for anything I either said or did."

"Very well! Your blood be on your own head!"

"My blood?"

"Yes, your blood," he said. "I wouldn't be surprised if it comes to blood before we're through. Perhaps you'll oblige me with the loan of one of that arsenal of revolvers of which you spoke."

I let him have his old revolver, or rather, I let him have one of Papa's new ones. He put it in the hip pocket in his pants. An hour later, the expedition started in a four-wheeled car.

Chapter 29

Mr. Holt looked as if he was in somebody else's garments. He was so thin and wasted that the suit of clothes which one of the men had lent him hung upon him as if he was a scarecrow. I was almost ashamed of myself for having incurred a share of the responsibility of taking him out of bed. He seemed so weak and bloodless that I wouldn't have been surprised if he fainted on the road.

I'd taken care that he eat as much as he could before we started, as the suggestion of starvation which he had conveyed to one's mind was dreadful. I also brought a flask of brandy in case of accidents, but in spite of every-thing, I couldn't conceal from myself that he would be more at home in a sickbed than in a jolting cab ride.

It wasn't a cheerful ride. There was in Sydney's manner towards me an air of protection which I instinctively resented. He appeared to be regarding me as a careful and anxious nurse might regard a disobedient child.

Conversation distinctly languished. Since Sydney seemed disposed to patronize me, I was bent on snubbing him. The result was that the majority of the remarks which were uttered were addressed to Mr. Holt.

The cab stopped after what felt like an interminable journey. I was rejoiced at the prospect of its being at an end. Sydney put his head out of the window and a short parley with the driver ensued.

"This is Hammersmith Workhouse, it's a large place, sir. Which part of it might you be wanting?" the driver asked.

Sydney appealed to Mr. Holt, who put his head out of the window in his turn; he didn't seem to recognize our surroundings at all.

"We've come a different way. This isn't the way I went. I went through Hammersmith then to the shelter. I don't see that here."

Sydney said to the cabman, "Driver, where's the shelter?"

"That's on the other end, sir."

"Then take us there."

He did as instructed and when we'd arrived, Sydney appealed again to Mr. Holt. "Shall I dismiss the cabman, or are you not able to walk?"

"Thank you, I feel quite equal to walking, I think the exercise will do me good," Mr. Holt said.

So the cabman was dismissed, a step which we—and I, in particular—had subsequent cause to regret. Mr. Holt took his bearings and he pointed to a door which was just in front of us.

"That's the entrance to the casual ward," Mr. Holt said, "and that over it is the window through which the other man threw a stone. I went to the right, back the way I'd come." We went to the right. "I reached this corner." Mr. Holt looked around, endeavoring to recall the way he'd gone. A good many roads appeared to converge at that point, so that he might have wandered in either of several directions.

Presently, he arrived at something like a decision.

"I think this is the way I went. I'm nearly sure it is." He led the way, with something of an air of uncertainty, and we followed. The road he'd chosen seemed to lead to nowhere. We hadn't gone many yards from the workhouse gates before we were confronted by something like chaos. In front and on either side of us were large spaces of waste land. At some time in the past, attempts appeared to have been made at brick-making; there were untidy stacks of bilious-looking bricks in evidence. Here and there enormous weather-stained boards announced that ***This Desirable Land was to be Let for Building Purposes.*** The road itself was unfinished. There was no pavement, and we had the bare uneven ground for sidewalk.

It seemed to lose itself in space, and to be swallowed up by the wilderness of 'Desirable Land' which lay beyond. In the near distance there were houses, but they were on other roads. On the one road which we were actually on, there was a row of unfurnished structures on the right, at the end, but only two buildings were in anything like a fit state for occupation. One stood on either side, not facing each other; there was a distance between them of perhaps fifty yards. The sight of them had a more exciting effect on Mr. Holt than on me. He moved rapidly forward, coming to a standstill in front of the one located on our left, which was the nearer of the pair.

"This is the house!" he exclaimed. He seemed almost exhilarated. I confess that I was depressed. A more dismal-looking habitation one could hardly imagine. It was one of those dreadful jerry-built houses which, while they are still new, look old. It had quite possibly only been built a year or two, and yet, owing to neglect or to poverty of construction, or to a combination of the two, it was already threatening to tumble down.

It was a small place, a couple of stories high, and would have been I should think at least thirty pounds a year. The windows had surely never been washed since the house was built; those on the upper floor seemed either cracked or broken. The only sign of occupancy consisted in the fact that a blind was down behind the window of the room on the ground floor. There were no curtains. A low wall ran in front, which had apparently at one time been surmounted by something in the shape of an iron railing, as a rusty piece of metal still remained on one end. But since there was only about a foot between it and the building, which was practically built on the road, whether the wall was intended to ensure privacy or was merely for decoration wasn't clear.

"This is the house!" Mr. Holt repeated, showing more signs of life than I had seen in him before.

Sydney looked the house up and down. It apparently appealed to his aesthetic sense as little as it did to mine. "Are you sure?" he asked.

"I'm certain," Mr. Holt said.

"It seems empty," I said.

"It seemed empty to me that night, that's why I got into it in search of shelter," Mr. Holt said.

"Which is the window which served you as a door?" Sydney asked.

"This one." Mr. Holt pointed to the window on the ground floor, the one which was screened by a blind. "There was no sign of a blind when I first saw it, and the window was open, it was that which caught my eye."

Once more Sydney surveyed the place, in comprehensive fashion, from roof to basement, then he scrutinized Mr. Holt.

"You're quite sure this is the house? It might be awkward if you proved mistaken. I'm going to knock at the door, and if it turns out that the mysterious acquaintance of yours doesn't live here, we might find an explanation difficult." "I'm sure it's the house, certain! I know it. I feel it here, and here," Mr. Holt said. He touched his chest and his forehead. His manner was distinctly odd. He was trembling, and a fevered expression had come into his eyes.

Sydney glanced at him in silence for a moment, then he bestowed his attention on me. "May I ask if I may rely on your preserving your presence of mind?"

The mere question ruffled my plumes. "What do you mean?" I asked.

"Exactly what I said. I'm going to knock at that door, and I'm going to get through it somehow. It's quite within the range of possibility that when I'm through, there'll be some strange happenings, as you've heard from Mr. Holt. The house is commonplace enough on the outside, but it may not be so within. You may find yourself in a position in which it will be of the utmost importance that you keep your wits about you."

"I'm not likely to let them stray," I said.

"Then that's all right. Do I understand that you propose to come in with me?" Sydney asked.

"Of course I do, what do you suppose I've come for? What nonsense you're talking.

"I hope that you'll still continue to consider it nonsense by the time this little adventure's done," he said.

That I resented his impertinence goes without saying, to be talked to in such a strain by Sydney Atherton, whom I'd kept in subjection ever since he was in knickerbockers, was a little trying. Still, I'm forced to admit that I was more impressed by his manner, or his words, or by Mr. Holt's manner, or something, than I should have cared to be.

I hadn't the least notion what was going to happen, or what horrors that woebegone-looking dwelling contained. But Mr. Holt's story had been of the most astonishing sort, and my experiences of the previous night were still fresh, and now that I was so close with the unknown, and though it was broad daylight, it loomed before me in a shape for which I wasn't prepared.

A more disreputable-looking front door I'd never seen. It was in perfect harmony with the remainder of the establishment. The paint was peeling, the woodwork was scratched and dented, and the knocker was red with rust.

When Sydney took it in his hand, I was conscious of quite a little thrill. As he brought it down with a sharp rat-tat, I half expected to see the door fly open, and disclose some gruesome object glaring out at us.

But nothing of the kind took place. The door didn't budge, nothing happened. Sydney waited a second or two, then knocked again. After another second or two he knocked once more. There was still no sign of anyone within taking note of our presence.

Sydney turned to Mr. Holt and said, "It seems as if the place is empty."

Mr. Holt was in the most peculiar condition of agitation, and it made me uncomfortable to look at him.

"You don't know, you can't tell; there may be someone there who hears and pays no heed," Mr. Holt said.

"I'll give them another chance." Sydney brought down the knocker with thundering reverberations. The din must have been audible half a mile away. But from within the house there was still no sign that anyone heard. Sydney came down the step. "I'll try another way. I may have better fortune at the back."

He led the way around to the rear, Mr. Holt and I following in single file. Once there the place seemed in even worse condition than the front. There were two empty rooms on the ground floor at the back. There was no mistake about their being empty, as without the slightest difficulty we could see right into them. One was apparently intended for a kitchen and wash-house combined, the other for a sitting room. There wasn't a stick of furniture in either, nor the slightest sign of human habitation.

"Not only is it plain that no one lives in these charming apartments, but it looks to me uncommonly as if no one has ever lived in them," Sydney said.

To my thinking Mr. Holt's agitation was increasing every moment. For some reason of his own, Sydney took no notice of it whatsoever, possibly because he judged that to do so would only tend to make it worse.

An odd change had even taken place in Mr. Holt's voice, and he spoke in a sort of tremulous falsetto, "It was only the front room which I saw."

"Very good; then, before very long, you will see that front room again," Sydney said and rapped with his knuckles on the glass panels on the back door. He tried the handle and when it refused to yield he gave it a vigorous shaking. He tapped the dirty windows again, but as far as succeeding in attracting attention was concerned, it was all entirely in vain.

Then he turned again to Mr. Holt, half mockingly and said, "I call you to witness that I've used every lawful means to gain the favorable notice of your mysterious friend. I must therefore beg forgiveness if I try something slightly unlawful for a change. It's true that you found the window already open, and in my case it soon will be again." He took a knife out of his pocket, and with the open blade, forced back the catch on the window. Then he lifted it up.

"Behold!" he exclaimed. "What did I tell you? Now, my dear Marjorie, if I go in first and Mr. Holt follows me, we'll be in a position to open the door for you."

I immediately saw through his plan.

"No, Sydney, you'll go in first, and I'll go in after you through the window, before Mr. Holt. I don't intend to wait for you to open the door."

Sydney shook his head, as if grieved at my want of confidence in him. But I didn't mean to be left in the lurch, to wait their pleasure, while on pretence of opening the door they searched the house. So Sydney climbed in first, and I second. It wasn't a difficult operation, since the window sill was only four feet off the ground. Mr. Holt came in last. Once we were in, Sydney put his hand up to his mouth, and shouted, "Is there anybody in this house? If so, will he kindly step this way, as there's someone who wishes to see him."

His words went echoing through the empty rooms in a way which was almost uncanny. I suddenly realized that if, after all, there did happen to be someone in the house, and he was at all disagreeable, our presence on his premises might prove rather difficult to explain. However, no one answered. While I was waiting for Sydney to make the next move, he diverted my attention to Mr. Holt.

"Holt, what's the matter with you? Man, don't play the fool like that!"

Something was the matter with Mr. Holt. He was trembling all over as if attacked by a shaking palsy. Every muscle in his body seemed to twitch at once. A strained look had come over his face, which wasn't nice to see. He said, as with an effort, "I'm all right. It's nothing."

"Oh, is it nothing? Then perhaps you'll drop it. Where's that brandy?" I handed Sydney the flask. "Here, swallow this," he told Mr. Holt, who swallowed the cupful of neat spirit which Sydney offered without an attempt at parley. But beyond bringing some remnants of color to his ashen cheeks, it seemed to have no effect on him whatever. Sydney eyed him with a meaning in his glance which I was at a loss to understand.

"Listen to me, my lad," Sydney said. "Don't think you can deceive me by playing any of your tricks, and don't delude yourself into supposing that I'll treat you as anything but dangerous if you do. I've got this…" He showed the revolver of Papa's which I'd lent him. "Don't imagine that Miss Lindon's presence will deter me from using it."

Why he addressed Mr. Holt in such a way surpassed my comprehension. Mr. Holt, however, showed no resentment. He'd suddenly become more like an automaton than a man. Sydney continued to gaze at him as if he would have liked his glance to penetrate to Mr. Holt's soul.

"Keep in front of me, if you please, Mr. Holt, and lead the way to this mysterious room in which you claim to have had such a remarkable experience," Sydney said. Then he asked me in a whisper, "Did you bring a revolver?"

I was startled. "A revolver? The very idea! How absurd you are!"

Sydney said something which was so rude—and so uncalled for—that it was worthy of Papa in his most violent moments. "I'd sooner be absurd than a fool in petticoats." I was so angry that I didn't know what to say, and before I could say it he added, "Keep your eyes and ears open, and be surprised at nothing you see or hear. Stick close to me. And for goodness sake, remain in control of as many of your senses as you can."

I hadn't the least idea what was the meaning of it all. To me there seemed nothing in the house to make such a bother about. Yet I was conscious of a fluttering of the heart as if there soon might be something. I knew Sydney sufficiently well to be aware that he was one of the last men in the world to make a fuss without reason, and that he was as little likely to suppose that there was a reason when in fact there was none.

Mr. Holt led the way, as Sydney instructed, to the door of the room which was in the front of the house. The door was closed. Sydney tapped on it but all was silence. He tapped again. "Anyone in there?" he demanded.

As there was still no answer, he tried the handle. The door was locked.

"The first sign of the presence of a human being we've had in here, as doors don't lock themselves. It's just possible that there may have been someone about the place at some time or another after all."

Grasping the door handle firmly, he shook it with all his might, as he'd done with the back door. So flimsily was the place constructed that he made even the walls tremble.

"Within there—if anyone is in there—if you don't open this door, then believe me I will." There was no response. So be it! I'm going to gain admission one way or another."

Putting his right shoulder against the door, he pushed hard. Sydney is a big man, and very strong, and the door was weak. Shortly, the lock yielded before the continuous pressure and the door flew open.

"So! It begins to occur to me, Mr. Holt, that your story may not have been such pure romance as it seemed," Sydney said.

It was plain enough that, at any rate, the room had been occupied, and recently, and if his taste in furniture could be taken as a test, by an eccentric occupant to boot. My own first impression was that there was someone living in it still, as an uncomfortable odor greeted our nostrils, which was suggestive of some evil-smelling animal.

Sydney seemed to share my thought. "A pretty perfume, on my word! Let's shed a little more light on the subject, and see what causes it. Marjorie, stop where you are until I tell you."

I'd noticed nothing peculiar about the appearance of the blind which screened the window, but it must have been made of some unusually thick material, for the room was strangely dark. Sydney entered with the intention of drawing up the blind, but he'd scarcely taken a couple of steps when he stopped.

"What's that?"

"It's it," Mr. Holt said in a voice which was so unlike his own that it was scarcely recognizable.

"It? What do you mean by 'it'?"

"*The Beetle!*"

Judging from the sound of Mr. Holt's voice, Sydney was at once in a state of odd excitement. "Oh, is it! Then, if this time I don't find out the how and the why of that charming conjuring trick, I'll give you leave to write me down as an ass, with a great, big A."

He rushed farther into the room; apparently his efforts to lighten it didn't meet with the immediate success which he desired. "What's the matter with this confounded blind? There's no cord! How do you pull it up? What the…" In the middle of his sentence, Sydney ceased speaking.

Suddenly Mr. Holt, who was standing by my side on the threshold of the door, was seized with such a fit of trembling that fearing he was going to fall, I caught him by the arm. A most extraordinary look was on his face. His eyes were distended to their fullest width, as if with horror at what they saw in front of him. Great beads of perspiration were on his forehead.

"It's coming!" he screamed.

Exactly what happened I don't know. But as he spoke, I heard proceeding from the room, the sound of buzzing wings. Instantly I recalled my experience of the night before. As I did so, I was conscious of a most unpleasant feeling in my stomach.

Sydney swore a great oath, as if he were beside himself with rage. "If you won't go up, then you shall come down."

Failing to find a cord, he seized the blind from below and dragged it down. It came, roller and all, clattering to the floor. The room was bathed in light. I hurried in. Sydney was standing by the window with a look of perplexity on his face which, under any other circumstances, would have been comical. He was holding Papa's revolver in his hand, and was glaring around the room, as if at a loss to understand how it was he didn't see what he was looking for.

"Marjorie!" he exclaimed. "Did you hear anything?"

"Of course I did. It was that which I heard last night, which so frightened me."

"Oh, was it? Then, by…" In his excitement Sydney must have been completely oblivious of my presence, for he used the most terrible language. "When I find it there'll be a small discussion. It can't have gotten out of the room. I know the creature's here. I not only heard it, I felt it brush against my face. Holt, come inside and shut that door."

Mr. Holt raised his arms, as if he were exerting himself to make a forward movement, but he remained rooted to the spot on which he stood. "I can't!" he cried.

"You can't. Why?"

"It won't let me."

"What won't let you?" Sydney asked.

"*The Beetle*!"

Sydney moved until he was right in front of Mr. Holt, then surveyed the man with eager eyes. I was standing at Sydney's back and I heard him murmur, "By George! It's just as I thought! The beggar's been hypnotized! Can you see it now?" he asked Mr. Holt.

"Yes."

"Where?"

"Behind you." As Mr. Holt spoke, I again heard quite close to me that buzzing sound. Sydney seemed to hear it, too, and it caused him to swing around so quickly that he all but knocked me off my feet.

"I beg your pardon, Marjorie, but this is of the nature of an unparalleled experience, did you hear something just then?"

"I did, distinctly; it was close to me, within an inch or two of my face," I replied. We stared about us, then back at each other; there was nothing else to be seen.

Sydney laughed, doubtfully. "It's uncommonly odd. I don't want to suggest that there are visions about, or I might suspect myself of a softening of the brain. But it's off nonetheless. There's a trick about it somewhere, I'm convinced, and no doubt it's simple enough when you know how it's done, but the difficulty is to find that out. Do you think our friend over there is acting?"

"He looks to me as if he were ill."

"He does look ill. He also looks as if he was hypnotized. If he is, it must be by suggestion, and that's what makes me doubtful, because it will be the first plainly established case of hypnotism by suggestion I've encountered." He turned to face Mr. Holt and yelled, "Holt!"

"Yes."

"That," Sydney whispered in my ear, "is the voice and that is the manner of a hypnotized man, but on the other hand, a person under influence generally responds only to the hypnotist, which is another feature about our peculiar friend which arouses my suspicions." Then, aloud he added, "Don't stand there like an idiot, Holt, come inside the room."

Again Mr. Holt made an apparently futile effort to do as he was bid. It was painful to look at him; he was like a feeble, frightened, tottering child who wanted to come but couldn't.

"I can't," Mr. Holt said.

"Let's have no nonsense, my man! Do you think this is a performance in a booth, and that I'm to be taken in by all the humbug of the professional mesmerist? Do as I tell you and come into the room." Sydney demanded.

There was a repetition, on Mr. Holt's part, of his previous pitiful struggle; this time it was longer sustained than before, but the result was the same.

"I can't!" he wailed.

"And I say you can, and will! If I pick you up and carry you, perhaps you won't find yourself as helpless as you wish me to believe." Sydney moved forward to put his threat into execution, but as soon as took his first step, Mr. Holt began to convulse all over.

Chapter 30

I was standing in the middle of the room, Sydney was between the door and me, and Mr. Holt was in the hall, just outside the doorway. As Sydney advanced towards him, he was seized with a kind of convulsion, and had to lean against the side of the door to save himself from falling. Sydney paused, and watched. The spasm went as suddenly as it came, and Mr. Holt became as motionless as he was only seconds before. He stood in an attitude of feverish expectancy, his chin raised, head thrown back, his eyes glancing upwards with the dreadful fixed glare which had come into them ever since we'd entered the house.

He looked to me as if his every faculty was strained in the act of listening. Not a muscle in his body seemed to move; he was as rigid as a figure carved in stone. Presently, the rigidity gave place to what seemed like causeless agitation.

"I hear!" he exclaimed in the most curious voice I'd ever heard. "I come!"

It was as though he was speaking to someone who was far away. Turning, he walked down the hallway to the front door.

"Hey!" Sydney cried. "Where are you off to?"

Sydney and I hastened to follow. Mr. Holt was fumbling with the latch, and before we could reach him, the door was open and he was through it.

Rushing after him, Sydney caught him on the step and held him by the arm. "What's the meaning of this little caper? Where do you think you're going now, Holt?"

Mr. Holt didn't turn and look at him. He said, in the same dreamy, faraway, unnatural tone of voice, while keeping his unwavering gaze fixed on what was apparently some distant object which was visible only to himself, "I'm going to him. He calls me."

"Who calls you?"

"The Lord of the Beetle."

Whether Sydney released his arm or not I can't say. As Mr. Holt spoke, he seemed to me to slip away from Sydney's grasp. Passing through the gateway and turning to the right, he commenced to retrace his steps in the direction we'd come.

Sydney stared after him in unequivocal amazement. Then he looked at me and said, "Well, this is a fine mess! Now what's to be done?"

"What's the matter with him?" I inquired. "Is he mad?"

"There's method in his madness if he is," Sydney replied. "He's in the same condition in which he was that night I saw him come out of Paul's window. He should be followed; he may be going to that mysterious friend of his. But on the other hand, he might not be, and it may be nothing but a trick of our friend the conjurer's to get us away from this house. He's fooled me twice already, I don't want to be fooled again, and I distinctly don't want him to return and find me gone. He's quite capable of taking the hint and leaving for good. But I can't ignore a clue to as fine a mystery as I've ever come across."

"I can stay," I said.

"You? Alone?" He eyed me doubtingly, evidently not altogether relishing the proposition.

"Why not? You can send the first person you meet, policeman, cabman, or whoever it is to keep me company. It seems a pity now that we dismissed that cab."

"Yes, it does seem a pity." Sydney was biting his lip. "Confound that fellow! How fast he moves."

Mr. Holt was already nearing the end of the road.

"If you think it necessary, by all means follow to see where he goes. You're sure to meet someone you can send before you've gone very far."

"I suppose I will. You won't mind being left alone?" he asked.

"Why should I? I'm not a child."

Reaching the corner, Mr. Holt turned and vanished out of sight.

Sydney gave an exclamation of impatience. "If I don't make haste I'll lose him. Fine, I'll do as you suggest and dispatch the first individual I come across to hold watch with you."

"That'll be all right."

He started off at a run, shouting to me as he went, "It won't be five minutes before somebody comes!"

I waved my hand to him. I watched him until he reached the end of the road. Turning, he waved to me. Then he vanished, as Mr. Holt had done.

Leaving me alone.

Chapter 31

My first impulse after Sydney's disappearance was to laugh. Why should he display anxiety on my behalf merely because I was to be the sole occupant of an otherwise empty house for a few minutes, and in broad daylight, too! To say the least, the anxiety seemed unwarranted.

I lingered at the gate for a moment or two, wondering what was at the bottom of Mr. Holt's peculiarities, and what Sydney really proposed to gain by acting as a spy on Mr. Holt's wanderings.

I turned to re-enter the house, and as I did so, another problem suggested itself to me: what connection, of the slightest importance, could a man in Paul Lessingham's position have with the eccentric being who had established himself in such an unsatisfactory dwelling place?

Mr. Holt's story I'd only dimly understood, and it struck me that it would require a great deal of understanding. It was more like nonsense, an outcome of delirium, than a plain statement of solid facts. To tell the truth, Sydney had taken it more seriously than I expected him to. He seemed to see something in it which I emphatically did not. What seemed dubious to me, seemed clear as print to him. So far as I could judge, he actually had the presumption to imagine that Paul—my Paul—was mixed up in the very mysterious adventures of poor, weak-minded, hysterical Mr. Holt, in a manner which was hardly to his credit.

Of course, any idea of the kind was purely and simply balderdash. Exactly what bee Sydney had got in his bonnet I couldn't guess. But I did know Paul. Just let me find myself face to face with the fantastic author of Mr. Holt's weird tribulations, and I would do my best to show him that whoever played pranks with Paul Lessingham trifled with danger.

I'd returned to that historical front room which, according to Mr. Holt, had been the scene of his most disastrous burglarious attempt.

Whoever had furnished it had had original notions of the resources of modern upholstery. There wasn't a table in the place, no chair or couch, nothing to sit down on except the bed. On the floor there was a marvelous carpet which was apparently of eastern manufacture. It was so thick and pliant that moving over it was like walking on thousand- year-old turf. It was woven in gorgeous colors, and covered with…

When I discovered what it actually was covered with, I was conscious of a disagreeable sense of surprise. It was covered with beetles!

All over it, with only a few inches of space between each, were representations of some peculiar kind of beetle; it was the same beetle over and over, too. The artist had woven his undesirable subject into the material with such cunning skill that as I continued to gaze, I began to wonder if by any possibility the creatures could be alive.

In spite of the softness of the texture, and the art—of a kind—which had been displayed in the workmanship, I rapidly arrived at the conclusion that it was the most uncomfortable carpet I'd ever seen. I wagged my finger at the repeated portrayals of the—to me—unspeakable insect.

"If I'd discovered you were there before Sydney left, I think it just possible that I would have hesitated before letting him go."

Then there came a feeling of revulsion and I shook myself and muttered, "You ought to be ashamed of yourself, Marjorie Lindon, to even think such nonsense. Are you all nerves and morbid imaginings, you who have prided yourself on being so strong-minded! A pretty sort you are to do battle for anyone. Why, they're only make believe!"

Half involuntarily, I drew my foot over one of the beetles. Of course it was nothing but an image, but I seemed to feel it squelch beneath my shoe. It was disgusting.

"Come!" I cried. "This won't do! As Sydney would phrase it; am I going to make an idiot of myself?"

I turned to the window, looking at my watch. It was more than five minutes since Sydney had left. That companion of he promised to send ought to be already on the way. I decided to go and see if he was coming.

I went to the gate. There wasn't a soul in sight. It was with such a distinct sense of disappointment that I was in two minds in what to do. To remain where I was, looking, with gaping eyes, for the policeman, or the cabman, or whoever it was Sydney was dispatching to act as my temporary associate, was tantamount to acknowledging myself as a simpleton, while I was conscious of a most unmistakable reluctance to return into the house.

Common sense, or what I took for common sense, however, triumphed, and after loitering for another five minutes, I did go inside again.

This time, ignoring to the best of my ability the beetles on the floor, I proceeded to expend my curiosity—and occupy my thoughts—in an examination of the bed.

It only needed a very cursory examination, however, to show that the seeming bed was, in reality, none at all, or if it was a bed after the manner of the Easterns' it certainly wasn't after the fashion of the Britons'. There was no framework, nothing to represent the bed stand. It was simply a heap of rugs piled indiscriminately on the floor. A huge mass of them there seemed to be, of all sorts, shapes, sizes, and materials.

The top one was of white silk, in quality exquisite. It was huge, yet with a little compression, a person might almost have passed it through a proverbial wedding ring. So far as space admitted I spread it out in front of me. In the middle was a picture; whether it was embroidered on the substance or woven in it, I couldn't quite make it out. Nor at first, could I gather what it was that the artist had intended to depict. There was a brilliancy about it which was rather dazzling. By degrees, I realized that the lurid hues were meant to be flames, and when I'd gotten so far, I perceived that they were by no means badly imitated either. Then the meaning of the thing dawned on me; it was a representation of a human sacrifice. In its way, as ghastly a piece of realism as I could see.

On the right was the majestic seated figure of a goddess. Her hands were crossed on her knees, and she was naked from her waist upwards. I fancied it was meant for Isis. On her brow was perched a gaily-appareled beetle—that ubiquitous beetle—forming a bright spot of color against her coppery skin; it was an exact reproduction of the creatures which were imaged on the carpet. In front of the idol was an enormous fiery furnace. In the very heart of the flames was an altar. On the altar was a naked white woman being burned alive. There could be no doubt as to her being alive, for she was secured by chains in such a fashion that she was permitted a certain amount of freedom, of which she was availing herself to contort and twist her body into shapes which were horribly suggestive of the agony which she was enduring; the artist seemed to have exhausted his powers in his efforts to convey a vivid impression of the pains which were tormenting her.

"A pretty picture, on my word!" I said. "A pleasant taste in art the garnitures of this home suggest! The person who likes to live with this kind of thing, especially as a covering to his bed, must have his own notions as to what constitutes agreeable surroundings."

As I continued staring at the thing, all at once it seemed as if the woman on the altar moved. It was preposterous, but she appeared to gather her limbs together and turn half over.

"What can be the matter with me? Am I going mad? She can't be moving!"

If she wasn't, then certainly something was; she was lifted right into the air. An idea occurred to me and I snatched the rug aside to see what lay behind it.

As I did so, the mystery was explained!

A thin, yellow, wrinkled hand was protruding from amidst the heap of rugs; it was its action which had caused the seeming movement of the figure on the altar. I stared, confounded. The hand was followed by an arm, the arm by a shoulder, the shoulder by a head, and the most awful, hideous, wicked-looking face I'd ever seen even in my most dreadful nightmares. A pair of baleful eyes were glaring up at me.

I understood what was happening in a flash of startled amazement. Sydney, in following Mr. Holt, had started on a wild goose chase after all. I was alone with the occupant of the mysterious house, the lead actor in Mr. Holt's astounding tale.

He'd been hidden in the heap of rugs the entire time.

PART 4

Extracted From The Casebook of Augustun Champnell, Confidential Agent

Chapter 32

The conclusion of the matter has been extracted from the casebook of Augustun Champnell, confidential agent.

On the afternoon of Friday, June 2, I was entering in my casebook some memoranda having reference to the very curious matter of the Duchess of Datchet's Deed-box. It was about two o' clock. Andrews came in and placed a card on my desk. On it was inscribed, *Mr. Paul Lessingham.*

"Show Mr. Lessingham in," I said.

Andrews did as I instructed. I was of course, familiar with Mr. Lessingham's appearance, but it was the first time I'd had with him any personal communication.

He held out his hand to me. "You're Mr. Champnell?"

"I am."

"I believe that I haven't had the honor of meeting you before, Mr. Champnell, but I have had the pleasure of meeting your father, the Earl of Glenlivet."

I bowed.

He looked at me as if he was trying to make out what sort of man I was. "You're very young, Mr. Champnell."

"I've been told that youth isn't of necessity a crime."

"And you've chosen an odd profession, one in which someone hardly looks for juvenility."

"You yourself, Mr. Lessingham, aren't very old. In a statesman one expects gray hairs. Still, I'm sure I'm at a sufficient age to be able to help you."

He smiled. "I think it's possible. I've heard of you more than once, Mr. Champnell, and always to your advantage. My friend, Sir John Seymour, was telling me only the other day that you've recently conducted for him some business of a very delicate nature, with much skill and tact, and he warmly advised me if ever I found myself in a predicament to come to you. I find myself in such a predicament now."

Again I bowed.

"A predicament, I fancy, of an altogether unparalleled sort," he said. "I take it that anything I might say to you will be as though it were said to a priest. Would I be correct in that assumption?"

"You may rest assured of that."

"Good. Then to make the matter clear to you, I must begin by telling you a story, if I may trespass on your patience to that extent. I'll try not to be more verbose than the occasion requires."

I offered him a chair, placing it in such a position that the light from the window would shine full on his face. With the calmest possible air, as if unconscious of my design, he carried the chair to the other side of my desk, then twisted it right around before he sat on it. Now the light was at his back and on my face. Crossing his legs and clasping his hands on his knee, he sat in silence for some moments, as if turning something over in his mind.

He glanced around the room. "I suppose, Mr. Champnell, that some peculiar tales have been told in here."

"Some very odd ones indeed. I'm never appalled by strangeness. It's my normal atmosphere."

"And yet I should be disposed to wager that you've never listened to so strange a story as that which I'm about to tell you now. So astonishing, indeed, is the chapter in my life which I'm about to open up to you, that I have more than once had to take myself to task and fit the incidents together with mathematical accuracy in order to assure myself of its perfect truth." He paused. There was about his demeanor the suggestion of reluctance which I uncommonly discover in individuals who are about to take the skeletons from their cupboards and parade them before my eyes.

His next remark seemed to point to the fact that he perceived what was passing through my thoughts. "My position isn't rendered easier by the circumstance that I'm not of a communicative nature," he said. "I'm not in sympathy with the spirit of the age which craves for personal advertisement. I hold that the private life even of a public man should be held inviolate. I resent, with peculiar bitterness, the attempts of prying eyes to peer into matters which, as it seems to me, concern myself alone. You must, therefore bear with me, Mr. Champnell, if I seem awkward in disclosing to you certain incidents in my career which I'd hoped would stay locked in the secret vault of my own heart; at any rate until I was carried to the grave. I'm sure you'll suffer me to stand excused if I frankly admit that it's only an irresistible chain of events which has forced me to make of you a confidant."

"My experience tells me, Mr. Lessingham, that no one ever comes to me until they have no choice in the matter. In that respect, I'm regarded as something worse even than a doctor."

A wintry smile flitted across his features, it was clear that he regarded me as a good deal worse than a doctor. He drew in a breath and began to tell me one of the most remarkable tales which I'd ever heard. As he proceeded, I began to understood his reluctance to speak. On the mere score of credibility he must have greatly preferred to have kept his own counsel. For my part I own, unreservedly, that I would have deemed the tale incredible had it been told me by some stranger that had come in off the street, instead of by Paul Lessingham.

Chapter 33

He began slowly, halting sometimes to gather himself, and by degrees his voice grew firmer, the words coming from him with greater fluency.

"I'm not yet forty. So when I tell you that twenty years ago I was a mere youth, I'm stating what's a sufficiently obvious truth. It's been twenty years ago since the events of which I'm going to speak transpired.

"I lost both my parents when I was a lad, and by their death I was left in a position in which I was, to an unusual extent in one so young, my own master. I was ever of a rambling turn of mind, and when at the mature age of eighteen, I left school, I decided I should learn more from travel than from sojourn at a university. So, since there was no one to say no, instead of going either to Oxford or Cambridge, I went abroad. After a few months I found myself in Egypt. I was down with fever at Shepheard's Hotel in Cairo. I'd caught it by drinking polluted water during an excursion with some Bedouins to Palmyra.

"When the fever had left me I went out one night into the town in search of amusement. I went, unaccompanied, into the native quarter, not a wise thing to do, especially at night, but at eighteen one isn't always wise, and I was weary of the monotony of the sick room, and eager for something which had in it a spice of adventure. I soon found myself in a street which I've reason to believe no longer exists. It had a French name, and was called the Rue de Rabagas. I saw the name on the corner as I turned into it, and it has left an impression on my memory which is never likely to be obliterated.

"It was a narrow street, and of course a dirty one, ill-lit, and apparently at the moment of my appearance, deserted. I'd gone perhaps halfway down its tortuous length, wondering what fantastic whim had brought me into such unsavory quarters, and what would happen to me if—as seemed extremely possible—I lost my way. Suddenly, I heard sounds which came from a house which I was passing, sounds of music and singing.

"I paused and stood a while to listen. There was an open window on my right, which was screened by latticed blinds. From the room which was behind these blinds the sounds were coming. Someone was singing, accompanied by an instrument resembling a guitar, and singing uncommonly well."

Mr. Lessingham stopped. A stream of recollection seemed to come flooding over him. A dreamy look came into his eyes.

"I remember it all as clearly as if it were yesterday. How it all comes back, the dirty street, the evil smells, the imperfect light, the girl's voice filling the air. It was a girl's voice, full and sweet. She sang a little tune, which just then, half of Europe was humming—it occurred in an opera which they were acting at one of the Boulevard theatres, 'La P'tite Voyageuse.' The effect, coming so unexpectedly, was startling. I stood and heard her to the end.

"Inspired by I know not what impulse of curiosity, when the song was finished, I moved one of the lattice blinds a little aside, so as to enable me to get a glimpse of the singer. I then found myself looking into what seemed to be a sort of cafe, one of those places which are found all over the continent, in which women sing in order to attract customers. There was a low platform at one end of the room, and on it were seated three women. One of them had evidently just been accompanying her own song, as she still had an instrument of music in her hands, and was striking a few idle notes. The other two had been acting as an audience. They were attired in the fantastic apparel which the women who are found in such places generally wear. An old woman was sitting in a corner, knitting; I took her to be a regular customer. With the exception of these four the place was empty.

"They must have heard me touch the lattice in the window, or seen it moving, for no sooner did I glance within than the three pairs of eyes on the platform were raised and fixed on mine. The old woman in the corner alone showed no awareness of me. We looked at one another in silence for a second or two, then the girl with the harp called out to me,

'Entrez, monsieur! Soye lé bienvenu!'"

"I was a little tired but rather curious as to where I was, the place struck me, even at that first momentary glimpse, as hardly in the ordinary line of that kind of thing. So not unwilling to listen to a repetition of the former song, or to another sung by the same singer, I said, 'On one condition; that you sing me another song.'

" 'Ah, monsieur, with the greatest pleasure in the world I'll sing you twenty,' she said, and she was almost, if not quite, as good as her word. She entertained me with song after song. I may safely say that I have seldom if ever heard melody more enchanting. All languages seemed to be the same to her. She sang in French and Italian, German and English, and in tongues with which I was unfamiliar. It was in these Eastern harmonies that she was most successful. They were indescribably weird and thrilling, and she delivered them with a verve and sweetness which was amazing. I sat at one of the little tables with which the room was dotted, listening and entranced.

"Time passed more rapidly than I supposed. While she sang I sipped the liquor with which the old woman had supplied me. So enthralled was I by the display of the girl's astonishing gifts that I didn't notice what it was I was drinking. Looking back I can only surmise that it was some poisonous concoction of the old woman. That one small glass had the strangest effect on me. I was still weak from the fever which I'd only just succeeded in shaking off, and that no doubt had something to do with the result. But as I continued to sit, I was conscious that I was sinking into a lethargic condition, against which I was incapable of struggling.

"After a while the original performer ceased, her companions took her place, and she came and joined me at my table. Looking at my watch, I was surprised to see the lateness of the hour. I rose to leave but she caught me by the wrist.

" 'Don't go,' she said. She spoke English of a sort, and with the queerest accent. 'All is well with you. Rest a while.'

"Her touch had on me what I can only describe as a magnetic influence. As her fingers closed upon my wrist, I felt as powerless in her grasp as if she held me with bands of steel. What seemed an invitation was virtually a command. I had to stay whether I wanted to or not. She called for more liquor, and at what again was really her command, I drank of it. I don't think that after she touched my wrist I uttered a single word. She did all the talking, and while she talked, she kept her eyes fixed on my face. Those eyes of hers! They were a devil's. I can positively affirm that they had on me a diabolical effect. They robbed me of my consciousness, of my power of volition, of my capacity to think; they made me as wax in her hands. My last recollection of that fatal night is of her sitting in front of me, bending over the table, stroking my wrist with her extended fingers, staring at me with her awful eyes. After that, a curtain seems to descend, and then there comes a period of oblivion."

Mr. Lessingham ceased talking. His manner was calm and self-contained enough, but in spite of that I could see that the mere recollection of the things which he told me moved him to his foundations. There was eloquence in the drawn lines around his mouth, and in the strained expression of his eyes.

So far his tale was sufficiently commonplace. Places such as the one which he described abound in the Cairo of today, and many are the Englishmen who have entered them to their exceeding bitter cost. With that keen intuition which has done him yeoman's service in the political arena, Mr. Lessingham at once perceived the direction my thoughts were taking.

"You've heard this tale before then?" he asked. "No doubt far too often. The traps are many, and the fools and the unwary aren't few. But take note, the oddness of my experience is still to come. You must forgive me if I seem to stumble in the telling. I'm anxious to present my case with as little exaggeration as possible. Though I fear some exaggeration unavoidable. My case is so unique, and so out of the common run of our everyday experience, that the plainest possible statement must smack of the sensational.

"As you may have guessed, when understanding returned to me, I found myself in an apartment with which I was unfamiliar. I was lying, undressed, on a heap of rugs in a corner of a low-pitched room which was furnished in a fashion which, when I grasped the details, filled me with amazement. By my side knelt the Woman of the Songs. Leaning over, she covered my mouth with kisses. I can't describe to you the sense of horror and of loathing with which the contact of her lips gave me. There was about her something so unnatural, so inhuman, that I believe even then I could have killed her with as little sense of moral turpitude as if she'd been some noxious insect.

" 'Where am I?' I exclaimed.

" 'You're with the children of Isis,' she replied. What she meant I didn't know, and don't to this day. 'You're in the hands of the great goddess, of the mother of men.'

" 'How did I come here?'

" 'By the loving kindness of the great mother.'

"Of course I don't pretend to give you the exact text of her words, but they were to that effect. Half raising myself on the heap of rugs, I gazed about me, and was astounded at what I saw.

"The place in which I was, though the reverse of lofty, was of considerable size. I couldn't conceive where it could be. The walls and roof were of bare stone, as though the entire massive room had been hewed out of solid rock. It seemed to be some sort of temple, and was redolent with the most extraordinary odor. An altar stood in the center, fashioned out of a single block of stone. On it a fire burned with a faint blue flame, and the fumes which rose from it were no doubt chiefly responsible for the prevailing perfumes. Behind it was a huge bronze figure, more than life-size. It was in a sitting posture, and represented a woman. Although it resembled no portrayal of a woman I'd ever seen either before or since, I came afterwards to understand that it was meant to be Isis. On the idol's brow was poised a beetle. That the creature was alive seemed clear, for as I looked at it, the beetle opened and closed its wings.

"If the one on the forehead of the goddess was the only live beetle which the place contained, it wasn't the only representation. The image was modeled in the solid stone of the roof, and depicted in flaming colors on wall hangings. Wherever I looked it rested on a scarab. The effect was bewildering. It was as though I saw things through the distorted view of a nightmare. I asked myself if I wasn't still dreaming, that my appearance of consciousness wasn't after all a mere delusion, and if I'd actually regained my senses.

"And, here, Mr. Champnell, I wish to point out, and to emphasize the fact, that I'm not prepared to positively affirm what portion of my adventures in that extraordinary and horrible place, was in actuality not the product of a feverish imagination. Had I been persuaded that all I thought I saw was indeed fact, I would have opened my lips long ago no matter what the consequences to myself might have been. But there is the crux. The events were so incredible, and my condition was such an abnormal one. I was never really myself from the first moment to the last. That I've hesitated, and still do hesitate, to assert where precisely fiction ended and fact began.

"With some misty notion of testing my actual condition I attempted to get off the heap of rugs on which I reclined. As I did so the woman at my side laid her hand against my chest, lightly. But had her gentle pressure been the equivalent of a ton of iron, it couldn't have been more effectual. I collapsed and sank back on the rugs to lay there, panting for breath, wondering if I had crossed the border line which divides madness from sanity.

" 'Let me get up! Let me go!' I gasped.

" 'Nay,' she murmured, 'stay with me yet a while, O my beloved.'

"And again she kissed me."

Once more Mr. Lessingham paused, as an involuntary shudder went over him. In spite of the evidently great effort which he was making to retain his self-control, his features were contorted by an anguished spasm. For some seconds he seemed at a loss to find words to continue.

When he did go on, his voice was harsh and strained.

"I'm altogether incapable of even hinting to you the nauseous nature of that woman's kisses. They filled me with an indescribable repulsion. I look back at them with a feeling of physical, mental, and moral horror, even across an interval of twenty years. The most dreadful part of it was that I was totally incapable of offering even the faintest resistance to her caresses. I lay there like a log. She did with me as she wished, and in agony I endured."

He took his handkerchief from his pocket, and although the day was cool, he wiped the perspiration from his brow.

"To dwell in detail on what occurred during my involuntary sojourn in that fearful place is beyond my power. I can't even venture to attempt it. The attempt, were it made, would be futile, and to me, painful beyond measure. I seem to have seen all that happened in a fog, with about it all an element of unreality. As I've already remarked, the things which revealed themselves, though dimly, to my perception, seemed too bizarre, too hideous to be true.

"It was only afterwards, when I was in a position to compare dates, that I was able to determine what had been the length of my imprisonment. It appears that I was in that horrible den for more than two months, two unspeakable months. The entire time there were comings and goings, a phantasmagoric array of eerie figures continually passing back and forth before my hazy eyes. What I judge to have been religious services took place, in which the altar, the bronze image, and the beetle on its brow, figured largely. Not only were they conducted with a bewildering confusion of mysterious rites, but if my memory is in the least degree trustworthy, they were orgies of nameless horrors. I seem to have seen things take place that at the mere thought of them, the mind reels and trembles.

"Indeed it's in connection with the cult of the obscene deity to whom these wretched creatures paid their scandalous vows that my most awful memories seem to be associated. It may have all been a mirage born of my half-delirious state, but it seemed to me that they offered human sacrifices."

When Mr. Lessingham said this, I pricked up my ears. For reasons of my own, which will immediately transpire, I'd been wondering if he would make any reference to a human sacrifice. He noted my display of interest, but misunderstood the cause.

"I see you start. I don't wonder why. But I repeat that unless I was the victim of some extraordinary species of double sight—in which case the whole business would resolve itself into the fabric of a dream—I saw on more than one occasion a human sacrifice offered on that stone altar, presumably to the grim image which looked down on it. And, unless I'm mistaken, in each case the sacrificial object was a woman, naked, as white as you or I, and before they burned her they subjected her to every variety of outrage of which only the minds of demons could conceive. More than once since then I've seemed to hear the shrieks of the victims ringing through the air, mingled with the triumphant cries of their frenzied murderers, and the music of their harps.

"It was the cumulative horrors of such a scene which gave me the strength, or the courage, or the madness, I know not which it was, to burst the bonds which bound me, and which even in the bursting, made of me even to this hour, a haunted man.

"There had been a sacrifice, unless as I've repeatedly observed, the whole thing was nothing but a dream. A woman—a young and lovely Englishwoman, if I could believe the evidence of my own eyes—had been savaged and burned alive, while I lay there helpless, looking on. When the business was concluded, and the ashes of the victim had been consumed by the participants, the worshippers departed.

"I was then left alone with the Woman of the Songs, who apparently acted as the guardian of that slaughterhouse. She was, as usual after such an orgy, more a devil than a human being, drunk with an insensate frenzy, and delirious with inhuman longings. As she approached to offer to me her loathed caresses, I was suddenly conscious of something which I hadn't felt before when in her company. It was as though something had slipped away from me, some weight which had oppressed me, some bond by which I'd been bound. I was filled with a sense of freedom, to a knowledge that the blood which coursed through my veins was after all my own, and that I was master of my own destiny.

"I can only suppose that through all those weeks she'd kept me there in a state of mesmeric stupor, and by taking advantage of the weakness which the fever had left behind, and by the exercise of her diabolical arts, that she hadn't allowed me to pass out of a condition of hypnotic trance.

"But now, for some reason, the cord was loosened. Possibly her absorption in her religious duties had caused her to forget to tighten it. So as she came towards me, she approached a man for the first time in many days who was his own man. She seemed totally unconscious of anything of the kind. As she drew nearer to me, she appeared to be entirely oblivious of the fact that I was anything but the fibreless, emasculated creature which, up to that moment, she'd made of me.

"But she knew it when she touched me, when she stooped to press her lips to mine. At that instant the accumulating rage which had been smoldering inside me through all those leaden, torturing hours, sprang into life. "Leaping off my bed of rugs, I wrapped my hands around her throat—then she knew I was awake! She quickly strove to tighten the mental noose which she'd suffered to become unduly loose. Her baleful eyes were fixed on mine. I knew that she was putting out her utmost force to control me, but I fought with her like one possessed, and I won—in a fashion. I compressed her throat with my two hands as if they were an iron vice. I knew that I was struggling for more than life, that the odds were against me, that I was staking my all upon the rolling of the dice.

"Tighter and tighter my pressure grew around her neck. I didn't know if I was truly killing her until suddenly…" Mr. Lessingham stopped. He stared with fixed, glassy eyes, as if the scene was being re-enacted in front of him. His voice faltered. I thought he would break down, but with an effort, he continued, "Suddenly, I felt her slipping from between my fingers. Without the slightest warning she instantly vanished, and where not a moment before she had been, I now found myself confronting a monstrous beetle, a huge, writhing creation of some wild nightmare.

"At first the creature stood as high as I did. But as I stared at it, in stupefied amazement, as you may easily imagine, the thing dwindled while I watched. I didn't stop to see how far the process of dwindling continued, for acting as a stark raving madman, I got to my feet and fled as if all the fiends in Hell were nipping at my heels."

Chapter 34

"How I reached the open air I can't tell you," Mr. Lessingham continued. "I have a confused recollection of rushing through vaulted passages, through endless corridors, of trampling over people who tried to stop me, and the rest is blank.

"When I again came to myself I was lying in the house of an American missionary named Clements. Apparently I'd been found at early dawn, stark naked, in a Cairo street, and picked up for dead. Judging from appearances I must have wandered for miles, all through the night. Where I'd come from or where I was going, none could tell, and I couldn't tell myself. For weeks I hovered between life and death. The kindness of Mr. and Mrs. Clements wasn't to be measured by words. I was brought to their house a penniless, helpless, battered stranger, and they gave me all they had to offer, with no expectation of an earthly reward. Let no one pretend that there is no Christian charity under the sun. The debt I owed that man and woman I was never able to repay. Before I was properly myself again, and in a position to offer some adequate testimony of the gratitude I felt, Mrs. Clements was dead, drowned during an excursion on the Nile, and her husband had departed on a missionary expedition into Central Africa, from which he never returned.

"Although my physical health returned, for months after I'd left my hospitable hosts I was in a state of semi-imbecility. I suffered from a species of aphasia. For days I was speechless, and could remember nothing, not even my own name. When that stage had finally passed and I began to move more freely among my fellows, for years I was but a wreck of my former self. I was visited, at all hours of the day and night, by frightful visions; though I know not whether to call them visions. They were real enough to me, but since they were visible to no one but me, perhaps that's the word which best describes them. Their presence invariably plunged me into a state of abject terror, against which I was unable to even make a show of fighting. To such an extent did they embitter my existence, that I voluntarily placed myself under the treatment of an expert in mental pathology. For a considerable period of time I was under his constant supervision, but the visitations were as inexplicable to him as they were to me.

"By degrees, however, they became rarer and rarer, until at last I flattered myself that I had once more become as other men. After an interval, to make sure, I devoted myself to politics. Since then I've lived, as they phrase it, 'in the public eye.' Private life, in any peculiar sense of the term, I've had none."

Mr. Lessingham stopped talking. His tale wasn't uninteresting, and to say the least of it, I was curious. But I still was at a loss to understand what it had to do with me, or what was the reason he'd come to see me. Since he remained silent, as if the matter as far as he was concerned was at an end, I told him so.

"I presume, Mr. Lessingham, that all this is but a prelude. At present I don't see where it is that I come in."

He was silent for a few moments, and when he finally spoke his voice was grave and somber, as if he were burdened by a weight of woe.

"Unfortunately, as you put it, all this has been but a prelude. Were it not so I wouldn't now stand in such pressing want of the services of a confidential agent, that is, of an experienced man of the world, who's been endowed with phenomenal perceptive faculties, and in whose capacity and honor I can place complete confidence."

I smiled, the compliment was a pointed one. "I hope your estimate of me is not too high."

"I hope not, for my sake, as well as for your own. I've heard great things of you. If ever a man stood in need of all that human skill and acumen can do for him, it's myself."

His words aroused my curiosity. I was conscious of feeling more interested than before. "I'll do my best for you, sir. A man can do no more."

"Excellent." He looked at me long and earnestly. Then leaning forward, he lowered his voice and said, "The fact is, Mr. Champnell, that quite recently events have happened which threaten to bridge the chasm of twenty years, and to place me face to face with that plague spot of the past. At this moment I stand in imminent peril of becoming again the wretched thing I was when I fled from that den of devils. It's to guard me against this that I've come to you. I want you to unravel the tangled thread which threatens to drag me to my doom, and when unraveled, to sunder it forever in two."

"Do explain further," I said. To be frank, for the moment I thought him mad.

"Three weeks ago," he said, "when I returned late one night from a sitting in the House of Commons, I found on my study table a sheet of paper on which there was a representation—marvelously like—of the creature into which, as it seemed to me, the Woman of the Songs was transformed as I clutched her throat between my hands. The mere sight of it brought back one of those visions of which I've told you, and which I thought I'd done with forever. I was convulsed by an agony of fear, and thrown into a state approximating to a paralysis of both mind and body."

"But why?"

"I can't tell you. I only know that I've never dared to allow my thoughts to recur to that last dreaded scene, lest the mere recurrence drive me mad."

"What exactly was this that you found on your study table? Was it merely a drawing?"

"It was a representation, produced by what process I can't say, which was so wonderfully, so diabolically like the original, that for a moment I thought the thing itself was on my table."

"Who put it there?"

"That's precisely what I wish you to find out," he said. "What I wish you to make it your business to ascertain. I've found the thing, under similar circumstances, on three separate occasions on my study table, and each time it's had on me the same hideous effect."

"Each time after you returned from a late sitting in the House of Commons?"

"Exactly," he nodded.

"Where are these—what shall I call them—illustrations?"

"That, again, I can't tell you."

"What do you mean?"

"Exactly what I say. Each time, when I recovered, the thing had vanished."

"Sheet of paper and all?"

"Apparently, though on that point I couldn't be positive. You'll understand that my study table is apt to be littered with sheets of paper, and I couldn't absolutely determine that the thing hadn't stared at me from one of those. The illustration itself certainly had vanished."

I began to suspect that this was a case rather for a doctor than for a man of my profession, and hinted as much. "Don't you think it's possible, Mr. Lessingham, that you've been overworking yourself so that you've been driving your brain too hard, and that you've been the victim of an optical delusion?"

"I thought so myself; I may say that I almost hoped so. But wait till I've finished. You'll find that there is no loophole in that direction."

He appeared to be recalling events in their due order. His manner was studiously cold, as if he were endeavoring, despite the strangeness of his story, to impress me with the literal accuracy of each syllable he uttered.

"The night before last, on returning home, I found in my study a stranger," he said.

"A stranger?"

"Yes. In other words, a burglar."

"A burglar? I see. Go on."

He'd paused and his demeanor was becoming odder and odder.

"On my entry he was engaged in breaking into my bureau. I need hardly say that I tried to stop him. But I couldn't."

"You couldn't? How do you mean 'you couldn't'?"

"I mean simply what I say. You must understand that this was no ordinary felon. Of what nationality he was I can't tell you. He only uttered two words, and they were certainly in English, but apart from that he was dumb. He wore no covering on his head or feet. Indeed, his only garment was a long, dark-flowing cloak which, as it fluttered about him, revealed that his limbs were bare."

"An unique costume for a burglar," I said.

"The instant I saw him I realized that he was in some way connected with that adventure in the Rue de Rabagas. What he said and did proved it to the hilt."

"What did he say and do?"

"As I approached to effect his capture, he pronounced aloud two words which recalled that awful scene the recollection of which always lingers in my brain, and of which I never dare to permit myself to think. Their very utterance threw me into a sort of convulsion."

"What were the words?"

Mr. Lessingham opened his mouth and then snapped it closed. A marked change took place in the expression of his countenance. His eyes became fixed and staring, resembling the glassy orbs of the somnambulist. For a moment I feared that he was going to give me an object lesson in the 'visions' of which I'd heard so much. I rose to offer him assistance but he motioned me back.

"Thank you. It will pass." His voice was dry and husky, unlike his usual silver tones. After an uncomfortable interval he managed to continue. "You see for yourself, Mr. Champnell, what a miserable weakling, when this subject is broached, I still remain. I can't utter the words the stranger uttered, I can't even write them down. For some inscrutable reason they have on me an effect similar to that which spells and incantations had on people in tales of witchcraft."

"I suppose, Mr. Lessingham, that there is no doubt that this mysterious stranger wasn't himself an optical delusion?"

"Scarcely. My servants can prove the contrary."

"So your servants saw him?"

"Some of them, yes. Then there's the evidence of the bureau. The fellow had smashed the top right in two. When I examined the contents I learned that a packet of letters was missing. They were letters which I'd received from Miss Lindon, a lady whom I hope to make my wife. This, also, I tell you in confidence."

"What use would he be likely to make of them?"

"If matters stand as I fear they do, he might make a very serious misuse of them. If the object of these wretches, after all these years, is revenge, they would be capable, having discovered what she is to me, of working Miss Lindon a fatal mischief, or at the very least, of poisoning her mind."

"I see. How did the thief escape, did he, like the illustrations, vanish into thin air?"

"No, he escaped by the much more normal method of crashing through the drawing room window, and clambering down from the verandah and into the street, where he ran right into someone else's arms."

"Into whose arms, a constable's?"

"No, into Mr. Atherton's arms, Sydney Atherton."

"The inventor?"

"The same. Do you know him?" he asked.

"I do. Sydney Atherton and I are friends of a good many years' standing. But Atherton must have seen where he came from. And anyhow, if the man was in the state of undress which you've described, why didn't Atherton stop him?"

"Mr. Atherton's reasons were his own. He didn't stop him, and so far as I can learn, he didn't attempt to stop him. Instead, he knocked at my front door to inform me that he'd seen a man climb out of my window."

"I happen to know that, at certain seasons, Atherton is an odd fish, but that sounds very odd indeed."

"The truth is, Mr. Champnell, that if it weren't for Mr. Atherton, I doubt if I would have troubled you even now. The accident of his being an acquaintance of yours makes my task easier."

He drew his chair closer to me with an air of briskness which had been foreign to him before. For some reason, which I was unable to fathom, the introduction of Atherton's name seemed to have enlivened him. However, I wasn't long to remain in the darkness. In half a dozen sentences he threw more light on the real cause of his visit to me than he'd done in all that had been said before. His bearing, too, was more businesslike and to the point. For the first time I had some glimmerings of the politician as he's known to all the world; alert, keen and eager.

"Mr. Atherton, like myself, is also a suitor for Miss Lindon's hand in marriage. Because I've succeeded where he has failed, he's chosen to be angry. It seems that he's had dealings, either with my visitor or with some other of his acquaintance, and he proposes to use what he's gleaned from him to the disadvantage of my character. In fact, I've just come from Mr.

Atherton and from hints he dropped I conclude that probably during the last few hours he's had an interview with someone who was connected in some way with that lurid patch in my career, and that this person made so-called revelations which were nothing but a series of monstrous lies. That these so-called revelations Mr. Atherton has threatened, in so many words to place before Miss Lindon, is an eventuality which I wish to avoid. My own conviction is that there is at this moment in London an emissary from that den in the Rue de Rabagas—for all I know it may be the Woman of the Songs herself.

"Whether the sole reason of this individual's presence is to do me injury I'm as yet in no position to say, but that it's supposed to cause me mischief is plain. I believe that Mr. Atherton knows more about this person and whereabouts than he's been willing to admit. So I want you to ascertain these things on my behalf; to find out what, and where, this person is, to drag her or him, out into the light of day. In short, I want you to effectually protect me from the terrorism which threatens once more to overwhelm my mental and my physical self, which bids to destroy my intellect, my career, my life, my everything."

"What reason have you for suspecting that Mr. Atherton has seen this individual of whom you speak, has he told you so?"

"Practically, yes."

"I know Atherton well. In his not infrequent moments of excitement he's apt to use strong language, but it goes no further. I believe him to be the last person in the world to do anyone an intentional injustice, under any circumstances whatever. If I go to him, armed with credentials from you, and when he understands the real gravity of the situation—which it will be my business to make him do—I believe that of his own accord he will tell me as much about this mysterious individual as he knows."

"Then go to him at once," he said.

"I will, and when I have the answers you seek, I'll be in touch." I rose from my seat, and as I did so, someone rushed into the outer office with a din and a clatter. I heard Andrews' voice, along with another voice, become distinctly audible, though Andrews' voice was raised in vigorous expostulation.

But it was raised seemingly in vain, for presently the door of my own particular sanctum was thrown open with a crash, and Mr. Sydney Atherton himself came dashing in, conspicuously under the influence of one of those not infrequent 'moments of excitement' of which I'd just been speaking.

Chapter 35

Mr. Atherton didn't wait to see who might or might not be present, and without even pausing to take a breath, he broke into full cry on the instant, as he did occasionally.

"Champnell! Thank God I've found you in! I need you at once! Don't stop to talk, just stick your hat on and put your best foot forward, I'll tell you all about it in the cab."

I endeavored to call his attention to Mr. Lessingham's presence, but without success. "My dear fellow…"

He cut me short. "Don't 'dear fellow' me! None of your jabber! And none of your excuses either! I don't care if you've got an engagement with the Queen; you'll have to chuck it. Where's that damn hat of yours, or are you going without it? Didn't I tell you that every second wasted may mean the difference between life and death? Do you want me to drag you down to the cab by the hair of your head?"

"I'll try not to constrain you to quite so drastic a resource, and I was coming with you in any case. I only wanted to call your attention to the fact that I'm not alone. Mr. Lessingham's here, too."

In his haste Mr. Lessingham had gone unnoticed. Now that Atherton's observation was particularly directed to Mr. Lessingham, he started, turned, and glared at my latest client in a fashion which was scarcely flattering.

"Oh! It is you, is it? What the hell are you doing here?" Before Lessingham could reply to this most unceremonious query, Atherton, rushing forward, gripped him by the arm. "Have you seen her?"

Mr. Lessingham, not unnaturally nonplussed by the other's curious conduct, stared at him in unmistakable amazement. "Have I seen whom?" he asked.

"Marjorie Lindon!"

"Marjorie Lindon?" Mr. Lessingham paused. He was evidently asking himself what the inquiry meant. "I haven't seen Miss Lindon since last night. Why do you ask?"

"Then Heaven help us! As I'm a living man I believe he, she, or it has gotten her!" Atherton said.

His words were incomprehensible enough to stand in copious need of explanation, as Mr. Lessingham plainly thought. "What is it that you mean, sir?"

"I believe that Oriental friend of yours has gotten her in her clutches, if it is a 'her,' hell, who knows what the infernal conjurer's real sex may be."

"Atherton! Explain yourself!" Suddenly Mr. Lessingham's tones rang out like a trumpet call. "If damage comes to her I'll be fit to cut my throat, and yours!" What Mr. Lessingham did next surprised me. I imagine it surprised Atherton even more. Springing at Atherton like a tiger, he caught him by the throat. "You, you hound! What have you done? If so much as a hair on her head is injured you'll repay it to me ten thousand fold! You mischief-making, meddling, jealous fool!"

Mr. Lessingham shook Sydney as if he was a rat, then flung him headlong to the floor. It reminded me of nothing so much as Othello's treatment of Iago. Never had I seen a man so transformed by rage. Mr. Lessingham seemed to have positively increased in stature. As he stood glowering down at the prostrate Atherton, he might have stood for a materialistic conception of human retribution.

Atherton was more surprised than hurt. For a moment or two he lay quite still. Then, lifting his head, he looked up at his assailant. Raising himself to his feet, he shook himself, as if he was checking to see if all his bones were whole. Putting his hands up to his neck, he rubbed it gently, grinned, and said, "By God, Lessingham, there's more in you than I thought. You are a man after all. There's some holding power in those wrists of yours; they've nearly broken my neck. When this business is finished, I'd like to put on the gloves with you and fight it out. You're wasted on politics. Damn it, man, give me your hand!"

Mr. Lessingham didn't give Atherton his hand. Atherton took it and gave it a hearty shake with both of his. If the first paroxysm of his passion had passed, Mr. Lessingham was still sufficiently stern.

"Be so good as not to play with me, Mr. Atherton. If what you say is correct, and the wretch to whom you allude really has Miss Lindon at her mercy, then the woman I love—and whom you also pretend to love—stands in imminent peril not only of a ghastly death, but of what is infinitely worse than death."

"The hell she does!" Mr. Atherton wheeled around towards me. "Champnell, haven't you got that hat of yours yet? Don't stand there like a tailor's dummy, move yourself! I'll tell you all about it in the cab. And, Lessingham, if you want to come with us, I'll tell you, too."

Chapter 36

Three in a cab is not, under any circumstances, the most comfortable method of conveyance, especially when one of the trio happens to be Sydney Atherton in one of his 'moments of excitement', as Mr. Lessingham and I both quickly found out.

Sometimes he sat on my knees, sometimes on Lessingham's, and frequently, when he unexpectedly stood up and all but precipitated himself to fall out, he stood up. In the eagerness of his gesticulations, first he knocked off my hat, then he knocked off Lessingham's, then his own, then all three together, once his own hat rolling into the mud. He sprang into the road without previously going through the empty form of advising the driver of his intention to pick it up. When he turned to speak to Lessingham, he thrust his elbow into my eye, and when he turned to speak to me, he thrust it into Lessingham's. Never, for one solitary instant, was he at rest, or either of us at ease. The wonder is that the gymnastics in which he incessantly indulged didn't sufficiently attract public notice to induce a policeman to put at least a momentary halt to our progress. Had speed not been of primary importance, I would have insisted on the transference of the expedition to the somewhat wider limits of a four-wheeler.

The explanation of the causes of his agitation was apparently more comprehensible to Lessingham than it was to me. I had to piece this and that together under considerable difficulties, but slowly I arrived at something like a clear notion of what had actually taken place.

Atherton commenced by addressing Lessingham, and thrusting his elbow into my eye. "Did Marjorie tell you about the fellow she found in the street?" Up went his arm to force the trap door open overhead, and off went my hat. "Driver, go faster! If you kill the horse I'll buy you another!"

We were already going much faster than legal, but that wasn't a matter of the slightest consequence.

Lessingham replied to his inquiry, "No, she didn't."

"You know the fellow I saw coming out of your drawing room window?"

"Yes."

"Well, Marjorie found him the morning after in front of her home, in the middle of the street. It seems he'd been wandering around all night, unclothed, in the rain and the mud, in a condition of hypnotic trance."

"Who's the gentleman you're alluding to?" Lessingham asked.

"He says his name's Holt, Robert Holt."

"Holt? Is he an Englishman?"

"Very much so. He'd lost his job and was stone broke! Then he got the boot from the shelter because it was full, the poor devil!"

"Are you sure?"

"Of what?"

"Are you sure that this man, Robert Holt, is the same person whom, as you put it, you saw coming out of my drawing room window?"

"Sure! Of course I'm sure! Think I didn't recognize him? Besides, there was the man's own tale, told by him personally."

"You must remember, Mr. Atherton, that I'm fully in the dark as to what has happened. What has the man, Holt, to do with the errand on which we're bound?" Lessingham asked.

"Am I not coming to it? If you'd let me tell the tale in my own way I'd get there in less than no time, but you keep on cutting in. How the hell do you suppose Champnell is to make head or tail of the business if you persist in interrupting? Now, where was I? Oh yes. Marjorie took the beggar in and he told his tale to her. She sent for me; caught me on the steps after I'd been lunching with Dora Grayling. Holt retold his yarn—I smelled a rat— saw that a connection possibly existed between the thief who'd been playing conjuring tricks off on to me and this interesting party down Fulham way."

"What party down Fulham way?" Lessingham asked.

"This friend of Holt's; am I not telling you? There you go again, you won't let me finish! When Holt slipped through the window to get out of the rain, the dusky-colored charmer caught him in the act, doctored him up in a trance, then sent him out to commit burglary by proxy. I said to Holt, 'Show us this little house you came across, young man.' Holt was game, then Marjorie said that she wanted to go and see it too. I said, 'You'll be sorry if you do.' But it did the exact opposite. After that she'd have gone no matter what. I never did have a persuasive way with women. So off we went, Marjorie, Holt, and I. We spotted the house in less than no time, and invited ourselves in by the kitchen window. The house seemed empty. Presently Holt became hypnotized before my eyes, the best established case of hypnotism by suggestion I've ever encountered. Then he started off on a pilgrimage of one. Like an idiot I followed, leaving Marjorie to wait for me."

"Alone?" Lessingham asked.

"Yes, alone! Am I not telling you? Great Scott, Lessingham, in the House of Commons they must be hazy to think you smart! I said, 'I'll send the first sane soul I meet to keep you company.' But as luck would have it, I never met one, only kids and a baker, who wouldn't leave his cart, or take it with him either. I'd covered pretty nearly two miles before I came across a policeman, and when I did the man thought me mad, or drunk, or both. By the time I'd got myself within nodding distance of being run in for obstructing the police in the execution of their duty, without inducing him to move a single one of his twenty-four-inch feet, Holt was out of sight. So, there was nothing left for me to do but return to Marjorie, but when I did I found the house empty and Marjorie gone."

"I don't quite follow," Lessingham said.

"Of course you don't quite follow," Atherton replied, "and you'll follow still less if you keep interrupting. I checked the entire house inside and out, shouted myself hoarse but Marjorie was gone. As I was coming down the stairs for about the tenth time, I stepped on something hard which was lying in the hallway. I picked it up, it was a ring; this ring."

He held it up so we could see. The ring was bent, and I assumed it was from when Atherton had stepped on it. Mr. Lessingham wriggled to one side to enable him to see better, then he made a snatch at it.

"It's mine!" he cried.

Atherton pulled back so the ring was out of Lessingham's reach. "What do you mean, it's yours?"

"It's the ring I gave Marjorie for an engagement ring. Give it me! Unless you wish me to do you violence in the cab."

With complete disregard of the limitations of space, or of my comfort, Lessingham gripped Atherton by the wrist and seized him, Atherton yielding just in time to save himself from being ejected into the street. Relinquished of his treasure, Atherton turned and surveyed Lessingham with something like a glance of admiration.

"Damn it, Lessingham, I never would have believed there was that much fire inside you."

Lessingham seemed to pay no attention to Atherton whatever. He was surveying the ring, which Atherton had trampled out of shape, with looks of the deepest concern.

"Yes, it is Marjorie's ring! The one I gave her! Something serious must have happened to her before she would have dropped my ring and left it lying where it fell."

Atherton went on, "When it was clear that there she wasn't, I tore off to find out where she was. I came across old man Lindon, but he knew nothing. I rather fancy I startled him in the middle of Pall Mall, because when I left he stared after me like one possessed, and his hat was lying in the gutter. I went home but she wasn't there. I asked Dora Grayling, she'd seen nothing of her. No one had seen anything of her, she'd vanished into thin air. Then I said to myself, 'You're a first-class idiot. While you're looking for her like a lost sheep, the betting is that the girl's in Holt's friend's house the whole bloody time. When I was there, the chances are that she'd just stepped out for a stroll, and that now she's back again, and wondering where on earth I've gone!' So I made up my mind that I'd go back and see, because the idea of her standing on the front doorstep looking for me, while I was going off my nut looking for her was too funny to laugh. On my way it struck me that it would be a good idea to pick up Champnell, because if there's a man who can find a needle in a haystack, it's the great Augustus Champnell." He looked up and added, "Ah, it looks like were finally here." Turning to the driver he said, "Now, cabman, don't go driving further on. We're here, for this is the magician's house!"

Chapter 37

The cab pulled up in front of a tumbledown cheap 'villa' in an unfinished cheap neighborhood, the entire place a living monument to the defeat of the speculative builder.

Atherton leaped out onto the grass-grown rubble which was meant for a footpath.

"I don't see Marjorie looking for me on the doorstep," he said anxiously.

I, too, saw nothing but what appeared to be an unoccupied ramshackle brick abomination. Suddenly Atherton yelled out, "Hey! The front door's closed!"

"What do you mean?" I asked.

"Why, when I left before after not finding her I left the front door open. It looks as if I've made an idiot of myself after all and Marjorie's returned; at least let's hope that I have." He knocked.

While we waited for a response I questioned him. "Why did you leave the door open when you left?"

"I don't really know," he replied. "I imagine it was with some dim idea of Marjorie being able to get in if she returned while I was absent, but the truth is I was in such a rush I really don't quite remember."

"I suppose there's no doubt that you did leave it open?" I asked.

"Absolutely none, on that I'll stake my life."

"Was it open when you returned from your pursuit of Holt?" I asked.

"Wide open. I walked straight in expecting to find her waiting for me in the front room. I was shocked when I found she wasn't there."

"Were there any signs of a struggle?" I asked.

"None, there were no signs of anything. Everything was just as I'd left it, with the exception of the ring which I trod on in the hallway, and which Lessingham now has."

"If Miss Lindon has returned, it doesn't look as if she's here," I stated.

It didn't, unless silence had such meaning. Atherton had knocked loudly three times without succeeding in attracting the slightest notice from anyone within.

"It strikes me that this is another case of seeking admission through that window at the back." Atherton then led the way to the rear. Lessingham and I followed. There was barely a yard, still less a garden, and there wasn't a fence of any sort to serve as an enclosure and to shut off the house from the wilderness of wasteland. The kitchen window was open. I asked Atherton if he'd left it so.

"I don't remember." While he spoke, he scrambled over the sill. We followed. When he was in, he shouted at the top of his voice, "Marjorie! Marjorie! Speak to me, Marjorie, it's me, Sydney!"

The words echoed through the house. Only silence answered. He led the way to the front room. Suddenly he stopped and cried, "Wait! The blind's down!"

I'd noticed when we were outside that the blind was down at the front room window.

"It was up when I left, that I'll swear to," Atherton said. "That someone's been here is obvious, let's hope it was Marjorie." He'd only taken a step forward into the room when he again stopped short to exclaim, "My stars! What's this? Why, the place is empty, everything's gone!"

"What do you mean? Was it furnished when you left?" I asked.

The room was empty enough then.

"Furnished? I don't know that it was exactly what you'd call 'furnished,' but the owner of this house had a taste in upholstery which was all his own. There was a carpet, a bed, and lots of things for the most part, I should say, were distinctly Eastern curiosities. But it's all gone now." Atherton was staring around as if he found it difficult to credit the evidence of his own eyes.

"How long ago is it since you left?" I asked.

He referred to his watch. "Something over an hour, possibly an hour and a half. I couldn't swear to the exact time, but it certainly isn't more that that."

"Did you notice any signs of packing up?"

"Not a sign." Going to the window, he drew up the blind, speaking as he did so. "The odd thing about this business is that when we first got inside, this blind wouldn't draw up at all, so since it wouldn't go up, I pulled it down, roller and all. But now it draws up as easily and smoothly as if it had always been the best blind ever made."

Standing at Atherton's back, I saw that the cabman was signaling to us with his outstretched hand. Atherton perceived him too. He threw up the sash.

"What's the matter with you?" he called.

"Excuse me, sir, but who's the old gent?"

"What old gent?"

"Why, the old gent peeping through the window of the room upstairs?"

The words were hardly out of the driver's mouth before Sydney was through the door and racing up the staircase. I followed rather more soberly, as his methods were a little too flighty for me. When I reached the landing, he was dashing out of the front room and rushing into the one at the back, then through a door at the side. He came out shouting, "What's the idiot mean about an 'old gent'! I'll old gent him if I get him! There's no one about the place!" He returned into the front room, I at his heels.

That certainly was empty, and not only empty, but it showed no traces of recent occupation. The dust lay thick on the floor, and there was that moldy, earthy smell which is so frequently found in homes which have been long untenanted.

"Are you sure, Atherton, that there's no one at the back of the place?" I asked.

"Of course I'm sure. You can go and see for yourself if you like; do you think I'm blind?" Throwing up the window, he addressed the driver, "What do you mean with your old gent at the window? What window?"

"That window, sir."

"You're dreaming, man! There's no one here."

"Begging your pardon, sir, but there was someone there not a minute ago," the driver said.

"It's your imagination, driver. It was the slant of the light on the glass, or your eyesight's defective."

"Excuse me, sir, but it's not my imagination, and my eyesight's as good as any man's in England, and as for the slant of the light on the glass, there ain't much glass for the light to slant on. I saw him peeping through that bottom broken pane on your left hand side as plainly as I see you. He must be somewhere about, he can't have gotten away. He's at the back. Ain't there a cabinet or somethin' where he could hide?"

The cabman's manner was so extremely earnest that I went to see for myself. There was a cabinet on the landing, but the door of it was wide open, and it was obviously empty. The room in back was small, and despite the splintered glass in the window frame, it felt stuffy and devoid of air. Fragments of glass kept company with the dust on the floor, together with a choice collection of stones, bricks, and other detritus. In the corner stood another cabinet, but a momentary examination showed that this was as bare as the other. The door at the side, which Atherton had left wide open, opened onto a closet, and that was empty. I glanced up; there was no trap door which led to the roof; no practicable nook or cranny in which a living being could lie concealed.

I returned to Atherton's side to tell the cabman so. "There's no place in which anyone could hide in here, and there's no one in either of the rooms; you must have been mistaken, driver."

The man shook his head. "Don't tell me! How could I come to think I saw something when I didn't?"

"One's eyes are apt to play tricks; how could you see what wasn't there?" I said.

"That's what I want to know. As I drove up, before you told me to stop, I saw him looking through the window, the one you're at right now. He had got his nose glued to the broken pane, and was staring as hard as he could stare. When I pulled up, off he ran; I saw him get up off his knees and go to the back of the room. When the gentleman took to knocking, back he came to the same old spot and flopped down on his knees. I didn't know what you all was up to—you might be bum bailiffs for all I knew—and I supposed that he wasn't so anxious to let you in as you might be to get inside, and that was why he didn't take no notice of your knocking, while all the while he kept a eye on what was going on.

"When you went around to the back, he got up again, and I reckoned that he was going to meet you, and perhaps give you a bit of his mind, and that presently I should hear a ruckus or that something would happen. But when you pulled up the blind downstairs, to my surprise he came back once more. He shoved his old nose right through the break in the pane, and he wagged his old head at me like a chattering magpie.

"That didn't seem to me quite the civil thing to do; I hadn't done no harm to him, so I told you that he was there. But for you to say that he wasn't there, and never had been, blimey! That cops the biscuit. If he wasn't there, all I can say is I ain't here, and my horse ain't here, and my cab ain't neither. Damn it, the bloody house ain't here either!"

He settled himself on his perch with an air of the most extreme ill usage, he'd been standing up to tell his tale. That the man was serious was unmistakable. As he himself suggested, what inducement could he have to tell a lie like that? That he believed himself to have seen what he declared he saw was plain. But on the other hand, what could have become in the space of fifty seconds of his 'old gent'?

Atherton asked, "What did he look like, this old gent of yours?"

"Well, that I wouldn't hardly like to say. It wasn't much of his face I could see, only his eyes really, and they wasn't pretty. He kept a thing over his head all the time, as if he didn't want to be seen."

"What sort of a thing?" I asked.

"Why, one of them cloak sort of things, like them Arab blokes used to wear what used to be at Earl's Court Exhibition, you know!"

This piece of information seemed to interest my companions more than anything he'd said before.

"A burnoose do you mean?" I asked.

"How am I to know what the thing's called? I ain't up in foreign languages, it ain't likely! All I know is that them Arab blokes what was at Earl's Court used to walk around in them all over the place. Sometimes they wore them over their heads, and sometimes they didn't. In fact if you'd asked me instead of trying to make out that I was seeing things, I would have said that the fella I saw was an Arab bloke. When he got off his knees to sneak away from the window, I could see that he had his cloak thing, what was over his head, wrapped all around him."

Mr. Lessingham turned to me, all quivering with excitement. "I believe that what he says is true!"

"Then where can this mysterious old gentleman have gotten to, can you suggest an explanation? It's strange, to say the least of it, that the driver should be the only person to see anything of him."

"Some devil's trick has been played, I know it. I feel it! My instinct tells me so!" Lessingham said.

I stared at him. In such a matter one hardly expects a man of Paul Lessingham's character to talk of 'instinct.'

Atherton stared too. Then suddenly, he burst out, "By the Lord, I believe he's right, the whole place reeks to me of foul doings; it did as soon as I put my nose inside this house. He moved towards the door and as he went he slipped, or seemed to, all but stumbling to his knees. "Something tripped me up, what's this?" He was stamping on the floor with his foot. "There's a board loose. Come and lend me a hand, one of you and help me get it up. Who knows what mystery lays beneath?"

I went to his aid and together we pried it out of its place, while Lessingham stood by and watched us. Once it was removed, we peered into the cavity it disclosed.

There was something there.

"Why, it's a woman's clothing!" Atherton said.

Chapter 38

It was a woman's clothing, beyond a doubt. It had been tossed in as if the person who had placed it there had been in a desperate hurry. An entire outfit was there: shoes, stockings, body linen, corsets, even hat, gloves, and hairpins. These latter were mixed up with the rest of the garments in a strange confusion. It seemed plain that whoever had worn those clothes had been stripped to the skin.

Lessingham and Atherton stared at me in silence as I dragged the items out and laid them on the floor. The dress was at the bottom. It was a pretty shade of blue, bedecked with lace and ribbons, as is the fashion of the hour, and lined with sea-green silk. It had perhaps been a charming dress once and that a very recent one, but now it was all soiled, creased, torn and tumbled.

"My God!" Atherton cried out, "it's Marjorie's, she was wearing it when I saw her last!"

"It is Marjorie's!" Lessingham gasped. He was clutching at the ruined dress, staring at it like a man who has just received a death sentence. "She wore it when she was with me yesterday; I told her how it suited her, and how pretty it was!"

There was silence then. The dress was an eloquent find; it spoke for itself. The two men gazed at the heap of feminine glories; it might have been the most wonderful sight they'd ever seen.

Lessingham was the first to speak; his face had all at once grown gray and haggard. "What's happened to her?"

I replied to his question with another. "Are you sure this is Miss Lindon's dress?"

"I'm sure," Lessingham said, "and if further proof is needed, here it is." He'd found the pocket in the dress and was turning out the contents. There was a small change purse, which contained money and some visiting cards on which were her name and address, a small bunch of keys, with her nameplate attached, a handkerchief, with her initials in a corner. The question of ownership was placed beyond a doubt.

"You see," Lessingham said, exhibiting the money which was in the purse, "it's not robbery which has been attempted. Here are two ten-pound notes, and one for five, besides gold and silver; over thirty pounds in all."

Atherton, who had been turning over the accumulation of rubbish between the joists, proclaimed another find. "Here are her rings, and watch, and a bracelet, no, it certainly doesn't look as if theft was the reason for her disappearance."

Lessingham was glowering at him with knitted brows. "I have to thank you for this."

Atherton was unwontedly meek. "You're hard on me, Lessingham, harder than I deserve, I'd rather have thrown away my own life than to see her suffer or put in harm's way."

"Yours are idle words. Had you not meddled this wouldn't have happened," Lessingham snapped. "If anything has befallen Marjorie Lindon you'll account for it to me with your life's blood."

"So be it," Atherton said. "If harm has come to Marjorie, God knows that I'm willing enough that death should come to me."

While they argued, I continued to search. A little to one side, under the flooring which was still intact, I saw something gleam. By stretching out my hand, I just managed to reach it.

It was a long plait of a woman's hair. It had been cut off at the roots, so close to the head in one place that the scalp itself had been cut, so that the hair was clotted with blood. They were so occupied with each other that they took no notice of me.

I had to call their attention to my discovery. "Gentlemen, I fear that I have here something which will distress you; isn't this Miss Lindon's hair?"

They recognized it instantly. Lessingham, snatching it from my hands, pressed it to his lips. "This is mine. I shall at least have something to remember her." He spoke with a grimness which was a little startling. He held the silken tresses at arm's length. "This points to murder, foul, cruel, causeless murder. As I live, I'll devote my all—money, time, reputation—to gaining vengeance on the wretch who did this deed."

Atherton added, "Amen to that!" He lifted his hand. "As God is my witness!"

"It seems to me, gentlemen, that we move too fast, to my mind it doesn't by any means of necessity point to murder," I said. "On the contrary, I doubt if murder has been done. Indeed, I don't mind saying that I have a theory of my own which points the other way."

Lessingham caught me by the sleeve. "Mr. Champnell, tell me your theory."

"I will, a little later. Of course it may be altogether wrong, though I bet it's not. I'll explain my reasons when we come to talk of it. But at present, there are things which must be done."

"I vote for tearing up every board in the house!" Atherton cried. "And for pulling the damn place to pieces. It's a conjurer's den. I wouldn't be surprised if the cabby's old gent is staring at us all the while from some peephole of his own."

We examined the entire house, methodically, so far as we were able, inch by inch. Not another board proved loose, and to lift any of the others that were nailed down required tools, and those we had none. We checked all the walls.

They were the usual lath and plaster constructions, and showed no signs of having been tampered with. The ceilings were intact; if anything was concealed in them it must have been there for some time, as the cement was old and dirty. We tore the closet to pieces, examined the chimneys, peered into the kitchen oven and the copper, and in short, we pried into everything which, with the limited means at our disposal, could be pried into, without result.

At the end we found ourselves dusty, dirty, and exhausted. The cabman's 'old gent' remained as much a mystery as ever, and no further trace had been discovered of Miss Lindon.

Atherton made no effort to disguise his chagrin. "Now what's to be done? There seems to be nothing in the place at all, and yet if there is, it's the key to the whole confounded business."

"In that case I'd suggest that you should stay and look for it," I said. "The cabman can go and look for the requisite tools, or a workman, to assist you if you like. For my part it appears to me that evidence of another sort is, for the moment, of paramount importance. I propose to commence my search for it by making a call at the house which is across the way."

I'd observed on our arrival, that the road only contained two houses which were in anything like a finished state, the one which we were in, and another, some fifty or sixty yards further down on the opposite side. It was to this home I referred. Both men immediately proffered their companionship.

"I'll come with you," Mr. Lessingham said.

"I as well," Atherton echoed. "We'll leave this place in charge of the cabman; I'll pull it to pieces afterwards." He went out and spoke to the driver and I watched from the front door.

"Driver, we're going to pay a visit to the little house over there, you keep an eye on this one," Atherton said. "And if you see a sign of anyone around the place, living or dead, give me a yell. I'll be on the lookout, and I'll be with you before you can say Jack Robinson."

"You bet I'll yell, sir. I'll raise the hair right off you, I will." The driver grinned. "But I don't know if you gents are hiring me by the day. I want to change my horse, he should have been in his stable a couple of hours ago."

"Never mind your horse, let him rest a couple of hours extra tomorrow to make up for those he's lost today," Atherton said. "I'll take care you don't lose anything by this little job, or your horse either. By the way, look here, this will be better than yelling."

Taking a revolver out of his pants' pocket, he handed it up to the grinning driver.

"If that old gent of yours does appear, you take a shot at him. I'll hear that easier than a yell. You can put a bullet right through him if you like, I give you my word it won't be murder," Atherton said.

"I don't care if it is," the driver declared, handling the weapon like a man who was familiar with firearms. "I used to fancy revolver shooting when I was with the colors, and if I do get a chance, I'll put a shot through the bloke's ass, if only to prove to you that I'm no liar."

Whether the man was in earnest or not I couldn't tell, nor whether Atherton meant what he said in answer.

"If you shoot him I'll give you fifty pounds," Atherton said.

"All right!" the driver laughed. "I'll do my best to earn that fifty!"

Chapter 39

That the house over the way was tenanted was plain to all the world. At least one occupant sat gazing through the window of the second floor front room. An old woman in a cap, wearing one of those large, old-fashioned caps which grandmothers used to wear tied with strings under the chin. It was a bow window, and as she was seated in the bay looking right in our direction, she could hardly have failed to see us as we advanced, indeed she continued to stare at us all the while with placid calmness. I knocked once, twice, and yet again without the slightest notice being taken of my presence.

Atherton gave expression to his impatience in his own peculiar vein, "Knockers in this part of the world seem intended for ornament only, nobody seems to pay any attention to them when they're used. The old lady must be either deaf or dotty." He went out into the road to see if she still was there. "She's looking at me as calmly as you please. What does she think we're doing here, I wonder, playing a tune on her front door by way of a little amusement? Madam!" He took off his hat and waved it to her. "Madam! Might you notice that we're here at your front door!" he looked away. "Perhaps she's so deaf that nothing short of a cataclysmal uproar will reach her."

She immediately proved, however, that she was nothing of the sort. Hardly had the sounds of my further knocking died away than, throwing up the window, she thrust out her head and addressed me in a fashion which, under the circumstances, was as unexpected as it was uncalled for. "Now, young man, you needn't be in such a hurry!"

"Pardon me, madam," Atherton explained, "it's not so much a hurry we're in as pressed for time, this is a matter of life and death."

She turned her attention to Atherton, speaking with a frankness for which he was unprepared. "I don't want none of your impudence, young man. I've seen you before, you've been hanging about here the whole day, and I don't like the looks of you, and so I'll let you know it. That's my front door, and that's my knocker. I'll come down and open when I like, but I'm not going to be hurried, and if the knocker's so much as touched again, I won't come down at all." She closed the window with a bang.

Atherton seemed divided between mirth and indignation. "That's a nice old lady, on my honor, one of the good old crusty sort. Agreeable characters this neighborhood seems to grow, a sojourn hereabouts should do one good. Unfortunately I don't feel disposed just now to stand and kick my

199

heels in the road." Again saluting the old dame by raising his hat, he shouted to her at the top of his voice, "Madam, I beg ten thousand pardons for troubling you, but this is a matter in which every second is of vital importance, would you allow me to ask you one or two questions?"

Up went the window and out came the old lady's head. "Now, young man, you needn't put yourself out to holler at me. I won't be hollered at! I'll come down and open that door in five minutes by the clock on my mantelpiece, and not a moment before."

The speech delivered, down came the window.

Atherton looked rueful, he consulted his watch. "I don't know what you think, Champnell, but I really doubt if this old fossil can tell us anything worth waiting another five minutes to hear. We mustn't let the grass grow under our feet; time is getting on."

I was of a different opinion, and said so. "I'm afraid, Atherton, that I can't agree with you. She seems to have noticed you hanging about all day, and it's at least possible that she's noticed a good deal which will be worth hearing. What more promising witness are we likely to find? Her house is the only one which overlooks the one we've just quitted. I'm of the opinion that it may not only prove well worth our time to wait five minutes, but also that it would a good idea not to offend her. She's not likely to afford us the information we require if you do."

"Good. If that's what you think I'm sure I'm willing to wait, only it's to be hoped that that clock upon her mantelpiece moves quicker than its mistress."

Presently, when about a minute had gone by, he called over to the cabman. "Seen a sign of anything?"

The cabman shouted back, "Never a sign, you'll hear gunshot when I do."

Those five minutes did seem long ones. But at last Atherton, from his post of vantage in the road, informed us that the old lady was moving. "She's getting up, she's leaving the window. Let's hope she's coming down to open the door. That's been the longest five minutes I've ever known."

I could hear uncertain footsteps descending the stairs. They came along the hall. The door was opened—on the chain—and the old lady peered at us through a crack of about four inches.

"I don't know what you young men think you're after, but have all three of you in my house I won't. I'll have him and you…" A skinny finger was pointed to Lessingham and me, then it was directed towards Atherton. "But not him. So if it's anything particular you want to say to me, you'll just tell him to go away."

On hearing this Atherton's humility was abject. His hat was in his hand and he bent himself double. "Suffer me to make you a million apologies, madam, if I have in any way offended you. Nothing, I assure you, could have been farther from my intention, or from my thoughts."

"I don't want none of your apologies, and I don't want none of you neither. I don't like the looks of you, and so I tell you. Before I let anybody into my house you'll have to sling your hook somewhere else."

The door was banged in our faces. I turned to Atherton and said, "The sooner you go the better it will be for us. You can wait for us over the way."

He shrugged his shoulders, and groaned, half in jest, half in earnest. "If I must I suppose I must. It's the first time I've been refused admittance to a lady's house in all my life! What have I done to deserve this thing? If you keep me waiting long I'll tear that infernal den to pieces!" He sauntered across the road, viciously kicking the stones as he went.

The door reopened. "Has that other young man gone?"

"He has," I replied.

"Then now I'll let you in. I wont have that man inside my house." The chain was removed and Lessingham and I entered. Then the door was refastened and the chain replaced. Our hostess showed us into the front room on the ground floor. It was sparsely furnished and not too clean, but there were chairs enough for us to sit on, which she insisted on our occupying.

"Sit down, do, I can't abide to see folks standing; it gives me the fidgets."

As soon as we were seated, without any overture on our parts she said, "I know what you've come about, I know! You want me to tell you who lives in the house across the road. Well, I can tell you, and I dare bet a shilling that I'm about the only one who can."

I inclined my head. "Indeed. Is that so, madam?"

She was huffed at me. "Don't madam me. I can't bear none of your lip service. I'm a plainspoken woman, that's what I am, and I like other people's tongues to be as plain as mine. My name's Miss Louisa Coleman; but I'm generally called Miss Coleman, I'm only called Louisa by my relatives."

Since she was between seventy and eighty, and looked every year of her apparent age. Miss Coleman was evidently a character. If we were serious about getting information out of her, it would be necessary to allow her to impart it in her own manner, as to endeavor to induce her to impart it in anybody else's would be time well wasted. We had Atherton's to show for it.

She started with a sort of roundabout preamble. "This property is mine; it was left me by my uncle, the late George Henry Jobson. He's buried in Hammersmith Cemetery just over the way, he left me the whole of it. It's one of the finest building sites near London, and it increases in value every year, and I'm not going to sell it for another twenty, by which time the value will have more than trebled, so if that is what you've come about, as lots of people do, you might have saved yourselves the trouble. I keep the boards standing, just to let people know that the land is for sale, though, as I say, it won't be for another twenty years, when it'll be for the erection of high-class mansions only, same as there is in Grosvenor Square. No shops or public houses, and none of your shanties. I live in this place just to keep an eye on the property, and as for the house over the way, I've never tried to rent or sell it, not until a month ago, when one morning I got a letter. You can see it if you like."

She handed me a greasy envelope which she ferreted out of a capacious pocket which was suspended from her waist, and which she had to lift up her skirt to reach. The envelope was addressed, in unformed characters, *Miss Louisa Coleman, The Rhododendrons, Convolvulus Avenue, High Oaks Park, West Kensington.* I felt, if the writer hadn't been of a humorous turn of mind, and drawn on his imagination, and this really was the lady's correct address, then there must be something in a name.

The letter within was written in the same straggling, characterless calligraphy of a servant girl. The composition was about on a par with the writing.

The undersigned would be obliged if Miss Coleman would rent her empty house. I don't know the rent but I have sent fifty pounds. If you need more I will send it. Please address, Mohamed el Kheir, Post Office, Sligo Street, London.

It struck me as being as peculiar an application for a tenancy as I remembered to have encountered. When I passed it on to Lessingham, he seemed to think so too.

"This is a curious letter, Miss Coleman," Lessingham said.

"So I thought, and still more so when I found the fifty pounds inside. There were five, ten-pound notes, all loose, and the letter not even registered. If I'd been asked what was the rent of the house, I would have said at the most, not more than twenty pounds, because between you and me, it needs a good bit of fixing up, and is hardly fit to live in as it stands."

I'd had sufficient evidence of the truth of this, altogether separate from the landlady's frank admission.

"Why, for all he could have done to help himself I might have kept the money, and only sent him a receipt for a quarter. And some folks would have done that, too, but I'm not one of that sort myself, and wouldn't care to be. So I sent this person—I never could pronounce his name and never will—a receipt for a year." Miss Coleman paused to smooth her apron, and consider. "Well, the receipt should have reached him on Thursday, as I posted it on Wednesday night. That Thursday after breakfast, I thought I'd go over the way to see if there was any little thing I could do, because there wasn't hardly a whole pane of glass in the place, when I looked across the road to see that the man was already there, at least as much as he ever was in, which so far as I can make out, never has been anything particular. How he had got in, unless it was through a window in the middle of the night, is more than I would care to say. There was nobody in the house when I went to bed, that I would swear to, yet there was the blind up at the parlor, and what's more, it was down, and it's been down pretty much ever since.

" 'Well,' I said to myself, 'for right down impertinence this beats anything, why he's in the place before he knows if I'll let him have it. Perhaps he thinks I haven't got a word to say in the matter. Fifty pounds or no fifty pounds, I'll soon show him.' So I slipped on my bonnet and walked over there and banged at the door.

"Well, I've seen many people banging since then, and how they've kept it up has puzzled me. Some for more than an hour. I banged and I banged, and I kept on hammering, but it wasn't no more use than if I'd been hammering at a tombstone. So I started rapping at the window, but that wasn't no good either. So I went around behind, and I banged at the back door, but I couldn't make out anyone inside. So I said to myself, 'Perhaps the man ain't in, but I'll keep an eye on the house, and when he's in I'll take care to have a word with him.'

"So I come back home, and as I said I would, I kept an eye on the house all day, but never a soul went either in or out. But the next day, which it was a Friday, I got out of bed about five o'clock to see it was raining, when I saw a man coming down the road. He had on one of them dirty-colored bed-cover sort of things, and it was wrapped all over his head and around his body, like as I've been told, them there Arabs wear, and indeed, I've seen them myself at West Brompton, when they was in the exhibition there. It was quite fine, and I saw him as plainly as I see you. He came skimming along at a tear of a pace, pulls up at the house over the way, opens the front door, and lets himself in.

" 'So,' I said to myself, 'there you are. Well, Mr. Arab, or whoever you may be, I'll take good care that you don't go out again before you've had a word from me. I'll show you that landladies have their rights, like other Christians, in this country, however it may be in yours.' So I kept an eye on the house, to see that he didn't go out again, and nobody ever did. Between seven and eight I went and knocked at the door.

"If you'll believe me, no more notice was taken of me than if I was one of the dead. I knocked and hammered until my wrist was aching, I daresay I hammered twenty times, and then I went around to the back door, and I hammered at that one, but it did no good. I was so angry that I was being treated as if I was nothing and nobody, by a dirty foreigner no less, who went about in a bed-gown through the public streets, that it was all I could do to stop myself from screaming.

"I went around to the front again, and I started knocking at the window with every knuckle on my hand, and I called out, 'I'm Miss Louisa Coleman and I'm the owner of this house. You can't deceive me, I saw you come in, and you're in now. If you don't come and speak to me this moment I'll have the police here.'

"Suddenly, when I was least expecting it, and was knocking my very hardest at the pane, up goes the blind, and then the window, too. Before I knew it, the most awful-looking man I'd ever seen put his head right into my face; he was more like a hideous baboon than anything else, let alone a man. I was shocked, and I fell back and sat down on the little wall, and all but tumbled head over heels backwards. He started shrieking in a sort of English, and in such a voice as I'd never heard the like—it was like a rusty steam engine.

" 'Go away! Go away! I don't want you here! I won't have you, ever! You have your fifty pounds, you have your money, that is the whole of you, that is all you want! You come to me no more! Never! Never no more! Or you be sorry! Go away!'

"I did go away, as fast as my legs would carry me. What with his looks and voice, and the way he went on, I was nothing but a mass of trembling. As for answering him back, or giving him a piece of my mind, as I'd meant to, I wouldn't have done it for even a thousand pounds. I don't mind confessing, between you and me, that I had to swallow four cups of tea straightaway before my nerves were steady.

"I've never rented that house before, and now I've done it with a vengeance, so I have. If that there new tenant of mine isn't the greatest villain that ever went un-hung it must be because he's got near relations what's as bad as himself, because two families like his I'm sure there can't be in this world.

"After a time I cooled down, because I'm one of them sort that likes to see both sides of a question. After all, he had paid his rent, and fifty pounds is fifty pounds, I doubt if the whole house is worth much more, and he can't do much damage to it whatever he does.

"I shouldn't have minded, so far as that went, if he'd set fire to the place, for between ourselves, it's insured for a good bit over its value. So I decided that I'd let things be as they were, and see how they went on. But from that hour to now I've never spoken to the man, and never want to again. That ugly face of his will haunt me if I live to a hundred. I've seen him going in and out at all hours of the day and night, that Arab's a mystery if ever there was one. He always goes tearing along as if he's running for his life. Lots of people have come to that house, all sorts of men and women— they've mostly been women—and even little children.

"I've seen them knock and knock at the front door, but never have I seen one of them be let in or taken any notice of, and I've scarcely taken my eye off the house since he's been inside it. Over and over again in the middle of the night I get up to have a look, so that I don't miss much that's taken place.

"What puzzles me is the noises that come from the house. Sometimes for days there's not been a sound. It might have been a house of the dead for all the noise it made. But then, all through the night, there have been yells and screeches, squawks and screams. I've never heard nothing like it. I've thought more than once that the devil himself must be in that front room, let alone all the rest of his demons. And as for cats! Where they've come from I don't know. I didn't use to notice hardly a cat in the neighborhood till that there Arab came—there isn't much to attract them—but since he came there's been dozens. Sometimes at night there's been herds about the place, screeching like mad. That Arab must be fond of 'em. I've seen them inside the house, too, at the windows, upstairs and downstairs, as it seemed to me, a dozen at a time."

Chapter 40

Miss Coleman paused, as if her narrative was approaching a conclusion, so I judged it expedient to make an attempt to bring the record as quickly as possible up to date.

"I take it, Miss Coleman, that you've observed what has occurred in the house today," I said.

She tightened her nut-cracker jaws and glared at me disdainfully, her dignity ruffled. "I'm coming to it, aren't I? If you'll let me. If you've got no manners I'll learn you some. One doesn't like to be hurried at my time of life, young man."

I was meekly silent. Plainly, if she was to talk, everyone else had to listen.

"During the last few days there have been some strange goings on across the road," she said. "That Arab has been flitting about like a man possessed. I've seen him going in and out twenty times a day. This morning…" She paused to fix her eyes on Lessingham. She apparently observed his growing interest as she approached the subject which had brought us there, and resented it.

"Don't look at me like that, young man, because I won't have it," she snapped. "And as for questions, I may answer questions when I'm done, but don't you dare to ask me before, because I won't be interrupted."

Up to then Lessingham hadn't spoken a word, but it seemed as if she was endowed with the faculty of perceiving the huge volume of the words which he'd left unuttered.

"This morning as I've said already…" She glanced at Lessingham as if she defied his contradiction. "When that Arab came home it was just on the stroke of seven. I know what was the exact time because when I went to the door to see the milkman, my clock was striking the half hour, and I always keep it thirty minutes fast. As I was talking to the milkman, he said to me, 'Hello, Miss Coleman, how's your friend coming along?' 'What friend?' I asked, for I ain't got no friends around here, nor I hope, any enemies neither.

"And I looks around, and there was the Arab coming tearing down the road, his bedcover thing all flying in the wind, and his arms straight out in front of him. I never did see anyone go at such a pace. My goodness," I said, 'I wonder he doesn't do himself injury.' 'I wonder someone else don't do him an injury," the milkman said. 'The very sight of him is enough to make my milk go sour.' Then he picked up his pail and went away quite grumpy, though what that Arab had done to him is more than I can say. I've always noticed that milkman's temper was rather short. I wasn't pleased with him for speaking of that Arab as my friend, which he never was, and never will be.

"Five people went to the house after the milkman was gone, and that there Arab was safe inside; three of them was business-type people, that I know, because afterwards they came to me. But of course - none of them got a chance with that there Arab except of banging at his front door.

"Now I'm coming to this afternoon," she said after looking at me and the impatience I must have been showing despite myself. I thought it was about time, though for the life of me, I didn't dare to hint as much.

"Well, it might have been three, or it might have been half past, anyhow it was around there when up comes two men and a woman in a cab; one of the men was that rude young man that's a friend of yours. 'Oh,' I said to myself, 'here's something new in callers. I wonder what it is they're wanting.' That young man that's a friend of yours, he starts banging on the door, as was the custom was with everyone who came, and as usual no more notice was taken of him, though I knew that the Arab was inside."

At this point I felt that at all hazards I had to interpose a question. "You're sure he was indoors?"

She took it better than I feared she might. "Of course I'm sure. I'd seen him come in at seven, and he'd never left since, for I don't believe that I'd taken my eyes off the place for two minutes together, and I'd never caught sight of him. If he wasn't inside, where was he then?"

For the moment, so far as I was concerned, the query was unanswerable. She triumphantly continued, "Instead of doing what most did when they'd had enough of banging and leaving, these three went around to the back of the house, and they must have gotten in through the kitchen window, woman and all, for all of a sudden the blind in the front room was pulled not up, but down— dragged down it was, and there was that young man of yours standing with it in his hand.

I wondered where could that Arab be. And whatever could he be thinking of, to let them go on like that and say nothing.

"About five minutes later, the front door opened, and a young man— not the one that is your friend, but the other one comes running out, through the gate and down the road, as stiff and upright as a grenadier. I never saw anyone walk more upright and as fast. At his heels comes the young man who's your friend, and it seems to me that he couldn't make out what this other was doing. It looked like there had been a quarrel between them two. The young man what's your friend stood at the gate, all of a fidget, staring at the other man as if he couldn't think what to make of him, and the young woman, she stood on the doorstep, staring after him, too.

"As the second young man left and turned the corner and was out of sight, all at once your friend seemed to make up his mind, and he started off running as hard as he could, and the young woman was left alone. I expected, every minute, to see him come back with the other young man, and the young woman, and by the way she hung about the gate, she seemed to expect it, too. But no, nothing of the kind. So when, as I expect, she'd had enough waiting, she went into the house again, and I saw her pass the front room window. After a while she came back outside to the gate, and she stood looking, but nothing was to be seen of either of the young men. When she'd been at the gate I daresay five minutes, back she went into the house, and I never saw nothing of her again."

"You never saw anything of her again? Are you sure she went back into the house?" I asked.

"As sure as I am that I see you."

"I suppose that you didn't keep a constant watch on the premises?" I said.

"But that's just what I did do. I felt something odd was going on, and I made up my mind to see it through. And when I make up my mind to a thing like that I'm not easy to turn aside. I never moved off the chair at my bedroom window, and I never took my eyes off the house, not till you come knocking at my front door."

"But since the young lady is certainly not in the house at present, she must have eluded your observation, and in some manner, have left it without your seeing her," I said, Lessingham nodding in agreement.

"I don't believe she did, I don't see how she could have' there's something strange about that house, since that Arab's been inside it. But though I didn't see her, I did see someone else," she said.

"Who was that?" Lessingham asked.

"A young man."

"A young man?" I repeated.

"Yes, a young man, and that's what puzzled me, and what's puzzled me ever since, for I never did see him leave."

"Can you describe him?" I asked.

"Not his face, for he wore a dirty cloth cap pulled down right over it, and he walked so quickly that I never had a proper look. But I'd know him if I saw him, if only because of his clothes and his walk."

"What was there peculiar about his clothes and his walk?" I asked.

"Why, his clothes were old, torn, and dirty, ones that a ragman wouldn't have given a thank you for, and as for fit, there wasn't none, they hung on him like a scarecrow. As for his walk, he walked off just like the first young man had done; he strutted along with his shoulders back, and his head in the air, so stiff and straight that my kitchen poker would have looked crooked beside him."

"Did nothing happen to attract your attention between the young lady's going back into the house and the coming out of this young man?" I asked.

Miss Coleman thought it over for a moment. "Now that you mention it there was something, though I'd have forgotten all about it if you hadn't asked me, that comes of your not letting me tell the tale in my own way. About twenty minutes after the young woman had gone inside, someone put up the blind in the front room, which that young man had dragged right down, I couldn't see who it was for the blind was between us, and it was about ten minutes after that that the young man came marching out."

"And then what followed?" I asked, finally getting to the matter at hand.

"Why, in about another ten minutes that Arab himself comes scooting through the door."

"The Arab?"

"Yes, the Arab! The sight of him took me clean aback. Where he'd been, and what he'd been doing with himself while those people played hi-spy about his premises I'd have given a shilling out of my pocket to have known, but there he was, as large as life, and carrying a bundle."

"A bundle?" I asked.

"Yes, a bundle, on his shoulder, like a muffin-man carries his tray. It was a large thing, and you never would have thought he could have carried it, and it was easy to see that it was as much as he could manage. It bent him nearly double, and he went crawling along like a snail. It took him quite a while to get to the end of the road."

Mr. Lessingham leaped up from his seat, crying, "Marjorie was in that bundle!"

"I doubt it," I said.

He moved around the room distractedly, wringing his hands. "She was! She must have been! God help us all!"

"I repeat that I doubt it," I said. "If you'll be advised by me you'll wait a while before you arrive at any such conclusion."

All at once there was a tapping at the window pane. Atherton was staring at us from without., "Come out of there, you fossils!" he shouted through the glass! "I have news for you!"

Chapter 41

Getting up in a fluster, Miss Coleman, went hurrying to the door. "I won't have that young man in my house. I won't have him! Don't let him dare put his nose across my doorstep."

I endeavored to appease her. "I promise you that he won't come in, Miss Coleman. My friend here, and I, will go and speak to him outside."

She held the front door open just wide enough to enable Lessingham and me to slip through, then she closed it after us with a bang. She evidently had a strong objection to any intrusion on Atherton's part.

Standing just outside the gate, Atherton saluted us with a characteristic vigor which was scarcely flattering to our late hostess. Behind him was a constable. "I hope you two have been in with that old woman long enough. While you've been gossiping I've been doing; listen to what this officer's got to say."

The constable, his thumbs thrust inside his belt, wore an indulgent smile on his face. He seemed to find Atherton amusing. He spoke in a deep bass voice, as if it issued from his boots. "I don't know that I've got anything to say."

It was plain that Atherton thought otherwise. "You wait till I've given this pretty pair of gossips a lead, Officer, then I'll trot you out." He turned to us. "After I'd poked my nose into every dashed hole in that infernal den, and been rewarded with nothing but a pain in the back for my trouble, I stood cooling my heels on the doorstep, wondering if I should fight the cabman, or get him to fight me, just to pass the time away—for he says he can box, and he looks it—when who should come strolling along but this magnificent example of the metropolitan constabulary." He waved his hand towards the policeman, whose grin grew wider. "I looked at him and he looked at me, and when we'd had enough of admiring each other's fine features and striking proportions, he said to me, 'Has he gone?' I said, 'Who?' He said, 'No, the Arab.' I said, 'What do you know about any Arab?' He said, 'Well, I saw him on Broadway about three-quarters of an hour ago, and then seeing you here, and the house all open, I wondered if he'd gone for good.' With that I almost jumped out of my skin, though you can bet your life I never showed it. I said, 'How do you know it was he?' He said, 'It was him right enough, there's no doubt about that. If you've seen him once, you're not likely to forget him.' I asked, 'Where was he going?' 'He was talking to a cabman, a four-wheeler one. He was carrying a great bundle and wanted to take it inside with him. The cabman didn't seem to want it.' That was enough for me, I grabbed this officer and dragged him across the road to you two fellows like a flash of lightning."

Since the policeman was six feet three or so, and more than sufficiently broad in proportion, he scarcely seemed the kind of figure to be dragged anywhere if he didn't want to go.

Still, even allowing for Atherton's exaggeration, the news which he'd brought was sufficiently important. I handed the officer my business card, and said, "Well, officer, probably, before the day's over, a charge of a very serious nature will be against the person who has been residing in the house over the way. In the meantime, it's of the utmost importance that a watch should be kept on his movements. I suppose you have no sort of doubt that the person you saw on Broadway was the one in question?"

"Not a bit. I know him as well as I do my own brother, we all do upon this beat. He's known amongst us as the Arab. I've had my eye on him ever since he came here. An odd fish he is. I've always said that he's up to some game or other. I never came across one like him for, always coming and going in all sorts of weather, at all hours of the night, always tearing along as if for his life. As I was telling this gentleman, I saw him on Broadway, well, now about an hour ago, perhaps a little more. I was coming on duty when I saw a crowd in front of the District Railway Station, and there was the Arab, having an argument with the cabman. He had a bundle with him, five or six feet long. He wanted to take this bundle with him into the cab, and the cabman wouldn't let him."

"You didn't wait to see him drive off," I asked.

"No, I hadn't time. I was due at the station. I was cutting it pretty fine as it was."

"You didn't speak to him, or to the cabman?"

"No, it wasn't any business of mine you understand. The whole thing just caught my eye as I was passing."

"And you didn't take the cabman's number?" I pressed.

"No, well, as far as that goes it wasn't needed. I know the cabman, his name and all about him; his stable's in Bradmore."

I whipped out my notebook. "Give me his address."

"I don't know what his Christian name is—Tom, I believe—I'm not sure. Anyhow his surname's Ellis and his address is Church Mews, St John's Road, Bradmore, I don't know his number, but anyone will tell you which is his place, if you ask for Four-Wheel Ellis. That's the name he's known by among his pals because of his driving a four-wheeler."

"Thank you, Officer. I'm obliged to you," I said. Two half-crowns changed hands. "If you'll keep an eye on the house and inform me of anything which takes place there during the next few days, you'll do me a great service. You'll find my address on the card I gave you."

We'd clambered back into the cab, and the driver was just about to start, when the constable was struck by a sudden thought. "One moment, sir, I almost forget the most important bit of all. I did hear the Arab tell Ellis where to drive him to, he kept saying it over and over again, in that weird lingo of his. 'Waterloo Railway Station, Waterloo Railway Station.' Ellis said, 'All right, I'll drive you to Waterloo Railway Station right enough, only I'm not going to have that bundle of yours inside my cab. There isn't room for it, so you put it on the roof.' 'To Waterloo Railway Station,' the Arab said, 'I take my bundle with me to Waterloo Railway Station, I take it with me.' 'Who says you don't take it with you?' Ellis said. 'You can take it, and twenty more besides, for all I care, only you don't take it inside my cab, put it on the roof.' 'I take it with me to Waterloo Railway Station,' the Arab said again, and there they were, arguing, and neither seeming to be able to make out what the other was saying, and the people all laughing."

"Waterloo Railway Station, you're sure that was what he said?" I asked.

"I'll take my oath to it, because I said to myself, when I heard it, 'I wonder what you'll have to pay for that little lot, for the District Railway Station's outside the four-mile radius.' "

As we drove off I was inclined to ask myself, a little bitterly—and perhaps unjustly—if it weren't characteristic of the average London policeman to almost forget the most important part of his information, or at any rate to leave it to the last and only to bring it to the front on having his palm crossed with silver. As the cab rode along, we three had what occasionally approached a warm discussion.

"Marjorie was in that bundle," Lessingham began in the most mournful of tones, and worried face.

"I doubt it," I observed.

"She was, I feel it. I know it. She was either dead and mutilated, or gagged and drugged and helpless. All that remains is vengeance."

"I repeat that I doubt it."

Atherton added, "I have to say that I agree with Lessingham."

"You're wrong, both of you," I said.

"It's all very well for you to talk in that cock-sure way, Champnell, but it's easier for you to say I'm wrong than to prove it," Atherton replied. "If I'm wrong, and if Lessingham's wrong, how do you explain the Arab's extraordinary insistence on taking that bundle inside the cab with him? If there wasn't something horrible in that bundle of his, of which he feared discovery, why was he so reluctant to have it placed on the roof?"

"There was probably something in it which he was particularly anxious not be discovered, but I doubt if it was anything of the kind which you suggest," I said.

"Marjorie was in the house alone, and now she's missing and her clothing and hair is found hidden away under the floor. Then this scoundrel sallies forth with a huge bundle, the officer saying it's five or six feet long, a bundle which the Arab regards with so much care that he insists on never allowing it to be, for a single instant, out of his sight and reach. What's in the thing? Don't all the facts most unfortunately point in one direction?"

Mr. Lessingham covered his face with his hands, and groaned. "I fear that Mr. Atherton's right."

"I don't agree."

Atherton at once became heated. "Then perhaps you can tell us what was in the bundle?"

"I fancy I could make a guess at the contents."

"Oh you could, could you, then, perhaps for our sakes, you'll make it, and not keep saying the same thing! Lessingham and I are interested to hear your opinion."

"It contained the bearer's personal property: that and nothing more," I stated. Atherton opened his mouth for rebuttal but I held up my hand to stop him. "Wait! Before you yell at me, hear me out. If I'm not mistaken as to the identity of the person whom the constable describes as the Arab, I say that the contents of that bundle were of much more importance to him than if they'd consisted of Miss Lindon, either dead or alive. More so, I'm inclined to suspect that if the bundle was placed on the roof of the cab, and if the driver did meddle with it, and did find out the contents and understand them, he would have been driven out of hand, stark staring mad."

Atherton was silent as reflected. I imagine he perceived there was something in what I said. "But what has become of Miss Lindon?" he asked.

"I fancy that Miss Lindon, at this moment, is somewhere else. I don't just now know exactly where, but I hope very shortly to be able to give you a clearer notion. No doubt she'll be attired in a dirty pair of boots, a filthy, tattered pair of trousers, a ragged, unwashed shirt, an ancient, shapeless coat, and a frowsy peaked cloth cap."

They stared at me, opened-eyed.

Atherton was the first to speak. "What on earth do you mean?"

"I mean that it seems to me that the facts point in the direction of my conclusions rather than yours—and that very strongly, too. Miss Coleman asserts that she saw Miss Lindon return into the house, and that within a few minutes the blind was replaced at the front window, and that shortly after a young man, attired in the costume I've described, came walking out the front door. I believe that young man was Miss Marjorie Lindon."

Lessingham and Atherton both broke out into interrogations, with Atherton as usual, the loudest. "But man alive! What on earth should make her do a thing like that? Marjorie, the most modest girl on all God's earth, to walk about in broad daylight in such an outfit, and for no reason at all! My dear Mr. Champnell, you're suggesting that she first of all went mad."

"She was in a trance," I said.

"Good God! Champnell!"

"Well?"

"Then you think that villain did get hold of her?" Atherton asked.

"Undoubtedly," I said. "Here's my view of the case, but keep in mind it's only a hypothesis and you must take it for what it's worth. It seems to me quite clear that the Arab, as we will call him for the sake of identification, was somewhere about the premises when you thought he wasn't."

"But where? We looked upstairs and downstairs, everywhere—where could he have been?" Atherton asked.

"That, at the present time, I'm not prepared to say, but I think you may take it for granted that he was there. He hypnotized the man Holt and sent him away, intending for you and Miss Lindon to go after him, and so get rid of you both."

"The hell he did, Champnell! You think me a fool!" Atherton yelled.

"Let me finish. As soon as the coast was clear, he discovered Miss Lindon was still in the house, and who I expect, was surprised. So he hypnotized her."

"The fiend!" Lessingham scowled.

"The devil!" Atherton added.

"He then constrained her to strip out of her clothes," I said.

"The wretch!" Lessingham hissed.

"The fiend!" Atherton said again.

"He cut off her hair and hid it and her clothes under the floor where we found them—where I think it probable that he already had some old male clothes concealed."

"By God! I wouldn't be surprised if they were Holt's. I remember the man saying that he was stripped of his clothes, and certainly when I saw him, and when Marjorie found him, he had nothing on but an odd sort of cloak. Can it be possible that the Arab could have sent Marjorie Lindon, the daintiest damsel in the land, into the streets of London dressed in Holt's old clothes!"

"As to that, I'm not able to give an authoritative opinion, but if I understand you correctly, it's at least possible. Anyhow, I'm disposed to think that he sent Miss Lindon after the man Holt, taking it for granted that Holt had eluded you. And he did elude you, as you yourself have admitted."

"That's because I stopped to talk with that mutton-headed constable. I'd have followed Holt to the ends of the earth if it hadn't been for that."

"Precisely," I said. The reason is immaterial, it's the fact with which we're immediately concerned. Holt did elude you, and I think you'll find that Miss Lindon and Mr. Holt are together at this moment."

"In men's clothing?"

"Both in men's clothing, or rather, Miss Lindon is in a man's rags."

"Good God! To think of Marjorie like that!" Atherton cried.

"And where they are, the Arab isn't very far off either," I added.

Lessingham caught me by the arm. "What diabolical mischief do you imagine he proposes to do to her?"

"Whatever it is, it's our business to prevent his doing it."

"Where do you think they've been taken?" Lessingham asked.

"That will be our immediate business to discover, and at any rate, we've arrived at Waterloo."

Chapter 42

I turned towards the booking office on the main departure platform. As I did, the chief platform inspector, George Bellingham, with whom I had some acquaintance, came out of his office. I stopped him and said, "Mr. Bellingham, will you be so good as to walk with me to the booking office and instruct the clerk in charge to answer one or two questions which I wish to put to him. I'll explain to you afterwards what their exact importance is, but you know me sufficiently to be able to believe me when I say that they refer to a matter in which every moment is important."

He turned and accompanied us into the interior of the booking office.

"To which of the clerks, Mr. Champnell, do you wish to put your questions?" he inquired.

"The one who issues third class tickets to Southampton."

Bellingham beckoned to a man who was counting a pile of money, and apparently seeking to make it tally with the entries in a huge ledger which lay open before him. He was a short, slightly-built young fellow, with a pleasant face and smiling eyes.

"Mr. Stone, this gentleman wishes to ask you one or two questions," Bellingham said.

"I'm at his service."

"I want to know, Mr. Stone, if in the course of the day, you've issued any tickets to a person dressed in Arab attire," I said.

His reply was prompt. "I have, by the last train, the 7.25, three singles."

Three singles! Then my instinct has told me rightly. "Can you describe the person?" I asked.

"I don't know that I can," he said, "except in a general way. He was uncommonly old and ugly. I can tell you one thing about him, though, he had a great bundle with him, and as it bulged out in all directions its presence didn't make him very popular with other people who wanted tickets too."

Undoubtedly this was our man. "You're sure he asked for three tickets?"

"Positive. He said three tickets to Southampton; he laid down the exact fare, nineteen and six—and held up three fingers—like that. Three nasty looking fingers they were, with nails as long as talons."

"You didn't see who his companions were?" I asked.

"I didn't try to look. I gave him his tickets and off he went, with the other people grumbling at him because that bundle of his kept getting in their way."

Bellingham touched me on the arm. "I can tell you about the Arab Mr. Stone speaks of. My attention was called to him by his insisting on taking his bundle with him into the carriage. It was an enormous thing; he could hardly squeeze it through the door, and it occupied the entire seat. But as there weren't as many passengers as usual, and he wouldn't or couldn't be made to understand that his precious bundle would be safe in the luggage van along with the rest of the luggage, and as he wasn't the sort of person you could argue with to any advantage, I put him in an empty compartment, bundle and all."

"Was he alone then?" I asked.

"I thought so at the time; he said nothing about having more than one ticket, or any companions, but just before the train started two other men—English men—got into his compartment, and as I came down the platform, the ticket inspector at the barrier informed me that these two men were with him, because he held tickets for them, which as he was a foreigner, and they seemed English, struck the inspector as odd."

"Could you describe the two men?"

"I couldn't, not particularly, but the man who had charge of the barrier might. I was at the other end of the train when they got in. All I noticed was that one seemed to be a common enough looking bloke and that the other was dressed like a tramp, all rags and tatters, a disreputable looking person he appeared to be."

"That," I said "was Miss Marjorie Lindon, the lovely daughter of a famous house, and the wife-elect of a coming statesman. I want you to do me a service, Mr. Bellingham, which I assure you that you'll never have any cause to regret. I want you to wire instructions down the line to detain this Arab and his companions and to keep them in custody until the receipt of further instructions. They aren't wanted by the police yet, but they will be as soon as I'm able to give certain information to the authorities at Scotland Yard. But as you'll perceive for yourself, until I'm able to give that information every moment is important. Where's the Station Superintendent?"

"He's gone. At present I'm in charge," Bellingham replied.

"Then will you do this for me? I repeat that you'll never have any reason to regret it."

"I will if you'll accept all responsibility."

"I'll do that with the greatest pleasure."

Bellingham looked at his watch. It's about twenty minutes to nine. The train's scheduled for Basingstoke at 9.6. If we wire to Basingstoke at once, they should be ready for them when they come."

"Good!"

The wire was sent and we were shown into Bellingham's office to await results. Lessingham paced agitatedly back and forth. He seemed to have reached the limits of his self-control, and to be in a condition in which movement of some sort was an absolute necessity. Meanwhile the unpredictable Atherton, leaned back in a chair, his legs stretched out in front of him, with his hands thrust deep into his pants pockets. He stared at Lessingham, as if he found relief to his feelings in watching his companion's restlessness. For my part, I drew up as full record of the case as I deemed advisable, which I then dispatched by one of the company's police to Scotland Yard.

Then I turned to my associates and said, "Now, gentlemen, it's past dinner time. We may have a journey in front of us. If you'll take my advice you both should have something to eat."

Lessingham shook his head. "I want nothing."

"Nor I," Atherton echoed.

I stood up. "You must pardon my saying this, but surely you of all men, Mr. Lessingham, should be aware that you won't improve the situation by rendering yourself incapable of seeing it through. Come and eat."

I got them to the refreshment room and I dined, after a fashion. Mr. Lessingham ate a plate of soup with difficulty, and Atherton nibbled at a plate of the most unpromising looking 'chicken and ham,' he proved, indeed, more intractable than Lessingham, and wasn't persuaded to tackle anything more.

I was just about to have some cheese and crackers when Bellingham came hastening in, his hand holding telegram. "The birds have flown the coop," he cried.

"Flown! How?"

In reply he gave me the telegram. I glanced at it. It said 'Persons described not in the train. Guard says they got out at Vauxhall. Have wired Vauxhall to advise you.'

"That's a level-headed chap," Bellingham said. "The man who sent that telegram. His wiring to Vauxhall should save us a lot of time, we should hear from there directly. Hello! What's this? I shouldn't be surprised if this is it."

A porter had entered, and he handed an envelope to Bellingham. All three of us kept our eyes fixed on the inspector's face as he opened it. When he perceived the contents, he gave an exclamation of surprise.

"This Arab of yours, and his two friends, seem rather a curious lot, Mr. Champnell," Bellingham said.

He passed the paper on to me. It took the form of a report. Lessingham and Atherton, regardless of forms and ceremonies, leaned over my shoulder as I read it. "Passengers by 7.30 Southampton, on arrival of train, complained of noises coming from a compartment in coach 8964. Stated that there had been shrieks and yells ever since the train left Waterloo, as if someone was being murdered. An Arab and two Englishmen left the compartment in question, apparently the party referred to in wire just to hand from Basingstoke. All three declared that there was nothing wrong. They had been shouting for fun. Arab gave up three third singles for Southampton, saying in reply to questions, that they had changed their minds and didn't want to go further. As there were no signs of a struggle or violence, there was no cause for detention, and they were allowed to pass. They took a four-wheeler, No. 09435. The Arab and one man went inside, and the other man sat on the front with the driver. They asked to be driven to Commercial Road, Limehouse. The cab has since returned. Driver says he dropped them off, at their request, on Commercial Road, at the corner of Sutcliffe Street, near the East India Docks. They walked up Sutcliffe Street, the two Englishmen in front and the Arab behind, took the first turning to the right, and after that he saw nothing of them. The driver further states that all the way the Englishman inside, who was so ragged and dirty that the driver was reluctant to carry him, kept up a sort of wailing noise which so attracted the driver's attention that he twice had to see what was the matter, and each time was told it was nothing. The cabman is of opinion that both the Englishmen were of weak intellect. We were of the same impression here. They said nothing, except at the seeming instigation of the Arab, but when spoken to both stared and gaped like lunatics. It may be mentioned that the Arab had with him an enormous bundle, which he persisted in spite of all objections, on taking with him inside the cab."

As soon as I finished reading the report, and perceived what I believed to be— unknown to the writer himself— its hideous inner meaning, I turned to Bellingham and said, "With your permission, Mr. Bellingham, I'll keep this communication, it will be safe in my hands. You'll be able to get a copy later, but for now I may need the original to show the police. If any inquiries are made for me from Scotland Yard, tell them that I've gone to Commercial Road, and that I'll report my movements from Limehouse Police Station."

Minutes later, Atherton, Lessingham and myself were once more traversing the streets of London by cab.

Chapter 43

It's a bit of a drive from Waterloo to Limehouse, and it seems longer when all your nerves are tingling with anxiety to reach your journey's end, and the cab I'd hit upon proved to be not the fastest I might have chosen.

For some time after our start, we were all silent. Each of us was occupied with his own thoughts.

Then Lessingham, who was sitting at my side, said to me, "Mr. Champnell, you have that report."

"I have."

"Will you let me see it once more?"

I gave it to him. He read it once, twice, and then again. I purposely avoided looking at him as he did so. Yet all the while I was conscious of his pallid cheeks, the twitched muscles of his mouth, the feverish glitter of his eyes, this leader of men, whose predominate characteristic in the House of Commons was immobility, was rapidly changing into an hysterical woman. The mental strain which he'd been recently undergoing was proving too much for his physical strength, and the disappearance of the woman he loved was to be the final straw. I felt convinced that unless something was done quickly to relieve the strain upon his mind, he was nearer to a state of complete mental and moral collapse than even he knew. Had he been under my orders, I would have commanded him at once to return home, but conscious of how things were, such a direction would be futile, so I decided to do something else instead. Feeling that suspense was for him the worst possible form of suffering, I resolved to explain, so far as I was able, precisely what it was I feared, and how I proposed to prevent it.

Presently there came the question for which I'd been waiting, and in a harsh, broken voice which no one who had ever heard him speak on a public platform, or in the House of Commons, would have recognized as his, he said, "Mr. Champnell, who do you think this person is of whom the report from Vauxhall Station speaks as wearing rags and tatters?"

He knew perfectly well who it was, but I understood the mental attitude which induced him to prefer that the information should seem to come from me.

"I hope that it'll prove to be Miss Lindon," I said.

"You hope!" He gave a sort of gasp.

"Yes, hope, because if it is, I think it possible, even probable, that within a few hours you'll have her again enfolded in your arms."

"Pray to God that it may be so! Pray to God!"

From the tremor which was in his tone, I was persuaded that in his eyes were tears. Atherton stayed silent. He was leaning half out of the cab, staring straight ahead.

After a while Lessingham spoke again, as if half to himself and half to me. "This mention of the screams on the railway, and of the wailing noise in the cab; what must this wretch have done to her? How my darling must have suffered!"

That was a theme on which I myself scarcely ventured to allow my thoughts to rest. The notion of a gently-nurtured woman being at the mercy of that fiend, possessed—as I believed that so-called Arab to be possessed—of all the paraphernalia of horror and of dread, was one which caused me tangible cringing of the body. Where had those shrieks and yells of which the writer of the report spoke come from? What had caused the Arab's fellow passengers to think that murder was being done? What unimaginable agony had caused them? What speechless torture? And the 'wailing noise,' which had induced the London cabman to see what was the matter; what anguish had been the cause of that? The helpless woman who had already endured so much, endured, perhaps, that to which death would have been preferred! Locked up in that rattling, jolting box on wheels, alone with that diabolical Arab with the enormous bundle, which was but the lurking place of nameless terrors, what might she not, while being borne through the heart of civilized London, have been made to suffer? What had she been made to suffer to have kept up that continued 'wailing noise'?

It wasn't a theme on which it was wise to permit my thoughts to linger, and particularly it was clear that it was a theme from which Lessingham's thoughts should have been kept as far away as possible.

"Come, Mr. Lessingham, neither you nor I will do ourselves any good by permitting our reflections to flow in a morbid channel. Let's talk about something else. By the way, weren't you due to speak in the House tonight?"

"Yes, I was due, but what does it matter?"

"But have you acquainted no one with the cause of your nonattendance?"

"Acquaint! Whom should I acquaint?"

"My good sir! Listen to me, Mr. Lessingham. Call another cab, or take this one, and go at once to the House. It's not too late. Deliver the speech you've undertaken to deliver and perform your political duties. By coming with me you'll be a hindrance rather than a help, and you may do your reputation an injury from which it may never recover. Do as I counsel you, and I'll undertake to do my best to give you good news by the time your speech is finished."

He turned on me with a bitterness for which I was unprepared. "If I were to go down to the House and try to speak in the state in which I'm in now, they would laugh at me. I'd be ruined."

"Perhaps, but don't you run an equally great risk of being ruined by staying away?" I asked.

He gripped me by the arm. "Mr. Champnell, do you know that I'm on the verge of madness? Do you know that as I'm sitting here by your side, I'm living in a dual world? I'm going on and on to catch that…that fiend, and I'm back again in that Egyptian den, upon that couch of rugs, with the Woman of the Songs beside me, and Marjorie is being torn and tortured and burned before my eyes! God help me! Her shrieks are ringing in my ears!"

He didn't speak loudly, but his voice was nonetheless impressive on that account.

I did my best to be stern. "I admit that you disappoint me, Mr. Lessingham. I've always understood that you were a man of unusual strength, but you appear instead to be a man of extraordinary weakness; with an imagination so ill-governed that it reminds me of nothing so much as feminine hysterics. Your wild language is not warranted by circumstances. I repeat that I think it's quite possible that by tomorrow morning she'll be returned to you."

"Yes, but how? As the Marjorie I've always known, as I saw her last, or something else entirely?"

That was the question which I'd already asked myself; in what condition would she be when we'd succeeded in snatching her from her captor's grip? It was a question to which I'd refused to supply an answer.

To him I lied by implication. "Let's hope that with the exception of being a trifle scared, she'll be as sound of mind and body as before."

"Do you believe that she'll be like that, untouched, unchanged, unstained?" he asked.

Then I lied right out; it seemed to me necessary to calm his growing excitement. "I do."

"You don't!"

"Mr. Lessingham!"

"Do you think that I can't see your face and read in it the same thoughts that trouble me? As a man of honor do you care to deny that when Marjorie Lindon is restored to me, if she ever is, you fear she'll be but the mere soiled husk of the woman that I knew and loved?"

"Even supposing that there may be a modicum of truth in what you say, which I'm far from being disposed to admit, what good will it do by talking about such things?"

"None, none at all, unless it be the desire of looking the truth in the face," he said. "For, Mr. Champnell, you mustn't seek to lie to me, nor try to hide things from me as if I were a child. If my life is ruined, then it's ruined, just let me know it, and look me in the eyes when you tell me so. That is what I want."

I was silent. The wild tale he'd told me of that foreign hell, oddly enough, had thrown a flood of light on certain events that had happened some three years ago to another family and which had ever since remained shrouded in mystery.

What had occurred was this:

Another family containing three people, two sisters and their brother, who was younger, were members of a decent English family and going on a trip around the world. They were young, adventurous, and—not to put too fine a point on it—foolhardy. The evening after their arrival in Cairo, by way of what is called 'a lark,' in spite of the protests of people who were better informed than themselves, they insisted on going for a ramble through the native quarter alone.

They went, but they never returned. Or, rather the two girls never returned. After an interval the young man was found again, or what was left of him. A fuss was made when there were no signs of the girls re-appearance, but as there were no relations, nor even friends of theirs, but only casual acquaintances on board the ship by which they had traveled, perhaps not so great a fuss as might have been was made. Anyhow, nothing was discovered. Their widowed mother, alone in England, wondering how it was that beyond the receipt of a brief wire acquainting her with their arrival at Cairo, she had heard nothing further of their wanderings. She placed herself in communication with the diplomatic people over there, to learn that to all appearances, her three children had vanished off the face of the Earth.

Then a fuss was made, with a vengeance. So far as one can judge the whole town and neighborhood was turned pretty well upside down. But nothing came of it, so far as any results were concerned, the authorities might just as well have left the mystery of the vanishing alone.

Then, three months later, a youth was brought to the British Embassy by a group of friendly Arabs who asserted that they had found him naked and nearly dying in some remote spot in the Wady Haifa desert. It was the brother of the two lost girls. He was as close to dying as possible without actually being dead when they brought him to the Embassy, and in a state of indescribable mutilation. He seemed to rally for a time under careful treatment, but he never again uttered a coherent word. It was only from his delirious ravings that any idea was formed of what had really occurred.

Shorthand notes were taken of some of the utterances of his delirium. Afterwards they were submitted to me. I remembered the substance of them quite well, and when Mr. Lessingham began to tell me of his own hideous experiences they came back to me more clearly still. Had I laid those notes before him, I have little doubt but that he would have immediately perceived that seventeen years after the events which had left such an indelible scar on his own life, this youth—he was little more than a boy—had seen the things which he'd seen and suffered the nameless agonies and degradations which he'd suffered. The young man was perpetually raving about some indescribable den of horror which was identical to Lessingham's temple, and about some female monster, whom he regarded with such fear and horror that every allusion he made to her was followed by a convulsive paroxysm which taxed all the ingenuity of his medical attendants to bring him out of.

He frequently called for his sisters by name, speaking of them in a manner which inevitably suggested that he'd been an unwilling and helpless witness of hideous tortures which they had undergone. Then he would rise in bed, screaming, "They're burning them! They're burning them! Devils! Devils!" At those times it required all the strength of those who were in attendance to restrain his maddened frenzy.

The youth died in one of these fits of great preternatural excitement, without having given utterance to one single coherent word, and by some of those who were best able to judge, it was held to have been a mercy that he did die without having been restored to full consciousness, for no doubt his nightmares would have been terrible to behold for the rest of his life.

Then tales began to be whispered about some devoted sect, which was stated to have its headquarters somewhere in the interior of the country—some located it in this neighborhood, and some in that—which was stated to still practice, and to always have practiced, in unbroken historical continuity, the debased, unclean, mystic, and bloody rites of a form of idolatry which had had its birth in a period of the world's history which was so remote, that to all intents and purposes it might be described as pre-historic.

While the ferment was still at its height, a man came to the British Embassy who said that he was a member of a tribe which had its habitat on the banks of the White Nile. He asserted that he was in association with this very sect, though he denied that he was one of the actual sectaries. He did admit, though, that he'd assisted more than once at their orgies, and declared that it was their constant practice to offer young women as sacrifices—preferably white Christian women, with a special preference, if they could get them, to young English women. He vowed that he himself had seen with his own eyes English girls being burned alive. The description which he gave of what preceded and followed these foul murders appalled all those who listened. He finally wound up by offering, on payment of an agreed upon sum of money, to guide a troop of soldiers to this den of demons, so that they should arrive there at a moment when it was filled with worshippers who were preparing to participate in an orgy which was to take place during the next few days.

His offer was conditionally accepted. He was confined in an apartment with one man on guard inside and another on guard outside the room. That night the sentinel without was startled by hearing a great noise and frightful screams issuing from the chamber in which the native was interned. He summoned assistance. The door was opened. The soldier on guard within was stark-staring mad, and he died within a few months, a gibbering maniac to the end. The native was dead. The window, which was a very small one, was securely fastened inside and strongly barred without.

There was nothing to show by what means entry had been gained. Yet it was the general opinion of those who saw the corpse that the man had been killed by some wild beast. A photograph was taken of the body after death, a copy of which is still in my possession. In it are distinctly shown lacerations about the neck and the lower portion of the abdomen, as if they had been produced by the claws of some huge and ferocious animal. The skull is splintered in half a dozen places, and the face is torn to ribbons.

That was more than three years ago. The entire business has remained as great a mystery as ever. But my attention has once or twice been caught by trifling incidents, which have caused me to more than suspect that the wild tale told by that murdered native had in it at least the elements of truth. Which have even led me to wonder if the trade in kidnapping wasn't being carried on to this very day, and if women of my own country weren't still being offered up on that infernal altar. And now, here was Paul Lessingham, a man of world-wide reputation, of great intellect, of undoubted honor, who had come to me with a fully unconscious verification of all my worst suspicions!

That the man spoken of as an Arab, and who was probably no more an Arab than I was, and whose name was certainly not Mohamed el Kheir, was an emissary from that den of demons, I had no doubt. What was the exact reason of his presence in England was another question. Possibly part of the intention was the destruction of Paul Lessingham, body, soul and spirit, and possibly another part was the procuring of fresh victims for that long-drawn-out holocaust. That this latter object explained the disappearance of Miss Lindon I had no doubt. That she was taken by her captor, the personification of evil, to suffer all the horrors at which the stories pointed, and then to be burned alive amidst the triumphant yells of the attendant demons, I was certain. That the wretch, aware that the pursuit was in full swing, would stop at nothing which would facilitate the smuggling of the victim out of England, was clear.

My interest in the quest was already far more than a merely professional one. The blood in my veins boiled at the thought of such a woman as Miss Lindon being in the power of such a monster. I may assuredly claim that throughout the entire business I was urged forward by no thought of fee or reward. To have had a part in rescuing that unfortunate woman, and in the destruction of her cursed persecutor, would have been reward enough for me. One isn't always, even in strictly professional matters, influenced by strictly professional instincts.

The cab slowed and a voice descended through the trap door. "This is Commercial Road, sir, what part of it do you want?" the driver inquired.

"Go to Limehouse Police Station," I said.

We were driven there. I made my way to the usual inspector behind the usual pigeon-hole.

"My name is Champnell. Have you received any communication from Scotland Yard tonight having reference to a matter in which I'm interested?"

"Do you mean about the Arab? We received a telephonic message about half an hour ago," the Inspector behind the desk said.

"Since communicating with Scotland Yard this has come to hand from the authorities at Vauxhall Station. Can you tell me if anything has been seen of the person in question by the men of your division?" I asked.

I handed the Inspector the 'report.' His reply was laconic. "I'll inquire." He passed through a door into an inner room and the 'report' went with him.

"Beg pardon, sir, but was that a Arab you was a-talking about to the Inspector?" The speaker was a gentleman unmistakably of the gutter-snipe class. He was seated on a chair. Close at hand hovered a policeman whose special duty it seemed to be to keep an eye on his movements.

"Why do you ask?"

"I beg your pardon, sir, but I saw a Arab myself about an hour ago, leastways he looked like as if he was a Arab," he said.

"What sort of a looking person was he?"

"I can't hardly tell you that, sir, because I didn't never have a proper look at him, but I know he had a bloomin' great bundle with him. It was like this, here. I was comin' around the corner, as he was passin', I never saw him till I was right atop of him, so that I accidentally ran into him! I was down on my back in the middle of the road before I knew where I was and he was at the other end of the street. If he hadn't knocked me more'n half silly I'd been after him, quick, I tell you, and asked him what he thought he was a-doin' of, but before my senses was back again, he was out of sight!"

"You're sure he had a bundle with him?"

"I noticed it most particular," came the reply.

"How long ago do you say this was? And where?"

"About an hour ago, perhaps more or less."

"Was he alone?"

"It seemed to me he was bein' followed, like there was a bloke keepin' close at his heels, though I don't know what his little game was, I'm sure. Ask the policeman, he knows, he knows everything the policemen do."

I turned to the policeman. "Who is this man?" I gestured to the man before me.

The policeman put his hands behind his back and threw out his chest. His manner was distinctly affable. "Well, he's being detained upon suspicion. He's given us an address at which to make inquiries, and inquiries are being made. I shouldn't pay too much attention to what he says if I were you. I don't suppose he'd be particular about a lie or two."

This frank expression of opinion aroused the indignation of the gentleman on the chair. "There you are! At it again! That's just like you coppers, you're all the same! What do you know about me? Nothing! This gentleman ain't got no call not to believe me, it's all the same to me if he do or don't, but it's true what I'm sayin', all the same."

At this point the Inspector re-appeared at the pigeon-hole. He cut short the flow of eloquence. He addressed me. "None of our men have seen anything of the person you're inquiring for, so far as we're aware. But if you like, I'll place a man at your disposal, and he'll go around with you, and you'll be able to make your own inquiries."

Suddenly, a wildly excited young ragamuffin came dashing in from the door leading to the street. He gasped out, as clearly as he could for the speed which he had made, "There's been murder done, Mr. Policeman, some Arab's killed a bloke."

The policeman gripped him by the shoulder. "What's that you say?"

The youngster put up his arm, and ducked his head instinctively, as if to ward off a blow. "Leave me alone! I don't want none of your handlin'! I ain't done nothin' to you! I tell you he has!"

The Inspector spoke through the pigeon-hole. "He has what, my lad? What do you say has happened?"

"There's been murder done, it's right enough, there was! Up at Mrs. Henderson's, in Paradise Place, some Arab's gone and killed a bloke!"

Chapter 44

The Inspector said to me, "If what the boy says is correct, it sounds as if the person whom you're seeking may have had a finger in the pie."

I was of the same opinion, and apparently, so were Lessingham and Sidney.

Atherton collared the youth by the shoulder which the policeman had left disengaged. "What did this murderer look like?"

"I dunno! I haven't seen him! Mrs. Henderson, she says to me! 'Gustus Barley,' she says, 'a bloke's been murdered. That there Arab what I chucked out half an hour ago has murdered him and left him behind up in my back room. You run as hard as you can and tell them there dratted police what's so fond of shovin' their dirty noses into respectable people's houses.' So I comes and tells you. That's all I know about it."

We went four in a cab which had been waiting in the street, to Mrs. Henderson's in Paradise Place, the Inspector, myself, Lssingham and Atherton. "The policeman and 'Gustus Barley' followed on foot.

"Mrs. Henderson keeps a sort of lodging-house, a 'Sailors' Home' she calls it," the Inspector explained. "It doesn't bear the best of characters, and if you asked me what I thought of it, I'd say in plain English that it was a disorderly house."

Paradise Place proved to be within three or four hundred yards of the Station House. So far as could be seen in the dark it consisted of a row of houses of considerable dimensions, and also of considerable antiquity. It opened on to three stone steps which led directly into the street. At one of the doors stood an old lady with a shawl drawn over her head. This was Mrs. Henderson. She greeted us with garrulous volubility. "So you've come, have you? I thought you never was a-comin' that I did." She recognized the Inspector. "It's you—Mr. Phillips, is it?" Perceiving us, she drew back a little "Who's these men? They ain't coppers?"

Mr. Phillips dismissed her inquiry, curtly. "Never you mind who they are. What's this about someone being murdered?"

"Shhhh!" The old lady glanced around. "Don't speak so loud, Mr. Phillips. No one knows nothin' about it as of yet. The people what's in my house is most respectable, most! And they couldn't abide the notion of there being police about the place."

"We quite believe that, Mrs. Henderson." The Inspector's tone was grim.

Mrs. Henderson led the way up a staircase in desperate need of repairs. It was necessary to pick our way as we went, and as the light was bad, stumbles were frequent.

Our guide paused outside a door on the topmost landing. From some mysterious recess in her apparel she produced a key. "In here. I locked the door so that nothing might be disturbed. I know how particular you policemen are."

She turned the key. We all went in; us in front this time and she behind.

A candle was guttering on a broken and dilapidated single nightstand. A small iron bedstead stood by its side, the clothes on which were all tumbled and tossed. There was a chair with a hole in the seat, and that, with the exception of one or two chipped pieces of stoneware, and a small round mirror which was hung on a nail against the wall, seemed to be all that the room contained. I could see nothing in the shape of a murdered man. Nor, it appeared, could the Inspector.

"What's the meaning of this, Mrs. Henderson? I don't see anything here."

"He's behind the bed, Mr. Phillips. I left him just where I found him. I wouldn't have touched him, nor have let anybody else touch him neither, because as I say, I know how particular you policemen are."

All four of us went hastily forward. Atherton and I went to the head of the bed, Lessingham and the Inspector leaned right across the bed and over the side. There, on the floor in the space which was between the bed and the wall, lay the murdered man. At sight of him an exclamation burst from Atherton's lips. "It's Holt!"

"Thank God!" Lessingham cried. "It isn't Marjorie!" The relief in his tone was unmistakable. That the man was dead was plainly nothing to him in comparison with the fact that it wasn't Marjorie.

Pushing the bed more into the center of the room, I knelt down beside the man on the floor. A more deplorable spectacle than he presented I've seldom witnessed. He was decently clad in a gray tweed suit, white hat, collar and necktie, and it was perhaps this fact which made his extreme emaciation all the more conspicuous. I doubt if there was an ounce of flesh on his body. His cheeks and the sockets of his eyes were hollow. The skin was drawn tightly over his cheek bones, and the bones themselves were showing through. Even his nose was wasted, so that nothing but a ridge of cartilage remained. I put my arm beneath his shoulder and raised him from the floor; no resistance was offered by the body's gravity, he was as light as a little child.

"I doubt," I said, "if this man has been murdered. It looks to me like a case of starvation, exhaustion, or possibly a combination of both."

"What's that on his neck?" the Inspector asked, he was kneeling at my side.

He referred to two abrasions of the skin, one on either side of the man's neck.

"They look to me like scratches. They seem pretty deep, but I don't think they're sufficient in themselves to cause death," I said.

"They might be, joined to an already weakened constitution. Is there anything in his pockets? Let's lift him onto the bed," the Inspector said.

We lifted him on to the bed, the body light as a feather. While the Inspector was examining the corpse's pockets—to find them empty—a tall man with a big black beard came bustling into the room. He proved to be Dr. Glossop, the local police surgeon, who had been sent for before our leaving the Station House.

His first pronouncement, made as soon as he commenced his examination, was under the circumstances, sufficiently startling.

"I don't believe this man is dead. Why didn't you send for me directly when you found him?" he asked. The question was put to Mrs. Henderson.

"Well, Dr. Glossop, I wouldn't touch him myself, and I wouldn't have him touched by no one else, because as I've said before, I know how particular the policemen are," she said.

"Then in that case, if he does die you'll have had a hand in murdering him. That's all," the doctor said with a deep frown.

The lady snickered. "Of course, Dr. Glossop, we all know that you'll always have your joke."

"You'll find it a joke if you have to hang, as you ought to, you…" The doctor said the rest to himself, under his breath. I doubt if it was flattering to Mrs. Henderson. "Have you got any brandy in the house?"

"We've got everything in the house for them as likes to pay for it—everything." Then, suddenly remembering that the police were present, and that hers weren't exactly licensed premises, she added, "Leastways we can send out for it if anyone gives us the money, being as is well known, we're always willing to oblige."

"Then send for some! If this man dies before you've brought it I'll have you locked up as sure as you're a living woman," the doctor threatened.

The arrival of the brandy didn't take long, and the man on the bed had regained consciousness before it came. Opening his eyes, he looked up at the doctor bending over him.

"Hello, my man! That's more like it! How are you feeling?" the doctor asked.

The patient stared hazily up at the doctor, as if his sense of perception wasn't yet completely restored, as if this big bearded man was something altogether strange.

Atherton bent down beside the doctor and said to Holt, "I'm glad to see you looking better, Mr. Holt. You know me don't you? I've been running around after you all day."

"You're…you're…" Holt's eyes closed, as if the effort at recollection had exhausted him. He kept them closed as he said, "I know who you are. You're the gentleman."

"Yes, that's it, I'm the gentleman, name of Atherton. Miss Lindon's friend. And I daresay you're looking pretty well done up, and in want of something to eat and drink; here's some brandy for you."

The doctor had some in a tumbler. He raised the patient's head, allowing it to trickle down Holt's throat. He swallowed it mechanically, motionless, as if unconscious of what it was that he was doing. His cheeks flushed, the passing glow of color caused their condition of extraordinary and extravagant attenuation to be more prominent than ever. The doctor laid Holt back upon the bed, feeling his pulse with one hand, while standing and regarding his patient in silence. Then, turning to the Inspector, he said to him softly, "If you want him to make a statement he'll have to make it now, he's going fast. You won't be able to get much out of him, he's too far gone I wouldn't rush him but get what you can."

The Inspector came to the front of the bed, a notebook in his hand. "I understand from this gentleman…" He signified Atherton. "That your name's Robert Holt. I'm an Inspector of Police, and I want you to tell me what has brought you to this condition. Has anyone been assaulting you?"

Holt, opening his eyes, glanced up at the speaker mistily, as if he couldn't see him clearly, let alone understand what it was that he was saying.

Atherton, stooping over Holt, tried to explain better. "The Inspector wants to know how you got here. Has anyone been doing anything to you? Has anyone been hurting you?"

Holt's eyelids were partially closed. Then they opened wider and wider. His mouth opened, too. On his skeleton features there came a look of panic and fear. He was evidently struggling to speak. At last the words came. "*The Beetle!*" He stopped. Then, after an effort, cried out again. "*The Beetle!*"

"What's he mean?" the Inspector asked.

"I think I understand," Atherton answered, then turning again to Holt, he said, "Yes, I hear what you say, the beetle. Well, has the beetle done anything to you?"

"It took me by the throat!" Holt gasped.

"Is that the meaning of the marks upon your neck?" Atherton asked.

"The beetle killed me." His eyelids closed and he relapsed into a state of lethargy.

The Inspector was puzzled, and said, "What's he mean about a beetle?"

"I think I understand what he means, and my friends do too," Atherton replied. "We'll explain afterwards. In the meantime, I think I'd better get as much out of him as I can, while there's time."

"Yes," the doctor said, his hand upon the patient's pulse, "while there's time. There isn't much—only seconds."

Atherton tried to rouse Holt from his stupor. "You've been with Miss Lindon all the afternoon and evening, haven't you, Mr. Holt?"

Atherton had penetrated the man's consciousness. His lips moved, in painful articulation. "Yes, all the afternoon and evening. God help me!" Holt cried.

"I hope God will help you, my poor fellow. You've been in need of His help if ever a man was. Miss Lindon is disguised in your old clothes, isn't she?" Atherton asked. Behind him, Lessingham leaned closer, anxious to hear Holt's answer.

"Yes, in my old clothes. My God!" Holy answered.

"And where is Miss Lindon now?"

Holt had been speaking with his eyes closed. Now he opened them wide, and there came into them a look of abject terror. He became possessed by uncontrollable agitation, half raising himself in bed. Words came from his quivering lips as if they were only drawn from him by the force of his anguish, "The beetle's going to kill Miss Lindon."

A momentary paroxysm seemed to shake the very foundations of his being. His entire body quivered. He fell back onto the bed. The doctor examined him while we all waited in silence.

"This time he's gone for good, there'll be no getting him back again," the doctor said.

I felt a sudden pressure on my arm, and found that Lessingham was clutching me. The muscles of his face were twitching. He trembled.

I turned to the doctor and asked, "Doctor, if there is any of that brandy left? And if so, will you let me have it for my friend?"

Lessingham disposed of the remainder of the brandy, and I rather think it saved us from a scene.

The Inspector said to the woman of the house, "Now, Mrs. Henderson, perhaps you'll tell us what all this means. Who is this man and how did he come to be here, and who came in with him, and what do you know about it all? If you've got anything to say, say it now, only you'd better be careful, because it's my duty to warn you that anything you say may be used against you."

Chapter 45

Mrs. Henderson put her hands under her apron and smirked. "Well, Mr. Phillips, it do sound strange to hear you talkin' to me like that. Anybody would think I'd done something the way you're goin' on. As for what happened, I'll tell you all happily. And as for bein' careful, there ain't no call for you to tell me to be that, for that I always am, as by now you should know."

"Yes, I do know. Is that all you have to say?" the Inspector asked.

"Really, Mr. Phillips, what a man you are for catching people up, you really are. Of course that ain't all I've got to say, ain't I just a-comin' to it?"

"Then go ahead, please."

"If you press me so you'll muddle me up, and then if I do happen to make an error, you'll say I'm a liar, when goodness knows there isn't a more truthful woman in Limehouse."

Words plainly trembled on the Inspector's lips, which he refrained from uttering. Mrs. Henderson cast her eyes upwards, as if she sought inspiration from the filthy ceiling.

"So far as I can swear, it might have been a hour ago, or it might have been a hour and a quarter, or it might have been a hour and twenty minutes."

"We're not particular as to the exact seconds," the Inspector said.

"I heard a knockin' at my front door, and when I went to open it, there was an Arab man with a great bundle bigger than himself, and two other men along with him. This Arab man says, in that weird foreign way them Arab men talk, 'A room for the night, a room.' Now I don't much care for foreigners, and never did, especially them Arabs, which their habits ain't my own, so I as much hints the same. But this here Arab, he didn't seem to quite follow my meaning, for all he did was to say as he said afore, 'A room for the night, a room.' And he shoves a couple of half crowns into my hand. Now it's always been a motto of mine that money is money, and one man's money is as good as another man's. So, not wishing to be disagreeable—knowing other people would have taken 'em in if I hadn't, I shows 'em up here. I was downstairs maybe half an hour, when I heard a shindy comin' from his room—this room."

"What sort of a shindy?" the Inspector asked.

"Yelling and shrieking—oh my gracious, it was enough to set your blood all curdled, for ear-piercingness I never did hear nothing like it. We do have troublesome people in here, like they do elsewhere, but I never did hear nothing like it before. I listened for about a minute, but it kept on, and kept on, and every moment I expected the other patrons in the house to start complainin', so up I came and I thumped at the door, but I was ignored."

"Did the noise keep on?"

"Keep on! I should think it did keep on! Lord love you! Shriek after shriek; I expected to see the roof fall in."

"Were there any other noises? For instance, were there any sounds of struggling, or of blows?" the Inspector asked.

"There weren't no sounds except for a man hollerin'."

"One man only?"

"One man only. As I said before, shriek after shriek. When I put my ear to the panel there was a noise like some other man was blubbering, but that weren't nothing, as for the hollerin', you wouldn't have thought that nothin' what you might call hummin' could have kept up such a screechin'. I thumped and thumped and at last when I thought that I would have to have the door broken down, the Arab said to me from inside, 'Go away! I pay for the room! Go away!' So I said, 'Pay for the room or not pay for the room, you didn't pay to make a scene'! And what's more I said, 'If I hear it again, out you go! And if you don't go quiet I'll have somebody in that will make you!'"

"Then was there silence?" the Inspector asked.

"So to speak there was, only there was this sound as if someone was blubberin' and another sound as if a someone was panting for his breath."

"Then what happened?" the Inspector asked.

"Seeing that, so to speak, all was quiet now, I left. In another quarter of a hour, or it might have been twenty minutes, I went to the front door to get some air. And Mrs. Barker, who lived over the road at No. 24, she came to me and said, 'That there Arab man of yours didn't stop long.' I looked at her, 'I don't quite follow you,' I said, which I didn't. 'I saw him come in,' she said, 'and then, a few minutes back, I see him go again, with a great bundle he couldn't hardly stagger under!' Oh,' I said, 'That's news to me, I didn't know he'd gone, nor see him go.' Which I didn't. So, up I came again, and sure enough, the door was open, and it seemed to me that the room was empty, till I come upon this poor young man who's lying behind the bed."

There was a growl from the doctor. "If you'd had any sense, woman, and sent for me at once, he might have been alive at this moment."

"How was I to know that, Dr. Glossop? I couldn't tell. My finding him there murdered was quite enough for me. So I ran downstairs, and I nipped old Gustus Barley, who was leaning against the wall, and I said to him, 'Gustus Barley, run to the station as fast as you can and tell 'em that a man's been murdered, that Arab's done and killed a bloke.' And that's all I know about it, and I couldn't tell you no more, Mr. Phillips, not if you was to keep on askin' me questions for hours."

"Then you think it was this man..." The Inspector motioned towards the bed. "Who was shrieking?"

"To tell you the truth, Mr. Phillips, about that I don't hardly know what to think. If you asked me, I'd have said it was a woman. I ought to know a woman's holler when I hear it, if anyone does. I've heard enough of 'em in my time, goodness knows. And I should have said that only a woman could have hollered like that and only when she was raving mad. But there weren't a woman with him. There was only this man what's murdered and the other man, and as for the other man I'll say this, that he hadn't have a bit of clothes to cover him. But, Mr. Phillips, however that may be, that's the last Arab I'll have under my roof, no matter what they pay, and you mark my words on that one."

Mrs. Henderson, once more glancing upward to ceiling, as if she imagined herself to have made some declaration of a religious nature, shook her head with much solemnity.

Chapter 46

As we were leaving the house, a constable gave the Inspector a note. Having read it he passed it to me. It was from the local office. I read it aloud: "Message received that an Arab with a big bundle has been noticed loitering about the neighborhood of Saint Pancras Station. He seemed to be accompanied by a young man who had the appearance of a tramp. The young man seemed ill. They appeared to be waiting for a train, probably to the North. Shall I advise detention?"

I scribbled on the flyleaf of the note. "Have them detained. If they've gone by train, have a special train in readiness for us."

In a minute we were again in the cab. I tried to persuade Lessingham and Atherton to allow me to conduct the pursuit alone, but it was in vain. I had no fear of Atherton's succumbing, but I was afraid for Lessingham. What was more almost than the expectation of his collapse was the fact that his looks and manner, his whole bearing actually, was beginning to tell upon my nerves. I foresaw a catastrophe of some sort. Of the curtain's fall on one tragedy we'd just been witnesses but that there was worse, much worse, to follow I didn't doubt. Optimistic anticipations were out of the question, that the man we were chasing would relinquish his prey uninjured, and no one, after what we'd seen and heard could possibly believe otherwise. Should a necessity suddenly arise for prompt and immediate action, I felt that Lessingham would prove a hindrance rather than a help.

But since moments were precious, and Lessingham wasn't to be persuaded to allow the matter to proceed without him, all that remained was to make the best of his presence.

The great arch of Saint Pancras was in darkness, and an occasional light seemed to make the darkness feel even heavier. The station seemed deserted. I thought, at first, that there wasn't a soul about the place, that our errand was in vain, and that the only thing for us to do was to drive to the police station and pursue our inquiries there. But as we turned towards the booking office, our footsteps ringing out clearly through the silence and the night, a door opened and a light shone out from the room within, A voice inquired, "Who's that?"

"My name's Champnell. Has a message been received from me from the Limehouse Police Station?" I asked.

"Step this way," the voice said.

We entered a small office, of which one of the railway inspectors was apparently in charge. He was a big man, with a thick black beard with streaks of white. He looked me up and down, as if doubtfully. Lessingham he recognized at once and he took off his cap and said, "Mr. Lessingham, I believe?"

"I'm Mr. Lessingham. Have you any news for me?"

I fancy, by his looks, that the official was struck by the pallor of the speaker's face, and by his shaky voice. "I'm instructed to give certain information to a Mr. Augustus Champnell."

"I'm Mr. Champnell. What's your information?"

"With reference to the Arab about whom you've been making inquiries. A foreigner, dressed like an Arab and with a large bundle in tow, took two single thirds for Hull by the midnight express."

"Was he alone?" I asked.

"It's believed that he was accompanied by a young man of very disreputable appearance. They weren't together at the booking office, but they'd been seen together previously. A minute or so after the Arab entered the train, this young man got into the same compartment—they were in the front wagon."

"Why weren't they detained?" I asked.

"We had no authority to detain them, or a reason, until your message was received a few minutes ago. We at this station weren't aware that inquiries were being made about them."

"You say he booked passage to Hull. Does the train run through to Hull?" I asked.

"No, it doesn't go to Hull at all. Part of it's the Liverpool and Manchester Express, and part of it's for Carlisle. It divides at Derby. The man you're looking for will change either at Sheffield or at Cudworth Junction and go on to Hull by the first train in the morning. There's a local service."

I looked at my watch. "You say the train left at midnight. It's now nearly —twenty-five past. Where is it now?"

"Nearing Saint Albans; it's due there at 12.35."

"Would there be time for a wire to reach Saint Albans?"

"Hardly, and anyhow there'll only be enough railway officials their to receive and dispatch the train. They'll be fully occupied with their ordinary duties. There won't be time to get the police there."

"Could wire to Saint Albans to inquire if they were still on the train?" I asked.

"That could be done, certainly. I'll have it done at once if you like.

"Where's the next stop from there?"

"Well, they're at Luton at 12.51. You see, there won't be much more than twenty minutes by the time you've got your wire off, and I don't expect there'll be many people awake at Luton. Sometimes at these country places there's a policeman hanging around the station to see the express go through, but on the other hand, very often there isn't, and if there isn't, probably at this time of night it'll take a good bit of time to get the police on the premises. I tell you what I'd do."

"What's that?" I prodded.

"The train is due at Bedford at 1.29—send your wire there. There should be plenty of people at Bedford, and there'll be time to get the police to the station."

"Very good. I instructed them to tell you to have a special train ready; have you got one?"

"There's an engine with steam up in the shed. We'll have it all ready for you in less than ten minutes. And I tell you what, you'll have about fifty minutes before the train is due at Bedford. It's a fifty mile run. With luck you'll get there about the same time the express does. Should I tell them to get ready?"

"At once," I said. While he issued directions through a telephone to the engine shed, I drew up a couple of telegrams.

Upon completing his orders, he turned to me and said, "They're coming out of the siding now—they'll be ready in less than ten minutes. I'll see that the line's kept clear. Have you got those wires?"

"Here's one, this is for Bedford."

It said, Arrest the Arab in the train due at 1.29. When leaving Saint Pancras he was in a third class compartment in front wagon. He has a large bundle, which detain. He took two third singles for Hull. Also detain his companion, who is dressed like a tramp. This is a young lady that the Arab has disguised and kidnapped while in a condition of hypnotic trance. Give her medical assistance and take her to a hotel. All expenses will be paid on the arrival of the undersigned, who is following by special train. As the Arab will probably be very violent, a sufficient force of police should be waiting. Augustus Champnell.

"And this is the other. It's probably too late to be of any use at Saint Albans, but send it there anyway, and also to Luton."

The wire said, *Is Arab and companion in the train which left Saint Pancras at 13.0? If so, don't let them get out till the train reaches Bedford, where instructions are being wired for arrest.*

The Inspector rapidly scanned them both. "They should do your business, I'd think. Come along with me. I'll have them sent at once, and we'll see if your train's ready," he said.

The train wasn't ready, nor was it ready within the prescribed ten minutes. There was some hitch about a saloon. Finally we had to be content with an ordinary, old-fashioned first class carriage. The delay, however, wasn't altogether time lost. Just as the engine with its solitary coach was approaching the platform, someone came running up with an envelope in his hand.

"Telegram from Saint Albans," the messenger said.

I tore it open. It was brief and to the point.

Arab with companion was in train when it left here. Am wiring Luton.

"That's all right. Now unless something unforeseen takes place, we should have them soon."

I went forward with the Inspector and the guard of our train to exchange a few final words with the driver.

The Inspector explained what instructions he'd given. "I've told the driver not to spare his coal but to take you into Bedford within five minutes after the arrival of the express. He says he thinks that he can do it."

The driver leaned over his engine, rubbing his hands with an oily rag. He was a short, wiry man with gray hair and a grizzled moustache, with about him the bearing of semi-humorous, frank-faced resolution which is noted about engine-drivers.

"We should be able to do it. The gradients are against us, but it's a clear night and there's no wind. The only thing that'll stop us will be if there's any shunting on the road, or any luggage trains. Of course, if we're blocked, we're blocked, but the Inspector says he'll clear the way for us."

"Yes," the Inspector said, "I'll clear the way. I've wired down the road already."

Atherton broke in, "Driver, if you get us into Bedford within five minutes of the arrival of the mail there'll be a five-pound note to divide between your mate and you."

The driver grinned. "We'll get you there in time, sir, even if we have to go clear through the shunters. It isn't often we get a chance of a five-pound note for a run to Bedford, and we'll do our best to earn it."

His mate waved his hand in the rear of the car. "That's right, sir!" he cried. "We'll have to trouble you for that five-pound note."

As soon as we were clear of the station, it began to seem probable that, as the second man put it, Atherton would be 'troubled.' Journeying in a train which consists of a single carriage attached to an engine which is flying at topmost speed is very different from being an occupant of an ordinary train which is traveling at normal speed. I'd discovered that for myself before, and tonight it was impressed on me more than ever. I expected at any moment that we were going to be derailed. It was hard to believe that the carriage had any springs, as it rocked and swung, jogged and jolted. Of smooth traveling there was none. Talking was out of the question, and for that, I personally was grateful. It was difficult to keep our seats, too, and every moment our position was being altered as we were jerked backwards and forwards, up and down, and this way and that. The noise was deafening. It was as though we were being pursued by a legion of shrieking, bellowing, raging demons.

"Champnell!" Atherton shrieked. "He does mean to earn that fiver. I just hope I'll be alive to pay it him!" He was only at the other end of the carriage, but though I could see by the distortion of his face that he was shouting at the top of his voice, I only caught a word or two of what he was saying.

Lessingham's contortions were a study to watch as he held on for dear life. And one thing was absolutely certain, that if we did crash while going at that speed, no doubt we would all be killed. As I watched Lessingham, it seemed to me that he was getting a firmer hold of the strength which had all but escaped him before, and that with every jog and jolt of the train he was becoming more and more of the man he once was.

On and on we went clashing, smashing, roaring, rumbling down the tracks. Atherton, who had been trying to peer through the grime-covered window, strained his lungs again in the effort to make himself heard. "Where the devil are we?" he yelled.

Looking at my watch, I screamed back at him, "It's nearly one, so I suppose we're somewhere near Luton."

Then came a shrill whistle from the engine, and a second later we were aware of the application of the Westinghouse brake. Of all the jolting that we'd already suffered was nothing compared to this! The mere reverberation of the carriage threatened to shake our bodies into their component parts. Feeling what I felt helped me to realize that with the retarding force on which the vacuum brake must be exerting, it didn't seem at all surprising that the train would have been brought to an almost instant stand still.

Simultaneously, all three of us were on our feet. I let down my window and Atherton let down his. He shouted out, "I should think that the Inspector's wire hasn't had it's proper effect, it looks as if we're blocked—or else we've stopped at Luton. It can't be Bedford."

It wasn't Bedford, that much seemed clear. Though at first from my window I could make out nothing, I was feeling more than a trifle dazed. There was a singing in my ears, and the sudden darkness was impenetrable. Then I became conscious that the guard was opening the door of his compartment. He stood on the step for a moment, seeming to hesitate. Then, with a lamp in his hand, he descended onto the tracks.

"What's the matter?" I asked.

"Don't know, sir. It seems as if there was something on the road. What's up there?" he asked to the man on the engine.

The reply was, "Someone in front there's waving a red light like mad. Lucky I caught sight of him; we would've been clean on top of him in another second. It looks as if there's something wrong. Here he comes."

As my eyes grew more accustomed to the darkness, I became aware that someone was making haste along the six-foot way, swinging a red light as he came.

Our guard advanced to meet him, shouting as he went, "What's the matter! Who's that?"

A voice replied, "My God! Is that George Hewett. I thought you were coming right on top of us!"

Our guard said, "What! Jim Branson! What the devil are you doing here? What's wrong? I thought you were on the twelve out; we're chasing you."

"Are you? Then you've caught us. Thank God for it! We're a wreck."

I'd already opened the carriage door. With that, all three of us clambered out onto the line, myself first, then Atherton and Lessingham.

Chapter 47

I moved to the stranger who was holding the lamp. He was in official uniform. "Are you the guard of the 12.0 out from Saint Pancras?" I asked.

"I am."

"Where's your train? What's happened?"

"As for where it's, there it is, right in front of you. What's left of it, anyway. As to what's happened, why, we're wrecked."

"What do you mean by you're wrecked?" I asked.

"Some heavy loaded trucks broke loose in front and came running down the hill on top of us."

"How long ago was it?"

"Not ten minutes," he said. "I was just starting off down the road to the signal box, it's a good two miles away, when I saw you coming. My God! I thought there was going to be another crash."

"Was there much damage done?" I asked.

"As far as I can make out they're matchboxed up in front. I feel as if I was all broken up inside of me. I've been in the service going on for thirty years, and this is the first accident I've been in." It was too dark to see the man's face, but judging from his tone he was either crying or very near to it.

Our guard turned and shouted back to our engine, "You'd better go back to the box and let 'em know!"

"All right!" came echoing back.

The special train immediately commenced retreating, whistling continually as it went. All the countryside must have heard the engine shrieking, and everyone who did hear must have understood that on the line something was seriously wrong.

The smashed train was wreathed in darkness; the force of the collision had put out all the carriage lamps. Here was a flickering candle, there the glimmer of a match, but these were all the lights which shone on the scene. More for illumination than for warmth, people were piling up debris by the side of the tracks, for the purpose of making a fire.

Many of the passengers had succeeded in freeing themselves, and were moving around the area, but the majority still appeared to be trapped. The carriage doors were jammed, and without the necessary tools it was impossible to open them. Every step we took our ears were filled with piteous cries. Men, women and children appealed to us for help.

"Open the door, sir! In the name of God, sir, open the door!" Over and over again, in all sorts of tones.

The guards vainly tried to appease the half-frenzied passengers.

"All right, sir! If you'll only wait a minute or two, madam!" the guard called. "We can't get the doors open without tools; a special train's just started off to get them. If you'll only have patience there'll be plenty of help for every one of you directly. You'll be quite safe in there, if you'll only keep still."

But that was what the passengers found most difficult to do—keep still!

In the front of the train it was chaos. The trucks which had done the mischief—there were afterwards shown to be six of them, together with two guards' vans—appeared to have been laden with bags of Portland cement. The bags had burst, and everything was covered with a gritty dust. The air was full of it, the dust getting into our eyes and half blinding us.

The engine of the express had turned a complete somersault. It vomited forth smoke, steam and flames, and every moment it seemed as if the woodwork of the carriages immediately behind and beneath would catch fire.

The front coaches were, as the guard had put it, 'matchboxed.' They were nothing but a heap of debris, telescoped into one another in a state of apparently inextricable confusion. It was broad daylight before access was gained to what had once been the interiors. The condition of the first, third class compartment revealed an extraordinary state of things.

Scattered all over it were pieces of what looked like partially burned rags, and fragments of silk and linen. I have those fragments now. Experts have assured me that they're neither silk nor linen, but of some other material.

On the cushions and woodwork—especially on the woodwork of the floor—were huge blotches, stains of some sort. When first noticed they were damp and gave out a most unpleasant smell. One of the pieces of woodwork is still in my possession, with the stain still on it.

Experts have inspected it, too, with the result that opinions are divided. Some maintain that the stain was produced by human blood, which had been subjected to a great heat. Others say that it's the blood of some wild animal, possibly of some creature of the cat species.

Yet others affirm that it's not blood at all, but merely paint. While a fourth describes it as, I quote the written opinion which lies in front of me: 'caused apparently by a deposit of some sort of viscid matter, probably the excretion of some variety of lizard.'

I was the first one through, and in a corner of the carriage I saw the body of what seemed to be a young man wearing the clothes of a tramp, and beside it a large insect leg, far larger than anything that should or could exist. It was lodged between two wooden beams, which was part of the structure of the compartment, and no doubt became lodged there in the crash.

The body was Marjorie Lindon.

Though there was a thorough search of the compartment contained, those two things were all that was found.

Chapter 48

It's been several years since I bore my part in those events, or I wouldn't have felt justified in sharing them now.

Marjorie Lindon still lives. She was still alive when found in the compartment and extricated from among the debris of the wrecked express.

The restoration of her health did not take weeks or months though, it was a matter of years.

I believe that, even after she was physically restored—in itself a tedious task— she was under medical supervision as a lunatic for something like three years. All that skill and money could do was done, and in time—which is truly the greatest healer— the results were entirely satisfactory.

Her father is dead, and has left her in possession of the family estates. She's married to Paul Lessingham.

Nothing has been said to her about the fateful day on which she was— consciously or unconsciously—led through London in the tattered clothes of a vagabond. She herself has never once alluded to it.

With the return of sanity the affair seems to have passed from her memory as if it had never happened; which is fortunate. No doubt what actually transpired will never be fully known, and what really occurred in the railway carriage.

What became of the Arab who all but killed her, who he was—if it was a 'he,' which is extremely doubtful—where he came from, where he went, what was the reason of his presence here, to this day these things remain unanswered.

Paul Lessingham hasn't since been troubled by his old tormentor. He's ceased to be a haunted man. But nonetheless, he continues to have what seems to be complete dislike for the subject of beetles, nor can he himself be made to speak of them. If they're mentioned in a general conversation, and he can't immediately change the subject, he will if possible, get up and leave the room.

His wife is the same on this subject. I have reason to believe that there still are moments in which he harks back, with something like physical shrinking, to that awful nightmare of the past, and in which he thanks God that it's in the past.

I still have the large insect leg, and other than Atherton and myself, no one else has ever seen it. When I had found Miss Lindon and had spotted the leg, I quickly pulled it from its trap and hid it within my jacket. Why I did this is still unknown to me, but something in that split second before the rescue workers filed in behind me told me that some things man wasn't ready to see—or believe.

Before closing, I would like to mention one more thing of interest. This tale has never been told, but I have unimpeachable authority for its authenticity.

During the recent expeditionary advance towards Dongola, a group of native troops which was encamped at a remote spot in the desert was woken one night by what seemed to be the sound of a loud explosion. The next morning, at a distance of a couple of miles from the camp, a huge hole was discovered in the ground, as if blasting operations on an enormous scale had recently been carried on. In the hole and around its edge, were found fragments of what seemed to be bodies; credible witnesses have assured me that they were bodies of neither men nor women, but of creatures of some monstrous growth. I prefer to believe, since no scientific examination of the remains took place, that these witnesses ignorantly, though innocently, were incorrect.

One thing is sure. Numerous pieces both of stone and metal were seen, which went far to suggest that some curious subterranean building had been blown up by the force of the explosion. Especially where there were portions of molded metal which seemed to belong to what must have been an immense bronze statue. They were picked up also, more than a dozen replicas in bronze of the whilom sacred scarabaeus.

That the den of demons described by Paul Lessingham had that night at last come to an end isn't an hypothesis which I'd care to advance with any degree of certainty. But that these things which lay scattered, here and there, on that treeless plain were the evidences of its final destruction there is no doubt in my mind. By putting this and that together, the facts seem to point that way.

Sydney Atherton has married Miss Dora Grayling. Her wealth has made him one of the richest men in England. She began, the story goes, by loving him immensely; I can attest to the fact that he loves her just as much. Their devotion to each other contradicts the pessimistic nonsense which supposes that every marriage must be of necessity a failure. He continues his career as an inventor. His investigations into the subject of aerial flight, which have brought the flying machine within the range of practical politics, are on everybody's tongue.

The best man at Atherton's wedding was Percy Woodville, now the Earl of Barnes. Within six months afterwards, Percy married one of Mrs. Atherton's bridesmaids.

It was never fully shown how Robert Holt came to his end. At the inquest the coroner's jury was content to return a verdict of 'died of exhaustion.' He is buried in Kensal Green Cemetery, under a handsome tombstone, the cost of which, had he had it in his pockets, might have indefinitely prolonged his days.

It should be mentioned that the portion of this strange story narrated by Robert Holt was compiled from the statements which Holt made to Atherton, and to Miss Lindon when she found him and took him in.

Miss Lindon's contribution to this story was written by her own hand. After her physical strength had come back to her, and while mentally she still hovered between the darkness and the light, her one relaxation was writing. Although she would never speak of what she'd written, it was found that her theme was always the same. She confided to pen and paper what she wouldn't speak of with her lips. She told, and re-told, and re-told again, the story of her love, and of her tribulation so far as it's contained in the present volume.

On the subject of the curse of the beetle, I don't propose to pronounce a confident opinion. Atherton and I have talked it over many a time, and at the end we have never come to a foregone conclusion, despite the large insect leg we have both inspected for hours on end. I believe we both know where the truth lies but neither of us wants to fully come to that conclusion, as that is the stuff of nightmares.

But despite this, experience has taught me that there are indeed more things in Heaven and Earth than are dreamed of in our philosophy, and I'm quite prepared to believe that the so-called beetle which others saw, but I never did, was a creature born neither of God nor man.

ABOUT THE AUTHORS

Anthony Giangregorio is the author of 46 novels and children's books, almost all of them about zombies, and has edited over 40 anthologies and books.

His work has appeared in Dead Science & Metahumans vs. the Undead by Coscomentertainment, Dead Worlds: Undead Stories Volumes 1-7, and Wolves of War by Library of the Living Dead Press. He also has stories in End of Days: An Apocalyptic Anthology Vol. 1-5, the Book of the Dead series Vol. 1-6 by LDP, Zombie Zoology by Severed Press, and two anthologies with Pill Hill Press.

He's also the creator of the 10 book action/zombie series titled "Deadwater" and the apocalyptic series "Warriors of the Apocalypse." His action/horror novel "Dead Rage" is being optioned for a movie at this time.

Richard Marsh (1857-1915) was the pseudonym of the British author born Richard Bernard Heldmann. He's best known for his supernatural thriller "The Beetle: A Mystery," published in the same year as Bram Stoker's "Dracula" and initially even more popular. "The Beetle" remained in print until 1960.

Heldmann was educated at Eton and Oxford University. He began to publish short stories, mostly adventure tales, as Bernard Heldmann, before adopting the name Richard Marsh in 1893.

Several of the Marsh's novels were published posthumously.